HELICOPRION

A NOVEL BY MICHAEL COLE

SEVERED PRESS
HOBART TASMANIA

HELICOPRION

WWW.SEVEREDPRESS.COM

ISBN: 978-1-922551-96-2

CHAPTER 1

After years in captivity, the fish had finally mastered the open ocean. No longer was it confined by dull grey steel walls, nor was it subject to the prodding and conduct of its handlers. Now, it was free to roam wherever it pleased.

It had taken a day for the creature to adjust to living on its own. For years, it had grown adjusted to swimming in endless circles in its man-made environment. Such a routine nearly foiled its escape when it first entered open water. Only the aggressive actions of its handlers in their attempt to recapture it broke the habit. First, it learned to fight. In that fight, it learned the taste of human blood. These land-dwelling creatures were as edible as any fish in the sea.

Second, it learned the secret of survival. The beast did not contemplate its existence beyond the natural drive to swim and eat, but it was now aware that the open ocean was the environment best suited for its needs. It was like a bird leaving the nest for the first time. It no longer saw the humans as caretakers who dropped pieces of grouper into its enclosure. They were now among its growing list of enemies and prey.

Thirdly, it learned to utilize its sensory organs to their full potential. Its built-in instincts, programmed since birth, activated like a high-tech processing computer. The fish detected all kinds of alien scents coming from all corners of the ocean. Its lateral line detected movement from other creatures inhabiting the sea. Its nose picked up the scent of blood, urine, and other fluids which served as a trail for potential prey.

In the twenty-four hours since its escape, the creature never fed. It proceeded east, gradually entering shallower waters. Here, prey was in abundance. The sunlight provided excellent visibility for its small eyes. Its lateral line detected intense water distortion from the surface. The fish moved in, cautiously, its nostrils taking in an unfamiliar scent which trailed from a large shape up above.

It was a vessel, similar to the ones used by its handlers. It was much larger than itself, and were the fish not driven by hunger, it would have turned away immediately. However, it watched another shape speeding along in tight circles nearby. This particular thing was fast, but predictable, moving in tight laps along the surface. It was much smaller, making an attack much more feasible. Spurred by the enticing scent, the fish moved in. The first few meters were taken with caution, as it waited for the right moment to strike in a burst of action.

****

"Oh, Jesus! I'm sorry, Kyle." Terrie Forbes got on her hands and knees like a measly servant. With a rag in hand, she wiped up the spilled wine. *How dumb of me*, she thought. She knew it was right by her foot; she had set it there *herself*. But the desire to enjoy the last days of summer break before returning to a mob of disorderly teenagers had clouded her judgement. All she wanted to do was get tipsy and forget about the approaching misery. "How expensive is this wine?"

Kyle laughed. "Oh, Terrie, don't worry about it."

"Not a chance," she replied.

The drone of the jet ski engine grew louder as her husband, Martin, steered close by. He brought the vehicle to a stop and looked at the red wine his wife had spilled forming a cloud in the water. From a dozen yards out, it resembled a cloud of blood trailing from a large whale.

Martin whistled at his wife, admiring her figure as she knelt over to clean the deck. "Ahoy, matey! Don't forget to sooge the captain's room when you're done!"

She looked up at him. "'Sooge'? What the hell kind of word is that?"

"You teach English. You should know?"

"Exactly, I teach *English*, you idiot. Sooge isn't a word."

"It is!" Martin exclaimed. "It's an old English word, I think. Used by sailors who had to clean the ship."

"Great. When we get home, why don't you remember to *Sooge* the dishes like you promised." She returned to scrubbing. She noticed he was still watching her. Worse—he had that shit-eating grin on his face. "Can I help you?"

"Turn just a little to your right." Reluctantly, she decided to indulge. "A little more…just a tad…THERE! Thanks!"

She looked down at herself, realizing she was giving him a straight view of her cleavage. Seven years of marriage, and every time he laid eyes on the goods, he acted like it was the first time.

"You're a pig!" She gave the deck one last wipe-down and returned to her lounge chair. She noticed Kyle laughing on the other side of the deck. He sat cross-legged with a margarita in hand, watching his marketing director dig himself into a hole. "I'd give you shit for being so immature in front of your boss, but then again—"

Kyle and Martin laughed simultaneously. "Except he taught me everything I know!"

"True that!" Kyle raised his glass.

Terrie shook her head, muttering, "Boys!" She looked back at Martin. "So, when's it my turn to ride that thing?"

Martin pretended to cough. "What's that, honey? I didn't catch what you said?!"

Terrie raised her middle finger as he sped away.

At least Martin learned other things from his mentor and employer than ogling women. Kyle might have been a goofball, but he was a very confident businessman. His plumbing supply company in Los Angeles was already doing well when Martin came aboard. Her husband was fresh out of college, where he majored in business, and accepted a sales position with the company, all thanks to Kyle Woodville, who saw potential in him. Good work led to increased revenue, which also resulted in lots of overtime and road miles. Terrie remembered complaining about those long hours in the first two years, but ultimately changed her point of view when the rewards came in. In 2018, Kyle announced he was opening up a new office, and that he had selected Martin to be the office manager. In the following six months, Kyle took Martin under his wing, and in January of 2019, Martin took command of the Amadea office. By year's end, the sales department alone brought in over five-hundred-thousand dollars in revenue. And despite the pandemic of the following year, he still managed to make an increase of another hundred-thousand.

Despite Martin's boyish antics, he was a kickass businessman. With a little bit of luck and patience, she might be able to quit her thankless job in the teaching industry. Four years ago, she would've balked at the idea of being a stay-at-home wife. Now? It's amazing how misery can change a person's point of view.

Every year seemed to cost her another piece of her soul. Kids these days gave her no hope for the future. It seemed everyone was self-centered, focused on their electronics, and only saw relationships as opportunities for sex. Any empathy she saw towards others was simply self-gratifying projection by people fixated on their own image. Subsequent job searches revealed that almost all nearby schools were just as bad, if not worse. Plus, the house was a constant mess, and they were considering having kids. Perhaps having someone home more often would be beneficial.

She watched her goofball husband ride around on his boss' jet ski. She couldn't judge too hard—that knucklehead was her best hope at getting out of teaching.

Martin performed his usual series of sharp turns, making more of an oval-shape than a circular turn.

Both she and Kyle winced as he leaned hard to the side.

"Hey! Careful there! Don't be overturning that thing!" Kyle shouted.

Martin waved, pretending to have understood what he said, and proceeded to zigzag around, splashing water with each change in direction.

They watched him ride for another couple of minutes. Finally, Terrie stood up, growing bored of sitting around. She waved to her husband.

"Hey! My turn! Bring it back around!" She could tell he was considering ignoring her under the guise of 'not hearing her'. However, he looked to be circling back.

Terrie smiled. Once in a while, her husband listened. Then again, there was no telling what kind of antics he'd pull on his way back to the yacht.

****

The fish waited. It had nearly struck when the target stopped, only to miss its opportunity when it proceeded to speed away. The thing above changed its routine into a long series of back-and-forth motions, making distance between it and the big vessel.

The shark watched. It recognized the motion of a wide turn. The object was circling back. On its way back to the boat, it continued the same wavy routine. The shark moved in, measuring its motions carefully. It lined itself up, aligning itself with the next point of angle.

The target was five meters away. With a flutter of its crescent-shaped tail, the shark launched itself like a rocket. Its pointed snout struck the object from underneath, flipping it over and launching its occupant into the water.

****

Martin's brain barely registered his predicament. One moment he was speeding across the ocean, then all of a sudden he was underwater. He sank a few feet before his lifejacket began pulling him up.

He broke the surface. He saw the jet ski floating upside down and cringed. He turned toward the yacht and saw a very irritated Kyle Woodville standing at the edge of the deck. Even Terrie was blushing, not working up the courage to watch the aftermath.

"I warned you, man," Kyle said.

Martin looked around. "I don't know what happened."

"Don't know what happened?! You made too sharp of a turn. *That's* what happened!" Kyle said. He tossed a rope out to him. "Wrap this around the handlebars and we'll pull it back in. Hopefully you didn't damage the engine."

Martin did as instructed and started swimming back to the yacht. Of course, his wife didn't miss the opportunity to cross her arms and do the usual 'tisk-tisk-tisk' sound.

Strangely, she stopped at the second tisk. Her face was not one of irritation but panic. She pointed a finger at him.

No, not *at* him, but *past* him!

Even more alarming was Kyle's equally terrified facial expression. That guy had served two combat tours in Iraq, gaining a purple heart for each one. He didn't scare easy.

Martin looked over his shoulder just in time to see the dorsal fin emerge. "SHIT!" He kicked out instinctively. The shark grabbed hold of his leg and took him under.

Air bubbles burst from his mouth as he screamed. In the blink of an eye, he could feel the teeth slice through muscle and tendon and strike his femur. It was nothing like how he imagined a shark bite would feel. He expected pressure along with individual piercings from dozens of teeth. This felt much more concentrated—a straight line, but only on one side of his leg, as though somebody was running a circular saw into his hamstring. Blood clouded around him. Another wave of pain struck.

Suddenly, he was released.

Martin didn't waste time figuring out what happened. The lifejacket pulled him to the surface, where he immediately kicked and stroked for the yacht. Within seconds, he felt immensely lightheaded, despite the overwhelming adrenaline. Each stroke was more sluggish than the last. Though he was kicking with both feet, he seemed to be drifting drastically to the right.

The sound of his wife screaming "Oh my God!" made him look back. The entire ocean behind him was practically red. As he continued to kick, he noticed that only his left foot was breaking the surface. He felt along his right leg, his fingertips finding nothing but tattered flesh and a piece of jagged bone protruding below the hip. Everything below was gone in a nice, nearly smooth cut, leaving a stump almost as flat as the end of a section of lumber.

"Catch!" Kyle shouted to him. Martin heard the splash of a rope land in front of his face. He reached out and grabbed it, allowing his boss to pull him back to the boat. In a few short moments, he was at the edge. Kyle and Terrie both reached down to grab him.

"Get him out of there!" Terrie cried. They each grabbed a hold of his jacket.

Right as they tugged, the predator emerged from the left Black eyes rolled back, its jaws parting wide. Terrie screamed as she witnessed a circular set of teeth close around her husband's midsection. Martin, who was near the point of passing out, came alive with an ear-piercing scream. Blood shot out from his belly, painting the deck, and those standing on it.

The subject of a match of tug-of-war, Martin writhed. Then, as quickly as it appeared, the shark dove, its tail spraying Terrie and Kyle with red seawater. They fell backward, their momentum hauling a noticeably lighter Martin aboard. Terrie righted herself and moved to kneel by her husband, only to freeze.

They were only successful in pulling half of him aboard. Everything below the torso, save for a few uncoiled intestines, had disappeared into the water. Under that red cloud, a dark, narrow silhouette sped away from the boat and disappeared into the distance.

Terrie fell backward. Kyle rushed to her side. Her eyes were open. She was breathing. Yet, it was like she was unconscious. He tapped her face repeatedly, only to realize she was lost in this catatonic state.

Terrie Forbes would achieve her wish of leaving her teaching job, as the following years would be spent in a psyche ward.

****

The beast continued toward the shallows. Though it had fed, it wasn't satisfied. It had a dual-instinct regarding humans. It viewed them as prey that made for sufficient sustenance. Also, having been prodded, lassoed, struck, and wrangled in the previous years, it viewed them as a threat that had to be destroyed on sight.

As the shark neared shore, new distortions in the water drew its attention. It turned south and followed the reefs to the new point of interest. These motions indicated slower prey, and more in abundance. One thing was for sure; they were human.

CHAPTER 2

It was a picture perfect day. The sky was clear, the ocean waves were gently brushing the shore, and there was just enough of a breeze to quell the summer heat. It had been two years since the Stuckey family moved to Amadea, California. So far, it lived up to their dreams. It was just busy enough to keep it from being considered a sleepy town, but it wasn't overcrowded either. It was located on the northern side of the state, less than an hour away from the border. There was more country out here as opposed to big cities like L.A. and San Francisco.

Allen Stuckey filled the grill with charcoal, covered it in lighter fluid, and ignited a towering flame. Mimicking Tom Hanks, he turned to his wife Katie, arms outstretched, and yelled, "*I* have made fire!"

"Well done. You have graduated to the rank of caveman," Katie replied. Allen admired his wife's figure as she stretched out in the lounge chair. Her blonde hair definitely fit their new 'California look'. She always stated she didn't think so. She was forty-two and though she had only gained six pounds since their wedding, in her eyes it may as well have been a hundred. Her wit, however, remained exactly the same as that special day twenty years ago.

Allen pulled the magazine from her hand.

"Excuse me!" she exclaimed. He ignored her struggles and laid on top of her. Her groans turned to giggles, her resistance to compliance. She wrapped her arms around her husband's neck and allowed the make-out to commence. Her insults towards him were only part of their banter. She was truly happy to be in such a fulfilling marriage after twenty years. In those two decades, she had witnessed friends, co-workers, and family members drift apart from their spouses. Those marriages either ended in divorce or in a standstill, in which the two parties were essentially roommates with no chemistry.

She closed her eyes and let Allen nip at her neck. "You know your brother'll be here any second, right?"

"Good. He can learn something."

Katie slapped his hand. "You're gross!"

Right then, they heard the back door slide open. Silence followed. Allen looked up to see their eighteen-year-old son Howard glaring at them.

"Okay…time to stick my eyes in the fire so I can burn this image out of my brain," Howard said.

Katie looked at Allen, then back at him. "Hey kiddo, without this magic, you wouldn't exist!"

Howard grimaced, leading to laughter from both his parents. He was surprised that it was his mother that made that phrase. Usually, it was dad who made the crude remarks.

He proceeded to the water, football in hand. "I might just have to let Brad sock me in the head with this thing."

They heard a car door shut from the other side of the house. Allen pushed himself off of his wife. "Speaking of which—"

"Oh, sure. For *him*, you'll act modest," Howard said.

"You're one to talk," Allen said, pointing at his son's swim trunks. "Your ass is practically hanging out of those things. If I didn't know better, I'd say you were hoping someone would notice. But, since it's your cousins coming over…"

Howard made a sickly expression on his face as he tightened his drawstring. "I told you what size I wear."

"Newsflash, 'Muscles', you have a car. Time to start buying your own shit."

"I'd happily do so, if goddamn textbooks didn't cost me every dime in the bank."

Katie sighed. It was hard to accept that her one and only baby boy had grown into a lean, adult man who was starting his journey into adulthood. It reminded her of her advancing age, as well as the regret of not having a second child. Allen, on the other hand, couldn't be happier. He was more focused on the fact that his son got through high school with a 3.1 GPA and managed to avoid knocking up any chicks. There were still the college flings to worry about, but Howard seemed to have pretty good judgement.

Allen returned to his grill and stirred the charcoal. He could hear his brother's family coming through the house toward the back door. It slid open, and the four of them stepped out.

"Good afternoon!" Gary said. His wife Sasha followed, carrying potato salad and deviled eggs in her arms. Gary, of course, carried the important thing: *Budweiser*.

Their kids, Brad and Danielle, were already dressed in their swimsuits. They saw Howard waist-deep in the water and immediately dashed out to meet him. Only the seventeen-year-old Danielle paused long enough to say hi to her aunt and uncle.

"Hey, kiddo!" Allen said. He watched the kids dart into the water. He turned to his brother Gary, while their wives proceeded to chitchat about work, hobbies, and life in general. He snatched the beer offered to him, smirking as he twisted the cap off. "Late, as usual."

Gary shook his head. "Why do you think?"

They both glanced to the water.

"Danielle or Brad?" Allen asked.

"*Both*!" Gary sipped his beer. "But mainly the older one. Danielle's mellowed out over the past year. Maybe the hormones are leveling out. I dunno." He shrugged.

Allen detected a hint of jealousy from his brother. Nothing serious. Gary simply wished Brad was as mild-mannered as Howard. Being a parent, he was undergoing the usual merry-go-round of guilt trips, questioning if he was a bad parent, whether he worked too much, whether he disciplined too harshly, or not harshly enough. Or was it simply a phase that would work itself out?

"So, what happened on the college end of things?" Allen asked.

"The kid's pissed off that he didn't get a football scholarship. Apparently, that's an excuse to not go." Gary sniggered. "According to him, at least. God, I swear, that kid's obsession with football is gonna be the death of me."

Allen watched as his nephew took the ball from Howard and reared it back. Both Howard and Danielle waded several yards into the water. By the time Brad let the ball loose, they were neck-deep. Danielle pushed Howard out of the way and caught the ball, then whooped victoriously. The group unanimously chuckled as she trash-talked Howard when he finally emerged from the water.

"Nice work, son! Getting your ass handed to you by a girl! Might as well play for the Patriots."

"Hey!" Gary, a Patriots fan, exclaimed.

The kids got into position again. Howard reciprocated the trash-talking with a few remarks about Danielle's hair and the dolphin tattoo which he referred to as a tuna.

The tactic seemed to work. They moved out, with Danielle attempting to block. This time, Howard used his superior height to reach over her head and snatch the ball.

"Ha-ha! It actually suits you to have that dolphin tattoo, considering you play as though you're in Miami."

"Ugh!" Danielle slapped him playfully across the chest. "Yeah, smartass?! It's easy for you to catch the ball when *this guy here* throws like he plays for the *Browns.*" She pointed her thumb at her brother.

Everyone laughed except Brad. He didn't look mad, but he wasn't amused either. The sting of failing to make it on the college team was still present. He caught the ball after Howard returned, then rose it high again.

"Alright, shorty! You wanna go long? Let's see if you guys can keep your heads above water!"

"Be careful!" Gary shouted from the grill.

Danielle and Howard started moving out, both attempting to block each other's view of the ball.

"Get off!" Danielle muttered, splashing water in her cousin's eyes. The tactic worked, getting his hand away from her face and allowing a clear view of the shoreline.

Brad let the ball loose. It was an impressive thirty-two yard throw, sending the ball on a long arch that led directly toward Howard's arms. Danielle was already struggling to stay above water, while Howard was still a whole head above her. Thinking fast, she clung onto his shoulder and pulled herself up, throwing his balance off. She reached out with her other arm and, to everyone's amazement, caught the ball with one hand, tucking it into her chest.

Sensing her cousin was about to fall, she pushed off of him and swam towards shore. The added force, on top of already being unbalanced, sent Howard reeling backward.

Danielle raised the ball and hollered triumphantly. She waited for Howard to surface so she could do her 'in your face' routine. As usual, the clumsy jock was taking forever to get back on his feet.

In the meantime, she would absorb the praises from the adults on shore. Danielle turned around with the ball still raised, then whooped at the crowd. Instead of clapping, she saw pointing fingers. Her uncle and dad were quickly approaching the shoreline, their faces displaying looks of intense shock and horror. Her aunt and mom stood up, the latter cupping her mouth as she gazed at the sea with widened eyes.

That's when she understood that they weren't pointing at her, but *past* her. Danielle turned around.

There was a swell of water, pushed by a massive submarine-shaped object. It was mostly submerged except for a two-foot long dorsal fin, and an even larger vertical caudal fin. A duo that only a shark could exhibit.

"Oh, God..."

Howard had landed square on his back, his feet floundering above him. For a moment, he stared at the glistening world above, bracing himself for the abuse he would receive upon surfacing. He just got beat by a five-foot-four art major. Hell, he wasn't even convinced Brad could've made the throw. Maybe if he had played like that in high school, he would've stood a better chance at a scholarship.

Right now, he wanted to get back at Danielle. He envisioned her hilarious squeal when being tackled into the water by him, as if he was a defensive lineman. The thought brought a smile to his face.

He rolled to his knees and knelt, ready to shoot up toward the surface. He paused, noticing the oncoming object speeding toward him. At first, it was just a shape in the distance. A moment later, it closed the distance like a projectile. Whatever air that remained in his lungs was driven out by the bone-splintering impact.

Howard writhed in agony as a circular object proceeded to slice into his hip. With little effort, the thing cut clean through, the bone barely offering any resistance. The world around him turned dark red, blinding him to the creature's next attack. The animal went for his neck. With a *crack* of the neck bone, Howard's head fell free from his shoulders.

"Oh, Jesus! Oh, God!" Allen screamed. Even from several yards out, he and his brother could see the red water. Gary proceeded to the edge of the dock then froze after witnessing a dorsal fin emerge from the center of the blood cloud. It turned and shot right for his daughter. There was no time to warn her. As though sucked through the seafloor, Danielle vanished beneath the surface.

The adults witnessed the thrashing of water and the rapid formation of a fresh red cloud. The women screamed, cupping their hands to their faces. Brad stood, dumbfounded and confused.

Gary leapt into the water and paddled to his daughter's aid. "I'm coming, sweetie! Daddy's coming!"

He dove where she went down. Between the sting of saltwater and the thick billowing mixture of blood and soot, he couldn't see much. He reached out into the tornado of chaos. Miraculously, he felt something. An arm or a leg. Either way, it was Danielle. He grabbed it and pulled. Right away, he was taken aback by the near weightlessness of the appendage. He raised it over the water. The blood drained from his face as he gazed at his daughter's severed arm.

Deep in shock, he never noticed the wall of red water rising in front of him. A cone-shaped snout broke through that wall, with an open jaw angled to the right.

A pair of hands grabbed him by the shoulder and yanked him backward right as the jaws slashed his belly like a battle axe.

"Come on! Get out of the water," Allen yelled. He was barely keeping it together, his eyes fixed on the huge thrashing movements between the floating array of body parts and clothes.

By the time they reached the shore, Allen was literally dragging his brother. Katie was in hysterics, screaming and grabbing her hair. Sasha pushed a dumbfounded Brad aside, then knelt by her husband. The sight of stringing intestines extending from his belly made her turn around and vomit.

"Call an ambulance!" a tear-filled Allen shouted. Nobody moved. Sasha had passed out, Brad was in shock, and Katie was lost in a hysterical mind-warp. Allen attempted compressions on Gary, but after the third round it was clear his brother, like his son and niece, was dead.

Allen fell on his rear, his head spinning, as he gazed at the world of carnage floating in front of him. In the middle of it all was the football, which drifted ashore, ultimately settling at Gary's limp foot.

CHAPTER 3

The pain was bad today. Staring at the grocery store shelf, Luke Jansen was stiff as a statue. He wasn't even thinking about the packaged meat in front of him. Instead, he pondered whether the damaged nerves in his face had become sentient, because they seemed to enjoyed firing whenever they felt like it. He could feel the skin on his left cheek stretch as he grimaced. Even after two years, he failed to grow used to it. But that was a minor issue compared to the pain.

Luke leaned on his cart, breathing slowly through his nostrils. He closed his eye, not wanting to see his reflection in the glass door of the frozen food aisle. Dwelling on the issue would only make the pain worse. He focused on the cool draft of the shelving behind him. It had a numbing effect, both to his face and psychology.

A scream snapped him out of his meditative trance. It was coming from his blindside. Luke pivoted to his left, his hand reaching for his holster. He eased up, seeing an embarrassed mother pulling her four-year old daughter away from him. She glanced back with a wince, mouthing "sorry". She couldn't bring herself to say it out loud—at this point, anything said would just make the situation more awkward.

She pushed her many items to the back of her cart, then set her daughter in the open space.

"What's wrong with that man, Mommy?"

"Shh! That's rude." The mother swung the cart around and, without looking back, hurried to the back of the aisle. The crowd of customers and staff, drawn by the screams, made a space for her to leave. "It's okay," the mother informed them. Still, their gazes went back to Luke.

He could hear a few murmurs, both in front *and* behind him. He turned around and saw another crowd gathered at the back of the aisle. A couple, less considerate people winced at the sight of him. Others were drawn to the sight of his Smith & Wesson model 29. The tip of the six-point-five inch barrel protruded through the end of the leather holster. Some turned and backed away nervously, even after seeing the badge clipped next to it that read *Amadea Police Department—Homicide.* Others, like the girl, were drawn to his face, even if only for a moment.

The pain worsened. Anger had such an effect.

Luke leaned toward them. "Boo!"

The crowd took the hint and broke apart. Within seconds, Luke Jansen was the only one standing in the aisle. His gaze returned to the meat he originally stopped in to get. Between him and the burgers was his reflection—the very thing he wished not to see. His one remaining eye squinted at the sight of charred flesh and the black patch on his left side. The hair had grown back along his temple, but it was grey rather than his natural brown.

The sight of himself only elevated his blood pressure all the more. No longer was he in the mood for burgers on the grill. Already, he could smell his own cooking flesh again, that of scorched fuel and metal, and that of—

Realizing where his mind was going, he walked out of the aisle, leaving his cart and the various groceries behind. Some staff member would take care of it. As far as Luke was concerned, it was what they were paid to do.

He arrived in the liquor section, grabbed a couple of bottles of *Jim Beam* and *Southern Comfort*, then checked out. Of course, there HAD to be a line, even in the express lane. While waiting, he endured a few double takes. At least the cashier managed to feign ignorance when he finally arrived at the checkout.

Luke carried the paper bag with a strangling grip as he stepped onto the lot. He entered his Dodge Journey, started it up, and steered for the exit. A simple left turn out, followed by a right turn after a mile, and he'd be home—and well into the process of self-medicating.

There was traffic on his police radio. As usual, he would've ignored it, but a specific word caught his attention. Did the patrolman say 'fatality'? He turned the radio up.

"...an absolute mess. Someone might want to alert the Chief. The major might wanna shut down the beaches."

The next voice was the dispatcher's. *"I just alerted EMS. They'll be on the way shortly."*

Luke quickly switched channels to Four, just in time to catch the traffic. *"...medical response to 4822 Lucero Drive. We have reports of a shark attack."*

Luke ignited the flashers, cut the wheel to the right, and sped for the coastline.

CHAPTER 4

Even two years after his transfer, Luke Jansen was not quite used to driving in a straight line without stopping every thirty seconds, REGARDLESS of whether the flashers were on or not. It was one positive change from his transfer from the LAPD. That, and everything else. He preferred the people; the culture; the lack of protests; hiring of actual qualified officers; the lack of 911 calls for non-emergency issues that oversensitive people proclaimed as such. There were less calls in general. Amadea had just enough crime for its police department to have its own Homicide Division, rather than rely on the County. Most were domestic violence issues, while the majority of the rest were gangs coming up from L.A. to conduct robberies, then retreating back to their safe havens.

After six minutes of leaving the store, Luke turned south on LeMay Street, which ran parallel to the coastline. Amadea's shores were mostly comprised of white sand beaches, along with a few rocky peninsulas.

For the first thirty seconds, he passed nothing but oceanfront homes. Afterwards, he neared the local harbor. The sight of an air-sea rescue helicopter speeding inland made him ease on the brakes. In the harbor were two Fire Rescue response boats. There were two cop cars and an ambulance parked near the pier.

What the hell was going on here? This wasn't Lucero Drive, yet there was an emergency response present *here* which equaled the one required for the recent call.

He didn't know what was happening, but by the glimpse he caught of a stretcher and a black body bag strapped over it, something serious had occurred. Luke cursed under his breath, having missed the entry lane. Without hesitating, he swung the vehicle into the exit lane. The driver of the truck coming up the drive swerved to the side and blared his horn before holding his middle finger to the window. As it was on his blindside, Luke never noticed it. He drove to a small parking area and stepped out.

He recognized Corporal Randy Shane standing next to the stretcher. The thirty-four year old patroller's face soured when he saw the Detective arrive on site. Captain Dalton Zeiler, a short and stocky, but confident leader of his shift of firefighters, was a little better at hiding his displeasure.

"Good afternoon, Detective," he said as Luke stepped onto the pier.

"What have we got?" Luke asked, ignoring the offered handshake. He angled his eye toward the bag.

"Guy was jet skiing and got hit by a shark," Corporal Shane said. Luke opened the bag and peered at the body, or rather, half a body inside. A couple of other patrolmen standing nearby had to turn away, unable to stomach the sight of the severed torso drained of blood. Intestines were coiled at the end of the bag like worms. The skin was wrinkled, pale, and deflated, and the eyes were swollen.

He looked back at the Corporal. "The shark attacked him *while* he was on the jet ski?"

Shane swallowed. He'd seen his fair share of corpses, but this one was one of the worst. He glanced down at it, then back at the Detective. The guy was worried about whether his fella was riding on the *jet ski* when the shark got him?!

He shrugged. "According to the witnesses, he took a spill before the shark attacked. He was probably riding around like an idiot."

Luke continued studying the corpse. He put on a rubber glove and inspected the bite wound. "Pretty clean cut."

"I would imagine so," Shane replied. "He WAS attacked by a shark."

"You sure? I don't see any tooth marks," Luke said.

"Uh? Pardon?" Shane looked at the corpse again, then shook his head. "Pardon me for pointing out the obvious, Detective, but I imagine those tooth marks you're looking for are on the missing half of the body that was *torn* away."

Luke's expression never wavered. "It's a straight line cut."

"Yeah? So?"

"Shark's teeth are sharp, but they're not clean cutters."

"Interesting observation, but it was a shark attack," Captain Zeiler said. He was sounding somewhat annoyed now. "Listen, your coroner has already been notified. He'll be able to give you more adequate details. Now, if you'd please...?" He motioned for Luke to step away so he could zip up the bag and complete the transfer into the ambulance.

Luke, however, never budged. He continued studying the cut. Even the spine looked like it had been sliced through, not broken. "If you're in such a hurry, why'd you bring the body all the way over here?"

Now, Zeiler was fully glaring at him. "What the hell are you talking about?"

"The attack happened in Lucero Drive, yet, you brought the body all the way down here. By boat."

The Captain scoffed. "Detective, that's a completely separate incident."

"You said that this was a shark attack. That's what I heard on the radio." Luke replied.

"Yes..."

"You're saying there were *two* shark attacks?"

"Wow! You really *are* a detective, aren't you!" The Captain mimicked applause. "Yes, two separate incidents. Both shark attacks. It's an unlikely scenario, but it does happen from time to time. We *do* live on the coast, after all. Now, would you mind?"

Luke finally stepped away from the stretcher. He removed his gloves and tossed them into a nearby trash can, then snapped his fingers at the Corporal, who reluctantly approached.

"I want all info on the witnesses. I wanna know what they were doing out there, whether there's any footage of the incident, their relationship with the victim—"

"One's his employer, the other's his wife," Shane replied. "They were hanging out on a yacht. It's Saturday… and *August*. What the hell do you think they were doing? It was a shark attack, Luke!"

Luke turned around. When first names were being used, that's when tempers were starting to get heated, unless the people using the names were friends. That was simple math for Luke, as he wasn't friends with anyone in this department to begin with.

"Still a case for the Homicide Division," Luke said. "Get those reports to my desk ASAP."

"I might have to run it by your Captain."

"Go ahead. Call her on her day off."

"Already did. She's over on Lucero. Do you not keep your radio on?" Luke didn't respond. He got into his Dodge and turned around. As he did, he noticed the cops and firemen speaking to each other. Some were shaking their heads in annoyance, others chuckling. Luke knew he was the subject of their griping. Shane never cared for him, nor did most of the patrollers in the department.

Luke's mind went to his recent session with the department shrink, mandated by his Captain. She questioned him regarding his lack of friendships, to which he stated that he preferred it that way. It kept life simpler and allowed him to remain objective. He never lost sleep over companionships with his fellow officers. Just pain.

"Have you been taking the gabapentin?" she asked.

"Makes me drowsy and dizzy. Some say it makes me moody." He remembered the smirk she made after that statement. It wasn't hard to imagine the phrases she had to suppress. In fact, Luke made a game of trying to guess what she wanted to say but couldn't. He settled on 'So, you're saying you take gabapentin every day?'

Hell, she probably could've gotten away with it. He wouldn't have bothered making a complaint, and even if he did, it likely would've been reviewed for thirty seconds before ending up in the shredder.

He eased on the brakes upon reaching the stop sign. Before taking a right turn onto LeMay Street, he noticed the group of patrolmen in his rear-view mirror. One was doing a 'bottoms-up' hand movement while chatting with the others. As he pulled onto the road, the whiskey bottles clanged together in their paper bag—almost as though *they* were mocking him too.

CHAPTER 5

When Luke arrived at 4822 Lucero Drive, he found that four squad cars, two ambulances, a Fire Rescue truck, and a van from Channel Eight Local News had beat him to the scene. In addition, he could see a utility boat and two Fire Rescue vessels in the water. He approached the yard and saw two officers at the front of the house. He could tell only one was instructed to be stationed there. He looked casual; unbothered. The other one, however, looked slightly purple. Luke assumed he saw something he wasn't used to seeing and decided to join his buddy to stand post in front of the house.

Both looked surprised to see him.

"Detective?" the non-sickly officer said. The words came out as a greeting, the tone was *What the hell are you doing here?* Luke glanced back at the vehicles, noticing a Ford Mustang at the front of the line.

"Where's Captain Raye?"

"Uh, back on the shoreline. With Detective Norton." They stepped aside as Luke entered the house. He passed through the living room, immediately noticing the family photos featuring a man, his wife, and their son. He was in his late teens by the looks of it, assuming these were current photos. One photo in particular showed another family, likely a friend or relative, with two kids; a boy and a girl. They were in their early-to-mid teens according to the photo, but the dust and chipping on the frame indicated it wasn't new.

He could hear commotion in the next room. He proceeded into the hallway, immediately finding a uniformed officer. Behind that officer was what appeared to be a dining room, where two women were weeping beyond control. Like the officer outside, he looked fairly disturbed. Luke knew the difference between awkwardness and disturbed, and this guy was definitely the latter.

The patroller stopped as soon as he noticed Luke. "Oh!"

"Has the body been taken away yet?"

"Which one?" the patroller replied.

Luke cocked his head back. "Beg your pardon?"

"You—you don't know?"

"Are you referring to the incident on the yacht?"

"Uh? No," the patroller said. "Three people were attacked here."

"*Three* people?" Luke said. The patroller nodded. "All shark attacks?" He nodded again. Luke stepped past him, taking one brief glance at the two women. Immediately, he recognized them from the photographs. The one in the photo with two kids had grown her hair out longer, but the waves and color was the same.

Luke stepped outside. There were numerous officers and paramedics near the shoreline. Standing outside the door was a nineteen-year old male who glanced at him, only to immediately look away. He bore a similar resemblance to the teen in the photo. From what he could see, there was no girl. Nor could he see the teen boy he noticed in the other photo.

With that in mind, he watched the boats anchored just beyond the reach of the dock. On the police boats, officers stood ready with rifles, cautiously watching the waters as recovery teams dove to the bottom. Meanwhile, the Fire Rescue team had lifted a body bag onto a stretcher.

Twenty feet to the left was Captain Brianna Raye of the Amadea Homicide Division. A woman in her mid-fifties, she aged remarkably well considering the stress the profession brought with it. As usual, Luke questioned the efficiency of her methods. She was nice, maybe *too* nice. Definitely the *good cop* in a good-cop-bad-cop routine. Her motherly tendencies seemed to come in handy in this case, however. She was talking to a tearful man in his forties—the male in the photo of three.

Luke gave the young man another brief glance. He was *not* the one in the photo of three, whom, judging by the age and family-photo style, was likely this tearful man's son.

A body bag, no young girl in the crowd, though her mother and brother were present, and a missing male teen—*three victims*.

Standing next to the Captain was Samuel Norton, a forty year old former Oregon State Trooper, who transferred to the California State Police in 2004 before again transferring to Amadea Homicide Division in 2017. According to him, it was because his wife had taken a job with the County Clerk's Office. Norton always wore a cocky grin on his face, especially when talking to other cops, like he thought of himself as smarter. Luke had checked his background and found it peculiar that the Captain of the Portland Police Department Homicide Division had worked with his father. Such connections always made Luke question the merit of a person's career elevation.

Media attention brought put merits into question. Norton loved being on the TV, and once again, he was demonstrating his willingness to speak to the reporter on site. Luke wasn't sure if it was ego or if he originally wanted to be a movie star but didn't have the chops, but Norton was always a little too eager to have the cameras on him. According to the Chief of Police, it was a good quality. "Maintain a positive image. Gain public trust."

Luke simply referred to that motto as perception mistaken as fact.

He noticed Norton tap the Captain with his finger, then point toward him. Brianna looked his way, sighed, then approached.

"Luke?"

"Cap." He wasn't looking at her, but at the divers.

"Whatcha doin' here?"

He glared at her. "Three dead bodies. Another in the harbor. I work in Homicide, as you do. I'm sure you can connect the dots."

"There's another dot you often remind us of," she replied. "It's your day off. Remember?"

"I was in the neighborhood," Luke said.

"Yeah?" Brianna placed her hands on her hips. "Making friends for once? Not often you leave your house on your off hours, with maybe one exception. I know *LeRoy's Cabinet* just got restocked. Saw the loading truck on my way over." Behind her, Norton snorted and turned away, placing a hand over his chin to conceal his smirk.

The nerves in Luke's face were firing. The Captain, notorious for being the nice lady, did not hesitate to pass judgement on him. "That's mean."

Sarcasm. Why was Brianna surprised? Whenever it wasn't outright insults, he resorted to his wit. Both were annoying.

"Go home. We've got this covered," she said.

"Oh, do you now?" Luke replied.

"It's a shark attack, Luke." Luke rolled his eye. She *always* referred to him by his first name. Considering the culture around the department, it was a telling sign of her opinion of him, despite the 'nice lady' demeanor.

"*Three* shark attacks. In this area alone, I might add." Luke raised his hands at the paramedics, who were starting to cart the stretcher away. "Hold up." They paused. Luke glared at them, his charred face giving him a demonic appearance which unnerved them enough to step back without argument. He opened the bag and gazed at the victim inside. Adult male—same as the one in the photo of four, judging by the narrow widow's peak and short trim.

"Luke, what are you doing?" Brianna said. Luke ignored her. Instead, he was fixated on the horizontal gash across the victim's abdomen. His stomach had been split wide open, as though someone had slashed him with a katana. Whatever had done it had broken a few lower ribs and exposed stomach tissue and everything around it, including the spinal column.

"He's literally been cut down to the bone."

"What?"

Luke turned to face her. "This wasn't done by a shark."

"Excuse me?"

"Okay, it *might* have been a shark—if it learned to use a cleaver."

"What are you implying?" Brianna said.

"I'm not implying anything. I'm *saying*, and have already *said*, and will *say again* that this wasn't done by a shark."

Brianna deliberately drew a breath before speaking again. She glanced over at the reporter. As luck would have it, he was listening in and taking notes.

"For Chrissake, Luke, it's not up for debate. We have witnesses confirming the presence of a shark."

"Oh!" Luke threw his hands up. "Case closed, then. Right?"

Brianna looked back at the resident. He was openly sneering in Luke's direction. She turned back to Luke. "We're gonna allow the coroner to do his job."

"Great. We'll waste two hours until he confirms what we already know. Actually, if it's McGibbeny, four to six. Add two more if he drops his wedding ring in there again."

"Luke—Detective!" She glanced back at the resident, then back at him. She spoke in a whisper. "Have a little respect. That man in the bag is—"

"His brother. And the other two that died were his son and niece.

Norton raised an eyebrow. "Who told you that?"

"Wasn't hard to figure out. What does that have to do with anything?"

"It has to do with a lot."

"Only if he's a suspect."

"God—" Brianna took another breath, then forced a smile. "What *are* you doing here, Luke?"

"Asking questions and making observations. It's what we're paid to do, isn't it?"

"Here's an observation: this isn't your case," she said. "How's your pain?" Luke snickered. That motherly voice was back.

"Just a little throbbing. Nice try in changing the subject. Almost made me forget to point out that the dead guy here doesn't have a shark bite wound."

"His name's Gary," Norton said

"Does his name have any effect on the type of laceration? And yes, that is a laceration. No tooth marks...looks more like somebody took a chainsaw across his gut."

"We saw the damn shark come at him, you son of a bitch!" Surprisingly, it wasn't the man who lashed out, but one of the women. It was the one with the longer hair. The dead guy's wife. The windows were open, making it easy to overhear from inside. She marched from the door and pushed against the patrollers who stepped in her path. 'We saw the dorsal! We watched it move in! We saw... there was that big swell! We saw it get—" she cupped her mouth and broke into tears, as did the man by the dock. The officers escorted her back into the house, along with her son.

"Nice work," Detective Norton said.

"Enough," Brianna said. Norton raised his hands and turned away. Brianna zipped the bag back up and waved the paramedics along. They eagerly carted the stretcher to the front of the house. "Luke, please go home."

"'A big swell' huh? So they actually *didn't* see the shark."

"They saw it, you idiot," Norton said. "We questioned them. They saw the dorsal fin and tail fin. They say it happened fast. Got one kid, then the other, then Mr. Stuckey."

"You don't find any of this strange?" Luke said.

"Yes, I admit it's a little off. But shark attacks do happen."

"What remains are there of the other victims?"

Brianna groaned. "It's not your concern, Luke. Go. Home... Please. We've got this taken care of."

Luke glanced about. "No other body bags. Were the other victims not yet found?"

"Luke..." She sighed, then lowered her voice again. "Our divers found some remains in the water."

Luke cocked his head. "*Some*?"

"Arms, legs...a head. It's not pretty."

"Wow. Is this shark a surgeon?" Luke remarked. The Captain glared at him, while internally questioning why she was even surprised to hear such a remark at this point. "Quit with that look. It's not like the movies. Sharks don't just devour people, especially in multiple numbers."

"We're suspecting it was maybe a small school of sharks," Norton said.

"Brilliant deductions. Have you seen any of these remains?"

"That's a job for the coroner," Brianna said.

"Not McGibbeny, right?"

"I know what you're doing." The Captain was visibly losing her patience. "Luke, I know how much pain you're in, and I also know cases are a way of distracting you from the pain. Hence, you're always looking at details with no relevance to your assigned case. Or unassigned."

"Except you don't know whether those details are relevant until after you solve the case. Last time I checked, when a detective doesn't examine every detail, he's less likely to solve the case."

"The case *is* solved. I'm getting sick of explaining this: *Shark attack*! A bizarre case, sure, but that's what it is."

"Based on witness testimony. Because…people don't lie? Or mistakenly identify something while under extreme duress?"

"And the people on the yacht?" Norton said. "They lying too?"

"Detective? Seriously?"

Norton sighed, then looked away, having realized the Captain didn't want to spark further interest from Luke.

"Relax, Captain, I'm aware of that incident too," Luke said. "And yes, it's very possible. People are often mistaken. It's kind of an unfortunate trait of the species. What I do know is that sharks don't saw people in half."

"What are you talking about? The shark tore that victim in two," Brianna said.

"Then came over here for seconds? Must be a damn hungry shark with no discretion about humans. By the way, I inspected the other victim. Anyone who knows anything about sharks beyond what they see on the *SYFY Channel* understands that, while shark teeth are indeed sharp, they're not clean cutters. Severe injuries are uncommon. Deaths even less so. And for a shark to completely rip its victims apart with clean cuts—"

"We're alerting the local fishermen and are sending maritime units out to hunt for it. We'll find the shark, cut it open, prove you're wrong. Then I'll talk myself out of firing you for interfering."

"The beaches closed?" Luke asked.

"No," Brianna said.

"Great. *Really* wise decision there."

"Knock it off, Luke," Brianna snapped. "The shark's full by now. It's not likely to attack again. BUT, we have nets set up just in case we're dealing with a school of sharks. We have men on patrol. Swimmers are safe. I've handled these types of situations before. This was either a great white or a tiger shark, or a pack of makos."

"Riiiight," Luke said. He read about it. 2013. Tiger shark attacked a sixty-two year old retiree on the southern peninsula. "Record sized tiger shark, and the guy didn't even lose a leg. You'd think you would've learned something about sharks from that little incident. Like what a shark bite looks like, for starters."

"Listen, Luke, stop while you're ahead. The Chief never wanted you in the department to begin with. I'm the reason you aren't working the night shift in some warehouse. But that can change if you keep pissing me off. Listen up: This isn't your case. Get the hell out of here. Norton and I have this covered."

Luke smirked. He'd heard the 'I'm-the-reason-you-even-have-a-job' guilt trip a hundred times in the last two years. Maybe he was too harsh; it was kind of true. Nobody wanted to work with him. The Chief made it clear he didn't want Luke patrolling the streets. "Our duty is to make people feel safe. Not increase their apprehension about cops," the guy openly said. The memory never failed to make Luke laugh. A big part of the whole 'acceptance' movement was not to pass judgement on someone based on their looks—unless it was someone you didn't like. Apparently, you were fair game. Brianna ultimately convinced the department to place Luke Jansen in the Homicide Division, where in Amadea, the cases were mainly cut and dry. He wouldn't be in the public eye, and he could coast for ten years then take an early retirement.

He started walking back to the house, pausing briefly to look back. "Hope you're ready to talk to *National Geographic*. They're bound to have questions about this, and you won't have the leverage of threatening their jobs." Figuring he had worn out his welcome with the residents, he walked around the side yard to the front, rather than step through the house again.

Norton shook his head and chuckled. It was both amusement and frustration. Usually, he kept his thoughts to himself, but this recent display by Jansen had put him over the edge.

"Captain?"

Brianna groaned. "What?"

"Feel free to yell at me, but I'm putting it straightforward: I think you were insane for putting this guy in our department. I mean, *you* of all people should know he's no good."

Brianna looked away. *There he goes, bringing up the L.A. thing again.* It seemed to be a more frequent topic as of late.

"I've never understood it. Why him?"

The Captain resisted the urge to shut him up. It wasn't good for subordinates to question the decisions of their superiors, especially in the presence of other cops. However, she understood everybody's confusion. She had fought hard for Luke's employment after his notorious incident in L.A. No department wanted him anywhere near them, yet she fought tooth and nail for him to be brought onto Amadea's team.

She rubbed her lower hip. Memory took hold. She closed her eyes. In that moment, she was back on night shift, fourteen years ago, in West Los Angeles. The radio call came in. Units in the West Valley Area were responding to a shootout which led to a standoff in an old strip mall. A request for backup was sent, to which she responded. Though dangerous, it sounded like a simple matter of forming a perimeter, letting the negotiator do his thing, then arrest the suspects. She followed instructions to move around to the back.

She remembered a voice on the radio, yelling at the commanding officer on scene. This person warned that these suspects would fight it out, as one was already being investigated for international human trafficking. He also warned of discovering a connection between these three suspects and a recent shipment of fully automatic weaponry and Kevlar-piercing rounds. A brief argument continued on the radio, as the warning voice warned the Lieutenant not to trust anything said by these wackos.

Still, the Lieutenant on scene tried to go with the negotiation route. Reports indicated that the suspects were responding, making the usual demands for a ride and escape route.

All of a sudden, there was shooting. Not in the front of the building, but in the back. Brianna recalled an intense sensation of heat in her left hip, which dropped her like a sack of potatoes. She could still feel the warmth of her own blood pumping from her body, and being so captivated by it, that she didn't realize her partner had also been hit until he fell beside her.

The next few moments was a mixture of shooting and adrenaline. The bandits had made their escape…all while negotiation seemingly continued at the front of the mall. As it turned out, they made a pre-recorded tape of general responses and demands, put it near a window while obscuring it from sight, then let it play to throw the officers off.

She would never forget the sight of those gunmen marching from the double doors, decked out in full body armor, shooting automatic weapons into the perimeter. Her heart skipped a beat when the muzzle of their weapons pointed at her. It seemed her fate was sealed; they'd execute her, steal her vehicle, and make a desperate run for the harbor.

There was the crack of a single shot. Death followed, but not for her. When her eyes opened, she saw one of the gunmen go down. The others turned to face the new threat. Another shot rang out, resulting in a fatal headshot in a second suspect. The third took a couple of rounds to the chest, which protected him from fatal injury, but still knocked him over. Outmatched, his companions dead, and all hope for escape lost, the remaining suspect opted for suicide. The final shot fired that night was his own, aimed up through the roof of his mouth.

Raye's vision was hazy at that point, but she vividly remembered seeing the detective wearing black jeans, biker boots, and a leather jacket stepping onto the scene. Smoke still trailed from the muzzle of his Carbine. It was the same detective that warned the officer in charge of inevitable action. He'd been investigating these people who were suspected of being part of a larger syndicate. From what she heard, they got sloppy with their methods and dumped a body in the harbor. Witnesses reported strange activity, and despite pushback from ranking officers, this same detective took it upon himself to make a dive. After three hours of searching, he located the body, shackled to a weight. She was a trafficking victim who likely presented too many problems. Regardless, it became a case for the Homicide Division, and ultimately led to a devastating shootout.

That day, Brianne Raye learned the sensation of a gunshot wound. She also learned the terrifying fear of seemingly-inevitable death, and the relief of having her life saved. Even after fourteen years, those memories were pure.

"Captain?"

She opened her eyes and watched the detective that saved her life disappear around the side of the house. How the mighty had fallen. The best of the best was now coasting through life, dedicating each day to isolation and painkillers. She feared where he'd be now if she didn't fight to get him a job with her department.

"Captain?"

Norton's voice quickly grew annoying. She turned around. "Don't worry about him, Detective. Don't question me on who I bring on ever again. You hear?"

Norton raised his hands in surrender. "Jeez! Whatever you say, boss."

Brianna proceeded to the house. There was nothing left to do here. She'd have to make a meeting with the Chief as well as the Mayor, then wait on the coroner's report.

When she arrived on the front lawn, she saw Luke's Dodge Journey still parked behind the line of police vehicles. Through the lower passenger window was something brown—a paper bag. Luke always carried regular groceries in plastic. A moment later, he did a U-turn and drove off.

Please Lord, let today not get any more complicated.

CHAPTER 6

"Oh my God!"

It was the most beautiful thing Dr. Elise Sheldon had ever seen. Lucky for her, she got to see it multiple times a week. Silver, the thirty-eight foot long humpback whale, had breached the shallow waters near LaFountain Reef. She twisted midair with such enthusiasm, it was as though she was deliberately showing off for her marine biologist observer up above. Never once did Silver quit her song while performing her dance. She hit the water with an enormous splash of bluish green water.

A residual mist swept over Elise. She laughed out loud and watched the mother glide under the surface. She could see a second, smaller shape swimming beside her. Silver's calf had grown a couple of feet since Elise last saw them.

"Want me to anchor here?"

Elise looked back at her nephew and personal assistant, Chad. "Um…YEAH!" They both smiled. The blonde twenty-two year old plopped the anchor. After fifty-feet, it settled.

Elise checked her rebreather and full-face mask. Every so often, her job managed to provide some degree of excitement. Saturday was always the one day out of the week she looked forward to, as it was the one where her work required her to be in the water. It was fairly routine: dive; collect measurements of various coral specimens, crabs, starfish; count populations of fish; collect water samples from various locations; return to the lab and spend the next six days analyzing.

She looked over at Chad. "You coming?"

"No thanks. I can see them from here," he said.

Elise scoffed. "You're actually telling me you'd rather watch from up here than swim with Silver?!"

"Well…" Chad shrugged.

"Oh, you little wuss."

Just like his mom, the kid was anxious regarding anything he was even vaguely unfamiliar with. Must be a genetics thing. Kathy suffered from anxiety, thus she struggled to break out of a basic routine. Her daily life consisted of the same general steps: wake-up, go to work, come home, cook dinner and tend to family, watch a show or read a book, sleep, repeat. Whenever they went on vacation, they always went to the same place. Always playing it safe. She and her husband always ate at the same three restaurants, because she was worried of trying a new option and not liking it.

Then again, maybe there was something to it. After all, it *was* trying something new that led to the car accident.

It was then that Elise experienced her own anxiety. Not only did she suffer the grief of losing her sister and brother-in-law, but was given custody of their one and only son.

Elise remembered being fourteen years old and jealous that her older sister Jaqueline had chosen her college friend to be Chad's godparent. She even stated, half-jokingly, that *she* should've been the one. Of course, her naïve mind at the time couldn't comprehend the responsibility of raising a child. Unfortunately, at the age of twenty-eight, she had no choice. Sadly, that friend was also in the car when the semi-truck ran the red light.

Elise had just graduated with her PhD in Marine Biology from the University of California Santa Barbara and was looking forward to taking a job heading a project to study migration patterns for seals in Antarctica to South America. Despite what people saw on TV or read in books, it was rather uncommon for marine biologists to regularly work on the water. Most of the time was spent in a lab, doing data work, looking over gene sequences and measuring the toxicity of the water. Thanks to her connections, and excellent performance during her research projects in graduate school, she managed to be among the ten percent of graduates that actually worked in the field.

Then came the news of the accident. In the blink of an eye, her nephew Chad Samson was without parents, and now she was the only thing he had left in the world. Hell, she was only fourteen years older than him. So much for those adventures that so many PhDs in the field dream of doing. He was only sixteen at the time; not a good age for her to be out of the country. So, she took a basic lab job. For the duration of Chad's remaining time in school, work was a basic nine-to-five, analyzing toxicology and plastic samples field workers brought in from the ocean. Not exactly her dream, but it proved to be worth it.

She and Chad bonded rather quickly. Unlike the typical teenager, he actually appreciated her sacrifice and even took an interest in her work. Elise was surprised that, despite the grief he felt, Chad adapted pretty well to the change in his life. There were no angry outbursts. A few instances of mourning and some anxiety, but no grudges toward his aunt and her rules. In fact, *she* was the one who had a harder time adapting. She was used to takeout, crappy frozen food, and not having the standard of cleaning up the house constantly. But now, she was the parent of a teenager in need of a good role model. So, she learned to cook. She learned about sports. She arranged time to attend his football games.

Two years later, he graduated high school. Four years after that, he was a semester off completing his Bachelor's Degree in Marine Science. It took a little goading, but he got through it. Now, he was faced with the decision to pursue his Master's, or settle for a gig as a research assistant. He was used to it, considering he already was one—for Aunt Elise.

Midway through his college years, she took a job in Amadea, monitoring levels of microscopic plastic in the coastal waters. Again, not exactly her dream job, but it was higher pay and still had regular hours, allowing her to help Chad through college. He was able to write the gig off as 'field work', a prerequisite for one of his advanced Oceanography courses.

Elise looked back at the whales. Silver was less than two hundred feet away and was swimming in gentle circles. The water around her was crystal clear, allowing an excellent topside view. Diving with these whales in water like this would be a majestic experience. She couldn't stand to let Chad miss out on this.

"They're not gonna hurt you, Chad. You should know this. Just think of them as...plus-sized angels," Elise said.

Chad laughed. "Unfortunately, all that analogy did was make me envision obese angels literally falling from Heaven."

Elise threw her head back in laughter. "You're too much, kid. But come on! It's not every day you get to do something like this."

"I know, I know..."

"Hey, this'll be a great bar story," she joked. "You can tell the ladies; 'Yeah, I totally swam alongside this huge humpback whale. It moved like a freight train under the water, but I didn't care. I swam up alongside it and clung to its flipper.'" She cleared her throat. Mocking a masculine voice seemed to turn her vocal cords into gravel.

"Wow, if only ladies were seduced as easily as you make them sound, Aunt Elise."

"Whoa! Whoa! Whoa! Who said anything about seducing?!" she exclaimed.

"Uh, YOU!"

"I did not!"

"Who sweet talks a girl like that, at a BAR, *without* the intention of getting some fuzz?"

Elise clenched her eyelids. "Wow! This conversation took a weird turn."

"Hey, you started it. Besides, I'm twenty-two...and full of hormones." He grinned. "However, I can improve on that idea. I'll go to the bar tonight and tell the ladies of the time I saved you from a hungry great white. 'I was so brave. My aunt was two minutes away from becoming shark chow, but I punched the shark in the eye and scared it away.' Mm-hmm! Yep! Real panty-peeler."

"Oh, Christ." Elise winced, which resulted in another obnoxious laugh from her nephew. It was obvious Chad was taking great pleasure in messing with her mind.

Their conversation made Elise understand what all parents go through when their kids grew up. Her sister's boy was all grown up now, and had girls on the brain. Took long enough; for a while, he avoided the topic of dating altogether. Too shy and, more specifically, timid. Just like his mom used to be. He was a work in progress, but that progress was indeed being made.

"*Back* to the subject about whales—"

"Don't you mean angels?"

"You're not getting out of this, mister. Get your rebreather on. I've got the camera. I'm gonna get a few shots of you swimming alongside Silver."

Chad's smile faded. "What if she doesn't take kindly to that?"

"You'll be fine, Chad. Silver's very used to humans. Just give her a few minutes to know you've come in peace, then slowly approach. I'll be right there with ya."

Chad let out an exaggerated sigh. "Alright." He collected his gear, checked his scuba tank, then slipped his mask and flippers on.

"By the way, I suppose in this 'hypothetical' scenario of telling stories in bars, you plan to omit the fact that that great white was only nine feet long? And that it was *me* who had to save *you*?!"

Chad stood up, complete in his diving gear. "I don't know what you're talking about," he lied through the commlink. Elise fastened her mask, tested her radio link, then moved to the diving platform. Before diving, she gave him one last glance.

"You're so full of shit."

After sharing another laugh, they dove in. With gentle strokes, they descended a dozen feet under the surface. The world below was so clear and gentle. She could see fish swimming directly below, like civilians casually going about their day in a major city. None of them were alarmed by the giant gliding about above them.

Silver was directly ahead, her forehead and back covered in barnacles. The runt moved alongside her. It immediately took an interest in the two humans who were approaching.

Immediately, Chad felt a little bit of apprehension. "I think they see us."

"Yep," Elise replied.

"You sure 'mom's' not gonna be a little bit defensive?"

"Chad, it's so incredibly rare for a person to be hurt by a humpback whale, that it's practically unheard of. Just take it slow. It's good that she sees us. Silver knows we're not predators. Just move in carefully—and watch out for the fluke. Catching a slap from that might hurt a little."

"A little?"

"I was being sarcastic." Elise took the initiative, moving her feet up and down like a dolphin. Silver slowed and turned toward her, continuing the majestic chorus of her song. Elise monitored the mother's body language. If she was uncomfortable, she would move away to avoid the humans. If interested, she would either move closer or stay in the same spot and allow the visitors to approach. Luckily, it appeared to be the latter case.

Silver cocked her head to the side, but only to aim her beautiful eye at Elise.

"Hi." She waved, as though Silver was an old friend. In a way, she was. Though she personally hadn't tagged the whale, she knew the researcher who did, and was given access to track the humpback's migrating patterns. She would typically visit the California coast during the months between May and November, then move south during the winter.

Elise swam over Silver's head and down along her back, then turned back around when she neared her fluke. Human and whale swam parallel, the larger creature deliberately keeping at a pace the human could keep up with.

"Wow," Chad's voice echoed through her receiver. The twenty-two year old was finally braving the venture.

"Come on. She doesn't bite," Elise said.

"No, she just gulps," Chad retorted.

"Only if you're plankton or shrimp," she replied. "Now get your ass over here. Don't be rude. Come say hi." The humpback let out a call, nodding her head. Chad raised his eyebrows. That coincidental movement was not literally an act of inviting him, but damn if his aunt didn't play it up as such. "She's waiting."

Chad moved in. He approached the whale from her right, coming up over Elise. He looked the mammal in the eye. "Good afternoon. Um...so, how's life? Catch the *Dodgers* game?"

He slowly moved with the whale as she continued north. It was a nice, steady swim, one that even an amateur diver could perform. For several meters they traveled side by side, with the youngster trailing a tad behind them. Finally, Silver decided to dive. She didn't have far to go, as it was only fifty-to-sixty feet deep around here. Chad waited to see what she was doing. The whale arched back up and ascended, stopping a few feet from the surface. She extended her flippers toward him.

For several moments, Chad froze, unsure of what the gesture meant.

"Psst! Dude!" his aunt hissed at him. He looked at her and saw that she was waving him toward the whale. "She wants to dance."

"She doesn't *actually* want to—"

"Shut up and touch her flipper! This is rare! You don't understand what you're missing!"

At this point, he was more afraid of his aunt's response than the actions of a thirty-two ton whale. He swam toward the whale and touched the flipper. It felt like a handshake between a mortal human and a titan, but not a malevolent ruler, but rather a nurturing spirit. A moment later, they glided together, moving along the surface where Silver took a breath.

Elise watched. She could see her nephew looking back at her. This time, however, it was not a nervous glance or a seeking of guidance, but an expression of excitement.

"You see this?" he asked.

"You're doing great! This is incredible, Chad." She proceeded to swim with the youngling, who also seemed to dance with her. The ritual continued for several minutes, which only felt like a few short moments. After which, Elise checked her watch. It was getting later in the afternoon, and they still had a few samples to collect and a few measurements to take. "Oh, damn it."

"What's going on?" Chad said.

"Unfortunately, we gotta get back to work. Say bye to Silver and the kid."

"Aw! But we just got going!" Chad said. A moment of silence followed. "Okay, that came out wrong."

"I was hoping you'd say that," Elise said.

Chad gave his goodbye by placing a hand on Silver's head. "Thanks for the dance."

Elise and Chad returned to the boat, exhilarated by what they had just experienced. Silver was still keeping close, casually moving with her young. Chad leaned over the portside to watch. The timid nature and unenthusiasm had disappeared completely. Instead, he looked like a marathon runner who came in first place.

"So...any chance we can take this boat out tomorrow?"

Elise dabbed her face with a towel. "You enjoyed it that much, huh?"

"Maybe."

She stood up. "I suppose we can arrange that. As for right now, we need to get back to work." She moved to the cockpit, then waited for the whales to move along, as humpbacks were known to be somewhat nervous around boats. She turned back to look at her nephew. "That was really cool, wasn't it? Bet you're glad I made you go."

"Once every so often you're right about something."

Elise scoffed. "Alright, smartass."

"Did you get pictures?"

"No."

"Aw, damn!"

"You don't need pictures! Just enjoy the moment while you're in it!"

"How am I supposed to impress the ladies with the story if I don't have pictures?!" Chad retorted. He thumped his fist against the gunwale, feigning anger. "Man, you were in the right spot for a wide shot too. All I needed to do was flash that photo, and the chicks at *David Daniel's* would practically be begging for it." He deliberately emphasized the use of the word 'it'. As intended, Elise fed his desire with a pained wrinkling of the face.

Shaking her head, she looked back at Silver. She had circled around and was now a hundred yards to the south. Elise started the engine and turned the boat north. "Maybe it *wasn't* a good idea to have you swim with the whales." It was a lie, of course. It was a great idea, and a beautiful memory that she would cherish eternally.

CHAPTER 7

After traveling three-quarters of a mile, they arrived at their destination. Chad anchored the boat and, for the final time that day, prepped to dive. It was the last section of reef they needed to take samples from. All day, they'd been making dives up along the coastline of northern California, ending with the northernmost part of LaFountain Reef, which lined up with the shores of Amadea. It was a hundred and twenty-feet deep around here. The bottom was alive with fish and crustaceans living in the northern edge of the reef.

There were four water samples needed from this region, and five specimens to take measurements from.

"Let's get this done and over with. I'm craving pizza," Chad said.

"I thought you were eager to go to the bar and impress the ladies," Elise replied.

"I would, but you screwed that up by not taking pictures."

"You're still on your soapbox about that, huh?" She slipped her harness on. "Maybe you can just try simple, pleasant conversation? Let the other person get to know you, rather than just try and get in their pants."

"Ha! You're one to talk! You've been on like two dates in the last four years, and hmmm…what was your complaint about both guys?" He put his finger to his chin and pretended to be deep in thought. "Oh right! You said they were *boring*!"

"I did not!"

"Sure you did! I remember you getting dropped off back home, *not* inviting him in—for which I'm grateful, by the way. You said bye, shut the door, then said, and I quote, "thank God that's over.""

"The guy wouldn't shut up about his accounting job."

"Case and point!" Chad exclaimed, pointing a finger at her.

"Be nice if you men would try listening for a change," she retorted. "Or, at least, find something interesting to talk about. Like, I don't know, diving with whales?!"

"They won't believe me," he said. "Hence, I needed the pictures."

"Oh, Chad. You're a goof." They stepped onto the diving platform. She thought for a moment. "Maybe *I* need some whale photos. Seems whenever I talk to dudes about what I do, they trail off after two minutes. Just my luck *you're* the only one who's ever taken an interest in my field of study. Then again, at least I don't have to pay ya!"

"Damn right you're paying me—in pizza."

"I guess I can live with that."

Aunt and nephew shared a fist bump then dove into the water. Schools of fish moved in to inspect them, quickly to lose interest and dart away. As they reached the bottom, Chad glanced to the north.

"I can hear Silver," he said.

"Yeah, their songs can travel for miles," Elise said. They allowed a few moments of the distant harmony.

"Better get them an agent. They sing better than a lot of the artists I've been hearing lately."

"There's something we can agree on," Elise said. They descended to the reef. The schools of fish busily moving about reminded Chad of college at noon. It was near-impossible to get anywhere through the crowds.

"Want me to get the crabs?" he asked.

"Nah, just get the water samples. I'll check the crabs and cucumbers. And hopefully I can get a photo of Ol' Murray."

"Oh, boy." Chad said. Murray the Moray Eel was not a particularly cooperative patient. The Institute required Elise to take measurements of him once a month in the year after being released into the wild. When originally found during a routine dive, Murray was found entangled in plastic loops used for cans of beer. Because of this, the poor creature failed to eat for several weeks and was literally starving. But, thanks to the biologists at Schmidt, he was nursed back to health and returned to his habitat.

"I'll collect the sample from zone thirteen while I'm over there," she said.

"Alright. See you in a couple of minutes."

Chad and Elise parted ways, the PhD following the signal for a two year old red rock crab before seeking out the eel. She dug around some large rocks, then found the crab nibbling on the remains of a green crab. Elise took a moment to admire the crustacean. As far as the crab was concerned, it was just having a simple meal. In terms of the ecosystem, however, it was providing an invaluable service. Green crabs had been listed among the world's hundred most invasive species, and were currently making waves to the California and Oregon coast. Efforts had been made by the authorities to slow the population growth with the use of traps, with some effect. Unfortunately, such a method had an effect of drastically reducing other species, including endangered ones. In a way, seeing this crab munch on its victim was uplifting. It was nature's way of maintaining balance. If only humans were so effective at helping to maintain such a balance as this simple red rock crab. The green crab it fed on had a fertilized egg sack, which its slayer also fed on. Thus, the rock crab had prevented over fifty-thousand new invaders from taking a foothold on the California coast.

"Sorry to interrupt your lunch, little fella." She took the measurement. "Twelve inches." She said it aloud for the audio recorder. Same as before, but still far better than her first measurement of the specimen a year ago.

She moved on to follow the sample of the next red rock crab. That was a trickier specimen to dig out, as it had burrowed itself into the rock bed.

"Oh, come on. Don't make this hard on me," she said, digging it out.

Chad's voice came through her receiver. *"Are the crabs outsmarting you, DR. Sheldon?"*

"You're very funny, Squirt!" She moved some rocks. The crab had practically made itself a little cave. She shone a light into the little tunnel. Surprisingly, she had a hard time seeing it. She lay parallel to the entrance, then pressed her head closer. It made her think of every horror movie cliché—don't look in the creepy tunnel! Something will jump out! She smiled at the thought, and felt stupid that she felt even the least bit apprehensive about it. It wasn't like crabs were known for leaping at people, claws agape and reach to shred flesh.

She leaned in, only to jump back and shrieked. It wasn't a crab that lashed out. Fish! All at once, the hundreds of fish around her had darted to the north, several of which blindly collided with her facemask in the process. She reeled backward, rolling down the small slope of reef.

"Aunt Elise? What's going on? You alright?" Chad said.

She settled on her back then shrieked again as the nerves in her leg flared up. She saw a small blood cloud seep from her suit. She leaned up and saw the piece of stony coral pressing its barb into her thigh. She pulled herself free, wincing hard. Every millimeter of movement was excruciating.

"Aunt Elise?" Chad continued.

"I'm alright," she said.

"You don't sound alright. I'm coming over."

Elise didn't bother talking him out of it. The flare in her leg did not falter. The sting of saltwater was now contributing to her misery.

It took a couple of minutes for Chad to find her. He gasped as soon as he saw the cloud of red rising from his aunt's leg. "Holy crap! You're hurt!"

"I'll be fine," she replied.

"What the hell happened?"

"The damn fish!" she exclaimed. "They all darted off. Hit me right in the face."

"I saw that. What the hell's going on?"

"I don't know," she said. "It's like they're running from something."

Chad pulled her up off the rock, then looked over his shoulder to the south. "Whatever it is, Silver doesn't like it either."

Elise looked up from her injured leg and took in the horrific sounds echoing from the distance. With the pain and chaos of falling over, the abrupt ending to Silver's song never registered in her ears. What she was listening to now was no song. They were cries of agony and despair.

"That's not normal, is it?" Chad said.

"No—no it's not," Elise muttered. For Chad, the uneasiness in her tone was just as worrisome as the cries themselves. She tried to swim, only to yelp in pain. "Damn it!"

"Can you make it?" Chad asked.

"I think I can." She tried swaying her flippers, only to cry out again. That piece of coral really stung her good. It hurt to even move her leg a little.

"I'm thinking not," Chad said. "We need to get you back to the boat. Let me help you."

"With all the stuff you're carrying? I don't think so," Elise said. "Head on up, tie a rope to the ladder, and bring it down to me. I'll climb on up."

"You sure? I can put your arm over my shoulder and help you swim up."

"Chad, it hurts for me to even move my leg," she said. She looked around. Whatever was causing the disturbance didn't appear to be anywhere nearby. "Just get the rope, please. I'd rather climb."

"You just want an upper body workout while you're at it," Chad quipped. He could see the shift in her cheeks as she pursed her lips at him. "Hey, when I stepped on an urchin, you were all about the jokes!"

"Yeah, duh! It's funny when it happens to *you*!"

Chad chuckled. "I see how it is." The cry from the south intensified, ceasing the moment of levity. Their hearts thumped. They couldn't see anything yet, but the distressed song seemed nearer. Chad started paddling. "Be right back."

He ascended to the surface, pausing every thirty feet for safety stops. Ascending was a tricky thing. Thirty feet of ocean may not seem like much; Elise didn't think so when she first learned to scuba dive. Then she experienced the bends for the first time—not fun.

In the few minutes that followed Elise watched as more fish evacuated the section of reef. Her heart thumped rapidly, the rushing blood intensifying the pain in her leg. She spotted a shape in the distance. It was far off, almost resembling a cloud. Her first instinct was to conclude it was a whale, yet, there was a strange buildup around it. A thin veil, almost like that from the blood that seeped from her leg. But this was *huge*, almost filling the entire background.

"Hey, I'm coming down," Chad said. Elise looked up at the boat overhead. Her nephew had broken the surface and was rapidly descending, rope in hand. He paused briefly, his gaze drawn to the phenomenon to the south. "Holy Jesus! What is going on?"

"I don't know. Let's just get out of here," Elise said. She groaned. Often, adrenaline dulled pain, allowing for struggling lifeforms to make their escapes from danger. In her case, however, it just made it worse. Even the slightest nudge made her thigh muscle feel like it was red hot.

Chad made his way down and gave her the rope. She wasted no time starting the climb. She made the first thirty feet easily. She paused for her safety stop. As she did, she noticed the shape take greater form. "Oh my God."

It was in fact a whale. Not just any whale; it was Silver. That bizarre veil filling the ocean behind was indeed her blood. The whale moved swiftly, red clouds pumping from lacerations in her back and fluke. Both biologists stared in horror. These wounds were not like anything a pod of orcas or a shark would inflict. They were long, deep cuts, as though she had been slashed with a large butcher's knife.

"What the hell happened? Where's her young?" Chad said.

"I don't know."

"There's nothing in the water that can do that to a whale," Chad said.

"Probably a damn boat propellor. Let's go. I'll get in touch with the scientist tracking her and inform them of—" She froze, her eyes locked on the large shape darting within the huge blood cloud. It glided effortlessly, tracking the injured whale, which was now passing a couple of hundred feet from them. It looked like a shark, but it couldn't have been. It was too large.

Her internal debate was quickly silenced as the creature appeared again. The crescent-moon shaped fin, the dorsal on its back; it was definitely a shark. Yet, it was *at least* thirty feet long, if not closer to forty.

"Did you see that?" Chad said.

"Yes." Elise proceeded to climb the rope. She made an additional six feet before stopping again. The shark appeared again and circled around Silver, who stopped. *Now* she hardly noticed the pain in her leg, as she was so fixated by the shape of the shark's lower jaw.

It can't be. It's impossible. I'm seeing things.

"What the hell is that?!"

Had Chad not spoken, Elise would've written the oddity off as a trick of the mind. But he saw it too. That circular-shaped set of teeth was real. That shark was real. More importantly, it should've been long dead. Yet, here it was. Alive.

Her fascination quickly reverted back to horror as the fish zipped at the whale. There was an echo of frantic movement. The shark cut the whale down her belly, then circled back around after completing its pass. It moved in again. With a slice of motion came another eruption of blood. Silver's right flipper fell away.

"My God! It's killing her!" Chad said.

"There's nothing we can do. Climb!" Elise said. Chad moved up another thirty feet, then paused. Elise started climbing past him. "Don't stop. Keep going."

"But what about the nitrogen buildup?"

"We *have* to get out of this water," Elise said.

"But—"

"No buts. That thing has no qualms about attacking larger animals. It might come after us next," she said. She grabbed him by the arm and shifted him up, the motion causing her leg to fire up again. Chad swam up for the boat, looking back to make sure his aunt was right behind him. At fifteen feet of depth, the decompression sickness hit. He felt woozy and stiff. A headache took hold, making his temples feel like they wanted to fly apart from each other.

Elise was feeling the same. Still, she continued her ascent, only looking back once at the horrific activity behind them. Silver was spiraling to the depths. Her fluke had been ripped away and there was a second gash in her belly. There didn't appear to be any movement. If she wasn't already dead, she would be with the shark's next attack. It closed in on her head and sliced with its jaws, running a deep laceration across her face. The placement of that cut would've caused water to rush down her blowhole. Elise could only hope that Silver had died already and be spared the sensation of drowning.

The shark followed the whale, then moved away as she settled on the reef. It was as though it had no interest in feeding; just killing. It was like a crazed maniac living under the sea, hellbent on inflicting harm to anything in its vicinity.

Suddenly, Elise was all too aware of the blood coming out of her leg, and the redirection of the shark's snout, which now pointed toward them.

"Oh no…Chad, MOVE! Get aboard the boat!"

She looked up, only to see her nephew floundering. He was clinging to the rope a few feet above her now. The sounds of gagging indicated he was trying not to vomit in his mask.

"Go. Move!"

"I can't. My head hurts."

Elise could feel the pain in her temples as well. Her vision was hazy. They had rushed the last fifty feet of this ascent. They were stuck between decompression sickness and being torn to bits by a shark. By the looks of it, they only had a shot of surviving *one* of those fates. She pushed Chad up. He threw his arms out, taking one handful of rope at a time.

Had his vision not been hazy, he would've realize he'd made it to the boat. Instead, he found out by clunking his head against the hull.

"Christ!" Elise grabbed him by the wrist as he fell away. He was barely conscious, his mouth agape. He was struggling to breathe. She grabbed the ladder and hauled herself onto the boat. Blood dripped from her nose as she pulled the mask away. She then shrieked as she balanced on both legs, but fought against it as she tried to haul Chad aboard. "Come on, kid! Grab the ladder."

Gritting teeth, Chad reached out, his slippery fingers coming off the side bar. He tried again, this time achieving a decent grasp. With her hand still on his other wrist, Elise moved up the ladder, then swung herself onto the deck. She leaned forward to pull him aboard. *Almost there.*

Like a rising volcano about to burst, a swell of water grew behind him. Beneath it was a large, dark blue shape. The snout broke the surface and snapped. Elise felt a brief tug, and suddenly, her nephew was gone. There was a splashing of red water to her right. Almost right away, she saw Chad. Her first instinct was to jump in after him, but stopped after he rolled with the swells. Everything under his shoulders and arms was gone in one clean cut.

She screamed his name, unable to take her eyes off the lifeless remains. Like a demented sadist hellbent on torturing the onlooker, the shark appeared again and snatched the upper torso, cutting it vertically down the center with its jaws, then consumed the halves.

Elise turned and stumbled across her deck. Shock, decompression sickness, and pain assaulted her at once. She fell against the radio, pulling the speaker mic to her lips.

"Mayday. Mayday." It was all she could mutter before passing out.

****

The fish circled the vessel, its stomach satiated with the contents of its recent kill. It moved slowly, detecting no vibrations from the vessel. After several minutes, the fish swam east.

After a few miles, it picked up new signals. These vibrations were widespread, as though a feeding frenzy was taking place in the shallows. The fish moved in close to investigate. It wasn't marine life, but the human species. There were hundreds of them, all oblivious to its presence. Like the ones it had slain earlier that day, they weren't on the land, but invading the sea like a cancer.

Only a thin veil of net separated it from its nearest target.

CHAPTER 8

"Subject one. Martin Forbes. Date of birth: September 4th, 1989. No remains below L4 vertebrae. Partial stomach tissue remaining. Lower ribs severed. Status of the tissue and bone around area of injury indicates that the instrument of use was a serrated edged object. With no other remains to examine, it is impossible to determine exactly what kind of instrument."

Captain Brianna Raye listened to the coroner narrate the report, which she held in her hands. On the outside, she looked neutral. Internally, she was throwing a fit. All she needed to hear was that this death was undoubtedly a shark attack. Simply the mention of 'instrument' indicated that the coroner, Dr. McGibbeny, wasn't certain.

"What about the others?" she asked.

McGibbeny shrugged. That annoyed the Captain. The doc always shrugged when thinking up an answer. He shook his head and removed the fog from his glasses. "Not enough remains to conduct a full detailed analysis. They were cut apart, with most vital organs and bones lost."

"Cut, or ripped?"

"Likely cut, but it's impossible to be certain. There was additional damage to the tissue from exposure to the seabed."

Brianna exhaled slowly. "And the last subject? Gary Stuckey?"

"That's the weirdest one," the doctor said. "He's suffered a deep laceration across the umbilical region. Colon was ruptured. Left and right lilac—"

"Yes, I already saw it," Brianna said. "Can you tell me what might have done it?"

"A large, edged weapon," the doctor said.

"Any idea what? Boat propellor, maybe?"

"No, there'd be multiple lacerations. This is just—one. Plus, the notes stated he was in shallow water. Considering the location of the wound, I don't think that's the case."

"Could a shark have done it?" Brianna said.

McGibbeny shrugged. "It's not consistent with a shark bite in terms of its form. BUT, there is an interesting thing that points in that direction."

"And that is?"

"I drew up some blood and tissue cultures from all victims, starting with Gary Stuckey. Tests came back positive for bacteria called Vibro Parahaemolyticus and Vibro Alginolyticus. Commonly found in the jaws of marine animals, including sharks. In recent years, biologists have cultured the jaws of great white sharks and found that their teeth were loaded with these bacteria. Considering Mr. Stuckey's exposure to the water was gravely limited, and taking into account that he lives inland, it's peculiar that he has such a strong amount of bacteria in his system."

"So, you're now saying it was a shark?" the Captain asked.

McGibbeny shrugged. “Normally, I’d question it. But the presence of the bacteria highly indicates that he was attacked by a shark. Nothing else in this region that I can think of can be responsible. Maybe the shark came at him, mouth agape, and sliced him while his brother pulled him back. I know I’m stretching logic here, but it’s the only thing I can think of.” He realized his answer wasn’t sufficient for the Captain. “Considering the eyewitness accounts of both parties, and my findings—yes, it was probably a shark attack.”

Brianna nodded. “Make sure that’s on the report. Thanks, Doctor.” She started walking away. She’d got the answer she wanted, in case Luke Jansen continued his tirade that it wasn’t a shark. He’d probably take issue with the fact that McGibbeny was the examiner—a doctor whom he considered incompetent. Still, she couldn’t help but think of some of the detective’s observations.

No, you’ve got your answer. Don’t overcomplicate things.

That inner voice almost won. Captain Raye was almost out the door. At the last second, she turned back to face the doc. “One last question. Subject one, Martin Forbes; you have any comments about the nature of the injury? Specifically, does the cut seem a little…too clean…for a shark bite?”

As usual, McGibbeny shrugged. “Frankly, I don’t have too much experience in shark injuries. The few I’ve delt with were from considerably smaller species. Whatever did this was clearly a large specimen. Depending on its bite power, I suppose it’s possible.” He didn’t sound convinced.

“Do you suspect one or more sharks?”

“*You’re* the detective,” McGibbeny said. “Considering the state of the remains, I can’t provide an exact bite radius.”

“Alright. Thanks.” The Captain exited the office then walked out into the parking lot. She found her vehicle, got in, and started the engine. She checked the time. It was a quarter past six. All she needed to do was speak to the police chief, who in turn would alert the mayor. Watches and advisories would be put out. The mayor would likely arrange a deal with local contractors to hunt the shark. The news surprisingly didn’t overblow the situation. They left the odd details out, simply stating that Amadea had been rocked by an odd series of shark attacks. There was more time spent on the latest so-called *Twitter* controversy, in which a bunch of accounts ganged up on one, misrepresenting and blowing a minor ‘offense’ out of proportion.

Before she could shift the lever to *drive*, her radio went off.

“Car Thirteen to Dispatch. Alert EMS to South Beach. We’ve got a shark attack. We’re evacuating the water now. Alert the Mayor’s Office.”

Tires screeched as Brianna sped the vehicle out of the lot and onto the road. From there, she took a left to cut through the suburban neighborhoods to avoid the heavier traffic.

“What the hell is going on?”

CHAPTER 9

A trembling hand lifted the *Southern Comfort* from the barbeque-stained living tray table. Its effect was hit-or-miss for Luke Jansen. Sometimes it helped dull his pain, other times it made him dwell on it even more. Today, it seemed to be the latter.

He took the next gulp, keeping his eye fixed on the voluptuous activity on the television screen. He tried to focus on the sight of wet, perky breasts of two twenty-something year old blondes as they caressed each other, their lips never parting. Yet, he felt no excitement, even as one worked her way down the other's chest.

Rather than be drawn to the gratuity that was front and center, his eye was fixated on the burning candlelight on the nightstand next to the ladies. The sensation of heat swept over his face. Images of scorched flesh flashed in his mind. For several moments, the wide shot continued, and in that time, his nerves taunted him with their damage.

Luke cursed under his breath. His distraction had reached a point where it was actively hurting him.

With a click of the remote, he turned the pay-per-view program off. He sat quietly in his living room chair, nearly oblivious to the garbage that littered his floor. Every so often, he'd attempt a cleanup, usually to stop after clearing the desk table or kitchen counter. Rarely did he feel the energy anymore. Life had become routine. Go to work, deal with police work, complete cases, piss off the Captain and judge, and waste time when there were no homicides. He didn't bother with social calls—the one or two he'd gotten since transferring.

On the floor near the ottoman, a snippet of newspaper lay. It had collected dust, grit, and mud stains from being stepped on by wet boots. In two years, it had never moved from that spot where he dropped it. Despite this, the image of thirty-three year old Morgan Laskey was clear as ever. He had a mustache in the photo they used, though he had shaved it two months later.

LAPD Homicide Detective killed. Partner injured in botched investigation.

He had seen the reports when they originally came out. They were unavoidable. His mind flashed back to his hospital room. There he was, lying in a hospital bed, his face still bright red from third-degree burns, unable to see from his left eye, while reporters tried shoving microphones and cameras in what was left of his face. It was through the barrage of questions that he found out Morgan had died of his injuries.

The questions were nothing to the public shunning that followed. The Captain of his division was quick to throw Luke under the bus. Like a hivemind, cops from all units and divisions joined the discourse. The worst stings by far came from Morgan's wife and parents, people he shared Thanksgiving dinner with, spent Christmas Eve with. Now, they thought him lower than a cockroach scurrying around a toilet bowl.

Luke's eye moved down to the paper. It had been mailed to him soon after he moved, likely by one of his former associates to remind him of his failure and legacy. The text other than the title was obscured by wear and grub. It didn't matter, however, as the narrative was implanted in his memory.

The sound of a police siren snapped him back to reality. He stood up and went to the window. A black Ford Mustang zipped across the road. Only one person in the department had such a vehicle. Captain Raye was heading west—right back to the coastal properties.

Like before, he found his radio and turned it on. What followed was a series of transmissions by officers announcing they were arriving on scene and stating what areas of the beach they were monitoring. One of which announced he was directing an ambulance to park by Reynold's Hot Dog stand.

Charley Reynold always set up his business on South Beach. Something was going on in the water.

Struck by curiosity, Luke switched on the internet and *Googled* news for Amadea, California. 'Breaking News' articles with *Shark Attack* somewhere in the article immediately popped up. One of which featured a brief video clip from a bystander's smartphone. He clicked on the link, then watched the twenty-second clip.

Immediately, the audio exploded with people yelling "shark!" The camera panned from people on shore to the buoys holding the anti-shark. Passing between two of them was a large dorsal fin. There was no sign of resistance. It was as though the net wasn't even there at all.

Screams erupted through the speakers as a female was knocked off her raft. A large caudal fin swung wildly, splashing red water into a panicking crowd of swimmers.

It was as though fate was deliberately taunting him Once again, he was proven wrong. It indeed *was* a shark causing these deaths. He was doomed to be ridiculed by Captain Raye and Detective Norton regarding his interference. He exited the tab, then moved the mouse to the lower left corner with intent to shut the computer down.

He paused.

A horizontal laceration. He thought of the corpses he inspected. He couldn't be definitive on the man that was bitten in half, though he still had his doubts. But the one on the property? No way in hell could a shark have done that.

He opened a new window and began researching shark bites and record history of attacks. What he uncovered were countless images of victims, most of which were taken in the hospital or on the beach after the attack. Almost none of these incidents, including those of the few victims who lost a limb, resembled the injuries of today's victims. A search for recorded shark attack incidents only resulted in one result for a victim bitten in half. The victim was an Australian surfer, who was killed in 2012 by a fifteen-foot great white shark. There were no images to compare to the jet skier.

Only now did his face hurt again. The relief ended as soon as he turned the volume back up on his radio. A few officers confirmed the sighting of the shark, stating it was moving back out to sea. He turned the radio off; no sense in reminding himself that he was wrong. There was no denying what he saw on the screen.

Case was closed. It was a killer shark.

CHAPTER 10

It was a few minutes after seven when Brianna Raye arrived at Town Hall for the press conference. Even as she pulled into the driveway, she was bombarded with questions by angry residents and press. The conference itself was due to start in twelve minutes. The mayor and chief's vehicles were already present. She parked next to them and pushed her way through the crowd.

"We're on top of the situation. We'll take your questions in the conference," she said. Trotting over hot asphalt, she made her way into the building. Once inside, she took a moment to neaten her formal uniform. Even after a shower and change of clothes, she still felt the wetness of fresh blood on her knees and arms.

The scene at the beach was a disaster of epic proportions. The shark was claiming a second life by the time she arrived. When boat patrols closed in, the fish circled around and disappeared into open sea. Injuries and fatalities didn't stop there. Panic had swept the beach. A stampede of people retreated from the water, resulting in numerous people suffering concussions from falls. Four people suffered heart attacks, two of which were twenty-feet out in the water. One was pulled out in time by family members, the other drowned. Bad went to worse as fights broke out, spurred by confusion and survival instincts gone haywire.

The reports of the attack itself were bogged down by the first wave of scrutiny against the police department. Already, reports were hitting the airwaves regarding the department's knowledge of the shark's presence. The cherry on top of the sundae for Brianna was the coverage taken on the Stuckey property. Footage of Detective Luke Jansen was aired, as well as recorded audio of him expressing his doubts that a shark was even responsible for the initial attacks. That was the final cannister of fuel that propelled the incident into national news.

People were more fixated about the police failure than the sensational fact that a single shark had caused so much death.

It was a quarter after seven when the conference commenced. Mayor Pedro Garza began with a statement, offering condolences to the families of the victims, and ensuring that all resources would be devoted to hunting the shark down. With the closing of his statement, he allowed Chief Claudio Pino to outline his plan of action.

Brianna stood by silently, listening along with everyone else as the Chief outlined his instructions. She clenched her hands behind her back, waiting for the inevitable 'throwing under the bus' moment. It would either come from him or the journalists—or both.

"I'll start out by explaining what we know so far," he said. "At four-nineteen P.M. today, a large shark, believed to be a great white, broke through the nets at South Beach. Two people were killed as a direct result of the attack.

One was a resident, Elizabeth Payton—thirty-two years of age, and the second was a vacationer from Colorado, Elijah Andrews—twenty-six years of age. In the panic that followed, there were three more fatalities, all from pre-existing medical conditions. Two were heart attacks and one stroke, though we're waiting on the medical examiners to confirm these.

"Regarding the issue at hand, we are announcing that all beaches in Amadea will be closed, and have advised neighboring coastal communities to do the same until the issue is resolved. I'd like to add my voice to the Mayor's in expressing we are devoted to leaving no stone unturned in ensuring the safety of our waters. However, our department lacks sufficient resources to conduct a large-scale hunt for a single shark, which could be anywhere in this ten-mile stretch of ocean. Therefore, we are announcing a fifty-thousand dollar reward to any fisherman who successfully catches and kills the shark. From what our advisors can determine from what we've observed so far, it prefers to hunt during the day. That said, we're instructing that nobody go out at night. This is clearly an unpredictable animal and I'd rather our contractors have the advantage of daylight when hunting it. Until it is successfully killed, the beaches will remain closed. Officers will be stationed at the beach twenty-four hours a day. Anyone in the water will be fined and possibly arrested.

"We are determined to solve this matter as quickly and efficiently as possible, and I thank everyone, local or otherwise, for their cooperation. With that said, I will take questions."

The crowd erupted at once, chattering over each other until one was selected.

"Chief, were there not any shark nets in place at the beach?"

"Yes there were. From what we can determine, the net was either sabotaged or otherwise compromised at that section. The shark located a gap in the net and made its way through."

"Did it not bite through?"

The Chief tried not to chuckle at that question. "Those nets are designed to withstand shark bites." He pointed out another reporter.

"Is it true that your department was already aware of the shark's presence, and yet chose *not* to close the beaches?"

"There was no reason to suspect that the beaches were unsafe at that time."

"'No reason'?!" another reporter shouted. "We're hearing that the shark had killed *four* other people prior to this."

"Yes, but we weren't aware of the flaw in the shark net. And frankly, this behavior is not the usual case for sharks. With respect to the previous victims, we were certain that the shark was done feeding."

An uproar from the crowd expressed the general condemnation of that response. They quieted down as an individual, not a reporter, but a common resident, shouted at the podium.

"Is it common practice for the police to not take action? What does the head of Homicide have to say? Word is she was investigating one of the previous attacks."

Brianna tensed as the Chief glanced in her direction. She knew that look. 'Your turn.' She stepped to the podium, taking a quick breath to remove any nervousness from her voice.

"I was on scene at the Stuckey property. I must reinforce the point our Chief has made. We were indeed certain that the shark would not attack again today, and that we would be able to track it down without closing the beaches and damaging the local economy."

"Is that truly the case? Or is it that you were accusing a member of the Stuckey family of murder?" another voice called out.

"I—beg your pardon? We've made no such accusation. That's a blatant misrepresentation and you should be ashamed of yourself."

"Lady, there's video of one of your detectives stating it was not a shark," another shouted.

"Another misrepresentation," Brianna replied. "He was questioning the irregularities of the attacks. Which, come on, *are* in fact irregular."

The Chief took to the podium, pulling the mic toward him. "I'd like to point out that Detective Luke Jansen was not part of that investigation and will be reprimanded for his interference."

Brianna glared at him. *Always confident in your leadership, until the heat is on, then you'll throw anyone under the bus, won't you?*

A female reporter to the right raised her hand. "Chief? What kind of shark was it?"

"As I stated before, we believe it was a great white. Unfortunately, everything happened so fast and there's hardly any video of the animal. But it should be easy to identify due to the fact it was very large."

"How big?" another asked.

"Can't really determine that at this point," he replied. "Some are saying it's a record-sized specimen, so that'll make it fairly easy to identify."

"What comment do you have about Dr. Sheldon?"

Chief Pino shared a confused glance with the mayor. "I'm not sure of your meaning?"

"She was a victim of the attack," another reporter said. "She states it was a prehistoric shark."

"Oh, that." The Chief shook his head. "Listen, I know there's a lot to be upset about, but are we really gonna entertain this kind of rhetoric?"

"She's a marine biologist—"

"Who's suffering from decompression sickness and trauma," Pino interrupted. "She was delirious when rescue teams located her. We're still working to determine what exactly happened regarding that incident. Until we do, please don't entertain that kind of nonsense."

As the Chief continued to spar with the reporters, Brianna slowly backed away, then turned around to find Detective Norton standing on the far side of the stage. She walked over to him and leaned over. "Were you aware of this?"

"Of what?" he asked.

"Of another attack? This Dr. Sheldon person?"

"EMS reported airlifting a patient. She had nitrogen build-up in her respiratory system. From what I hear, she ascended too fast."

"She saw the shark?"

"She claims she did. So I hear, at least. They flew her in during the chaos at the beach."

"Has anyone spoken with her?"

"Nobody in our department. I think a few reporters stuck their noses into the ER while she was being admitted. It gets worse, though. Sounds like she wasn't alone."

"What?"

"The paramedics reported to the patrol Sergeant, who passed it on to the Chief, who passed it on to me. From what it sounds, she was diving with somebody. And, well, they only found her."

"Great." Brianna shook her head. "We're gonna have to speak with her just to clear this up. Otherwise, the media will run with it."

Norton scoffed. "Why don't you put Jansen on it?"

"Stop with the jokes," she said sternly. "Right now, I think it's best to keep him as far from this case as possible."

"Why not just terminate him?" Norton said.

"Seriously, dude? You're awfully quick to draw on that," she replied.

"One could argue you're a little too eager to keep him onboard," he said. "Some might draw certain conclusions from *that*. Plus, I think the media's gonna hound the Chief about Jansen's idiotic statements."

"They weren't statements," Brianna said. Her voice unintentionally boomed, briefly drawing the attention of everyone in the crowd and on stage. It took a moment for the back and forth between Pino and the reporters to continue. With her voice lowered, Brianna leaned toward Norton. "What he said was stupid, but he didn't make a press conference and make pronouncements. And you know as well as I do that he wasn't accusing the family members."

"He wasn't ruling it out," Norton muttered.

"It was a hot mic moment, caught by people bloodthirsty for a scapegoat."

"Careful who you say that around," Norton said.

Brianna resisted the urge to roll her eyes. Arguing with Norton about Luke was like trying to convince *Celtics* fans to make friends in Los Angeles. Success was only a fantasy. "This Dr. Sheldon woman, is she at Amadea General?"

"Yes."

"Alright. Let's wait for this to finish up. We've got more work to do."

The Captain waited silently while Chief Pino concluded the press conference. "Thank you for addressing your concerns. We will inform you the moment the shark has been killed..."

****

"As we've stated, our highest priority is the safety of our civilians. Thank you. Have a good night."

Barton lit a fresh cigar. It wasn't often he smoked to mellow himself out. But the shit had hit the fan, and that fan was turned on high.

"Shut that damn radio off," he said, never once taking his eyes off the sunset in the horizon. He could hear footsteps of nervous men down on the main deck. They were all waiting for his response to the situation.

Only one was brave enough to climb up to the flybridge. Barton turned around to see his brother-in-arms, Dixon, staring at him.

"The boss is gonna be pissed," Dixon said.

"You think I don't know?" Barton drew on the cigar, then offered one to his friend. Dixon took one and lit it. He stood by his comrade and stared out into the water. They had to think of a solution fast, or things were bound to get worse.

"Perhaps it's not Thirteen doing the killing. Maybe it's just some great white, like what the news is reporting."

Barton spat his cigar. "*Six* deaths?! Maybe seven? All in an area that hasn't had a shark attack in seven years? Besides, the tracker shows that it's here. Clearly, it found an abundant food supply."

Dixon looked at the stogie floating in the water. "Those aren't cheap, you know."

"Right! Like it's such an issue. You hand those things out on the regular like candy. Practically your calling card."

"I'll buy you a whole freaking pack if you figure out a solution. We need to catch that thing now and get the hell out of here."

"You'll buy me a pack anyway. And we won't catch it now. At least, not tonight. Believe it or not, we've got bigger fish to fry. That scientist lady's gonna stir up the media unless we give them something to chew on." He lit a new cigar and took a long draw. "I know what to do. Contact home plate. Tell them to bring Number Four."

Dixon's eyes widened. "Boss won't be happy with that."

"Don't care. We're up shit creek. Catching Thirteen won't be enough. We need to give these people a scapegoat, or they'll be a headache forever." His eyes brightened as another thought came to mind. "Is Patterson still on site?"

Dixon laughed. "Yeah. Why?"

"You know what? *I'll* make the call. I know how to make that idiot useful."

Dixon followed him into the pilothouse. "Him? Useful? The guy who didn't repair the pen door when we ordered him to, thus causing all this? *Useful?!*"

Barton grinned. "Believe me, you'll love what I have in mind."

CHAPTER 11

Elise dreaded sleep. Anything longer than a blink would bring back that horrible image of Chad in the water. The nightmares began the moment she passed out on the boat. Now, it was late in the evening, and she was lying in a hospital bed, with night looming over her. The nurses instructed her to try and get some rest, and that she was physically well enough to be let out tomorrow as long as her condition continued to improve. It only took fifteen minutes in a decompression chamber to alleviate her symptoms. She still had a headache, but the doctor stated that it was due to stress.

She stared at the door, ignoring the food and water on her tray table. The very thought of eating made her nauseous. Her mind couldn't separate the mashing of the sandwich from the image of Chad getting chopped up by that shark's teeth. With quivering hands, she pushed the tray away.

There were people talking outside the door. She recognized one voice as the night-shift doctor. There were two others, a male and a female. Whoever they were, they sounded inquisitive. Considering the circumstances of her being in this hospital bed, it wasn't hard to deduce that they were police officers.

"Is this something that can wait until tomorrow? The patient has undergone a lot of stress in the past six hours or so," she heard the doctor say.

"We need to get an understanding of what occurred," the female cop explained.

"Watch the news. She says she was attacked by a shark," the doctor replied.

"Forgive us, Doctor, but we don't conduct investigations by what's reported on the news. We tend to go a little more in-depth," the male cop said.

"You'll probably get a more coherent story if you wait until tomorrow," the doctor said.

"Why's that?" the woman said.

"She might be delirious. She's been saying stuff about a helicop—uh, something."

"A helicopter?" the woman asked.

"No. She claims she was attacked by a prehistoric species of shark," the doctor said. "She might have some mental trauma. At the very least, she's in shock."

There were a few moments of silence before the male cop spoke to his partner. "Maybe he's right. If she's like this, we probably should hold off." The silence that followed indicated that the other cop was buying into the crap the doctor said.

Elise couldn't take it anymore. She leaned forward. "Is that the police?! Bring 'em in, please. I want to talk to them. And yes, I'm feeling well enough."

There was a sigh from the doctor. "Alright." He held the door open for the two officers, who were clearly detectives judging by their attire and badge. The word *Homicide* naturally made Elise slightly nervous. Would they consider her a suspect? After the day she'd experienced… everything she lost… that would be the icing on the cake.

The woman was ten-to-fifteen years older than the man, and seemed to show a little more concern. Both looked glassy-eyed. Considering the bits of news she'd caught, it had been a long day for the police department. On any other occasion, she would feel pity for them. Then again, none of them had lost their nephew whom they were raising as their own son. For all Elise cared, these cops could work twenty-four hours a day for the rest of the year, and it wouldn't compare to how miserable she felt now.

"Hi," she simply said.

"Good evening. I'm Captain Brianna Raye with the Amadea Police Department. This is Detective Norton. First, I'd like to express my condolences for your loss. Your vessel has been towed to your property in Vincent Cove, courtesy of the Wayne tugboat service. I hope you don't mind, first responders found your ID among your belongings in the vessel when they found you, which was how they knew where to deliver it."

Elise nodded. "Okay. Thank you."

"We'd like to ask you a few questions and get the details of what happened if you're feeling up to it."

"Okay."

"It's our understanding that it was your nephew that was with you?" Norton asked.

"Yes. Chad Samson."

"I'm sorry. If you provide his parents' contact info, we can alert them—"

"They passed away when he was a teenager," Elise said. "I was given custody of him, since I was the only family he had left. His dad was an only child. His paternal grandparents live in France. They've never met him."

"I see," Brianna said. She jotted down notes, then glanced at a clipboard. "So, you're a marine biologist?"

"Yes. I mainly work in a lab. I take samples from the reef every week and monitor the levels of microplastic in the area."

Brianna didn't bother trying to understand what that entailed. "That's what you were out doing today with Chad?"

"Yes." Elise closed her eyes to stop the tears, unwittingly doing the thing she so badly wanted to avoid. The image of that horrid shark flashed in her memory, making her shiver.

"Whoa!" Detective Norton said. "You alright? Need us to get the doctor?"

"No, no. I'm fine," she replied. She reached for her bottle of water. It was the only thing that would stay down. "It was a shark."

"How many sharks was it?" Norton said. Elise glared at him. What difference did that detail make? Chad was dead either way.

"One."

"What he means is, we've had an extremely unusual series of shark attacks today, including one on the South Beach. Due to the nature, we suspect there might be multiple sharks in the area."

"Just one," Elise said. Her memory flashed to its circular-shaped lower jaw. Her eyes widened in alarm. "You need to close the beaches!"

"Already done," Norton said.

"There'll be a large-scale hunt commencing tomorrow morning," Brianna said. "It's pretty clear we're looking for a great white."

"No, no, NO!" Elise said. "It's not a great white."

"Ma'am, with respect, considering its size and ferocity—"

"I saw it clear as day," Elise said. "It's not a great white. We're dealing with an extinct species—or, what we thought was extinct. It's called a Helicoprion." Norton scratched his head. The look in his eyes gave away his thoughts. *Looks like the doctor wasn't kidding about the hallucinations.* Elise swung herself out of bed. "I'm telling the truth."

"Whoa! Ma'am. Best to stay rested," Brianna said.

"I'm fine. I—" She coughed, then dry-heaved. With the Captain's help, she was repositioned into her hospital bed.

"What is a Helicoprion?" Norton asked.

Elise took a moment to regain control of whatever was left of her stomach contents. "Records show that it went extinct around two-hundred-fifty-million years ago."

"Ma'am, shhh," Brianna said.

"No, *listen*!" Elise said. "Its lower jaw is comprised of a singular row of teeth that are in a whorl. Like a damn circular saw. Researchers thought it might've been used for crushing shellfish, but it'll attack anything. It's a violent predator—"

"Dr. Sheldon, PLEASE listen," Brianna said.

"No, *you* listen," Elise said. "I watched it attack a humpback whale. I watched it come after Chad. I saw it—I—" Her voice started to break.

"Shhhhh." Brianna sat on the edge of the bed and put a hand on her shoulder. "You've been through a horrible experience. Please hear me out: you've suffered decompression sickness and psychological trauma. It's very understandable to see things that weren't present under such circumstances."

Elise looked away. "I see you're not gonna do anything about the shark."

"Like she said; there's a hunt taking place tomorrow morning," Norton said. "You'll see once they catch the shark, ma'am. I promise you there's no dinosaur swimming around out there. Just a big mean shark, which has maybe fifteen more hours to live."

"More importantly, if you keep making statements about a prehistoric shark, the doctors might require a psyche evaluation to let you leave. From what I'm told, you're doing well enough to go home tomorrow. Don't put yourself in a position to be forced to stay. Keep in mind, you weren't self-admitted to this hospital."

Elise pursed her lips. She thought of a few insults but kept them to herself. What good would lashing out do? Chad was still gone. In that moment, she put the shoe on the other foot. Of course nobody would believe her. Hell, had it been someone else saying the exact same thing to her, she'd be in disbelief.

"I'm sorry."

"Oh, no, sweetie. There's nothing to be sorry about," Brianna said. She and Elise shared a hug. The marine biologist appreciated the maternal nature of the detective. She didn't have anyone else to comfort her. "Do you have any other family at all?"

"I have people," Elise said. Brianna sensed the lie. She reached into her pocket and pulled out a business card and one for a grief counselor.

"Give me a call or text, and I can set you up with a good grief counselor," she said. "He's really good. You'll think he's family after two minutes of talking with him."

"I appreciate it," Elise said. They shared another hug before Brianna stood up from the bed.

"Don't hesitate to call if you need anything. Try to get some sleep, alright?" She started for the door. "Come on, Norton."

"Good night, ma'am," he said.

Elise nodded, leaned back against the pillow and watched the door shut.

****

Norton shut the door behind him and followed the Captain down the hall. She stopped briefly to let the MD know they were done, then made their way into the main hall.

"As though this day couldn't get weirder," he said.

"Just keep the report short and sweet," Brianna said. "Don't mention anything about a prehistoric shark—whatever she called it."

"A chainsaw shark, or something like that," Norton said. "Poor girl. Must've been so damn traumatic for her to envision something like that."

"Yes. And we don't need to add to her misery. Or ours. The Chief would laugh us out of his office if he read that in the report." She groaned. "Thank God the media didn't get a chance to talk with her."

"You think he'll want us to go a little more in-depth on this investigation?" Norton asked.

"No. With all the shark-related incidents that have occurred, it's pretty obvious what went down. There's no criminal history with that woman. Spent three years in the Army, completed her doctorate at the age of twenty-eight, hasn't even had a speeding ticket in all the years of living here. I gave the Schmidt Institution a call and got in contact with her supervisor, and he had nothing but good things to say. We'll run a check on Chad Samson to validate her story, but otherwise, there's nothing to indicate foul-play." They found the main lobby and went out to the lot. Brianna looked up at the evening sky. "Please, God, let it end tomorrow."

****

Elise stared at the ceiling, feeling more helpless than ever. That Captain was a well-meaning woman with a good heart. Unfortunately, there was no way of convincing the police of what was really out there. Already, her claims were being dismissed as a false memory, with the stress being used as the catalyst for her 'seeing things'.

"I saw it. I know I saw it." She wanted to make a series of phone calls. *Somebody* had to believe her. Maybe Doctor Hamden at Schmidt. He might hear her out. Tears streamed down her face. She didn't want to sleep. The thought of facing her nightmares was too much for her already fragile mind to handle. On the contrary, she couldn't exhaust herself either.

It was all beginning to sink in. Going home would be forever different. Going on the boat would never be the same. Every time she saw a *Star Wars* commercial, she wouldn't get to experience Chad's joy or criticism. Christmas and Thanksgiving would be dark and lonely.

Taking Chad into her life was the best thing she had ever done. Every time Elise looked to the sky, she always felt her sister was smiling down on her for stepping up to the plate. What was she feeling now? Elise found herself hoping that Heaven didn't exist, that way there was no chance her sister was angry. That only led to more despair. Without Heaven, there was no peace for Chad.

Elise put her head in her hands and wept. "I'm sorry, Kathy. I failed you. Please forgive me."

With the repenting came a desire to somehow make it right. Inaction would only worsen the pain. She needed to do something, and all she could think to do was make sure that shark was found and killed.

Maybe tomorrow.

CHAPTER 12

Even when asleep, the shark was active. Its tail swayed to and fro, gently gliding its eight-thousand-pound bulk above the coral reefs lining the coast. In this state, the fish could have easily been mistaken for a gentle giant. It was a passive being with no awareness for any existing life around it. Its stomach was hard at work breaking down the immense amount of protein it had consumed in the past twenty-four hours. Twice, it expelled waste through its lower intestinal tract, lining the reef with the indigestible garments worn by the humans.

It took no notice of the smaller creatures below as they scavenged the remains for anything edible. The crabs gathered by the droppings in large numbers, devouring whatever particles they could find. Some of the green crabs broke away from the group as some red rock crabs crashed the party. Most of the scavengers were able to break away. But such as life, there were a few unlucky members who could not outpace their pursuers. They were torn apart and consumed over the course of a few hours. King of their domain, the red rock crabs fed at their leisure, turning the soft flesh beneath the shell to pulp. They ate everything from the muscular tissue to the stomach contents.

After it completed its meal, one of the rock crabs continued scurrying along the rock beds. After an hour, its movements grew sluggish. Its vision weakened as did its sensory receptors. At two hours, its rear legs failed to function properly. Motor control continued to rapidly deteriorate. There was no sense of direction, no clue of where its den was located—and no clue that it was stumbling near the lair of a Pacific octopus.

The cephalopod lunged at the easy meal, trapping it under its tentacles and guiding it towards its beak. The eagle-like jaws made easy work of the shell. The red rock crab, which hours ago had been the ferocious predator, was now the helpless prey. Its misery came to a swift end as its flesh was slurped into the octopus' stomach.

Thus, with the progression of the food chain, the disease in which the crab carried was passed along. Within an hour, the octopus understood something was wrong. Like with its prey, it began losing motor control and eyesight. There was pain, as though its cellular system was fighting against itself. Thirty minutes later, the octopus began to spray ink uncontrollably. Fish passing by its cloud quickly darted away, but not before the substance passed through their gill slits—the water oxygenating their blood.

Muscular contractions occurred sporadically. For the cephalopod's brain, it was as though it was being bitten by a dozen small sets of jaws. Yet, it was alone in its little lair. Despite this, the creature felt an urge to flee. Filling its mantle with water, it jetted into the open ocean. The eight-legged creature was fleeing an enemy it could not comprehend. No matter how far it went or how fast it moved, the pain and misery followed. Only when its mind faded to the permanent darkness of death was the octopus freed from the torment. Its corpse settled in the shallows, where it would be nipped by a few scavenging fish. In a few hours, the bacteria in its body would release gases and raise its body to the surface, where the waves would wash it ashore.

Meanwhile, the food chain continued, just as it did every other day in the ocean. Fish that fed on the octopus or were exposed to its ink cloud continued to swim about. Some eventually died in the coral reef, while others ascended toward the surface. Their bodies floated on the surface, carried away by the tide, while others were doomed to be picked off by larger organisms, unaware of what lurked within the blood of their prey.

The cycle of death had begun.

CHAPTER 13

"You want a refill?"

Brianna Raye extended her empty coffee mug toward her husband, Kirk, who happily stepped into the living room with the pitcher. Sunday mornings, as long as work was routine and there was no major case to be solved, were the part of her week that she looked forward to the most. There was no such thing as police work. She was simply a lazy housewife who wanted nothing more than to eat eggs, drink coffee, and mindlessly scroll through the internet.

Kirk knew his wife well. Don't bring up her work, even if it was front and center on the local news. Just talk about the store, his buddies, make breakfast, and don't forget to bring her the sugar. Which he did. He grinned at the glare he received from his wife when he arrived with the coffee but no sugar jar.

"Be right back."

She smiled as soon as his back turned. Getting on his case for minor offenses was simply part of their daily banter. He returned with the sugar and put two scoops in her mug. Her smile widened as he stirred the contents into the coffee for her.

"Good boy," she quipped.

"Anything for my queen," he replied.

"Flattery will get you nowhere," she said.

"We both know that's a lie," he said. It was, but again going with their usual roleplaying, Brianna pretended it wasn't.

"Where's the kid?" she said. She looked over her shoulder to the back hallway which led to their son's bedroom. It was the tail end of summer break, so it was safe to assume he was taking advantage of his last week of freedom by sleeping in.

"I heard him up and about right before you got up," Kirk replied.

Brianna nearly spit her coffee. "Seriously?" She glanced about again. "Where'd he go?"

"Kid just got his license," Kirk said. "He said he was heading to the harbor."

This time, Brianna *did* spit her coffee. "The harbor?!"

Kirk dropped what he was doing and looked at her. He was alarmed, considering the look on her face was not part of their usual banter. She was actually irritated.

"Um, yes?" His wife picked up the real message in that question: *Is that a bad thing?*

"Why'd you let him go?"

"He's going on a boat with his buddies," Kirk said. "They go out all the time. Maybe not this early, but it didn't seem like such a huge deal."

"Oh, Jesus, Kirk. Don't you realize what's going on?"

"Yeeeaaahhh—didn't you make the rule that we don't talk about your cases?"

"You—" she stopped herself, looked to the floor and groaned, then raised her eyes back to him. "Yes. You're right."

"What's going on?"

"I'm sure you've at least heard of the killer shark incidents, right?"

"Yes," he answered. Brianna was somewhat surprised, as Kirk usually avoided the news like the plague. Too depressing, he often said. She used to disagree, stating it was better to be informed. Then she became a detective and saw the coverage of her cases, and then she realized watching the news was often the opposite of informing yourself.

Brianna found the remote and flipped the channel to the local news.

"What the hell's going on?" Kirk said.

"The Mayor's Office is offering a reward for anyone who kills the shark," she said.

"What does that have to do with Glenn and his buddies—ohhhhh!" It all came together. He sat by his wife and watched the coverage on Channel Eight Amadea Local News.

The Amadea Harbor was alive with fishermen, city staff, and journalists. Word of the hefty reward made its way through town like wildfire. Fishermen with oceanfront properties had a head start, and had already set out onto the water. A few boats could be seen from the pier by those who lived inland as they hustled on the docks to board their vessels.

The reporter on site went from fisherman to fisherman, each of whom were eager to get their fifteen seconds of fame by proclaiming how skilled they were at seamanship and fishing. It was like watching a sports convention, with each player bragging about their past scores and accolades.

It wasn't the interviews that Brianna was interested in. She watched the background intently. Unfortunately, there were too many bodies moving about. She wouldn't recognize Glenn unless he was front and center in the crowd.

Kirk pulled out his cell phone and dialed their son's number. "He's not picking up."

"Probably left it in his car. Or might be out on the boat already. Nobody gets decent service out on that water," Brianna said. The repeated deep breaths she took worried Kirk even more. He always saw her as a level-headed woman, always on top of whatever scenario life threw at her.

"These shark attacks—how bad *are* they?" he asked.

"Bad enough to gain this type of media coverage," she replied. She sighed. "Seven people were killed by it yesterday alone."

The coffee mug fell from Kirk's hand, shattering onto the floor. "*Seven*?!" She nodded. It was almost impressive how blind Kirk was to current events. Then she remembered he also stayed off social media as well as the news. Overall, she considered it smart, except this was the exception. Had he known, he would've prevented Glenn from heading to the harbor.

He pointed. "There!"

Brianna sat up. The damn mayor was in the center shot, blocking most of the pier behind him. After a few moments, the camera panned a little, granting a view of the many boats moving about. She realized it wasn't the pier that Kirk was pointing at, but a thirty-foot vessel with an Irish flag waving high. There was no doubt in their minds that it was Glenn's buddy's boat, the *Stephan*, named after the Irishman in *Braveheart.*

"Great! Just great!" Brianna said.

"No chance of getting in touch with him by phone while he's out there," Kirk said. He ran his hands through his hair. "He's on a boat. Is he really in that much danger? It's not like sharks are in the habit of attacking vessels."

"I don't want him out there," Brianna said.

"Then get on one of your police boats and go after him," Kirk said.

"They're all being used to patrol the shorelines," she replied.

"Can you use the radio? Order him to come in?"

"Malcolm is eighteen and legally owns the boat," she replied. "You know how they'll play this up if we call him. He'll pretend Glenn's not there, and we can't prove he's with him until they get back. To them, a fifty-thousand dollar reward is well worth the shit they'll catch for this little stunt."

"So, we're fucked?" Kirk asked.

"Hang on. I'm thinking," she replied.

"Now, do you agree that we should get our own boat?" Kirk said. Brianna closed her eyes. Was he seriously using this crisis as an excuse to finally buy a boat; something he'd been nagging for during the last two years? Then again, he wasn't necessarily wrong in this particular case.

They continued watching the news, as reporters concluded their interview with the mayor. They then proceeded to ask Chief Pino a couple of brief questions while he oversaw the operation commence.

"Yes, I believe by the end of today, life will go back to normal. As you can see, there are many professionals taking to the water. With such a widespread operation, it's highly likely the shark will be found," he said.

"Will the shark be dissected to ensure that it is indeed the one doing the killings?" the reporter asked.

"I'll speak with a few consultants, but considering how uniquely large the shark is, it probably will be an easy matter to identify it."

"Thank you, Chief." The reporter took the spotlight. *"As you can see, the operation is underway. And the police force is confident that—"* She paused and looked back over her shoulder, as several other journalists were suddenly rushing to one end of the pier. The camera panned, showing a gathering near one of the boats.

"What the hell's going on?" Kirk asked.

Brianna shook her head. "I don't know." They watched as the camera crew joined the crowd.

"Maybe someone's already got it," Kirk said, hopeful that it was the case. Brianna stood a couple of feet in front of the screen. As the camera approached the fishing boat, she realized *who* it was the reporters were so fascinated with.

"Oh, shit."

"Is that..."

"Yes," she said.

The reporter shouted into her microphone. *"Detective Luke Jansen? Is it true that you're joining the hunt for the shark?"*

The one-eyed detective glared at the crowd of curious journalists. *"Nah, I thought I'd come here on a busy Sunday morning and work on my tan."*

"Charming guy," Kirk said. "Can see why you had him transferred."

She shook her head. If only he knew *why*, he'd probably have a very different opinion. Hell, they were married when the mall shooting happened. In fairness, it was a memory they both tried to shield themselves from. Not just the incident itself, but the therapy, both physical and psychological, which followed. The two years that followed were not pleasant, especially for their marriage. Sometimes, certain facts—even important ones, were forgotten under such duress.

A new idea formed in Brianna's mind. She pulled out her phone and made a call, only for it to go unanswered. "Damn it!"

"I told you he's not gonna get the signal," Kirk said.

"I'm not calling Glenn," she said. She rushed into the bedroom, threw on a pair of jeans and a decent shirt, then hurried for the door. "I have a plan. Be right back. Or…just watch the TV. You'll probably see me on it." Before Kirk could respond, she was out the door. She boarded her Ford Mustang and sped toward the harbor.

CHAPTER 14

Luke Jansen stuffed a cigar in his mouth and chewed the end off. He could hear the clicks of cameras as reporters gathered on the dock. He pretended they weren't there as he arranged his supplies. There were a few gasps in the crowd as he leaned his twelve-gauge against the wheelhouse.

Typical anti-gun morons. Apparently, they expect me to cuff the shark and read it its rights.

"Hey, Luke! I see you're getting in on the fun as well!"

He looked up and saw a thirty-three-year-old man with thick brown hair, with a pen and notebook in hand. Luke didn't need to look at the ALC-8 press badge on his suit to know who he was. The snarky expression was enough. Anthony Zach liked to show up at every homicide case, no matter how cut and dry the investigation was. Even if the suspect was caught on site, even if he confessed, Anthony would always spin it. It seemed that guy was more hellbent on interfering with police work than he was to get a good story out. A story was often the proper word for the stuff he put out. He may as well make something up from scratch. That seemed to be the way of the world these days; get a few basic details of an event or incident then craft a narrative around it. It was not about spreading information, but getting clicks and attention.

"What are you doing here? Soup kitchen's *that* way. You'll find your free meal ticket there," Luke said.

"Now, why you gonna be like that for? I'm just covering a story," Anthony said, feigning offense.

"*Tor Forge* and *McMillan* are accepting submissions. Then again, they require talent, not just the ability to make something up." There was a time Luke would've been careful about what he said around such reporters. Nowadays, he didn't pay it a second thought. The guy was gonna write whatever the hell he wanted anyway. Showing up to the site was just a formality to make himself appear legitimate to the braindead readers.

"So, is it true that you're also heading out to catch the shark?" Anthony asked.

Luke stepped back onto the dock, only to collect the rest of his supplies. He yanked the chum bucket by the handle, 'accidentally' spilling some of the contents on Anthony's freshly shined shoes. "Whoops." He carried it back onto the boat. "It seems I answered that same question five times in the last three minutes, by five different reporters. Don't they teach you guys anything else?"

"They teach us to seek out irregularities. Such as the peculiar fact that a police detective who's on record stating that it was *not* a shark that is responsible for the killings, is now boarding his private vessel to hunt it. Does this mean you retract your previous statement?"

"Anyone with a brain would consider the irregularity to be the claim I made a statement when I never did. But then again, that would require people to *think*. But, in case there's anyone here who'll actually report the facts—I had questions in the beginning. The wounds on the victims weren't, and still aren't, consistent with a usual shark bite."

"So, why'd you change your mind?"

"Thanks to the magic of sight. I saw the snippet of footage of the beach attack. I know what a dorsal fin looks like."

"So, you're hunting it down out of guilt?" another reporter said.

Luke stared off into the distance. *Guilt. No reason to feel guilty except for the contrived and exaggerated reasons presented by the press.* There was no sense in arguing that fact. "Fifty-grand is fifty-grand." He snapped his fingers at Anthony, then pointed down at the dock. "Hand me that case of beer, will ya?"

Anthony looked down at the *Budweiser* on the dock, then chuckled. He passed it over the gunwale. "Whatcha gonna do with the money if you catch the shark?"

"What's it matter to you?"

"Just curiosity. I'm aware of the fundraiser being held for Diane Laskey in L.A."

Luke pulled a torch lighter from his pocket and held a flame to the tip of his cigar. The heat against his face was as taunting as Anthony's statement. He turned to face the journalist, tip glowing bright orange. After blowing a thick cloud of smoke, he awaited the inevitable question.

****

It wasn't often that Brianna used her flashers for personal convenience. Normally, it took twelve minutes in decent traffic to get from her house to the harbor. Twelve minutes was more than long enough for Luke to depart, and she couldn't risk missing him. Using the overheads proved to be a good option, as every traffic light she came across was turning red as she approached it.

When she arrived at the docks, she felt the area looked more like a fish-fry festival rather than a shark hunt. Everyone was fairly upbeat, with many lighting up cigars, tobacco pipes, and in many cases, weed. Cases of beer were passed about. Fishermen trash-talked with one another. Some were eager to be interviewed by the press, especially if the reporter was young and attractive.

She was amused to see several vendors on the dock attempting to sell fishing supplies and food to the fishermen and reporters. This event, sparked by the tragic deaths of multiple people, was being treated with the insouciance of a fishing tournament.

After scanning the area with her eyes, she located a group of reporters gathered around a stretch of dock. Their attention was fixed on one person. For someone to achieve this much attention solely with their presence, they were either highly respected or controversial. No doubt it was Luke Jansen they were talking to.

"Oh, thank God," she said to herself. She kept a brisk pace as she stepped onto the pier. As soon as she arrived, vendors were extending food and merchandise into her face.

"Here, ma'am! Try an omelet! Only seven-ninety-nine!"

"No thanks," she replied. Immediately, another vendor put himself in her way.

"Hi! Going out on the water! Try this fishing line! Really strong! Made to reel in fourteen-hundred-pound swordfish—" He looked down at her belt as she lifted her sweater a few inches, revealing her Glock and detective badge. He smiled nervously and got out of the way.

It seemed today was the day that Brianna was willing to exploit her police powers. She couldn't deny she enjoyed it. Good thing too, because she would have to use it to break up this unofficial press conference. By the time she neared the crowd, she saw the detective standing on the deck of his boat, having just received a remark from a local cockroach that passed as a reporter, Anthony Zach.

"My understanding is that the charity would go to funding her college education. You know, since her dad's not around to provide."

Brianna cringed. It was a tossup how Luke would respond to this. She said a silent prayer, asking God to alleviate his pain. That was usually the factor that determined his mood.

"You ought to start a Go-Fund-Me," he replied.

Brianna exhaled, relieved he didn't say anything too stupid. That respite was gone as another question was asked, this time by a short and stocky reporter with a high-pitched voice standing on the back of the dock.

"Excuse me, Detective Jansen. Is it true you're the same Detective Jansen who was investigating his partner, Morgan Laskey on accusations of accepting money through a human trafficking operation?"

Luke lowered the cigar. There was no point in denying it—the info was already out there. "Yeah."

"These accusations were proven to be false, correct?"

"Right."

The journalist proceeded to jot down notes. "If I recall, your partner was shot, correct?"

By the look on Luke's face, he was considering a dozen different responses, and possibly imagining a few violent repercussions for this leading question. Surprisingly, his answer was calm and direct, though it still conveyed his annoyance. "Burned. He was hit by a Molotov cocktail."

"I see. That explains the, uh—" the reporter pointed to the eyepatch, then quickly walked away, still jotting notes.

Despite his relatively relaxed demeanor, Brianna knew the detective was a ticking time bomb. He didn't like the press to begin with. She could only imagine his feelings regarding guys like Anthony Zach. She raised her badge and pushed herself through the group.

"Alright. Break it up. Give us space, I need to speak to the detective." The crowd did as instructed, but not without several of them snapping photos and giving inquisitive looks. Only Anthony remained on the pier.

"Hi, Captain. I thought this wasn't an official police operation."

"It's not," she replied. "Excuse us, please. I'd like to have a private word with Mr. Jansen."

Anthony simpered, then stepped away. The Captain made sure he was off the dock before turning her attention to Luke. "You alright?"

"Never better, now that you're here to pass me that roll of cable," Luke said. Brianna looked down at the loop full of 7x7 steel cable, then back at him.

"When did you get a boat?"

"Memorial Day," Luke said.

"Why? You get bored?"

"It's a good way to *not* be around people." He clapped his hands. "Chop! Chop! Cable time!"

"So, what's your plan? Attach that to a hook, draw the shark in with bait, and winch it close enough for a shotgun blast to the head?" she asked.

"It's not rocket science," Luke said. He leaned on the gunwale until the Captain finally passed the cable over to him. "What are you doing over here, anyway? Thinking of heading out yourself? There's fifty-grand to be had."

"Is that why you're doing this?"

"That, and I hear *Applebee's* is offering a free riblet platter to the winner. If that's not motivation, I don't know what is."

"You know what I'm talking about," she said. "You sleeping alright?"

"Like a baby," Luke said. "Is that why you're here? Playing doctor? Asking what my pain level is on a scale of one-to-ten? I see you're in plain clothes, so you're not here on business."

Brianna looked away. Only now was it dawning on her how ridiculous her request was going to sound, especially to a snarky son of a bitch like Luke.

"I've got my *eye* on you, Cap. And I don't like that look on your face," Luke said. "What the hell's on your mind?"

"I need a huge favor."

Luke tilted his head, aiming his right eye directly at her. "A favor? *What* favor?"

"Listen, you clearly know how dangerous this situation is. I know sharks don't generally attack boats, but I can't help but have a nervous feeling about this."

"Is the favor to listen to you ramble?" Luke said.

Brianna groaned. "I need you to go after someone for me."

"*Someone*?" Luke climbed up onto the dock then wiped his hands on a cloth. "The mayor made it an open contract. Anyone with a boat is allowed to go after that shark."

"Not if they're underage."

"They are if they have mommy and daddy's permission," he replied. "Considering nobody's reported their children taking their boat out, I'm guessing *you* have an issue with a disobedient boy." Brianna's silence and humiliated expression served as a 'yes'. Luke marched up the wooden steps to the upper level of the pier. "Isn't Brad like nineteen, now?"

"*Seventeen*," Brianna corrected him. "And his name is *Glenn*."

"Seventeen. You should be proud. Kid's taking initiative, which is more than ninety-percent of all other kids his age. I didn't know you guys had a boat for him to steal."

"We don't. He went out with a friend of his."

"Nothing I can do about that."

"I want you to go out there and bring him back. I couldn't care less about his buddy," Brianna said.

"I'm busy," Luke said. "Can't you see I'm going fishing? Besides, I have no idea what the boat looks like, which way it's going, how well your boy's gonna react to me bringing him aboard. Shouldn't Mommy and Daddy be taking care of this?"

"Like I said, we don't have a boat. And I can't reach him by phone." She reached into her pocket and pulled out a sheet of notebook paper. "I wrote the name of the boat and some distinct markings for you to find." She watched the slack-jawed expression as the detective bitterly gazed at the sheet. "Come on, Luke. After yesterday, you owe me a favor."

"Really?" He turned and walked toward the nearest vendor. "Four-egg omelet. Nice and greasy. Throw in some peppers, tomatoes, and mushrooms while you're at it."

"You got it." The chef went to work on his breakfast.

Brianna stepped beside him. "You *do* realize you caused the department a lot of grief, right?"

"No. The lovely journalists did that, remember? I recall making some very obvious observations. Which I still stand by, by the way. No way a great white caused a gash like the one in that guy's gut."

"Coroner says otherwise," Brianna said.

Luke chuckled. "Let me guess: McGibbeny?"

"Luke…"

"Dr. Path of Least Resistance, and 'Let me get done with this, so I can go home and watch *Jeopardy!*' Yeah, I'm sure his report is reliable."

"He found bacteria, commonly located from sharks' gums, in the victim's wound," she said. Luke's surprise was only visible for a moment. He deliberately watched the chef make the omelet, which gave him an excuse to not make eye contact. "You know, it'd be nice if you trusted my judgement once in a while."

"Yeah? Like you trusted *my* judgement. Good thing you don't live further north, or that hip would really annoy you during the winter."

The chef finished the omelet. "That'll be ten-fifty."

"She'll be taking care of that," Luke said, taking the fresh food wrapped in tinfoil. He turned to a very irritated looking Brianna. "You know, when you save someone's life, they owe you forever!" He walked away, leaving her to pay the bill.

Brianna bit her lip, and begrudgingly pulled her wallet out. "Ten-fifty? When I passed you earlier, you said seven-ninety-nine!"

The chef shrugged. "That was for plain omelet. He added toppings." Brianna groused under her breath, handed out some cash, then hurried back down to the boat.

"You'd think getting you a job here would've fulfilled that debt," she said. "Especially when you consider the misery that came with your hiring."

Luke stepped out of the wheelhouse. "Is that meant to win me over?"

"I'm asking you *please* do me this favor," she said. "I bought you breakfast. I'll even add coffee." She peeked into the boat and saw the six-pack of beer. "Jesus, Luke! It's not even nine o'clock in the morning!"

"I'm not drinking any. Yet. And, for your information, these trips tend to last all day," Luke retorted while munching on his omelet. He tossed the remainder on the console, then looked at the notes. "The *Stephan*? Irish flag. Do you have a serial number?"

"No. It'll stand out like a sore thumb."

"You don't see many sore thumbs out in the open ocean," Luke said.

"Good Christ! You're not trekking across the Pacific. Just search the nearby area. They were heading about northwest of here," she said. "Hell, would it help if I came with you?"

Luke coughed. "What?"

"I'll come with you. You brought up a fair point. He's *my* kid. I should be the one going after him. Luke, I really could use your help."

Luke stepped back into the wheelhouse. She heard him kick the wall and curse under his breath. Brianna smiled. She knew she'd won the debate. She climbed aboard and undid the mooring.

Luke started the motor and throttled the boat into the open sea. "If he doesn't agree to come back with us ASAP, then I'm cuffing the little bastard. No offense."

Brianna took a seat on deck and watched the water swishing past the hull. "None taken."

CHAPTER 15

It was twenty-minutes past nine when Elise checked herself out of the hospital. The hour prior to that consisted of a half-hour of physical therapy, which she argued was unnecessary, a session with a grief therapist who made all the usual checkbox statements, and a final evaluation with the MD. All she had was a slight lingering headache, and that had more to do with lack of sleep. She dozed off a few times over the night, getting just enough sleep to function, but there was no true rest. Every time she closed her eyes, she saw that whorl. Her hand clenched with each flash of the memory. She could still feel the pull against her wrist as Chad was yanked away.

The office clerk on duty was kind enough to phone a cab for her. Elise put on the appearance of a normal woman going about her day, not wanting to draw too much attention to herself. She even managed to chitchat with the driver during the ride home. It was simple conversation, talking about the weather, politics, tastes in food, etc. Only when they arrived at her home in the cove did the conversation get awkward.

The driver looked at the ocean, then whistled. "Best to stay out of the water. I hear there's a big ass great white out there. Killed a lot of people."

Elise stared through the windshield as though in a trance. After several seconds of silence, the driver looked back. The woman who seemed fairly nonchalant suddenly looked possessed. "You okay, ma'am?"

"Yes. I'm fine." What point was there in trying to convince him of the truth? He was simply a guy working his nine-to-five, with no real authority in the investigation. She paid the money then stepped out.

She froze in the driveway. The sight of Chad's grey Nissan LEAF Hatchback was like a ghost staring back at her. It would never be driven by its owner again. Elise's mind flashed to the last time Chad drove in the thing. It was yesterday morning. He had gone out to grab donuts for their weekly trip to collect samples. It was such an unassuming task Already, she wondered how things might've changed if she hadn't suggested the idea of getting breakfast. They would have left a half hour sooner. By the time they got to the northern part of the reef, the shark might not have been anywhere near that area. And Chad would be okay.

Elise wasn't sure how long she had been standing there, but her trance was deep enough for her to not notice the cab driver leave. The sight of her vessel was even more haunting. She couldn't bear to look at it. Chad's belongings were still on deck. She wanted everything to vanish. His belongings, his car, it almost made her feel like Chad was still around. She hadn't even considered what she would do with his stuff.

She walked with a slight limp. That damn coral injury. Why the hell did she not tough through it? Had she just ignored the pain and swam for the boat immediately, she would've gotten on the boat much sooner, and Chad would still be here.

After hesitating briefly at the doorway, she stepped into the house. Her home was similar, yet infinitely different. Empty was the only word that felt accurate. The whirlwind in her mind became a hurricane of emotion. That Xbox console, which she complained so much about after hearing him playing on it at two in the morning—she'd do anything to suffer that 'grief' again. Then there were the empty Mountain Dew cans on the side table that he always failed to put away. As recently as seventy-two hours ago, she had said she longed to see the day she wouldn't wake up and find empty pop cans lying around. Now, that 'be careful what you wish for' quote was whispering in her ear, as if a devil was propped on her shoulder.

She fell to her knees and wept. There was nobody to hug her, nobody to convince her it wasn't her fault. Sure, the police captain had given her a card. Big deal. As though a stranger had the power to make her feel better.

The only thing that brought any degree of comfort was knowing that the shark would be caught and killed. She always hated the idea of revenge, and greatly despised the killing of sharks. But everyone had a line, and hers was crossed and long behind her.

Her eyes went to the poster on the front wall above the entertainment center. The image was copied from a photo she took of the Great Barrier Reef when she was working on a project for her Master's Degree. In the photo were three blacktip reef sharks and a leopard shark, each swimming peacefully among a crowd of fish. She stared at the jawlines, then thought of yesterday's attacker.

It was a whorl. She *saw* it. "That shark was a Helicoprion," she said aloud to the empty room. She heard the words as they came out, then rubbed her forehead. That headache was there since she woke up at the hospital. The nurses and doctors stated it was due to stress, as well as residual effects from the improper surfacing technique. Her memory of the last twenty-four hours was incredibly hazy. Every thought was clouded by the reality of Chad's death, despite her attempts to block it out. It was a classic symptom of the first stage of grief.

Staring at the wall, she began to question herself. Did she see a Helicoprion? Or were the doctors and detectives right, and she had just imagined it? The scientist in her started asking questions: How could a fish that large go unseen until now? Where did it come from? How has it remained so unchanged without any significant evolution if it truly survived the last two-hundred-and-fifty million years?

Yet, she knew what she saw. Or did she? It was already becoming a blur, probably because her mind wanted to shield her from the gristly images of Chad being cut down to size.

She couldn't deny it sounded insane. Maybe everyone else was right. Maybe it was just a large violent great white. She peered out the window at the ocean. There were at least three fishing boats in view, and so many more beyond them.

Whichever shark it was, someone would find it. They *had* to. It didn't matter what species it was. Great white; Helicoprion; mako; tiger; hell, it could be a goddamn megalodon for all she cared. As long as it was captured and killed.

She grabbed her keys and got in her SUV, and sped for the harbor. That bastard shark would soon be brought in, and she wanted to see it in the flesh. Maybe then, she would have some measure of peace.

CHAPTER 16

Brianna leaned over the side of the boat, coughing after losing the rest of her breakfast. Had it been any other occasion, she would have remembered to take some Dramamine before departing.

As she regained control, she could feel Luke's eyes on her back. The prick just stood there, finishing off the rest of his omelet as she emptied her guts.

"Does it taste good?" she groaned.

"Eh." He shrugged. "He went a little light on the mushrooms. Want a bite?" Brianna proceeded to dry heave, much to his amusement. "You know you didn't have to come, right?"

"Yeah, sure! Like you would've actually gone after Glenn yourself," she replied. She spat into the water, then stood up straight. "You would've played the whole 'oh, I couldn't find him' excuse, while chumming for your fish."

"Hey, *Mommy*, last I checked, your kid isn't my responsibility," Luke said. "Besides, I say it's good. Maybe this'll make him a man."

"Or chowder," Brianna said. "He doesn't know his way around a boat, let alone how to hunt for a man-eating fish. Which *you* didn't believe in twenty-four hours ago, by the way."

Luke reached into a drawer and found a can of chili. He yanked on the pull tab, and aimed the open can at the police captain. The aroma, which normally wouldn't have had an effect, reignited the dry heaves. She was back over the side in a heartbeat.

"Wait till you see the chum," he quipped.

"I swear, I'm gonna turn *you* into chum," she said between gags. She regained control and found a place to sit. "Son of a bitch. Whew!" She closed her eyes for a minute and focused on the cool breeze. When she opened them, she noticed Luke with a spoon in hand, eating the chili right out of the can. "That's disgusting."

"What?" he said, shrugging. "Can't let it go to waste."

"Is this your grand plan? To torture me?"

"Ah, yes! You got me! I *knew* your kid was gonna run off this morning to go hunt an oversized killer fish and that you would be desperate to run after him like a puppy! So, I got on my boat, bought a bunch of bait—"

"And beer!"

"Irrelevant... Then loaded my boat, arranged to be ambushed by the bloodsucking leeches society calls reporters—JUST so you could see me on TV and come beg for a ride on my boat. I'm so good, I even made you forget to take Dramamine, so you'd be as sick as a woman in her first trimester. And you sprang the trap like a mouse seeking cheese. Speaking of which..." He reached into the cooler and found a block of cheese. "Want some?" Brianna looked away. The thought of food made her head spin. Grinning ear-to-ear, Luke stepped into the wheelhouse again, then emerged with a little grey box. "Here." He tossed it into her lap.

Brianna grimaced, holding the box of Dramamine up at him. "You had this the whole time?!"

"Sorry. I was so focused on finding Ben that it just slipped my mind."

"*Glenn*," she said. She didn't even know why she was offended by that. Luke obviously knew his name and was just messing around to make the trip miserable for her. She took the Dramamine and washed it down with some water. Hopefully this pill would work on the faster side, only taking thirty minutes to take effect. With her luck, it'd be over an hour before she felt any change. "Sorry. I guess it's just the nausea talking. Thank you for helping me. I appreciate it—even if I see it as you returning the favor."

"Never did anything wrong to begin with," Luke said. "But you're welcome, I guess."

"Maybe you're not responsible for the press blowing everything out of proportion, but you *did* interfere with the investigation. Norton and I had everything under control. You showing up because you wanted a distraction from your nerve pain threw everything out of whack."

Brianna leaned back. Remarkably, she felt her body was settling down already, probably because she already emptied everything. She didn't care at this point, as long as her insides no longer felt like a raging storm.

"Have you been keeping up on your sessions?"

Luke tossed the chili in a trash can. "Doesn't Dr. Leslie report that to you?"

"She reports that you show up. She doesn't state what goes on in the meetings. There's a policy of doctor-patient confidentiality in our city."

"She checks out my eyepatch," Luke said. "Apparently, she thinks scars are hot."

"Quit with the bullshit," Brianna said. "What do you guys talk about, really?"

"It's the same useless routine. She asks me how I'm sleeping, my hobbies, my pain level, tries to dig inside my head as though there's some complex background. Tells me a few feel-good stories of other patients, asks about my relationship with coworkers—that's always a short answer, thank God."

"How much do you guys talk about Morgan Laskey?" Brianna asked.

"You know, there's easier ways to get a pep talk with me than to chase after your kid," Luke said.

"Actually, there's not," Brianna said. "The fact that I was able to trap you here is just a convenient aspect to this whole scenario. This way, you can't run off and dodge the question as always."

"Thanks, but I have a mother," Luke said.

"In Jackson County Prison—not much use to you," she said. She instantly regretted bringing that up. Had she not been feeling both woozy and cranky, she would've caught herself. Bringing up his mother, who was serving thirty-five years for shooting his father, was probably not helpful in this case. Though, it did speak volumes as to why he became a homicide detective and was so fixated on attention to detail. She took a deep breath. "Besides, I think of myself more as an older sister. I'm not nearly old enough to be your mother."

"Well, *technically* you are, if, say... you got knocked up in the tenth grade..."

"Alright! Alright! You should know better than to bring up a woman's age—then again, it's *you* I'm talking to, so who am I fooling?" She stood up. "Probably another part of your plan to alienate yourself from everyone in the department. Not gonna work with me, Jansen."

"Doesn't have to. You're the Captain. I don't work with you, just under you. Hell, you shouldn't even have to leave your office," Luke said.

"Everyone in the department thinks you're an ass...well, you are, but I know why. You reject the idea of having another partner after what happened to Morgan."

Luke put a hand over his eye as he gazed into the distance. "I think I see your kid's boat."

"Nice try, but you're not getting out of this," Brianna said. "I think it's time you forgive yourself for what happened and move forward. The sooner you do that, the sooner your pain will go away, I think."

"Irish flag, you said," Luke said.

"You think I'm stupid, Luke?" He looked back at her. Briana pointed a finger. "Answer that, and you're fired!"

Instead of doing so, he approached the helm and turned the boat to starboard. Brianna's expression soured as she saw the *Stephan* drifting a couple hundred yards ahead of them. She groaned. The jerk was telling the truth after all.

Luke raised a pair of binoculars to his eye and gazed at the people aboard. He smirked. "The guy at the helm has one of those stupid looking neck-beards."

"That's...Glenn," Brianna said.

"Oh...Good looking kid," he said.

Brianna climbed to the fly deck, located above the wheelhouse, and observed the boat. She couldn't really judge Luke for his assessment of Glenn's appearance. She, in fact, hated that neckbeard look too.

The *Stephan* wasn't moving, aside from a slight drift. She could see Malcolm on the main deck. A scrawny little twerp, he was dressed in a red shirt and tan khakis. Red, perfect color for shark hunting. The bow was pointing west, with the portside facing Luke's vessel. Several yards behind the stern was a round red buoy, attached to a cleat on the transom by a rope. Around that buoy was a thick stream of chum mixture.

"Looks like chili," Luke joked.

Brianna burped, sucking in a deep breath to keep anything else from coming out. She stomped her foot, the vibration signaling her frustration. Naturally, all it did was add to Luke's amusement.

Glenn and Malcolm didn't see them coming, as their attention was fixed on something on their starboard side rather than their buoy.

"Should I make a "wee-u" noise, since we don't have a siren?" Luke said.

"Just bring us in close," Brianna said.

Luke scoffed. *I'm taking orders on my own boat.* He angled the boat and brought it alongside the *Stephan.* Malcolm and Glenn looked back, the teen's eyes bulging wide as he saw his infuriated mother deriding him with an icy stare.

"Mom?"

Luke opened his window. "You're caught, buster! Mommy's brought the wooden spoon! Time for an ass paddling!"

"What?" Malcolm muttered, caught off guard by the guy with the eyepatch. He looked at Glenn. "Does your mom always hang out with crazy friends?"

"Oh, Jesus." Brianna rubbed her eyes. "Shut up, Luke. And thanks for another age reference. As for you, Glenn: what the hell do you think you're doing?"

"What do you mean?" Glenn said.

"Don't play dumb! Do you not realize how dangerous this is? Hunting a killer shark? In a dinky boat like *this*, for godsake?!"

"Hey!" Malcolm said.

"Don't even argue, kid," Brianna said to him. Malcolm saw the sun's reflection on her badge, then flushed. He looked at his boat, then nodded. It was a little small. "Malcolm, I know you're a legal adult, so I can't order you to bring your boat in. But you, Glenn, you're coming aboard right now."

"But wait, Ma, there's something—"

Luke poked his head out again. "Listen, kid, I've got shit I wanna do today. Instead, I'm hunting you down like *Dog: The Bounty Hunter*. The longer you bellyache, the more pissed I'm gonna get. So, I'll put it this way. If you're not aboard in thirty seconds, I'll drag you over by the hairs of your chinny-chin-chin."

Glenn looked up at his mother, hopeful she'd put the crazy one-eyed guy in his place. Instead, she had her hands on her hips, her eyes now icy enough to give people in hell a chill.

"But there's something here," he said.

"Nice try," she said.

"Hang on," Luke said.

"Hang on? I thought you were in a hurry?" Brianna said.

Luke watched the body language of Glenn and Malcolm. He knew the various types of 'flustered' individuals presented when around cops. Some were nervous to be caught, usually presenting more shaky, jittery movements. Then there were the quieter types, who saw something bad that they weren't sure how to describe.

"He's seventeen. I thought seventeen-year-old teens were a little more combative with their mommies when they were being yelled at," he said. Brianna nearly followed her urge to argue. At the last second, she stopped herself, then studied the look on Glenn's face. Luke was right. Usually, in situations like this, Glenn would be combative from the start. He looked alarmed, but not solely due to her presence, or Luke's. She remembered seeing them gazing into the water as they approached. Something already had them disturbed.

"What's wrong, hon?"

Glenn pointed to the water on the starboard side of his boat. "Hang on, let me get out of the way." He throttled forward. The *Stephan* moved a few yards west, revealing the floating bodies bobbing in the waves.

Luke steered the boat closer, then stepped out on deck to look. There were three bottlenose dolphins, all dead. Their bodies were bloated with gas, meaning they had been dead for several hours. There were no wounds, no sign of struggle. There did appear to be some kind of infectious growth near their jaws, blowholes, and eyes, though it seemed simple enough to determine that was due to bacteria attacking their bodies.

"Goodness," Brianna said. She climbed down and looked over the gunwale. "Have you ever seen anything like this?"

"I've seen dead dolphins," Luke said. "But usually by themselves. Not fully intact, and not three in a group." He reached out with a pole and pulled one of them closer. "No bite marks, by the looks of it. Hard to say. Maybe they ate something that didn't agree with them."

"All *three*?" Brianna said.

"You have a better explanation?" Luke said. "Or should we put Norton on the case."

"Last we checked, we aren't in the business of investigating animal homicide."

"What about a call to the EPA?" Luke said.

"For what?" Brianna said. "They test the water weekly, to my understanding. There hasn't been a toxic spill anywhere near this area in years."

"Well, something happened to them. There's inflammation around the jawline. Discoloration near the eyes…"

"All which could be a side effect from, oh I don't know…being dead for a day?" She cupped her stomach, which still ached from the recent exertion. "I'll notify the Wildlife Services and see if they want to take a look at them. There's nothing I can do beyond that." She snapped her fingers at her son. "Alright, Glenn. Hop on over. We're heading home."

Now, her son looked combative. "Why can't I do this?"

"Because you have no clue what you're doing. And considering the number of hot pockets you eat, I'm doing that shark a favor by preventing him from getting indigestion after eating you. Now get your ass over here."

"You've been whining about me not getting a job for the last few months. Now that I'm actually trying to make money…"

"Oh, give me a break," Brianna said. "This isn't even in the same league as having a job. Something tells me Malcolm is putting in most of the work, anyway." Her son's friend accidentally let a small nod slip through. His shirt was stained with grease and oil from the chum bucket.

Glenn looked to his friend for support, but all Malcolm could offer was a shrug. No way was he going to argue with a police detective, and her crazy one-eyed henchman. The battle was lost. He throttled the boat around in a tight circle.

Suddenly, Malcolm pointed out to stern and shrieked. "Holy shit!"

Glenn eased off the throttle. "What?"

"The buoy! Something tapped it!" he said.

All fear of his mother's wrath vanished in the blink of an eye. Glenn hopped down to the main deck and found his friend's speargun.

"Glenn! Don't!" Brianna said.

The buoy bobbed again. It definitely was no swell causing these motions; it was being pulled from underneath.

Luke stepped onto the foredeck. "If that's the shark we're hunting for, kid, you're gonna need more than that little speargun."

The buoy vanished completely and the line went taut. Malcolm's boat started to swing slightly as the unseen creature started to run.

"We got it! It's caught on the hook," Malcolm exclaimed. "I just need to tire it out. Once it surfaces, we'll put a spear through its brain!"

Brianna looked down at Luke. "Get us in closer, you idiot. They're gonna get themselves killed!"

"Ah, I wouldn't worry about it," Luke said. "Shark as big as the one we're looking for would be spinning that dinky little boat around like a top. They probably hooked a tiger shark or a hammerhead."

The line continued to lash back and forth. It sank deeper, than began to rise. The water erupted as a twelve-foot long shortfin mako thrashed along the surface, jaws agape. Embedded in the roof of its mouth was the barbed hook, with bits of the tuna bait still dangling between its teeth.

"Nice work, kids," Luke quipped.

"Oh God," Brianna said. She glanced about, thankful there weren't any boats in sight. If someone got a photo of a high-ranking policewoman's son torturing an innocent shark, animal rights activists would ruin her.

"Hang on, I'll take care of it," Malcolm said. He aimed his speargun.

"What the hell do you think you're doing?" Brianna said.

Malcolm's face flushed. "Um, I don't see how else to handle it."

"You're not killing it," she said. "We'll figure out a way to free it."

"Yeah? Gonna put on some rubber gloves and pry that hook out from those snappers, are ya?" Luke said.

"You're not helping, Luke."

"I'm helping *a lot*, actually. I brought you out here, didn't I?"

"Forget it." She climbed down. "I'm calling Animal Control. Maybe they'll be able to send somebody out here."

"Fabulous. Dead dolphins, 'eh, forget about it.' A fish on a line, then it's, 'oh, the horror!'"

"The dolphins were already dead, Detective. The shark's still alive. Also, killing it is illegal. I'm making the call." She entered the pilothouse and adjusted the radio's knob to find the police channel.

A simultaneous outcry of "whoa!" from all three men outside drew her attention back to the shark. The line was tight and angling deep. Only this time, the boat literally was being dragged around to its side. Malcolm and Glenn went into a panic, the latter tripping over something and falling backward. The spear zipped aimlessly into open water, disappearing under the waves.

"Jesus, Luke! What's happening?"

The Detective already had his revolver drawn and pointed toward the water. As soon as the hammer cocked back, the boat settled. The buoy rose high and spun along the surface.

Malcolm stood on his feet, breathing deeply through his mouth. He watched the buoy for several seconds, making sure whatever was pulling on it was no longer there and not simply taking a break. Cautiously, he pulled the line closer. It came back with no resistance, though there was a little bit of weight that wasn't previously there.

He raised the buoy on deck and beheld the severed mako shark head that dangled from the hook. "Holy SHIT!"

Luke Jansen leaned forward. Bring your boat closer. I wanna get a look at that." The teens did as instructed, aligning their boat with Luke's. Malcolm held the head high so the detective could examine it. "That's our shark."

Malcolm looked at the head, confused. "I don't think this shark was the one that—"

"No, not *that* shark, you moron. I mean the shark that ate this one."

Brianna shook her head. "Oh, come on, Jansen. We can't know for sure."

"First of all, decide whether or not you're pissed at me, because first you call me by my last name, then my first. It's a little headache-inducing. Second, look at the wound. It's a clean-freaking-cut." He hurried to the other side of the deck and gazed far out into the water. "We literally just missed our target. It's somewhere out here." He thumped a fist against the guardrail. If only he had invested money into a fish finder.

"So freaking close!" Malcolm said.

"As close as you're gonna get," Brianna said. "We're gonna escort you back to town. Right now."

"Yeeeeah, my fifty-grand is swimming around out here," Luke said.

Brianna was near the point of seething. "No, we came out here to get Glenn. Then, you'll be free to get yourself killed fishing for that thing."

"We're literally within a quarter-mile of it," Luke said. "Tracking it down is no easy feat, and here we are with an actual lead. I might not get that again."

"I'm not gonna have Glenn remain out here when there's a shark that literally nearly brought his whole boat down," Brianna snapped.

"Luckily for you, you don't need my boat to escort him back to the pier," Luke said. "Hop on down. Ride with them. We both win."

Brianna couldn't deny he had a point. "Fine. Good luck, *Luke.*" She swung her legs over the gunwale and gently lowered herself onto Malcolm's boat. "Let's go, guys."

Malcolm didn't resist. He climbed up to the flybridge and steered the boat east.

Luke didn't waste time watching them leave. His attention was on the water. He replayed the motions of Malcolm's vessel in his mind. The fish had dragged the line to the northwest, meaning it was likely running in that direction.

"Alright, you bastard. You can run, but you can't hide."

He gunned the engine, speeding after the target, while simultaneously putting distance between himself and the closest humans in his proximity. That was an added bonus.

CHAPTER 17

Fred Conner was no stranger to being sick. In his forty-seven years of life, he suffered yearly flu bugs, a stomach bug every four years—as though it had a set schedule, stomach ulcers, kidney stones at thirty-eight, and a urinary tract infection a year later. Despite all this, he rarely missed a day of work. The only thing he hated worse than feeling like crap was losing out on making money. Being self-employed, the rules of economics were simple: you don't work, you don't eat. And Fred had quite the appetite, but it didn't match that of his two teenage sons. They were already hitting the track, getting in shape for the high school football season. With that on top of the typical teenager metabolism, they practically ate everything out of the refrigerator two days after it was restocked.

Since the age of sixteen, Fred only missed five days of work, three of which were during the kidney stone fiasco. Today, he feared he was looking at day six.

It didn't make sense. That morning, he felt perfect. He was up at four-thirty as usual, had some coffee and eggs, and was out on his boat at six. As far as he was concerned, he was feeling *more* energized than ever. Fifty-thousand dollars for catching a shark? That'd take care of his expenses for the next two years, making everything he brought in from fishing pure profit.

A half hour into his voyage, he found something floating in the water. It looked like a deflated rubber raft at first. Then he got closer and saw that it was a freaking dead octopus. It wasn't a sight he was used to. First of all, it was one of the biggest ones he ever saw, and usually, when they died they were quickly consumed by all the critters in the water. This fella showed signs of damage, but was intact for the most part.

There seemed to be a whitening around the mantle and tentacles, almost like bleach was poured on the thing. Despite his many years on the ocean, Fred wasn't the most familiar with cephalopods or their life cycles. Did dead octopuses always look like this? What the hell did it die from? Old age? On that note, he wasn't sure how long their lifespan typically was.

It was an easy matter to put from his mind. He didn't want to waste time and focus on a stupid octopus when there was a fifty-thousand dollar shark out there. With the rising sun, the rest of the world would soon be out in force.

Then came the discovery of dead fish floating along the water's surface. Just like the octopus, they had white blotches. This time, it was enough for him to stop and inspect the carcasses. With a net, he hauled some of the specimens aboard to get a look at them. The bleached spots were blistery, almost like the acne on his youngest son's face, but he'd never seen it on a fish. It wasn't just the face, but all over its body. Whatever it was, it was the same as the octopus. Perhaps they'd been dead a while and this was just some sort of fungal growth? It was the only thing that made sense, though barely. If something died in the ocean, it was doomed to become food for something else within a few hours. But Fred Conner was no biologist. He was just a simple fisherman trying to pay off his house, truck, and get his boys ready for college. He tossed the fish back to the water and resumed the hunt.

The next two hours went by normally. He found a location precisely between the reported location where that researcher was said to have been attacked, and South Beach. If the shark was swimming around anywhere, it'd probably be here. Those two hours were spent chumming and listening to the radio.

Then the nausea started creeping up on him. Fred was taken aback by this. Not since the age of seventeen had he ever been seasick. Almost every day in his life, he'd been on the water. He kept Dramamine handy in case he had a guest on board, but never needed it for himself. And no way was he sensitive to the chum. He'd been gutting fish for thirty years, and that included sharks. He'd been exposed to digestive contents which looked like something from some horror movie. Not once did he lose his cookies. If he got sick, it was always due to some stupid virus.

Twenty minutes after the symptoms started, what remained of breakfast found its way into the ocean. He hoped it was a simple case of bad eggs. Luckily, he kept Gatorade in the cooler. He sipped on that and continued his task. After all, he wasn't gonna let an aching stomach prevent him from scoring fifty-grand. Next came a mild case of vertigo. Nothing major at first, and he assumed it was from the electrolyte imbalance.

For the next hour, it got worse. He was starting to sweat heavily, and it wasn't from the heat. Lethargy came next, naturally, followed by irritation. Fred couldn't believe that of all three-hundred-sixty-five days in the year, *today* was the day he had to get sick. He tried toughing it out, chumming the water and praying he'd see something appear on the fish finder. More nausea tormented his stomach and the vertigo got worse. He could feel the fever rising as though a temperature knob was being twisted.

It got to the point where a half-full scoop felt as heavy as a bag of bricks. Even then, Fred tried to push forward. It wasn't until he tried singing along with the radio and was slurring his words that he realized this wasn't a simple case of stomach flu. Worried he was having a stroke, he tried to make his way to the wheelhouse, but ended up stumbling to the starboard side. He folded over the gunwale.

There he remained. For how long, he had no idea. He faded in and out of consciousness. Only the sound of an approaching motorboat and a female voice calling out to him pulled Fred back into reality.

****

"This is bullshit. BULLSHIT!" Glenn exclaimed.

"You nearly got capsized, and you *still* think I'm insane for coming after you?" Brianna said.

"We could've caught it, Ma. If the damn thing just surfaced, we could've put a spear through its eye and scored fifty Gs."

"Oh, don't act like you would've shared any of that with the household," Brianna said. She leaned against the transom, watching her son throw his little tantrum. Up on the flybridge, his buddy Malcolm kept quiet, while keeping the boat pointed southeast. "Listen, if you want to make some money, your dad needs some help with the shop. They should be getting a regular supply of stock coming in. He'd be happy to pay both of you to help unload."

"Yeah, no thanks," Glenn said.

Malcolm, however, looked over his shoulder. "Yeah? Any idea how much?"

"A hundred bucks for a couple hours work. And knowing him, he'll probably buy you lunch."

Malcolm directed his gaze at Glenn. "That doesn't sound too bad, actually."

Glenn's eyes pierced his friend like daggers. "You kidding? You're excited about a hundred bucks after we lost out on fifty-thousand?"

"Dude, we would've lost the shark regardless of whether your mother showed up or not." He looked at the badge on Brianna's belt then cleared his throat. "I mean, the police captain..."

Brianna couldn't help but chuckle. "It's alright, young man. I don't obsess with titles."

"What time does your husband want us there?" Malcolm asked.

"I'll have to double-check with him, but I'm pretty sure oh-nine-hundred," she said.

"Nine o'clock?" Malcolm asked. Brianna nodded. Yes, she tended to used military time, but was oh-nine-hundred really that hard to figure out? Glenn grumbled. Now that his friend agreed to the job, he was doomed to join in or else look like a jerk. Such a thing didn't bother him too much, unless it directly made someone else look good as a result. And right now, Malcolm was acting like the son his mother never had.

Malcolm noticed his friend's glare. "Hey man, a hundred bucks is a hundred bucks. Should be enough to cover fuel. Dad let me take his boat out, but said I had to cover the gas and bait myself."

"I thought this was your boat?" Brianna said.

"No. Dad just lets me use it, but I have to contribute to its maintenance. And I burnt up a hundred bucks worth of fuel. I thought it'd be a simple matter, since I was confident we'd catch that fish. But we all know how that turned out."

"Oh." Brianna shrugged. Up until now, she always thought of Malcolm as a spoiled semi-rich kid. *Some detective I am.* That sentiment was magnified with Malcolm's next statement.

"Uh, Mrs. Raye? Is that guy alright?"

She stood up and saw a forty-foot fishing vessel, the *Wild Wind.* She wasn't familiar with the boat itself, nor its owner who was slumped over the side. At first sight, it was obvious that this wasn't a simple case of seasickness or a hangover. This gentleman didn't look well at all.

"Mind taking us in closer?" Brianna asked. Malcolm steered the vessel to starboard, then decreased speed as they neared the fishing vessel. Brianna cupped her hands around her mouth. "Hello? Sir?" He lifted his head weakly. She raised her badge. "Amadea Police. Sir, are you okay there?" He didn't respond. His face was flushed, his eyes half-open. He heard her, but wasn't certain if his mind registered her words. "We're coming aboard to help you. Don't be alarmed."

"What's wrong with him?" Glenn asked.

"No idea," Brianna said. "You stay aboard. I'll check on him. Malcolm, do you happen to be certified in first aid?"

"Yes, I am," he replied.

"Okay good. I *might* need your help if you're willing."

"Yep, hang on." He lined the boat with the *Wild Wind* then climbed down. "Glenn, hand me that line, would ya?" Glenn passed him the rope and they tied the boats together to keep them from drifting. Malcolm and Brianna crossed over.

The man turned to look at them, then fell on his rear. His eyes were red, his lips chapped, and his pants wet from his bladder letting loose, and going by the smell, possible defecation.

Brianna knelt beside him. "Hi. I'm Captain Brianna Raye. I'm with the police. We saw you slouched over the side there. Can you tell me your name?"

The man mumbled. "Fred."

"Hi, Fred." She touched his forehead. "You don't look well. Can you tell me the date?"

"August. Twenty—"

Brianna waited a minute. He couldn't finish the day. She put a hand to his temple. "You've got a bad fever going on. You have any medical history?"

"Nothing major," he said.

"Taking any meds?" she asked. Fred shook his head. "Can you tell me what happened? Were you feeling this way all morning?"

"Just...happened grad-ity. Gracdy... grad-u-al-ly. Nausea. Fatigue. Got...Lizzy—fizzily—*dizzy*." He started to cough.

Brianna shook her head. Just listening to the man speak was more than enough to know he needed to be admitted to the hospital She had to debate what was faster, calling air-sea rescue or driving him there herself. She settled on the middle ground; take him to the harbor and call EMS along the way. By the time she got there, the ambulance would be ready.

"Alright, we'll take your boat in for you. Just rest." She hurried to the stern and looked to Glenn.

"Is he alright?"

"No," she said. "You think you can drive Malcolm's boat to the harbor? All you have to do is follow us. We're gonna drive this gentleman's boat."

"Yeah, I can do that," he said.

She looked back at Malcolm. "You comfortable with that?"

"Yeah. He knows how to operate it. He'll be fine," Malcolm said.

"Alright, thank you, young man." She patted his shoulder, then undid the line to separate the boats. "Just stay with him while I drive the boat." She hurried into the wheelhouse, spun the boat around until it pointed east, then gunned the throttle.

Malcolm put a hand on Fred's shoulder. "Just hang in there, buddy. Let us know if anything hurts."

"*Everything* hurts," Fred said. He coughed again.

Afraid the guy was about to vomit, Malcolm tried picking him up by the shoulders to lean him over the side. As Fred got to his feet, another huge uncontrollable cough took over his body. Saliva peppered Malcolm's face and eyes. The eighteen-year old spat and wiped his sleeve over his face.

"Shit!"

"Sorry," Fred said between coughs.

"Don't worry about it." He helped him lean over the side. "Just focus on that breeze."

"You alright?" Brianna asked. Malcolm gave a thumbs up. She continued looking back long enough to make sure Glenn was following them, then put her attention back on the path ahead. She grabbed the radio and started making her call to EMS.

All I wanted to do today was sit around and be lazy.

CHAPTER 18

Like a long brown tentacle, the chum trail stretched out for a quarter-mile from Luke's boat. With classic music beating from the radio and nobody else on the boat, Luke felt more relaxed than ever. He almost wanted to beat himself up for not taking the boat out more often. This was actually soothing. Nobody around; no cell service; not even noise from neighbors. Now to find that shark and bring home fifty-thousand bucks.

Despite making the boat purchase in May, he resented the maintenance and fuel costs that went along with it. But now that he was getting a taste of the solitude being on the water brought him, those costs didn't seem so bad. All he was lacking now was a beer. It was a little after eleven-thirty. Who cares if it was considered early? You only live once.

Luke dug into the cooler and pried one from the plastic loop. He cracked it open and took a gulp, then sat down on a chair. With the beer in one hand, he continued tossing scoopfuls of chum into the ocean. He watched it extend further to the north, like a squiggly line. His eye followed it to the horizon. There, his gaze remained, not focused on the soupy mixture, but the large boat far off in the distance.

It was roughly a mile away, but could still be seen with the naked eye. Luke went into the wheelhouse and found a pair of binoculars. He lifted it to his eye and checked out the vessel. It was some kind of yacht—not like anything anyone in Amadea owned. He hadn't memorized everyone's boat design, but something like this would stick out like a sore thumb. It wasn't anything extravagant as a superyacht, but it was still fairly large. Luke estimated it was almost two-hundred feet in length. Whether it was here for fishing, he couldn't tell at this distance. It was easy enough to assume it was some party boat that belonged to some rich guy. If that was the case, he didn't get the memo that these waters were off limits until further notice. Luke would've dismissed this as the case had it not been for the smaller fishing boat near the yacht.

They were close enough for the occupants to communicate in person. Luke's inquisitive nature was getting the better of him. Was this an argument? A chitchat? Did they know each other? Or was this fisherman yelling at the hotshot to get out of the local waters?

Or was he showing something off?

It wasn't long before the fishing boat started heading east. Whatever the occasion was, it was over. Luke kept an eye on the boat while he added to his chum trail. As the boat drew near, he noticed something large was hanging from the boom. He raised the binoculars again.

"Son of a bitch."

Dangling by its caudal fin was the biggest damned shark he'd ever seen. It was a great white, jaws slightly agape, the fish motionless. There were two people on deck, with a third driving the boat. They saw him watching them, then raised their beers. *Yeah, bitch! We caught the sucker!*

Of course, the fools were too self-absorbed to realize their observer was not watching them, but the fish. He followed the fish with his glasses, specifically its jaws. It was hard to know for sure, but it looked like most of its teeth were intact.

"Bastard just killed a mako shark. No fucking way it kept all its teeth." More importantly, its jaw didn't match the bite wounds on the victims. Then again, he wasn't sure what could inflict such a clean wound. In the reading he'd done, he learned that a great white's bite power wasn't much stronger than a human's. The main difference was those freakishly sharp serrated teeth. A bull shark, on the other hand, would be a little more believable. Their bite strength was significantly stronger. The problem, however, was they didn't get near the size of the chap seen in the footage.

Regardless, the ignorant crowd back at the harbor would declare this the shark without question. The Chief would declare the waters safe and send people out to the slaughter. Assuming the name of Amadea City wasn't tarnished already. It wasn't reputations Luke was worried about. No way was he letting this idiot get fifty-grand for catching the wrong fish.

He swung the boat around and followed these guys back to port.

CHAPTER 19

Elise Sheldon waited in the parking lot. Her attention was fixated on the paramedics, who hastily strapped a patient onto a stretcher and loaded him into the ambulance. She recognized the woman with him as the same police captain she spoke to yesterday. There were two young men accompanying her. The older one returned to his boat and left the area, while the younger one stayed with her. Probably her son.

Elise didn't step out of her car. She didn't want to talk to anybody, especially not the policewoman. Not that Elise thought lowly of her, but if she was recognized, the conversation would unavoidably focus on how she was coping—something she didn't want to talk about.

She wasn't here to socialize. The only thing she wanted said to her was the word that the fish was caught. Around a quarter to noon, that word swept through the harbor. The shark was caught and was being hauled to port. Finally, she would see the bastard and get some sort of closure. She needed it, or else sleep would be an impossible feat.

She stepped from her vehicle and hurried onto the pier. After ten minutes, someone pointed out that the boat was on the approach. It was coming in from the northwest, with another fishing vessel following closely as though in pursuit.

People pointed and shouted with excitement that they could see the dead shark. Elise watched the fish as the vessel docked. It was definitely a large specimen. Not *quite* as large as the fish she saw, but still pretty damn big. Its jaws would make short work of any human. She started to consider that maybe she was wrong. Yet, something in her gut knew the responsible fish had that strange jaw. She saw it. Then again, a great white this large was extremely rare. Also, what were the odds that someone would catch a shark this big following a series of attacks?

She stepped from the vehicle and followed the crowd to the dock. Cameras clicked so rapidly the pier sounded like a giant Geiger counter. Two proud fishermen stepped off the boat, exclaiming "We got the shark!" The leader wore a tank top, aviator sunglasses, had four days' worth of growth on his beard, and had a British accent.

The mayor and police chief were quick to congratulate the fishermen on their achievement. Reporters crowed around him, with Anthony Zach asking the majority of the questions.

"What's your name, sir?"

"Just call me Beau," the British man said.

"Hey, Beau! Well done, sir!" another reporter said.

The chief and mayor waited for the men to pose for a seemingly endless series of photographs before stepping in.

"Alright, alright, alright! Give us some space, will ya?" the Chief called out, waving his hand to the crowd. A few officers stepped in and guided the press back. Brianna stepped on the pier and was greeted by her boss' smile. "Captain! Looks like we found your perp!"

"Looks like it," Brianna said. She studied the jaw, then turned to the British man. "What'd you say your name was?"

"Beau."

"Beau—"

"Mott," the man said. *What business is it of yours, lady?* He managed to keep his upbeat demeanor.

"How'd you do it?" the mayor asked.

"Found him a few miles northwest of here. Hooked him with some bait, drew him to the surface, and put a few shells through his face!" Beau mimicked pumping a shotgun.

Brianna eyed the twelve-gauge openings in the shark's head. *Yeah, that would definitely do the trick.*

"He didn't take too well to it," the first mate said.

"No, he did not. But, what would you expect from a homicidal shark that's already killed so many?" Beau said.

As they spoke, Elise pushed her way through the crowd. She needed a closer look. It was as necessary to her psyche as air was to her survival. She forced her way between a few reporters, then was stopped by the line of cops.

"Excuse me, ma'am. You can't come any closer."

She didn't reply; she was right where she wanted to be. That didn't last long, however, as a few cameramen stepped in front of her. "Hey! Move!"

"Hey, lady. *You* move. We've got press credentials. Do you?"

"I just wanna see the damn thing," she said. It didn't take much time before voices raised and fingers pointed. Moments before it could escalate into a shoving match, the cops stepped in.

"Break it up! Come on!" They stepped in-between then focused on her. "Ma'am. Time to go."

"Just let me look," Elise said. "I'm simply trying to—"

"No, time to go," the other cop said.

"Dr. Sheldon?" Brianna said. The cops looked back at the homicide captain, then realized she recognized the person in question. Brianna wanted to ask 'what are you doing here?' but didn't want to draw any more press attention to the poor woman. If they realized she was attacked by the fish, they'd hound her for a statement. Still, she needed to separate her from the crowd. "It's alright, guys," she said to the cops.

Elise stepped between them. So much for not being recognized.

Brianna put a hand on her shoulder. "What are you doing here?" she whispered.

"I needed to see it," Elise said.

"Something wrong, Captain?" the chief asked.

"No, sir. Everything's fine," Brianna said.

"Doesn't look like it. Who's this?" the mayor said.

Brianna clenched her teeth. Better to answer and get this over with. Still, she would speak quietly enough to keep the press from overhearing. "She and her nephew were attacked yesterday. He didn't make it."

"Oh, I see," the chief said.

"Ma'am, my deepest condolences. But as you can see, we got the bastard," the mayor said triumphantly. He noticed Elise didn't look satisfied. "Does this not look like the one you saw?"

Elise took a deep breath. "Well, I don't know. The one I saw looked…" she noticed the look of apprehension on the Captain's face. *Don't say what I think you're gonna say.* Probably right. "…Different."

"Nonsense," Beau quickly said.

"Sir, if you would be respectful…" Brianna said.

"Disrespect is not the intent, ma'am. But if I can be straightforward, it's not like sharks this big are common. This is clearly some kind of record. It HAS to be the one."

"I concur," the mayor said.

"I concur you're all stupid!" another voice called out.

Elise turned around to see a man wearing an eyepatch push his way through the crowd. One tall reporter stepped in his path.

"Sorry, Jansen! Looks like somebody beat you to the punch!"

"Only a nitwit like you would think this hunt's over, Anthony." The one-eyed guy bumped him with his shoulder and approached the dead shark.

"Luke, what are you doing here?" Brianna said. There was a strain in her voice, like she had been asking that question a lot today.

"Detective, this doesn't concern you," the chief said.

"The hell it doesn't," Luke said.

"It's not your case," the chief said.

"To hell with the case. I'm speaking as a private contractor. You've offered a reward for the shark responsible for the attacks."

"Yeah?"

"Not a chance in hell this is the shark," Luke said.

"Give me a break!" Beau exclaimed. "Who's this guy?"

"Interesting, that's what I was about to ask *you,*" Luke said.

"Beg your pardon?"

Luke smirked. "I like your accent. Sounds like someone out of South London. *Definitely* not someone from around here."

"Got a prejudice against the English?" Beau asked.

"Couldn't care less," Luke said. "I do find it interesting that an outsider happens to be the one who supposedly brings us our fish."

"Not supposedly," Beau said. "And for your information: word got around. I'm from L.A. I think it's safe to state there's a fair number of accents down there. I heard about the shark yesterday and decided to bring my mates up and take a stab at killing it."

"More like a shot," the first mate said, sparking laughter from the crowd.

"Ha-ha-ha," Luke mocked. "So funny. Not as funny as the look on your face when you see that this *isn't* the right shark."

"Bollocks!" Beau said. "You're just jealous that you didn't bring it in."

"The bite wounds don't match the jaw on this bad boy," Luke said. "Captain, Chief, Mayor—the *real* killer is still out there. And it'll kill someone else if you declare these beaches safe."

Chief Pino turned red. He stepped forward and put a finger to the Detective's chest. "Jansen; I am *this* close…" he pinched his finger, leaving a sliver of space. Nothing else was said, but his meaning was clear.

"Chief?" Brianna said. "I'm not saying he's right, but he does bring up a point. We need to be sure."

The Chief glanced at the mayor, who was staring at Luke with contempt. He obviously wanted this quandary over and done with. But he couldn't argue against Brianna's logic. It would murder his political career to reopen the beaches and then have another fatal shark attack.

"Alright. Let's get most of these reporters out of here. We'll be conducting an autopsy to see what this shark has eaten in the last twenty-four hours." He looked at Elise. "Captain, we might want to get her out of here."

"Agreed." Brianna put her hands on Elise's shoulders. "Come on."

Before she went along, Elise turned toward this one-eyed detective whom she had never seen before now. This man, unlike everyone else, seemed to share her viewpoint, not in the suspicion that the shark was a Helicoprion, but in the belief that this shark was not the real killer.

"What kind of shark do you think did this?" she asked.

The guy shrugged, not even sparing her a glance. "No clue, lady. I'm no fish expert. But I do know patterns. Those jaws did not cut them people down to size."

Brianna cringed. She would've preferred a more sensitive choice of words from him, but it didn't appear to faze Elise. She guided the doctor away from the pier, while a bunch of cops instructed the crowd of reporters and civilians toward the lot.

Of course, the vendors proceeded to take advantage of the situation. Instead of omelets, it was burgers and hot dogs.

CHAPTER 20

By one-thirty that afternoon, a canopy had been raised over the pier. A tarp was laid out to collect all the innards. A veterinarian hired directly by the mayor's office arrived on site with a variety of surgical tools. His arrival prompted a series of taunts and jeers from the other fishermen, all of whom complained that they could easily have done the job and for cheaper.

Luke Jansen stood cross-armed at the pier. He casually watched the body language of the three outsiders who brought the shark in. The man who called himself Beau was on the pier, while the other two remained on the boat. Their smiles had vanished, and for the duration of the surgery, it seemed like a challenge to sit still. Nervous energy? Nervous for what? If shark guts made experienced fishermen queasy, then they weren't fishermen. If they were so confident this was the shark, then why be nervous? If they had a direct line of sight to the operation, he could assume they were dreading the sight of a partially digested human, but a wall had been erected with the canopy to help block the excessive sunlight. They had no direct view, hence Beau watched from the pier.

He, on the other hand, still kept a fairly confident demeanor, though not as flamboyant as before. Luke watched him stuff a pinch of chewing tobacco in his mouth. His jaw was rolling with the chewing motion. There it was: nervous energy, just hidden better. But it wasn't simply the type of nervous energy of someone awaiting the outcome of something; his eyes seemed to be glancing around toward the people around him. It wasn't simply unassuming glances at the crowd: each time his eyes moved from the shark, it was always in the direction of the cops, Brianna, the chief, mayor, or Luke himself. Luke had seen such actions all throughout his police career, mainly from people guilty of something and were watching their covering up of evidence be put to the test.

"You know this isn't the right shark, don't ya?" he said. Beau spat a wad of tobacco onto the pier and looked over at him.

"Suck it up, Detective. You're not getting the fifty grand. You'll have to find another means of paying your gambling debts. That's what you burnt out cops do, right?"

"I think he knows all too well what it's like to be burnt out!" one of his fellow fishermen said. Fingers pointed at Luke's face, drawing laughter, even from some of the cops.

"That's enough," Brianna said. She looked at Luke. "Please don't cause any more trouble."

"Only in today's day and age are facts considered problematic," Luke said.

"Speculation," Chief Pino said "Speculation which'll be put to rest in a few short moments." He winced as a horrid smell flooded the pier. The vet had made a long cut along the shark's belly. Blood and stomach fluid poured onto the tarp. In that moment, the crowd became harder to control, with cameramen trying to squeeze past the wall of cops for a photo.

The vet did more work to widen the wound and allow easier entry. Finally, it was time to dig in. The first things to flop on to the deck were mostly digested pieces of fish.

The mayor cleared his throat and stepped away, pretending he needed to make a call by holding his phone up. The chief fared well, until a bloody flipflop was pulled from the shark's stomach. He kept himself under control, allowing himself breaks to look away and 'monitor' the crowd.

The line of cops struggled to keep the press back. But with the reveal of a pair of severed legs being pulled from the shark, their job instantly got easier. Some snapped a few photos then hurried back toward the lot. For some, their vendor food consumed during the wait made a new comeback.

"Oh, heaven..." Chief Pino muttered. More human remains were pulled out. There were at least two people in there, both completely unidentifiable due to the state of their digestion.

"I'd say we have one female and one male," the vet said.

"The victims from the beach," Brianna said.

"What about the others?" Luke said. "There were three people killed on that property. And then there's that guy from the yacht..."

"One victim was pulled to shore from that wound to the belly—"

"Which had no chance of being caused by this shark," Luke interrupted.

"And the kids were torn to bits, and were not completely consumed.

"Also—" the vet raised a hand. He shone a light into the stomach, then looked at the detectives. "There's signs of inflammation."

"Meaning what?"

"Meaning it vomited at some point," the vet said. "Not to sound insensitive to the other victims, but between the Stuckey attack and the beach, it must've lost its cookies at some point. I will say this: the bite wounds from all victims are identical, meaning it was the same fish that did all of this."

"Not the guy with the gash in his belly," Luke said.

"Coroner's report says otherwise," the vet replied.

"Suck it up. You lost. Money goes to me and my mates," Beau said. "Even *you* can see what's been laid out in front of you. Time to admit defeat, Detective—and *maybe* I won't file a complaint for your derogatory remarks about my accent."

"Being offended is the way of the world these days," Luke said. He eyed the gaping wound in the shark. "Doc, is that all?"

"Yes."

"Funny there's no mako shark remains in there."

"There's bits and pieces—"

"No, this'll be fresh. I almost encountered the bad boy while I was out there. Couple boys accidently hooked a mako, and while it dove, something else got ahold of it. Bit everything below the head."

"Yeah? So what? Some other shark could've done it. Or rather, a killer whale could have. We've seen plenty of them out there this time of year," the first mate said.

"Out there? I thought you boys weren't from around here?" Luke said.

"He meant along the California coast, wanker," Beau said.

"Alright, that's enough," Chief Pino said. He turned to the crowd. "I am announcing officially that these men have successfully caught and killed the shark that brought so much pain and devastation to our city. We will provide watches all night, and the mayor and I will conduct a meeting in the coming hours to let you know when we will reopen the beaches."

The crowd erupted with questions, none of which the chief answered.

The mayor approached Beau. "Congratulations, sir. See my secretary and she'll make sure you get every dime of what you're owed."

"Suits me," Beau said. He shook the mayor's hand, then turned to face Luke. "Let me guess? You're gonna say something like 'don't show your *face* around here ever again'?"

"I wish he would. Then one of us could say, 'look who's talking'!" one of his companions called out. Luke blared an exaggerated laugh, then waved a hand to concede the argument.

"Chief, Mayor, if you guys wanna give people the green light to get slaughtered, that's up to you. Let me know when the next hunt starts."

Chief Pino, seething with anger, watched the detective step through the crowd of reporters. Already, they were shouting questions of whether the waters were still safe.

Great. Getting the beaches open today was no longer a possibility. With this rhetoric hitting the internet, we'll be lucky to be back to normal in a week.

"Captain Raye?"

"Yes, sir?"

"Meet me at the station in thirty minutes, please."

She clamped her jaw shut to prevent any disparaging comments from escaping. "Yes, sir."

Elise watched the one-eyed detective make his way through the crowd, while giving sarcastic answers to the horde of reporters. He knew something wasn't right about this, and even though he had given up the argument, he hadn't conceded the fact that there was something else in these waters.

She needed to speak with him. She forced her way through the crowd, raising a hand to get his attention. "Sir?!" She jostled a few reporters, knocking them aside. Her fast walk progressed into a run. By the time she got through the crowd, the man was standing beside the driver's side door of his Dodge Journey. "Sir?! Detective?!"

He gave her a brief, uncaring glance, then slid into his vehicle.

"No, wait!" Her words meant nothing to him as he drove off. "Damn it!" She heard laughter behind her. It was the tall reporter the detective told off. On his badge was the name *Anthony Zach*. "What's so funny?"

"No offense, but I've never seen anyone so eager to get that guy's attention before. Especially not a pretty lady such as yourself." He eyed her top to bottom. "You with the press?"

"No," she said. "That detective; what's his name?"

"Luke Jansen?" He laughed again. "You're probably the only person in town who doesn't know who he is. Trust me, you don't want anything to do with him. To be frank…and off the record, he's a burnt out detective from L.A. who frankly shouldn't even be working night shift security in a strip mall."

"Why?" she asked.

"You really wanna get involved with a guy who throws his partner under the bus before getting him killed?" Anthony said. He threw a peanut in his mouth and walked away.

Elise stood in silence. That reporter seemed to have knowledge of Luke Jansen. Judging by how willfully he ignored her, he didn't seem like the most pleasant of individuals. Maybe Anthony was right. Still, his observations stirred her uncertainty of what really killed Chad. She chased him down, "Sir?"

Anthony turned toward her. "Yeah?"

"Pardon me, I'm not quite caught up on everything that happened. What's this news about someone who died of a laceration?"

"The white attacked a family on their private beach," he said. "They're not sure how it happened, but the shark either slashed a guy with its teeth in an attempt to bite, or maybe swiped him with its tail. Either way, the guy was cut open all the way. Was pulled back by his brother, but died on the sand. Coroner confirmed bacteria from shark jaws in the wound, so it was definitely the fish."

Elise stared past him at the water. *A straight gash…from a shark's jaws…like what a Helicoprion's jaw could do.*

"Ma'am? You alright?" Anthony asked.

Elise snapped back into reality. "Oh, yes. Sorry."

"Who are you, actually?" he said.

"Just a curious bystander," she said. She turned around and returned to her vehicle.

Anthony didn't believe her, but didn't press the issue. With plenty of resources of his own, he'd get his answers. Somehow, this woman was connected to the events. He watched her pull out of the driveway, making sure to get a discrete photo of her license plate before resuming his current activities.

CHAPTER 21

Stepping foot on her vessel was almost as daunting a task as entering the house. Chad's belongings spread across the deck were a taunting reminder of their last moments together.

It almost took an hour just to brave the short walk. It was as though the very deck was poisoned. Fighting against her overwhelmed and exhausted mind, she boarded the vessel. Immediately, she felt paralyzed. Every item that belonged to Chad, every *hint* of his existence—it all reminded her of her failure. It hadn't even been twenty-four hours, and she already felt like a ticking time bomb.

Elise closed her eyes. There was only one thing she could do: shut it all off. She remembered being taught to do so during her stint in the U.S. Army. She meditated on deck for several minutes. When her eyes opened again, she felt like a machine. Cold, uncaring, seeing everything in front of her for what it was: inanimate objects used for different purposes and functions. She went into the pilothouse, and found her phone, which had lost most of its battery.

She took it into the house and plugged a charger into the kitchen outlet. With the phone hooked up, she began dialing a number. After four rings, the voicemail for Dr. Aaron Kent of the Schmidt Institute began its usual list of options.

It was Sunday. He wasn't in. BUT, she had his cell number. She dialed, waited, only for the call to go unanswered. Her blood began to rush. She hung up, waited a moment, then dialed again. Still no answer. *Goddamnit, Aaron. Answer the call!*

Third time was the charm.

"Hello?"

"Dr. Kent. This is Dr. Sheldon."

"Elise?!" His voice went from irritated to sympathetic in a heartbeat. *"You alright? How can I help?"*

"I'm fine, Doctor. Listen, there's something I need to address."

"I was notified yesterday by the Amadea Police Department. They were kind enough to explain what happened. I'm so sorry for your loss, Elise. Don't even bother coming into the lab tomorrow. I've already arranged cover for the month of September. Take time and heal. Please."

"I—thank you, sir. But that's not why I'm calling," she said. "We need to send an investigative team out into these waters. The shark that attacked me, that's been attacking everybody, it's not a great white."

"I beg your pardon?"

"I'm telling you. I saw it."

"Saw what?"

"It had a set of teeth in a whorl—it was a Helicoprion."

There was a pause. *"A Helicoprion?"*

"Yes! I'm serious."

"Oh, dear. Elise, please take the time to get with close friends and family."

"Doctor, I saw it with my own eyes."

"Elise, I know it'd be an insult to your intelligence to remind you that Helicoprion is long extinct. Listen, I can't even imagine the ordeal you've been through. It's so horrible. Yesterday was a horrible day altogether for your city, judging from what I've read. But, I doubt it's being caused by a resurrected species of shark."

"I watched it attack Silver, the humpback whale. I watched it slice her open with its jaws. It's out there, Dr. Kent! We need to put together a team to find it!"

"I—" Elise could imagine him shaking his head and rubbing a sweaty brow. Judging by his tone, he wanted nothing more than to get out of this conversation. Yet, considering the circumstances, he didn't want to be a jerk and simply hang up. *"Ma'am. I can't go to the board and ask for funding to search for a prehistoric shark, based on the testimony of, no offense, a professor under extreme duress. Besides, I checked the news. They caught the shark responsible."*

"That's not it. That's not the one that killed Chad. It's still out there, I'm telling you. The police won't do anything about it. That leaves you and me."

"Elise, listen to me very carefully. I'm going to forget this conversation ever took place. I won't even speak to my family about it. There is NO Helicoprion out there. I can't imagine the pain of what you went through, let alone had to witness. I haven't spoken to the doctors and police about your condition, but I have a feeling you've addressed these concerns to them, and that they believe the same thing I'm about to tell you: It was all a figment of your imagination. You're in shock. Please, get together with a grief counselor, a pastor, friend, ANYONE that can help you get through this. We have counselors at the campus, and I'll be more than happy to put you at the top of their schedule. Just say the word."

A hundred responses swirled in Elise's mind. She settled on "Thank you, I'll let you know." Then hung up. She tossed her phone on the counter and strolled through the empty house. On the bookshelf were pictures of her and Chad together. She couldn't bear to look at them or the pictures of her sister and brother-in-law.

She had failed to protect their son. The least she could do was uncover the truth about his death.

How can I do that when nobody will help me. Nobody even believes me. They're all willing to accept that the great white was the killer. She sat in the computer chair.

"Everybody but that detective. Maybe—MAYBE if I could just speak with him..." Yeah, he seemed like an asshole, but in her experience, assholes were often the ones who got results. And that asshole was the only one with the brains to question what he saw.

She needed to meet with him. Unfortunately, she had no idea where to find him. Being a scientist, Elise knew how to seek out answers. She remembered overhearing that police chief instructing Captain Raye to meet him in his office. They'd be there by now.

Elise hurried back to her truck. For the second time today, she left her house in a hurry.

CHAPTER 22

Dixon drained his cigarette to the butt, then flung it into the water. He leaned on the starboard side guardrail, watching his brother-in-arms return to the yacht. The *Namesake* pulled alongside the main deck, allowing Barton to cross over.

"You smell like fish," Dixon said.

"What'd you expect?" Barton replied. "I need a whiskey."

"He's hogging it all, boss," one of the crew said, pointing to Dixon.

Barton rolled his eyes. "Go figure." He climbed the ladder to the fly deck. Dixon was kind enough to have a scotch glass waiting for him on a tray table. Barton filled it and tossed it back.

"I saw the news reports," Dixon said. "Looks like 'some fisherman' caught the shark."

"Uh-huh." Barton took another. He looked frustrated.

"Something wrong? They *are* convinced, right?"

"Yeah-yeah," Barton said. "It just took longer than I hoped. There's this fucking one-eyed detective who thinks he's *Sherlock Holmes.* Basically made them drag the process out."

"You think they'll run DNA analysis of the two victims?"

"Boss made sure the bodies were FUBAR," Barton said. "Shouldn't be anything we should be worried about. We'll be long gone before the DNA analysis is complete." He looked toward the pilothouse. "Fix that glitch in the electro-transmitter?"

"Yep. Seems to be working just fine now," Dixon said.

"Be nice if it worked the first time. We wouldn't fucking be out here," Barton said. He lit a cigar and watched the water. "As long as it keeps the fucker from causing more trouble in the meantime."

"You want us to commence the operation?" Dixon asked.

"Not yet," Barton replied. "Let's wait until nightfall. I don't want to be seen by any of these Yanks still out hoping they'll win the big prize. That one-eyed prick at the pier did do us one small favor, I think. The authorities think everything's safe, but the ruckus the detective made was caught by the media, and there's still a little bit of fear being spread. So, as a precaution, they're gonna keep the beaches closed for a while. Which is good for us. Last thing we need right now is for our fish to kill another swimmer."

"Has there been any more word from that scientist woman who was attacked? If she spread the news that she saw it—"

"They've written her story off," Barton said. "They think she's nuts because her kid got munched. Let's keep it that way—hence we're waiting until nightfall to finish this. In the meantime, let's make sure our tranquilizer darts are ready. Have that IV drip on standby, because I'm not dosing the fish throughout the whole trip back. You're gonna be in the *Namesake* with Dirk and Vick."

"Why me?"

"Because it's your turn. I've been in it enough for one day," Barton said.

"You just want access to the good stuff," Dixon said, shaking the bottle of whiskey at him.

Barton cracked a smile. "So what if I do? Besides, brother, I need to supervise the operation from here. I can't let any of these idiots do damage to the thing. And since you're the best shot—other than me, I want you on the other boat as support."

"Whatever you say, brother," Dixon said. He raised his scotch glass and tapped it to Barton's. In a few hours, their job would be done with, and they would be back to supervising security operations at home plate. Neither of them minded. This was the first action of any kind they'd had in a couple of years. Other than that, it was fairly routine, which was fine with them.

"So, what's gonna happen with that fifty-grand?" Dixon asked.

Barton smiled. "You think I'm sharing it, you're out of your damn mind."

CHAPTER 23

For the second time today, Brianna's stomach was killing her. This time, it wasn't nausea, but hunger. After emptying herself out on Luke's boat, her body was now craving replacement sustenance. She would happily oblige herself, except instead of a drive-through, she was wasting her time in Chief Pino's office.

She endured twenty minutes of back-and-forth with him. The topic: whether Luke Jansen should be allowed to remain on the police force. As usual, she rose to his defense.

It was only because their working relationship was so valuable, Chief Pino didn't override her command and fire Luke himself. Despite their disagreement on this matter, he found Brianna to be an excellent policewoman and a valuable member of the department. But that defense was starting to wear thin regarding the tenure of Luke Jansen's employment.

"You see what he's done," Pino said, crossing a foot over his knee. "He's got the whole community in an uproar. We have major news stations covering this situation, and it's not positive press. People still don't think the beaches are safe. People all over the country are doubting the competency of our department. Tourism is already looking to go down next year. The mayor's been on my ass for the last twenty-four hours, and thanks to Jansen's show at the harbor, the *next* twenty-four hours. Prison inmates will have less sore asses than me by the time this finally blows over."

"And what if he wasn't wrong?" Brianna said.

"He *was* wrong," Pino said. "That was the shark. Even still he questions it."

"That's what a good detective does, Chief," Brianna said. "You should know. You were a good one in San Francisco."

Pino sat quietly. It wasn't the first time she brought that up in defense of Luke. Perhaps he had been behind a desk for too long. He couldn't argue that his concerns nowadays were political headaches rather than the tension of walking the beat and kicking in doors. Still, never once had he accused his fellow police officer of a crime he didn't commit. He had arrested cops, sure, but it was always in the act and during a proper investigation.

"It is possible to ask too many questions," he said.

"Is it?" Brianna asked. "What about the press? They've been after him since the Laskey case. Don't they have any accountability?"

"You speak as though he doesn't deserve it."

"He didn't kill his partner. It wouldn't have happened if the media hadn't—" Brianna raised a hand, signaling peace. "It doesn't matter at this point."

"Listen, Captain. I *know* why you hired him. You feel you owe him something. I don't agree, but I won't deny the simple fact that you probably wouldn't be here if not for him. That said, there does come a time where a guy like that becomes more trouble than he's worth."

Brianna shook her head. "I'm not canning him. I'm also not gonna hold his feet to the fire for the media's intentional over-sensational coverage. Be nice if someone held *them* accountable for once."

Pino nodded. *That* was something they agreed on.

"Keep a tighter leash on him. Keep him away from the cameras. Please. If this continues, I'll throw him to the wolves. I'm not kidding."

A hunger headache was settling in, worsening her mood. Brianna knew best not to respond with anything other than "Yes sir." Any other response she had in the chamber would probably get *her* thrown to the wolves.

"I gotta go. Husband's probably wondering where I am. I'll see you tomorrow."

She left the chief's office and walked to the main lobby. The officer at the desk raised her hand to get her attention.

"Excuse me, Captain Raye?"

Am I not allowed to eat?! Brianna counted to three before answering, once again suppressing any inappropriate remarks.

"Yes, Officer. What can I do for you?"

"We have a woman looking for you." She pointed to a woman seated in a chair on the right side. Brianna's irritation was pushed aside by compassion. It was Dr. Elise Sheldon.

"Thank you." She approached the doctor, who stood up.

"Captain. Sorry to bother you again."

"It's no problem. It seems like we keep running into each other, though. How can I help you?"

"I want to talk to that detective with the eyepatch. I'm told his name is Luke Jansen."

Brianna reared her head back in surprise. "Jansen?! Pardon me for asking, but what do you want to talk to *him* for?"

By the look on Elise's face, she didn't want to give the actual reason. "Just want to ask him a few questions."

"About…?"

Elise gave a half-hearted chuckle. "Please, just tell me where I can find him."

"He's not here, and it is against policy to give the private information of any staff to civilians." A technicality, but still the truth. Despite her respect for Luke, Brianna could not fathom any positive interaction between him and this grieving woman. "Listen, it's apparent that you don't want to tell me the truth. I'll just say this; whatever you want from Detective Jansen, you're not gonna get it. He's not a nice guy. Kind of an asshole, actually."

"But is he a good cop?" Elise asked.

"Pardon me?"

"Just answer, please."

Brianna was surprised at the swift change in Elise's attitude. She almost came off as one of the field instructors during the academy. Then she remembered that Dr. Sheldon was in the military. Such discipline comes in handy when focus is needed.

"Yes, I think so. Overall." *Please don't ask me to elaborate.*

"Okay. Thank you." Elise turned around and went for the door. Brianna groaned, then hastily followed her out.

"You mind if I ask where you're going?"

"I'm leaving the police station," Elise said.

Brianna scoffed. *Smartass. Maybe she and Jansen WILL get along with each other.* "Nice one. You know, it's not gonna get easier pursuing this ghost. The shark is dead, Doctor. Talk with one of our counselors. I'll set up an appointment for tomorrow morning, if you'd like."

"Thanks, but I'm doing fine," Elise said. She got in her SUV and started the engine.

Brianna remained standing in the lot until she was gone. On the one hand, she was relieved that the conversation was over. On the other hand, she was worried about what Elise would try. She had the look of a determined woman. Considering her motive, she would drive through Amadea all night until she found Luke.

CHAPTER 24

Once again, Anthony Zach's face was on the five o'clock news. Despite working for a local channel, his coverage of the incident and police response was receiving comments from all over the nation. He could almost feel himself elevating up the journalistic ladder. In a few years, he'd be on one of the prime time shows of CNN or FOX. At least, that was the goal. First, he'd have to find a way to wedge out one of the talking heads already in those slots.

After finishing up his half-hour, Anthony was heading out the front doors of the studio. Standing in front of him was a familiar face. He stared for a moment, making sure he recognized her. The sight of her SUV in the employee parking lot concluded that was the woman from the harbor.

"Uh, hi!"

"I need your help," she simply said.

"Okay," he said.

"That detective we spoke about, Luke Jansen, how can I find him?"

"Simple. Go to the police station in the morning and ask for him."

"I'm not interested in waiting. I want to speak with him *now*." She noticed the reporter tilt his head and raise an eyebrow. "Don't get any funny ideas."

"Excuse me," he said. "Mind if I ask why you want to speak with him?"

"I do, actually," she replied.

"Whoa. Okay then. So, why should I help you?"

"Because, *if* I'm right, you'll have the biggest story of the decade," she said. That eyebrow raised again. Anthony thought about what she said for a moment. He knew there was no way she would elaborate on what this story would be exactly. But he knew significance when he saw it, and this woman was undoubtedly positive she had the lead to something important. And, if it turned out she was just some psycho bitch with the hots for Jansen, that'd be a fun story too. Not as significant, but still something he could milk.

"He lives somewhere on the hills," Anthony said. "Don't have the exact address. Even if I did, I couldn't give it. But I may, or may not have tracked him to Nebraska Street, between Siefke and Ayres. Can't confirm or deny that he's on the north side, closer to Ayres than Nebraska. But, if someone were to go looking for him, I'm sure they'd spot that Dodge Journey he drives."

"Thank you," she said. She turned around and went straight for her vehicle. As she drove away, one of Anthony's cameramen stepped outside.

"Who was that?" he asked.

"Someone who just made this whole story much more interesting. Keep an ear on the police frequencies. I'm curious what this might entail."

"Police frequencies? Why? Is she trouble?"

"Trouble for somebody. But not us," Anthony said.

CHAPTER 25

The water temperature was just right. Warm, borderline hot, but not to the point of melting your skin off. Luke stripped naked and lowered himself into the tub. Though it didn't touch his face, there was something soothing about soaking in warm water that made the pain subside somewhat.

At least something was going his way today. Luke reached to the floor where his *Southern Comfort* sat, and brought the neck to his lips. It was his way of mourning the wasted day that just passed by. Fifty-thousand bucks passed him by, and on top of that, there was the wasted cost of fuel and bait.

Fuck it. I'm done with sharks.

Luke Jansen closed his eye and leaned back. He should've brought an audiobook or put some movie on his smartphone. Instead, he was left with his imagination. Naturally, he thought of past girlfriends, mainly focusing on the hotter ones. Then there were the ones he never got a chance to hook up with, and would never have a shot with in the future. It wasn't a matter of distance that kept him from having a chance with any of the gorgeous women he set his sights on. The true reason was staring back at him from the reflection in the bath faucet. Who the hell would hook up with *that*?!

Luke flicked some water at the image, then leaned back. He focused on the warm sensation of water. He could fall asleep in here. The idea didn't sound so bad, except the inevitability of waking up in cold water. Slowly but truly, the pain in his face began to subside.

Then came a knock on the door.

Luke opened his eye. "You've got to be kidding me." Hardly ten seconds went by before it was followed up with another knock. Still, he didn't move, hoping that by simply not answering, the person would give up and go away. But the knocks kept coming. Soon, they were followed-up by "Hello?! I know you're here. I see your vehicle!"

It was a female voice. The only woman he knew with the gall to show up on a Sunday afternoon was Captain Raye, and that wasn't her voice. Whoever she was, she didn't take the suggestion on the 'welcome' mat literally.

Not only did she get louder and less patient, but the knocks were heavier. Luke groaned. It had been ten minutes and this idiot wasn't taking the hint. And unfortunately, he couldn't tune out the knocking. He crawled out of the tub, patted himself down with a towel, then reached for his clothes. He stopped before putting them on, then cocked a grin as a new idea took form. He dropped his shirt, strolled out into the kitchen, found an apron, put it on, then went for the door. If someone wouldn't go away willingly, make them feel as uncomfortable as possible.

He pulled it open. The woman outside was in her mid-thirties, had brown hair tied back, wore jeans, a black tank top—and a very shocked expression on her face.

"Uh—hi."

Luke eyed her for a moment. Though he didn't know her, she did look familiar. Then it hit him: the girl who chased him in the harbor lot. How the hell did she know he lived here?

Great. A stalker. Should've considered that before answering the door with no clothes on.

"Didn't you read the mat?" he said.

The woman looked down. 'Go Away.' She honestly thought it was intended for laughs when she first saw it. The sound of a door slamming shut drew her eyes back up.

"Hey!" She started knocking again.

Luke waited a minute, realized she wasn't giving up, then opened it again. "Listen, lady. I may not know you, but trust me, I'm not your type. Now, go away."

The woman put a hand to the door, stopping him from slamming it shut.

"No. I need to talk to you."

"You do realize I'm a cop, right? With a bad temper and lots of guns."

The woman sniggered. "Yeah? Got one stashed in that little apron? Or in your ass?"

Luke stared blankly. This ploy wasn't working as he intended. "Listen, lady, it's getting late. Go stalk someone else."

"I'm not stalking. You're Luke Jansen, right?" she said.

"Nope. You'll find him on Rogatta Park. Has a Portland accent, real douchey."

"Nice try. You think I'm stupid? I'm a PhD, smartass."

"Some of the dumbest people I've ever met have PhDs," Luke said.

"Doesn't take a doctorate to know that Luke Jansen has one eye, a burnt face, a Dodge Journey, and a cocky attitude. Though, nobody warned me of the attire." Luke didn't offer a response. For several seconds, they stood in dead silence. "I'm Elise Sheldon."

"I didn't ask." Luke went to shut the door again, only for Elise to put both hands against it.

"Wait. I need to speak with you."

"Not interested. There's a neighbor down the street that'll give you the attention you crave. Not me." With a little added force, he overpowered her and latched the door, then twisted the lock. He ignored her angry pounding as he returned to the kitchen, where his *Jim Beam* was waiting.

He let a smile slip through. How interesting this desperate chick showed up right after he was fantasizing about women. Maybe God was helping him with certain needs. Then again, it did nobody any good to bang a stalker. That would lead to a certain kind of trouble that he wanted no part of.

"I'm not stalking you!" Elise shouted. "I tried to speak to you at the harbor. I need your help. It's about the shark. You know that shark didn't kill those victims. You know something's off about this case. I'm a marine biologist! You're right. That *wasn't* the shark."

That caught Luke's attention. He stood motionless in the kitchen, bottle inches from his lips. The pain in his face, which had returned during their interaction, was subsiding as curiosity took over. After a minute of contemplation, he opened the door again.

Elise almost looked like she was out of breath. "You believe it too, don't you? That shark wasn't the right one."

"The fish had two people in its gut, lady. Can't fake that."

"Yes, I know, but—"

"We can argue that another shark is out there, but fact of the matter is, that great white was the one that attacked the beach."

"The one that attacked—what about what you said at the pier?!" Elise said. "That whole time, even when the shark was gutted, you told them there was something wrong."

"Just saving face. I wanted the fifty-grand," Luke said. He went to shut the door again.

"A great white can't make straight-line cuts," Elise said. Luke stopped the door before it latched. His eye burned through the woman's brow, as though prowling for any lies. "But I know what can."

After a moment of consideration, Luke let her in. "You have five minutes."

Elise smiled nervously. "Thank you. Um, can it begin after you put some clothes on?"

Luke looked down at himself then back at her. "I'm covered up."

"Not enough."

First I'm told what to do on my own boat, now in my own house. By a STRANGER, this time!

"Fine. One sec." He returned to the bathroom and found his jeans and shirt. *This visit better be worth it.*

****

It dawned on Elise how trashy this place was when she went to sit down. There were crumbs on the couch, stains on the carpet. The tray table by the chair had barbeque stains on it. How miserable was this guy to live like this?

God, I should start a second career as a housecleaning service. I'd make bank with this guy alone.

Luke returned, dressed this time, thankfully.

"I see you've made yourself comfortable," he remarked.

"Not sure that's the right word, but sure," she replied. Luke didn't take a seat. He leaned against the chair and held his hand toward her.

"Go ahead. Tell me about the shark we're looking for." Elise suddenly grew nervous, something Luke took notice of. "I don't like that look on your face. It's the look of someone who knows she's full of shit."

"No! It's not that," Elise said. "It is pretty unbelievable, though. But it's the truth."

"Your five minutes is ticking," Luke said.

"The victims you saw. They all suffered clean cuts, correct? As though a chainsaw had been used, or some serrated edged blade?"

"Yes," he said.

"What if I told you there's a species of shark with a singular row of teeth on its lower jaw, designed in a whorl? Literally a circular saw made of teeth."

"I'd say I've never heard of such a thing, but then again, I'm no fish expert," Luke said.

"It can get between thirty and forty feet in length. It's called a Helicoprion, discovered by the Russian Geologist Alexander Petrovich. Literally means 'spiral saw'. The suspension of its jaw places the species in the chondrichthyan subgroup Euchondrocephali, more specially, a member of Eugeneodontida."

"Okay, okay, holy shit, lady. You lost me after 'forty-feet in length'," Luke said. "*Forty* fucking feet?"

"Yes. It's big. And deadly."

"There's some logic errors in what you presented me, Doc," he said. "If these things were around, they'd be as well-known as your everyday great white. That leads me to something else that doesn't pass the bullshit test. You said it was a Russian geologist that discovered the shark—being as you're a marine biologist, you know very well that geologists tend to study rocks, not fish. Which tells me you left something out. This heli-heli—spiral-tooth shark was discovered through *fossil evidence*. When I put that together with the fact that these sharks are fairly unknown, I conclude you're talking about a goddamn *prehistoric* shark."

Elise saw the reaction she so badly wanted to avoid. Even this detective—the one guy questioning the events that had taken place in the past thirty-six hours, wasn't believing her.

"I know it sounds unlikely…"

"More than unlikely," Luke said. He chuckled. "Jesus, I thought you were crazy. But I thought it was a stalker, obsessed woman type of crazy. Not someone talking that she thinks dinosaurs are coming back to life."

Elise stood up. "I don't just think this shark exists. I *know* it. I saw it with my own eyes."

Luke didn't waver. People often got made when called on their bullshit. "Yeah? When?"

"I—" Her voice broke. She looked away, regained control of her emotions, then looked him in the eye. "It killed my nephew. I watched it cut him with its jaw. Repeatedly."

Luke watched her in silence. He wondered if this woman was so crazy that she'd make something like that up. Or worse, fabricate it in her mind. Then he remembered the report of a marine biologist who was attacked out by the reefs.

"That was *you*?" he said. "You're the one they found passed out on their boat with the decompression sickness and the coral reef wound in her leg." He looked down and saw that she was somewhat favoring her right side. "It's a shame what happened. Clearly indicates your mind played tricks on you. It's understandable."

"I know what I saw. I've studied the ocean all my life. I know what a damn shark looks like."

"Under normal circumstances, sure," Luke said "Not when your head is about to explode. Not with God-knows what poison was in your system from the coral sting. And, to be straightforward, not while under the extreme stress of having your kid eaten in front of you. Sorry, Doc, but I'm not buying this spiel about a prehistoric shark." He took a quick drink of his bourbon. "Sorry for your loss. But I hate to break it to ya; you need a shrink. Not a detective."

Elise was turning red with anger. "I'm sick of everybody telling me I'm crazy."

"You're wrong. You're mad that everyone *thinks* you're crazy, but don't have the balls to say it outright," Luke said.

Elise wanted to slap him. It took everything not to. She knew right where to hit, too. But what good would it do? If anything, it'd confirm to him that she was unhinged.

"Detective, please. If this shark continues to swim on the loose, it can kill someone else."

"That's not what you're worried about. You just want to kill it because it killed your boy." He shrugged when she grimaced at him. "Hey, would you rather I make the claim that you consider yourself on the verge of the scientific discovery of the decade?"

Elise shook her head. The detective had a point. *That* probably would've earned the smack. Still, she didn't want to give up. She needed someone, *anyone* to believe her. Even if it was a cocky, insensitive son of a bitch like this guy.

"You know how to operate on the water. I need to track it down, but I need help. I have equipment on my boat. We can track the shark down, tag it, then figure out a way to kill it. That way we can keep what happened to Chad from happening to anyone else."

Luke shook his head. "Sorry. I've dealt with a lot of strange cases, but I don't buy this crap about a resurrected shark. Where the hell did it come from? How has it not been seen up till now? How the hell did it not evolve in those three-hundred million years? You'd think after all that time, the damn thing would look significantly different, right?"

Elise was simultaneously disappointed and impressed. The detective would probably make for an excellent scientist, the way he asked questions and considered all factors. That observation paled to the crushing sense of defeat. Not only was it obvious he wouldn't provide assistance, but his statement added to her inner turmoil. Self-doubt was hitting hard. But the scientist in her hit back:

"Aside from the whorl and the suspected length, we've had no idea what it looked like. The fossil record does not preserve the cartilage skeleton, thus there's no skeleton or other material to date with radiometric measures," she explained.

"Still seems like a paper-thin stretch," Luke said.

"Listen, nobody will help me. I need somebody who knows how to operate on the water and knows how to track. More importantly, I need someone who's a good shot. You can have all the credit. I don't care. I just want the thing caught and killed. Someone else can do the research afterwards. And you can have the credit for solving a case that everyone else thought closed. What do you think?"

"I think your five minutes are up," Luke said.

That was the final blow. The fact that he was holding the door open demonstrated he was finished with this discussion. Elise said nothing more; it'd just be emotional babble, which would only make her look more like a fool.

Before exiting, she stopped by the chair. She dug into her wallet, pulled out a photo, then placed it on the arm of the chair. Judging by this interaction, it wouldn't do much to persuade Luke, but she preferred letting him keep it. She couldn't bear to look at it. Silently, she walked out to her SUV.

Luke shut the door, then waited until he heard her pull out of the driveway. *Finally.* He peeked through the window, watched the woman drive off, then got back to his day.

"For the love of God. Now I can't even be home without idiots coming to my door. Might be time to move."

Over the next several minutes, he gradually put the conversation from his mind, though he still questioned how the hell she figured out where he lived. Someone gave her his location. Brianna knew where he lived, but she wasn't the type to relinquish it to strangers. Hell, she was more likely to lie and direct people *away* from him. She was smart like that. None of the other cops knew his exact address.

After thinking back on all visitors, it wasn't hard to guess who might have done it. Anthony Zach had tailed him a year or so back when he was reporting on a murder case which Luke was investigating. The guy was always digging for a story and was more than willing to put a spin on anything he could get his hands on. He saw Luke Jansen as a gold mine. A scar-faced detective with a controversial background, despised by almost everyone—there was a lot Anthony could milk from that. Whether his reports were true or not didn't matter. They got clicks on the internet and eyes on the TV screen.

Who the hell else is that asshat gonna send?

Luke considered returning to his soak. Yet, he couldn't help but glance repeatedly to his driveway. He wondered if that woman would turn back. Worse, what if Anthony Zach planned on sending others? The only thing worse than that would be if that moron showed up himself. Luke would probably shoot the prick, should he be dumb enough to do that. Just the thought alone made his temper flare, along with the nerves in his face. Pissed off and in pain; not a good combination. Luke probably *would* shoot the next person to show up.

"Great," he said to himself. Now he wouldn't be able to sleep knowing this. Seemed the only way to relax undisturbed was to change locations. He didn't mind the rocking of water. Looks like he was in for a second ride on his boat. He wouldn't go out far; just enough to anchor and catch a snooze until his alarm went off the next morning. The cool ocean breeze might do wonders for him.

Luke strapped his revolver to his hip. He never went anywhere without it. He packed a small cooler with ice, tossed his *Jim Beam* in it, as well as a couple of lunchmeat sandwiches. For good measure, he tossed in a bag of potato chips. The only healthy thing that made it into the cooler were a couple of bottles of water.

He went for the door, stopping only to double-check that he had everything. The keys, of course! By the computer desk. He crossed the living room, snatched them up, then spun on his heel to return to the door.

The sun had angled itself just right, its rays reflecting off the laminated image lying on the arm of his chair. Luke allowed himself a brief glimpse of the young man featured. Definitely that biologist's nephew. Even someone as cynical as Luke could see this kid seemed like a well-adjusted fellow. His shirt was freshly ironed, his hair combed to the right, his smile baring white teeth. Graduation photo, by the look of it.

Enjoy the easy life, kid. Give it time, that smile will turn to a scowl. Except, time was something that kid no longer had. It wasn't his smile that faded, but his aunt's. He stared at the image longer than he intended. *Definitely a ploy to appeal to my better nature. Lady DEFINITELY doesn't know me.*

He locked up, boarded his Dodge, and took down the street. A few hundred feet past the next intersection, he noticed a grey Toyota Highlander parked on the side of the road. Despite his inner voice telling him not to, he looked out his passenger window as he passed by it. The woman inside was looking back. Though the encounter lasted for a split-second, it was enough for Luke to know driving off was the right call. She had the look of a desperate woman thinking of a new way to plead her case.

"Find a shrink, lady." He took a left at the next intersection, purposely going the wrong way so it would not be obvious where he was going. Sometimes, it was nice to take the scenic route anyway.

****

"Asshole," Elise muttered. She leaned back in her seat and accepted her reality. The detective was actively avoiding her, nobody else believed her, worse—they thought she'd lost her damn marbles. She was on her own.

She knew her way around her boat, but she was no shark hunter. *First time for everything.* She had the tracking tags on the boat and a speargun to connect them to the fish. At least she had a first step. Then there was the question of killing the Helicoprion. She didn't own any firearms and would not be able to obtain one fast enough for her liking, unless she went through an illegal route. She wasn't that far gone.

However, she did have enough chemical supplies on hand; she could develop a poison and inject it into the shark's bloodstream. It was a high-risk plan, but could theoretically work. She could buy some supplies from the local fishermen to make chum and bait. But with daylight quickly dwindling, she would have to start immediately.

She sped for the harbor.

CHAPTER 26

Malcolm sat at the dinner table, staring at the mashed potatoes, carrots, and grilled chicken breast. He wasn't nauseous, but his stomach was putting out those early warning signals to kill any appetite. There was a faint headache taking hold, though nothing extreme yet. He took Excedrin when he first felt it coming, which probably didn't help the discomfort in his stomach. He peeled off a few thin slices of chicken and munched on a couple of carrots. So far, everything was staying down. He hoped he didn't catch a bug from that sick guy on the boat.

"You alright there?"

Malcolm looked up at his dad. "Hmm?"

"Your food. You've barely touched it." Mr. Barnhiser had already cleared his plate of two chicken breasts and a mountain of potatoes. The veggies served to fill in the cracks, and they were halfway gone. His wife, who sat across from him, was a slower eater, but always had a clear plate when finished. Both came from backgrounds where you only left the table if your plate was empty. It didn't matter to them if Malcolm was eighteen. He was still living under their roof, therefore the rules remained the same.

"Yeah, I'm alright." He realized he was between a rock and a hard place. He didn't want to admit he wasn't feeling good, since he was eager to go to Mr. Raye's shop tomorrow and make a little money. Yet, those warning signs in his stomach weren't lying. He knew eating was not in his best interest right now.

"Something wrong with your food?" his dad pressed.

"Nothing at all. Just...I think I'm gonna pack it in some Tupperware and take it with me tomorrow. Got a little side gig."

"Good. You owe me for that fuel and bait you cost me today," his dad said.

"That's the plan, actually," Malcolm said.

"Ease up, won't ya?" Mrs. Barnhiser said. Her husband registered the stern look.

He nodded. It wasn't the first time he was put in check, and not just by her either. He didn't mean any harm by his strict methods; he just didn't want Malcolm to end up like these other spoiled brats he'd been seeing in the college campuses. So many of them did not have any ambition or drive. He'd even known of kids—hard to think of them as the adults they technically were—suing the university he worked at because they thought they were guaranteed a job after graduation. It'd be a cold day in hell before he saw Malcolm turn out that way. But it had been brought to his attention that maybe he pushed too hard sometimes. The way the kid jumped to attention as though dad was a drill sergeant demonstrated that. Mr. Barnhiser didn't like to let his wife know she was right, but considering himself a TRUE academic, he wasn't the type to deny the truth either.

"Okay," he said. "Where ya working?"

"God a gig at Mr. Raye's store. I guess he's got some stock coming in and is willing to pay a hundred bucks or so to have it sorted out. Should cover the fuel."

Mr. Barnhiser nodded. "Nice work, bud. But why you not hungry now? Feeling sick?"

"No," Malcolm said. "Probably just an ulcer. I think I need some antacids."

"That's what happens when you drink those sodas all day long," his dad said. This time, Mrs. Barnhiser agreed.

"Nothing much. I'm gonna turn in early. Should wear off once I wake up. It just has my appetite in the dumps for now."

His mom got up and got him some Tupperware. "It's alright, sweetie." She took care of his plate. "How 'bout some water or Gatorade?"

"Thanks," he said. She brought him a bottle of each.

"If you're not feeling up to it tomorrow, don't go," she said.

Malcolm watched his dad munch on his carrots and green beans. The cost of fuel would hover over his head until it was paid off. Better to take care of it sooner rather than later.

"Nah, I'm fine. Thanks."

He went upstairs. Instead of going to his room, he went to the bathroom. He had already showered today, but felt the need to do it once more. Maybe it'd cleanse him of any lingering bacteria on his skin.

The shower was intended to be brief, but the steam accumulating in the stall felt too good. Instead of a shower, it was a steam bath. It helped to clear the sinuses and clear his pores.

Malcolm wasn't sure how long he was in there, but the fact that his father knocked on the door and asked, "Bud? You sure you're alright?" indicated it had been a while.

"I'm good," he replied. The hot water was running out anyway. He turned it off, stepped out and dried himself. He felt a tad better, but still felt mildly fatigued. He dug around the bathroom drawer and located his vitamins. He had already taken them that morning, but at this point, he didn't care. One day of overloading wouldn't kill him, but it might slow down whatever was fatiguing him. He downed a multivitamin, then a D3 tablet, then followed it up with a tangerine drink mix. As when he got sick with anything, he always loaded up with vitamins to give his immune system that extra boost.

Towel wrapped around his waist, he stared at the young man in the mirror. His left eye was bloodshot. How long was it like that? Couldn't have been long; his folks would've pointed it out. He tried to brush it off as a result of the steam bath. Whether such a thing was actually possible wasn't relevant.

Still, he was getting nervous. His eyes went back to that shelf. In a prescription bottle were a few pills of his dad's amoxicillin, given to him when he had stomach ulcers a year back. Malcolm had eyed the bottle when his symptoms first started, then *Googled* the use for those pills. 'Used to treat infections' was all he remembered.

"What the hell? It's not gonna hurt me." He took the bottle, downed a pill, and washed it down with water. Something about doing that made him feel better. Maybe whatever he had wasn't serious. Maybe the medicine and vitamins did the trick.

Malcolm went to his bedroom, changed into pajamas, and took some Benadryl to help him sleep.

He'd know in the morning.

CHAPTER 27

"You've got to be shitting me."

Luke Jansen strangled the steering wheel, watching the pier several yards ahead. Was some higher force at work? Was he doomed to encounter this Elise Sheldon woman repeatedly? Whatever the case was, his plan to take the scenic route had backfired. Had he just gone straight for the harbor, he'd be on the water already, oblivious to her whereabouts.

There she was, meeting with Ol' Hal in his supply shop. Like a countryside bait and tackle store, he always had the last-minute supplies that the local fishermen needed, whether it was bait, netting, cable lines, even hull patches. In the past twenty-four hours, he had made a killing, selling chum, rope, hooks, buoys, traps—for those that were foolish enough to use them. Even with the shark craze over…*mostly* over, the media was still milking it for all it was worth, Ol' Hal was still making bank.

He was helping Elise load up her vehicle with chunks of beef and three tubs worth of chum. Luke was too far away from identifying the other supplies, but he suspected he saw a hook, a roll of rope or chain, and something that resembled a rifle. Considering Hal didn't have an FFL, it was probably a speargun.

"Is this crazy woman seriously going after it herself?" Luke said. He thought of turning around and heading for home. What point would there be in going out on the water if the purpose was to *get away* from this woman?

Then he saw Elise's gaze turn toward him. Luke felt as though he'd tear the wheel from the car. Great! Of course, the shop had to be close to the dock where his boat was moored. If he was at the other end of the harbor, she'd never notice him, nor would he notice her.

Elise paid the man, got in her vehicle, and drove over to him. Luke considered speeding away, but in today's day and age, this lady would probably accuse him of stalking *her*. And knowing how eager the press was willing to gun for him…

She rolled down her window. "I thought I saw you."

"Too frequently," he replied.

"Having second thoughts?" she said.

"No."

"Then what are you doing here?"

"Ironically enough, trying to make sure I didn't have another encounter with you," Luke said. Elise leaned up and saw the cooler in his passenger seat.

"You're planning to sleep on your boat?"

"So what if I am? I appreciate my solitude. I imagine you appreciate the water. Or used to, at least," Luke replied. Elise didn't react; she knew the remark was meant to provoke. The guy must *really* dislike people.

"Can I ask you a question?"

"You just did," he retorted.

Elise thought about that, then smirked. She actually found that funny, despite her mood and growing distain for him.

"Are you aware if they're doing dental analysis on the victims they found?"

"I don't think so. They're relying on DNA tests. Don't know if you wanna hear this, but the skulls were too mashed up. Both victims lost a lot of their teeth due to trauma and dissolving acid."

"Interesting," Elise said. "Not a *single* tooth?"

"That's what I'm told," Luke said. "They'd been in the shark's gut for almost a day."

"Shouldn't affect the dental records," she replied. "Teeth are the most durable bone in the body. Hence, it's the only bone that's exposed."

Luke wished he had sped off. "So, what? Now you're telling me there's a conspiracy to make fifty-grand off a dead shark? Those guys just so happened to catch a record-sized great white and stuffed a couple of bodies in its gut?"

"No. I just think it's strange. Don't you find it strange? You're a detective, after all?"

"I'm only interested in cases I can solve," Luke said. "Despite what they might say, I'm not actually David Copperfield—and I can't interrogate a shark. Especially not a dead one. Or those fishermen. They're gone, and even if they weren't, they probably wouldn't want to speak with me anyway."

"Sounds defeatist to me," Elise said.

"Don't let my good looks fool you," Luke quipped. "Not everyone is flocking to have a meet-and-greet with me. In fact," he checked his watch, "your time's up!" He got out of his vehicle, grabbed his belongings, and started for the dock.

Elise opened her door to peer out at him. "Yesterday, you were interested in the strange details. The odd wounds. The frequency of attacks. Suddenly, it's as though you're buying into the narrative."

"I've been wrong before," Luke said. He glanced back at her. "Let it go. You'll sleep easier."

"You know what it's like to have trouble sleeping?" she asked. Luke wasn't sure if it was a genuine question or if she was trying to make a point. Either way, he wasn't interested. He continued to his boat, loaded it with his supplies, then started the engine. He throttled out of the harbor and turned south. A few miles down, he'd come near the South Beach, which was fairly barren as of right now. The recent deaths had made it somewhat taboo to hang around there.

Nice and quiet, with hardly anyone around. Exactly what Luke was looking for.

****

Elise stood on the pier, hoping for the slim possibility that the detective would change his mind and turn around. That didn't happen. The boat got smaller and smaller as it traveled further away, soon becoming a speck in the southwest sea.

"Nicer fellas for you to take interest in." She looked over at Ol' Hal, the bait store owner. He was wiping his greasy hands with a handkerchief after tossing a few bags of trash into the dumpster. "Sorry. Couldn't help but notice you talking to One-Eye over there."

"Not *that* kind of interest," Elise said.

"Good. I mean, not that it's any of my business," Hal said. "Nobody likes that fella, and for good reason."

Elise remembered something Anthony Zach had mentioned. "How well do you know that detective?"

"I know the stories."

"What's this news of him getting his partner killed?"

"According to the reports, his old buddy in L.A. got a bunch of money. One-Eye accused him of getting paid off by a human trafficking operation, which turned out to be bogus. Some think he was trying to get the cash for himself. Whatever the motivation, it all got out of hand, and a few vigilantes ambushed the partner, believing the scoop of him being a criminal. Heh, didn't surprise me at all that he was gunning for that fifty-grand reward today."

"How'd that injury happen?" Elise asked, pointing to her left eye.

"I believe it happened during the attack. I guess the guy deserves a tiny morsel of credit: he tried to save the partner, whatever his name was. Got cooked in the process. Guess he just wanted to blackmail him, not kill him. Everyone has the line they aren't willing to cross, I suppose. Still, serves him right for the false accusation. Takes a real dick to do that to his own partner."

"I suppose so," Elise said. "How'd the partner come across the money?"

Hal shook his head. "Reports never specified that."

Of course they didn't. Still, Elise found it to be an interesting insight. She knew enough to no longer pursue the detective. He wasn't interested in solving any cases that weren't cut-and-dry.

She would have to find the Helicoprion herself. She thanked Hal, then drove home. It was bound to be a late night. Good thing sleep wasn't something that came easy anyway.

CHAPTER 28

The glowing sun reached out over the horizon, its final gleams blinding before the day officially ceased, only to be taken over by the dark of night. During those final hours, the man named Barton had watched the water. Miles from shore, it was as though they had the entire ocean to themselves.

Exactly how I want it.

He had the helmsman direct them to the location of the underwater electro-transmitter they had installed on the seabed. The tracker showed that the target had been circling it for most of the day.

For Barton, these had been the slowest hours since his first tour in Afghanistan. He remembered hours upon hours of nothingness, and the few fights he had during those twelve months were hindered by political red tape. In the private sector, things were more streamlined. Go in, do the job, go out, payday. This current position had been the least exciting of his jobs, but it paid well for relatively simple work. And in a state of his life where he'd prefer to keep a low profile, simple and uneventful was preferred.

That was the root of the stress he felt. A part of him felt foolish for going undercover with the shark, but unfortunately it was a case where he was the only one who could pull it off. Many of the men below didn't even speak English, and those that did had thicker accents than his. Only a couple were American, and their faces were on the police watchlist. Most people that worked in this operation had some sort of baggage. In fact, they were the kind of people his employer desired. They weren't too heavily bound by morality, but not to the point where they couldn't be controlled. If they got out of line, it'd be a simple matter to make them disappear. Nobody in this operation had anyone waiting at home. If they 'went missing' nobody would raise the alarm. And being paid under the table, the government wouldn't take notice either.

If only reliable machinery was as easy to come across as personnel. At noon, the electro-transmitter had shorted out, forcing divers to hastily repair it. In that time, the fish branched out in search of prey. All the money in the world, yet they were still handicapped by the failures of technology. For the entirety of the afternoon into the evening, he waited tensely on the fly deck, hoping that the device would not fail. The longest hours since Afghanistan. Occasionally, the electrical discharge would weaken, causing the fish to lose interest, but overall, it held.

"We're ready to begin," Dixon said. He was on the fishing vessel with the two 'fishermen' who had accompanied Barton in delivering the decoy. Dirk was at the helm, Vick on deck ready to assist with whatever Dixon needed.

Barton looked down at the main deck. A dozen men were standing ready across the thirty-five foot wide space, some with harpoons loaded with sedatives, one at the winch, and others prepping the chum, bait, and buoy marker.

"Deactivate the transmitter. Start chumming. Put the bait out there and be ready to winch the bastard in."

The men got to work. The *Namesake* circled around, Dixon and Vick standing ready with harpoon guns.

Barton glanced down at the deck and saw one of his men approaching the transom with a high-powered rifle.

"What are you doing?" he said.

The man, roughly thirty-years of age, looked up at his superior. Any display of manly confidence dwindled with the sight of fiery eyes in the deck lights. "Uh, I just figured we'd want to use some precautions."

"Let *me* do the figuring," Barton said. "The specimen is NOT to be killed."

"But it's a maneater!" the man protested. "It's killed many people already. I'm not eager to die just to catch some creepy shark."

Barton stared the man down for several seconds. "Let me persuade you with this: If I hear a single gunshot, it'll be followed by a second…mine." He unholstered his Glock and pointed it down at him. The action removed any sense of doubt of his implication. The target was not to be harmed, even at the cost of their own lives. A few murmurs echoed across the deck, with men pointing at the gunman.

"Put it down, man. You're playing with fire," one said.

A Nigerian man shook his head at the offending crewmember. He looked up at Barton. The only reason he hadn't squeezed the trigger already was because he didn't want to attract attention from anyone possibly nearby. The Nigerian man looked back at his crewmate, who clearly had no grasp how lucky he was so far. "When did you come into this outfit?"

The crewman with the rifle raised an eyebrow. "Uh, a year ago?"

"Ah. So, you weren't with us in Nicaragua," the Nigerian man said. "Otherwise, you'd know." A Central American crewmember by the winch nodded. Nobody spoke about Nicaragua. That alone gave the rifle-bearing crewman an understanding of the kind of man it was who commanded this operation.

The man put the firearm away and returned to the transom, where he proceeded to toss chum out into the water.

Barton's rule was established. He holstered the pistol, then clicked his two-way radio. "*Namesake*, you got your eyes on that monitor?"

"Affirmative," Dixon replied. *"Looks like he's getting hungry. He's already beginning to ascend."*

"Good. I don't feel like waiting," Barton replied. "He'll probably take his time to examine the bait. Remember, he's not too fond of boats, so we're gonna pull forward to add a few meters of distance." He pounded the pilothouse door, signaling for the helmsman, who could hear him, to throttle ahead. The engine growled as the boat moved forward a few meters. As it did, two of the men on the main deck lifted a drum full of chum and tilted it into the water, creating a steady stream of enticing mixture. With the bow pointed south, they waited.

The target was maintaining a depth of fifteen meters. Dixon was right, it was being cautious.

Several minutes passed. Ten minutes became twenty, during which the moon seemed to get brighter and brighter. And all the while, the fish maintained the depth.

"Okay, what the hell?" one of the men said. Apparently, Barton wasn't the only one getting impatient.

"It's still here. It's interested, but for some reason he won't commit," he said. He looked across the water at Dixon, then at the world around them to double-check for witnesses. So far, so good.

"It's coming!"

Dixon barely finished speaking when the huge fish breached the surface. The men exclaimed in unison as forty-feet of prehistoric muscle flopped high over the water, then crashed down with an enormous splash. The hook set in and the line went tight. The boat leaned to stern, causing the men to stumble.

"Fish on!" Barton said. "Haul it in slowly. Keep that cable tight!" He lifted his radio. "*Namesake*, move in. He'll be coming up again any second."

"Roger that!"

****

Elise couldn't stand the silence. In the past few years, she had grown used to the casual chitchats between herself and Chad. Even during her quest to avenge him, she still caught herself looking over her shoulder with the intent to say something to him, only to remember he was no longer there.

Each time led to more intense anger. She looked down at the shaft of her speargun, which she had outfitted with a tracking device. That was only the first step in killing the shark.

Propped up against the transom was the Cap-Chur tranquilizer rifle. Used for immobilizing larger animals, particularly livestock, the weapon was the most ideal for piercing the Helicoprion's thick skin. An ordinary dart needle would likely snap upon impact. But instead of sedative, these darts were loaded with Strychnine. One dart would probably not contain enough poison to get the job done, but Elise wasn't taking any chances. There were numerous darts on standby, each loaded with Strychnine. There was no chance of getting the fish close enough for her to jab it with a stick, forcing the marine biologist to improvise. She had the tranquilizer rifle handy ever since she was hired with the Institute. On one occasion during grad-school, she joined an operation to free a whale from a drift net. The creature was thrashing about, making it impossible for the rescue team to free it. With no other choice, they had to tranquilize the animal with that very rifle. It was one of those occasions that always stuck in Elise's mind. Ever since, she had a Cap-Chur rifle on standby, in case she ever found herself needing to come to the rescue of another large marine animal.

Her finger itched to squeeze that trigger. She could envision the shark getting hit by the dart, then spiraling to the depths as the poison stopped its heart.

Impatience was taking hold. Elise had been out for several hours, and there was no sign of the Helicoprion. As far as she could tell, she was the only one out on the ocean. At least, she and one other vessel. She could see the deck light looking like a tiny speck of yellow in the distance. Considering the direction Luke Jansen went after departing the harbor, it was definitely his boat. It was closer to shore than she was, not too far from the southern docks on the south side of the beach. She wondered what he was doing. Was he asleep? Was he reading a book or watching a movie? Or was he looking for the shark too?

As long as he's dressed.

After what seemed like an eternity of chumming the water, she took a breather. Nothing was coming after the bait except for a bunch of smaller sharks. She considered moving somewhere else, but what point would it be. Sharks could smell a single drop of blood from a mile away. A thick trail like what she just made? The Helicoprion would smell that from anywhere along the Amadea coastline.

It was time to consider calling it a night. That thought naturally sparked the internal debate of whether she was crazy or not, as well as the concern of sleeping. She knew what dreams awaited her, and they were worse than the prospect of confronting the shark again.

Elise watched the smaller sharks nipping at the chunks of fish floating in the stream. There were a few animals splashing about, none of which were large. Everything she saw thus far was only big enough to serve as a snack for the predator.

As time went on, she noticed the peculiar motions in the splashing shark directly ahead. She saw the white underbelly as it passed across the chum trail. Its left pectoral fin would have acted as a dorsal were the fish able to move more graciously. However, it flopped with each swing of its caudal fin.

Curious, she aimed the spotlight down at the thing. It was a blue shark, fairly young judging by its six-foot length. Elise watched the shark's jerking motions. Something was definitely wrong with it. What it was, she had no idea. There were no outward injuries. Its tail and fins were intact and there were no malformations in its figure. Yet, it seemed to be in some kind of distress.

After a while, its motions brought it closer to the boat. Elise kept the light on it as best she could. The fish would disappear every few seconds, not from diving, but from sinking. It was dying, its muscles becoming increasingly rigid. It resembled a drowning swimmer struggling to keep himself afloat. Except this fish had no concept of what was happening to it. It simply followed its senses, which led it to Elise's chum trail and light.

What was more bizarre was the discoloration. The thing looked as though it had blistered skin around its jaws, as well as a few spots on its underbelly. She had never seen such a thing before. She had researched infectious diseases in sharks before. Some had been reported to have died from streptococcal bacteria, and in one case, a sandbar shark that was being tracked by researchers was found mysteriously dead. Autopsy results revealed that it had died of severe meningoencephalitis. None of these diseases created visible symptoms other than skinniness from malnourishment. This blue shark, however, looked anything but malnourished.

It was at the right weight it should be for its size. But it was dying, and whatever was killing it was internal. Finally, the shark disappeared under the water and never came back up. If it was still alive, it wouldn't be for long. It was the next thing Elise saw that confirmed this.

As she panned her spotlight back to the chum marker, she spotted something else floating nearby. Kingfish. Two of them. They were much smaller than the blue shark, but the silver scales reflecting her light made them easy to spot. These fish were drifting toward shore. She estimated they had been dead a couple of hours.

Questions took form in her mind. A dying blue shark with odd skin blisters along its gill slits; two dead kingfish—*three*—another drifted near the port quarter. It was much closer to the boat, allowing Elise to get a more detailed glance. Some of its scales had fallen off, the skin underneath discolored by infection. Whatever had killed it was actively killing the shark.

"What the hell?"

Whatever it was, it was unlike anything she had researched in her studies of underwater infectious diseases. That led to the next question: was it something in the water itself that was causing this? Was there a spill of some kind? She had been diving here for years and hadn't come across anything. If this was caused by an outside factor, it had to have moved into the area recently.

Around the same time as the shark's arrival.

Elise's palms turned sweaty. Maybe it was the exhaustion and emotional fatigue, but she couldn't shake the feeling that something was wrong. Really wrong.

****

Luke stared up at the night sky, which occasionally got hazy. The smoke from his cigar twisted high above his face like the fumes from a tiny volcano. The tobacco helped a bit to relax his mind. He was in complete silence, save for the lapping of water against the hull.

Despite his efforts to drift off into a deep slumber, his mind wandered back to the lost fifty-grand and the bizarre outsiders that won it. That led to a rabbit hole of issues his mind couldn't figure out. He thought of the mako shark Brianna's kid had hooked. The fishermen claimed they'd seen killer whales around here. The media and city government seemed happy enough with that explanation. It was possible; killer whales were more than capable of eating sharks that size. Still, he found it odd that they never saw them breach even from afar.

Then there was the state of the victims. He'd seem bodies in many different states of decay. In his years, he'd pulled corpses from collapsed and burnt buildings, found murder victims stuffed in dumpsters, where they rotted for weeks. And in most of these cases, if there was no identification, the medical staff was able to identify the victim within a few days. In this case however, it was looking like it would take a month. There was nothing else they could run on? Neither of these victims had any identifying features? No birthmark? Implant? No physical defects of any kind?

He still couldn't get over the idea that a single great white caused so much mayhem. To say it wasn't common was an understatement. It simply didn't happen. The closest thing to it occurred on the shores of New Jersey in 1916, and that was over a period of twelve days, not twelve hours.

Another hit of the *Southern Comfort* failed to budge his thoughts. *The case is over,* he told himself. *It's an odd shark attack, but a shark attack nonetheless. Unless you can prove the fishermen somehow found a twenty-something foot white and stuffed it with bodies, you have no case. Who cares, anyway?*

He took in another gulp of whiskey.

Wrong pipe. The instinctive suction of air only made it worse, as it caused him to inhale a cloud of cigar smoke.

"Fucking shit!" He rolled off the cot, landing on his hand and knees, coughing as though trapped in a burning building. He leaned over the side and spat into the water. Cursing and gagging, he miraculously managed to keep his stomach contents in place. He slowly caught his breath, staring into the water as his lungs slowly returned to normal. "I guess that's why you don't drink while lying down."

The coughing continued, like an echo in the distance. Luke listened intently. Was someone mocking him? Or just another night owl suffering a similar mishap at a coincidental time? The fact that it was going on nonstop for several minutes indicated the latter.

Luke straightened up and glanced around. There were no boats nearby, except for one further to the north—that biologist woman. But she was a considerable distance away, and the sound wasn't coming from over there. He looked toward shore and saw a porchlight come on.

Not any of your business. Don't concern yourself with it.

The continuation of the coughing and probable vomiting ended that internal debate. Luke grabbed a pair of binoculars and aimed it at the shoreline. It was hard to see, but there was someone near the porchlight. The resident was in a white t-shirt and what appeared to be sweats. Not clothes to go out at night, but the reflection of car keys in the porchlight confirmed he wasn't staying in.

A few seconds later, the guy fell to his knees.

Luke smirked. "Moron can't hold his drink, apparently." He watched the guy fumble about. Did he drop his keys? Or his beer bottle? Luke then eyed his whiskey. "Screw it, I can judge. I've never been so blackout drunk that I couldn't make it out the door." Saying that out loud brought another concern to mind. Luke squeezed his eye shut in frustration: if this person was really planning to drive in this state, he would certainly kill himself or someone else.

It was a possibility he couldn't ignore.

"Oh, damn it. *This* is why you mind your own business, Jansen." He checked the property with the binoculars and saw that there was a dock which he could use to secure his boat. With a resigned sigh, he hauled up the anchor and throttled the boat to shore.

When he arrived, he heard the strained sound of vomiting. Even from the dock, the vile stench was potent. Whatever the guy had eaten throughout the day was now in the grass. Luke secured the boat then stepped onto the dock. The man was still on his hands and knees.

"Howdy, friend. Seems like your tolerance for alcohol matches my tolerance for people," Luke said. The man looked over at him, his sickly face animated with astonishment. "Relax. I'm a cop. Heard you puking your guts up from all the way out there. Might wanna stick with light beer. They usually store it in the tampon aisle."

"I'm not drunk," the man said.

"We'll have to see about that," Luke said. He nudged the keys with his boot. "Going on a trip?"

"Hospital." The word came out in a raspy breath. This time, Luke suspected there was more to this situation than a simple weak stomach. He dug a small keychain flashlight from his pocket and shone it over the resident. The man's eyes were red and veiny. His skin was pasty white, with boils on his neck and right hand.

"Aw, shit!" He moved back to keep from being touched.

"Help me, please!" the man strained.

"Yeah, yeah, hold on, partner. What's your name and age?"

"Bradley Windle. Twenty-four."

"Any medical history?"

"Graves' Disease. I don't think this is—"

"Not interested in what you think," Luke interrupted. He dialed 9-1-1 on his phone. "Yeah, hi. I'm gonna need an ambulance at…" he circled to the front of the house to see the address, "Two-eleven-zero, Sayles Drive. Got a twenty-four year old here with a history of autoimmune disease. Looks to be having some kind of outbreak. Symptoms are intense nausea, fatigue, abrasions on the skin, possible fever."

"Copy that. Stay on the line, please. I'll be sending an ambulance right away."

"Right." Luke directed his attention back at Bradley. "How long you been feeling this way?"

"Woke up feeling fine," Bradley said. "Started feeling sick around noon."

"Eat anything weird?"

"Not unless you consider fresh crab weird," Bradley said. "Had some blue crab caught in a trap. Decided to have 'em for lunch. Been feeling shitty ever since."

"Yet, you waited this long to get yourself looked at?"

"I'm starting a new job tomorrow. I can't afford to miss work."

"Hate to break it to you, bud, but you're definitely calling in sick. Trust me, you're not just *feeling* shitty," Luke muttered.

"That bad?"

"Compared to what? A reanimated corpse?" He heard the operator return to the line. "Yeah?"

"Ambulance is en-route. ETA five minutes."

"Tell them to make it three."

****

Water surged over the transom, drenching the crew as the shark fought against the winch. Its head breached twice, displaying its immense jaw as though threatening the crew of its devastating power. Some backed away in fear, even though the fish was still a hundred feet away.

Barton, safe on the fly deck, wasn't concerned with the danger as he was the placement of the hook. Both times the fish surfaced, he trained his spotlight onto its mouth. The hook was deeply embedded in the upper jaw. Most of the bait had disappeared, either swallowed by the creature, or torn away by the repeated hacking of its teeth.

"*Namesake*, close in. Take your shot when ready," he radioed. He then directed his attention to the men with harpoon rifles below. "That goes for you guys down there as well."

As Dixon's vessel closed in, the shark attempted another dive. The *Queen's* winch strained, the gears generating smoke. Its operator pushed the lever forward to cease cranking and minimize inverse force, which would damage the mechanics. The best course of action would be to let the fish tire itself out. After exerting enough effort, it would ease up, allowing for the winch to pull it closer to the surface.

The line swung to port. The *Namesake's* helmsman, Dirk, cut the wheel to starboard, keeping them just out of reach. Dixon had the crossbow at eye-level. Near the tip of the spear was a plastic cannister with enough sedative to put down an elephant. Specially designed by the guys in white coats back at home base, the spear was essentially a giant tranquilizer dart.

"Come on up, damn you. I'm tired of this place," Dixon muttered. The damn fish was persistent. That line was so tight, he could walk on it. He grabbed the two-way radio. "Jesus, Barton. You suck at this." He could see his partner up on the fly deck, raising a middle finger to him.

"There's slack," Vick said. "It's tiring out."

Barton noticed this as well. "Winch it in," he said to the operator. There was a creaking sound of a lever being pulled, then the rattling of the gears reeling the fish to the surface.

The slack disappeared, resulting in a taut line. There was no tension beyond that of a heavy weight at the end of the cable. Like an anchor, the shark was gradually hauled toward the boat.

Dixon lowered his aim. At this rate, with the shark being pulled *away* from him, it looked as though one of the crewmen on the *Queen* would get the glory shot.

Vick pointed a finger at the line. "There's slack again."

He was right. The line was folding, yet, the winch was still cranking. Right as he realized what was happening, the dark blue shape emerged in the white stream of the spotlight.

"*Queen*, it's gunning toward you."

The transmission was lost under the tsunami of water that crashed against the yacht. The Helicoprion breached, its gargantuan snout slamming down hard on the transom, folding it inward. The beast turned its head to the side and swept its open jaw across the gunwale like an axe. The toothy whorl caught one of the crewmen across the waist, splattering blood and intestines onto the deck.

Screaming in agony, the man spun, his finger tensing against the trigger. The harpoon zipped from the barrel and punctured the winch operator through the neck. Tranquilizer fluid squirted from the exposed tip, mixing with blood and seawater below.

Spurred by the taste of blood and an overwhelming desire to rid itself of its captors, the fish continued thrashing about. Fragments burst from the gunwale as it continued to crumple. Another crewman attempted to fire his harpoon, only to lose his balance as the vessel dipped backward by the creature's weight. Staggering, he twisted to the left to catch his balance, only to accidentally jab another crewman with the tip of the spear. The man jumped back, but it was too late. The overdose of sedative triggered cardiac arrest. The crewman stumbled, one hand clutching his wound, the other his chest. The realization of what was happening was his final thought. The crewman fell face first, dead before he hit the deck.

Unable to reach any of the tasty humans above, the Helicoprion threw itself back into the water. It attempted another run, only to be stopped by the snag in its jaw. Repeated clamps of its blade-like jaws failed to free itself from the strange object embedded in the roof of its mouth.

Abandoning the effort, it angled itself upward for another attack on the humans. The smaller vessel was moving in, inadvertently planting itself within range. The shark ascended like a missile and struck the stern.

Barton heard the boom from under the *Namesake*. It was as though the vessel had turned into a catapult. The rear of the boat rose ten feet in the span of a heartbeat, flinging Dixon and Vick toward the cabin.

"Jesus!" he snarled. The boat settled, rocking to-and-fro with the waves. He waited long enough to make sure his friend wasn't hurt. Judging by the sound of frequent cursing, Dixon wasn't hurt too badly, but thoroughly pissed.

Down on the main deck, his men were lost in panic and confusion. The mayhem was amplified by another attack from the shark. Like an anti-tank round with what resembled a tracing wheel at its front, the beast struck the starboard quarter. There was an ear-piercing sound of metal folding inward.

Barton aimed his light over the side to see if there was any visible damage. Two crewmen ran onto the fly deck from the pilothouse.

"Engine's stalled, sir," one of them said.

"Go down below. Make sure we don't have a breach!" Barton said. The shark was circling around the rear, its fin slicing through the surface. A wide swing of its tail propelled it at the transom. This time, it didn't hammer its jaw down, rather it went for a direct collision.

The weakened transom exploded inward, splitting down the center, making way for the huge snout. With half its body on deck, the shark lashed its jaw.

Another crewman, who had fallen to his hands and knees during the crash, squealed as the jaw cut through his abdomen like a circular saw through a 4x4. His pelvic bone and spine split like toothpicks, the two halves flopping in a pool of his own blood.

The Helicoprion lashed its snout to the left, striking another crewman with enough force to throw him fifteen feet to the gunwale. The center of his back snapped on impact. Folded backward over the side, the paralyzed crewman stared wide-eyed into the night sky before gravity tugged him into the sea.

Barton threw his arms over his head. "Are you kidding me?! Could just ONE of you harpoon the prick!" Another thrash of the fish rocked the vessel, throwing the crew, including him, off balance. Barton grabbed ahold of the guardrail to keep from tumbling.

The crack of a rifle shot drew his attention back to the main deck. The fish thrashed with increased intensity, widening the gap in the transom, and generating mountainous waves with its caudal fin. Barton felt the forward motion of the boat. The fish was so strong, it was pushing a vessel four times its size. But that wasn't as alarming as the sight of the crewman chambering the rifle—the same fucking crewman whom he had warned earlier.

A second round punctured the shark's flesh near its lower jaw. A jet of blood gushed from the wound, provoking additional thrashes by the fish. It twisted its body, corkscrewing its way onto the deck. Its snout jabbed the man in the chest, knocking him backwards.

Only the desire to oxygenate its gills prevented the shark from continuing the attack. Its body bent like a snake as it redirected its mass to the transom, bursting the remaining jagged fragment from the deck as it threw itself into the water. The beast wasted no time darting to starboard, sensing the blood of the crewman with the broken spine.

Unbeknownst to it, the cable lashed across the deck. One crewman, who had fallen to his knees during the attack, opened his mouth to scream. There was no sound other than the *clunk* of his severed head against the deck. The rifle-wielding crewman watched the headless body spasm, still on its knees, the neck stump fountaining scarlet.

He shrieked, then aimed the rifle into the water and emptied the magazine.

The Helicoprion cut the dead human down to size and swallowed each piece, taking no notice of the bullets raining down over it. Most zipped past it, spiraling aimlessly to the depths. One, however, nicked its sensitive gill slits.

The fish tugged at the cable, still unable to pry it free. The roof of its mouth was now bleeding profusely from the puncture. Once again, it clamped down with its jaw. Over and over again, it hacked at the thing. Teeth scraped against metal, the inner muscles reeling the whorl inward to create a grinding motion. Little by little, they made progress. An incision was successfully made in the hook shaft, which gradually got deep enough to weaken it.

The Helicoprion turned around and raced to the east. With a heavy tug, the hook snapped at the weakened area. The fish was free once again.

"Sir, we've got a problem," Vick said. Dixon joined his fellow crewmen at the pilothouse. On the tracking monitor, the blip representing the shark was moving away from the vessel.

"Great! Just great!" He searched the deck and located his dropped radio. "*Namesake* to *Broken Arrow*, the fish is gone. I repeat, the fish is no longer on the cable. It's moving eastbound, roughly twenty-miles an hour."

Barton took five seconds, during which he took in a very deep breath. Good leadership was not displayed by screaming and shouting, though that was what he wanted to do in this moment.

He peered into the bridge. "What's the status on the engines?"

"Minimal damage, sir. We're functional."

"Follow the signal. Full speed."

"Aye-aye," the helmsman said.

Barton hurried through the stairway onto the main deck. By the time he arrived, the vessel was already turning around. Water sprayed over the busted transom, sweeping over the mangled bodies. There was a smell of innards, bowels, and salt. Some men had retreated into the forward deck or galley, while a few brave souls remained. And one foolish one.

He approached the crewman with the rifle. "My orders were clear. *No* shooting."

The man glared at him with bemusement. "You're shitting me, right?"

Barton's brow wrinkled. This crewman was on thin ice already, and seemed content with taking a blowtorch to that fragile layer.

"I don't have to justify my orders with you. This was what you're paid for. These were the risks. This asset is more important to our client than you'll ever know."

"It *killed* our men! Hans. Ricardo. Jaimie…"

"Occupational hazard. You know this, crewman."

The crewman looked to the water and saw the change in direction. "We're going after it? Even after what happened?!"

Barton took a step forward, leaving only a yard of space between them. "Either get with the program, or I'll find a way to make you useful."

The crewman studied his commander. The rifle quaked in his hands. *No way am I dying for someone's pet fish.*

Barton noticed the tremor in the muzzle. In a swift blur of action, the crewman pointed the rifle toward his commander. That motion was a snail's pace compared to Barton's. He grabbed the barrel and shifted the muzzle skyward, directing the crewman's shot toward the stars. The crewman grunted as Barton hammered the weapon against his forehead. It took two strikes to loosen his grip. Barton twisted the weapon like a baton, easily prying it from his enemy's grasp, then landed a third strike, this time with the butt of the weapon.

The crewman stumbled back into the remaining bit of transom. His vision was hazy, but he understood the sound of a cocking lever. With a deafening *bang* came an overwhelming sensation of heat, pressure, and pain in his abdomen. He folded over, feeling as though a rocket had just plowed through his intestines. Blood rained from his lower abdomen, inches from his groin. Mouth agape, he fell to his knees, holding his stomach as it threatened to fall through the wound.

Barton held the rifle at port arms, then shook his head scornfully. "Some idiots don't listen. Don't worry, I know how to make you useful." He faced the two other crewmen who stood with their arms behind their backs, awaiting instructions. "Retract the cable and attach it to a floating harness. Put *him* in it."

"Yes, sir. Shall we, uh…" the crewmember mimicked a finger pistol at their injured associate.

"No. The thing probably won't fall for the same trick. It needs live bait this time." He walked to the starboard side of the deck to speak with Dixon, who was traveling parallel with the yacht. "*Queen* to *Namesake*?"

"What's the plan?"

"Go after it. Draw it in. We've got new bait. Once the shark moves in, take the shot. Don't miss. You'll only have a split-second to harpoon it."

"You know me."

****

Elise was certain now. Those loud *pops* in the distance weren't firecrackers or thunder. She'd spent enough time on the range during her military stint to know what rifle shots sounded like.

"What the hell's going on over there?" Whatever it was, it was coming from the west. After a few minutes, she heard the sound of boat engines and shouting voices. She found a pair of binoculars and looked to the distance.

She saw lights—deck lights, from two separate vessels. Even with the glasses, she was too far away to make out what was going on. Nonetheless, a suspicion arose within her. Had these people just encountered the shark? If somebody was under attack, it was possible they didn't understand what they were up against.

There was a moment of consideration. She'd be moving *toward* the sound of gunfire. Not the wisest of moves.

I need to see it. Even if someone else kills it, I NEED to know it's dead.

Emotion trumped logic. Elise turned the boat and went full throttle toward the lights.

****

The *Namesake* went full throttle after the shark. Dixon shuffled through his supplies, locating a cattle rod they had brought along precisely for this kind of situation.

"Come on, baby. Don't lie. I know of your fetish for electrical shocks." He poked the water with the rod, sending mild surges of electricity into the Pacific.

"It's slowing down," Vick said.

"Take this." Dixon handed him the rod then grabbed his harpoon rifle. Vick continued sending shocks into the water, while Dirk, the helmsman, watched the monitor.

"It's circling around. Depths at twenty meters. Distance: seven-hundred feet." He slowed the boat.

The *Queen* was on approach, roughly five hundred feet behind Dixon's vessel. Barton stood on the foredeck, his own harpoon rifle in hand. Through the radio receiver, he received alerts regarding the shark's position.

"Angle twenty-degrees starboard. Prep the bait."

On the main deck, the injured crewman was fitted into a floating harness. His pleas for help fell on deaf ears. Despite the several casualties which continued to permeate the deck with their odor, they remained loyal to Barton and the mission. Death was no stranger to them. Nor was execution. It was part of the life they had chosen.

"Should've listened," the Nigerian man said.

"N-no. Don't."

Nothing else was said. The fool was thrown out into the water. He bobbed with the waves, his blood clouding the ocean around him. He cursed at his former associates who he thought were his friends, not realizing his rapid heartbeat and thrashing limbs only served to draw the fish in faster.

"One hundred meters. Closing in fast. The plan's working," the bridge crew announced.

"Ascending to ten meters. Five. He's coming up," Dirk radioed. He brought the *Namesake* within range. Dixon moved to the foredeck and centered the human bait with his iron sights.

The fish broke the surface with the haste of a submarine evading pursuit. Only, this gargantuan wasn't fleeing, but on the attack. Water rolled away in thick laps as it cut through the surface in a straight line toward its target.

Through the spotlights, the man saw the huge dorsal getting larger and larger, until it was secured by the rising snout. His scream was brief, as was the sound of the teeth slicing diagonally through his body.

Barton and Dixon simultaneously launched their harpoons. One struck the fish near the dorsal, the other near its caudal fin. The fish turned to dart away, and with just a few swings of its enormous tail, it gained several dozen yards of distance. But even a creature as aggressive and determined as the Helicoprion could withstand the drugs circulating in its bloodstream.

The beast had no understanding of what was happening to it. Even if it had the mental capacity, it wouldn't have had the time. The sedatives took hold within seconds. Motionless, and unable to remain afloat, the shark sank to the depths.

The two boats closed in. Barton was already strapping a scuba tank over his back. There was no time to get in a diving suit. He needed to get a harness onto that fish *now* before it suffocated. One of the crewmen provided him with a diver propulsion vehicle. Meanwhile, the others lowered the cable into the water. The broken hook had been replaced with a large tether to be strapped around the shark's tail. Once it was lifted to the boat, they would properly position the shark to be towed.

Dixon leaned over the guardrail of his boat and sniggered at his war buddy. "You sure you want to do that?"

"Hey, unless you'd rather go..."

Dixon waved a hand, dismissively. "No thanks. If the shark bites you in half, I'm claiming those cigars in your locker."

Barton reached into his pocket and pulled out two thick stogies, both encased in plastic tubes. "Once we're finally done with this, the next shipment's on me." He tossed one to Dixon, then handed the other to a crewman for safekeeping, then pointed a finger at him. "If I see you lighting that up, you'll be the fish's next meal."

"You got it," the crewman said.

"Aw, go ahead, man! Light it up! Not like he doesn't have a shit ton to spare!" Dixon shouted.

"You filthy cunt," Barton muttered. A delighted Dixon cackled as he stuffed the cigar back into his pocket. Barton suppressed his urge to make a few personal insults, but the job was yet to be complete. Just a few short minutes to go and they would finally be on their way back to the base.

He hit the water, swam toward the cable, then followed it down seventy-eight feet to the bottom. Each boat crew aimed their vessel down at the shark's location. Still, it was a hazy abyss. The rocky bottom at night resembled the surface of a distant planet. The water current around him added to this effect, making him feel like he was in high-gravity.

With a flashlight strapped to his shoulder, he panned around in search of the fish. It was lying on its side, its jaw agape. Its eyes stared blankly, giving the *almost* fearless mercenary pause. He pulled the harness to the creature's tail and strapped it tightly around the caudal fin.

Over the next several minutes, he ascended, pausing every thirty feet to adjust for pressure.

"Alright. Bring him up."

****

"What in the name of..."

Elise eased her vessel to a stop, then raised her binoculars to her eyes. As she suspected, there were two boats. They were roughly eight hundred feet away, their decks brightly lit, allowing her to see all hands. One was a large yacht, like those owned by rich CEOs. However, the deck was covered with mechanical equipment, including a winch. It was hard to see at this distance at night, but it almost looked as though the transom was heavily damaged. The second boat was much smaller—a thirty-foot fishing vessel with a crew of three.

Just like the one that brought in the great white...

They were bringing something up with the winch. The mechanical sound was faint from her location, but unmistakable nonetheless. Judging by the rigidness of the cable, there was something heavy on the other end.

Her hands started to shake. Keeping the binoculars steady was now tedious. Her heart was beating so fast she felt it would bruise her insides. A gigantic caudal fin emerged, attached to the cable by a thick tether. That's when she realized there was a diver in the water with it. Yet, the shark didn't move. It was either dead or unconscious.

A spotlight shone over its jaw, putting its teeth in full display. There it was. Elise was not crazy. The shark was an honest-to-God Helicoprion.

After watching the diver secure a huge harness around the shark's neck and dorsal fin, she concluded the latter. They wanted it *alive.*

"My God." These men didn't just stumble onto the shark's location. They were actively seeking it out. What was their connection? Did they discover it and were capturing it for study? Then why keep it top secret? Why no news of the initial discovery?

One of the crewmen's voices echoed across the night sky. "Hey! Eight o'clock!" Spotlights swept the ocean, settling on her boat.

"Oh, fuck."

She didn't know who they were, but she knew the tone. These people did not want to be seen. And judging by the way they were scrambling, they wanted to keep it that way. Hearing the motor of the fishing boat at full throttle reinforced that suspicion. The sound of gunfire confirmed it.

"Holy Christ!" Elise turned the boat around and sped for shore. She didn't care where she made landfall, as long as she put distance between herself and these people.

Whoever they were, they meant business. And had no qualms about murder.

CHAPTER 29

"So, you just happened to be in the neighborhood?" the paramedic asked. Luke clipped his badge back to his belt and watched the team load Mr. Bradley Windle into the ambulance. The paramedics knew at first glance he needed to be transported right away. Blood pressure was high, heart rate was at sixty-bpm, and his breathing was raspy. Then there were the outbreaks on his skin.

"What can I say? Breeze coming off the ocean keeping the temperature down. Perfect night for a stroll," Luke said.

The paramedic shut the back doors and made his way to the driver's seat. "Seems like you and Captain Raye are in competition with each other."

"Don't let her fool you. I'm clearly the better looking one," Luke quipped.

The medic snorted. "I mean, she called us in for a sick guy too. Had some sort of viral infection."

"Like this guy?"

"Yeah. Something seems to be going around."

Luke followed him to his seat. "Any word on how that other guy's doing?"

"Died twenty minutes ago," the medic said. Luke heard the unspoken message. *Gotta go now. Can't waste time talking.* The siren blared into the night sky as he steered the ambulance onto the road.

Luke watched it shrink in the distance, the red and white lights strobing against the trees. *Finally, that's over.*

A rapid series of *pops* drew his attention toward the ocean. "The hell?" One crack followed after another. Next thing he knew, there was rapid bursts, each louder than its predecessor. Gunfire. These weren't twenty-twos either; these were military-grade weapons.

Peddling his boots on the ground, Luke hurried to the dock. There was an average-sized yacht speeding toward the shoreline. That Elise Sheldon woman. Behind her was a thirty-five-foot fishing vessel, a smaller speedboat—possibly an inflatable Zodiac, and two jet skis. Beyond them was a large vessel. Even in the dark of night, there was no doubt in his mind that it was the same vessel he'd seen anchored to the northwest earlier that day.

And all of them were chasing Elise.

****

Back aboard the yacht, Barton threw his mask off and hurried below, barking orders into his radio with each step.

"You stupid idiots! Whoever started shooting, you've just butchered this whole operation!"

"Want us to call off the chase?" Dixon replied.

Barton stopped, gripping the guardrail so hard the screws holding it to the bulkhead started to come loose. "No. We're in fuckville now. Get her. Bring her in. Take her boat too. Can't leave any trace." He continued down the hangar. A team of four had already departed on the Zodiac, and one on a jet ski. Only one other remained.

He contemplated joining the chase, but backed off at the last second. With many of the crew dead and over a half dozen others going after the witness, the yacht was on a skeleton crew.

No. Let Dixon handle it.

****

Elise jumped at the sound of bullets crashing against her hull. The portside back window shattered, the projectile zipping past her into the bulkhead. She was gonna go for the docks to the right, but now her mind was in a frenzy. She had no guns to shoot back with. No body armor. The boat itself could only provide so much protection. Barricading inside would only prolong the inevitable. She needed to get to shore and get away.

The Zodiac and jet ski quickly caught up to her, while the fishing boat lagged behind. Automatic rifles pelted the starboard quarter. Elise ducked instinctively. That instinct served her well; she hadn't taken another breath before the back starboard window shattered and bullets nicked the front of the console where she stood.

She peeked through the windshield. The shore was just a couple hundred feet away. Automatic gunfire continued to mutilate her hull. This boat, her main connection to her lost nephew, was now under attack by these men. The very same men who had something to do with the Helicoprion that killed him.

Anger overcame panic. Elise swung the boat to starboard. There was a heavy *thump* from her hull connecting with something heavy. Outside, the man on the jet ski yelped. Immediately after was a loud splash. The propellors protested. They didn't stall, but they cut through something which resisted. It wasn't the jet ski—*that* would've stalled the propellors.

"Oh, damn!" a gunman on the boat shouted. Their expressions revealed that their attention was on their companion's eviscerated corpse, and *not* on her in this moment. Elise stood up to gauge their position. They were a hundred feet off, not enough for her to sideswipe them, but enough to create a barrier when she hit the shore.

She could feel the hull grazing against the sand. She turned the boat to starboard, angling the bow southeast, right into the path of the Zodiac. It struck the sandbar and came to a sudden stop. A moment later, the Zodiac crashed into the starboard hull.

Elise rushed outside. The men on the Zodiac had fallen forward, granting her a moment of opportunity to flee. She would need it, because the fishing boat was closing in fast. The men on board were armed with H&K submachine guns. As she turned, her shoe hit the tranquilizer. It had been flung forward when the boat ran aground. She snatched it up and leapt onto the beach.

Gunfire ensued, tearing up the deck where she stood.

"Damn it! Get after her!" the leader said.

Sand kicked high with each step. Elise knew she was out in the open with no cover. Up ahead were a few shops and a parking lot. Beyond that was the road.

Though late at night, there was bound to be at least one passing car she could flag.

She heard running feet splash the water and hit the sand. In about three seconds, a hail of gunfire would tear her down. She had one opportunity to delay that assault.

Spinning on her heel, Elise raised the tranq gun to eye-level. Four mercenaries had cleared the bow of her boat, each one holding a submachine gun. She launched the projectile.

The dart zipped across the three hundred feet of open space and struck one of the men in the left shoulder. The poison passed through his system like a raging river. He dropped to his knees as cardiac arrest sank in. His companions stood flabbergasted, not understanding what was happening to their friend until they saw the dart protruding from him.

Elise didn't watch: she was already racing up the beach. Fifty-feet south of her vessel, the fishing boat had stopped in the shallows. Two men disembarked, the third waiting by the helm like a getaway driver.

Almost there.

Bullets whistled past her ear, making her duck. She passed between two shops then hooked to the right. Bullets thumped against the siding and shattered the windows.

The marine biologist couldn't believe her situation. What was so important about this shark that even *witnesses* had to be murdered?

As the men cleared the shop, they resumed their gunfire. This time, Elise felt the hot burn of a round grazing her left thigh—right by her coral injury. No amount of adrenaline could block out the supernova of pain which dropped her like an anvil. Hands and knees in the grass, she tried to stand back up, only to be knocked back down.

The men crowded around her. One kicked her dart gun away then placed his weapon at her temple. One of them, a British man with a semi-circular scar on his left cheek, grabbed the barrel of the weapon and shifted it away.

"Not here," he whispered. He grabbed Elise by the shoulder and lifted her to her feet. "Take her to the boat."

Elise sprang to life. She plowed a fist into one gunman's groin, doubling him over. She pivoted to the right and struck another across the jaw. She turned to take on the scarred British man. He beat her to the punch, clocking her in the brow with his H&K.

"On second thought, so what if we leave a little blood?" He lined the muzzle up with her forehead.

Elise squeezed her eyes shut and awaited her reunion with her sister and nephew. The gunshot sounded off, but death did not come. Instead, she felt sand splashing against her temple. When she opened her eyes, the British man was stumbling forward, knocked off balance by a kick to his back, throwing his aim over to the earth beside her.

Luke Jansen threw himself into the crowd. A kick to the ribs sent one of the gunmen reeling backward. Luke planted a right hook to the bent-over merc's jaw, then pivoted left as another gunman raised his submachine gun. It was raised further than intended, not by the mercenary, but by Jansen, who grabbed it by the barrel and slammed it against his skull.

As he fought the merc for control of the weapon, the fifth gunman lined his muzzle up with his head. Luke thrust kick to his right, plowing his heel into the gunman's chest. The merc fell in a wild display of flailing limbs and the twirling of a dropped weapon.

He redirected his attention on the enemy in front of him. The gunman gritted his teeth in his effort to maintain control of the H&K. Time and time again, he tried to direct it to Luke's face, only to be outmuscled. Muscle strain led to clenching of the trigger finger. Bullets sprayed into the sky like fireworks, ceasing once the mag ran empty. Luke put his elbows to work. His right crushed the man's nose, the left knocking a couple of left crowns loose. A kick to the chest put him on the dirt.

Behind him, one of the other mercs was righting himself. In a single swift motion, Luke did an about-face, drew his revolver, and fired from the hip. The bullet punched through the mercenary's sternum, knocking him flat on the ground with the force of a speeding car.

Luke turned the revolver on the gunman nearest to the left, who had snatched his dropped weapon off the ground with intent of deadly use. His aim was redirected to the side after two .357 rounds pierced his chest. He spun once then fell to the dirt.

In the corner of his eyes, Luke saw the leader of the group take aim. He pivoted to his right and dove behind a nearby burger shop. Bullets missed him by inches. Those that were in his path were stopped by the brick wall of the small building.

Dixon emptied half his mag into the building, then turned his weapon toward the woman. To his surprise, she had already darted off toward the road. She was limping heavily, only gaining fifty-paces or so. He started to pursue, but stopped after a couple of yards.

Flashing red and blue lights illuminated the distance. From that same direction came the whirling sound of sirens.

"Fucking shit!" he growled. Everything that could've gone wrong in this mission had gone way beyond wrong. His two-way radio crackled at his hip.

"Abort. We've got too many eyes on us. Get back to the boats NOW!"

Dixon changed direction and fired a burst toward the one-eyed third party. His shots failed to hit their target, but they successfully drove him back behind the shop.

Vick was back on his feet and grabbing their surviving companion by the vest.

"Forget the others. Let's go," Dixon said.

Luke placed three fresh bullets in his cylinder. He took aim, only to realize the suspects were retreating down the beach. Cop cars came to a screeching stop near the lot. He'd let Elise brief them on the situation.

He sprinted behind the line of shops and made a turn for the beach. By the time he got there, the suspects were already nearing the shoreline. Past them was the fishing vessel, which was already turning around. Several hundred feet beyond that was the large boat, which was also in the process of turning around.

The three gunmen assembled at their Zodiac vessel. Seeing the detective sprinting toward the shore, one of them opened fire. Luke cocked the hammer and planted a round in the shooter's chest. A cloud of pink burst from the man's back. He dropped to his knees, gagging for breath.

The British man pointed his weapon. Before he could squeeze the trigger, a bullet from Luke's revolver punched through his neck. The criminal leader stared in awe at the blood spurting from his throat, then collapsed into the water.

The final mercenary pushed the Zodiac into the water then hopped inside. Pushing the engine to its max, he swung the boat around and disappeared into the distance.

From that black distance came the screams of an infuriated man.

****

"No! No! Goddamn you—you son of a bitch!" Barton snapped. Even as the yacht turned around, he kept his binoculars fixed on Dixon's body. Time seemed to slow down as he watched his brother-in-arms fall backwards into the water. Grief and anger consumed him, but not enough to break his focus. Dixon was dead, but their problems didn't end there. Vick was still on the beach. He was critically injured, but still alive.

They had traded one loose end for another. Vick was a good soldier, but he had his limitations. Standard police interrogations, he would withstand. However, this wasn't a standard case.

Barton adjusted the binoculars. Walking across the beach was that one-eyed cop from the pier. This prick was a shit-stirrer, and Barton had a sneaking suspicion that he would use unconventional means to get information from a suspect. And who the hell would know what the hell Vick might say under the influence of hospital drugs.

Whoever jumped the gun and fired those shots is gonna die a slow death. They could've simply left. If the witness reported them, there would have been a useless investigation at worst, which would have produced zero evidence connected to their operation. Now, there were a host of loose ends they needed to erase…including this vessel.

Barton marched into the bridge, pushed the helmsman out of the way, and grabbed the radio. "Home base. ID-Code: four-twenty-two-Bravo-niner. Get the boss on the line, ASAP. We need to arrange a pickup."

CHAPTER 30

"Jesus, Doc, you're *really* willing to go above and beyond to get my attention."

Holding the icepack to her forehead, Elise grimaced from Luke's unfunny remark. "You believe me now?"

"I never said that."

"It's real, Detective. I saw it again…"

"You say one more word about a helicopter shark, I swear I'll put on another apron." The surrounding paramedics and patrol officers stared with confusion. "Don't ask."

"Believe me, I won't." From around the corner of the ambulance came Brianna Raye. In her hand was a near-empty *Starbucks* coffee. She gave a reserved look at Elise, then at Luke. "I see she found you."

Luke tilted his head. "Wait a sec, did *you* tell her where I lived?"

"No, but it's clear she's more resourceful than I suspected." Brianna sighed. "So, who are these guys?"

"Oh, I don't know. Probably bill collectors," Luke said. He led her to the bodies behind the shop. They were covered with tarps, their weapons still lying on the ground where they had fallen.

Brianna knelt by one of them, then examined the weapon. "How many of these guys were there?"

"Not sure. Going by their equipment, they don't work for cheap."

"They don't look like soldiers," Brianna said.

"Probably because they're not supposed to," Luke replied. "You don't dress up in full tactical gear when you're trying to blend in."

"You don't shoot automatic weapons at people when you're trying to blend in," Brianna said.

"True, unless you're caught doing something you shouldn't be. We just don't know what that 'something' is."

"I know what it is," Elise said.

"Oh, for crying out loud," Luke said.

"What?" Brianna said.

"She thinks they captured a prehistoric shark," Luke said, his tone passive.

"Listen…" Elise stopped herself. It had been a long day. A long *two* days. "Listen—forget whether it's a Helicoprion. The fact is, whatever kind of shark they captured, it is the one that killed Chad, and those people on the beach. I don't know what they want with the shark, but they're covering something up."

Brianna looked to Luke and awaited his opinion.

"I didn't see anything about a shark."

"What were you doing here, then?"

"I was trying to get away from everybody," Luke retorted. "Seems every time I try, I invite more people into my life. I got her showing up at my house, dropping pictures of her nephew on my chair. I try to enjoy a little night cruise on my boat, then I hear this idiot coughing his lungs out because he ate some bad crab…"

"I beg your pardon?"

"Unrelated issue. Though I don't envy the guy. Whatever he caught from that crab might deter me from eating seafood for the foreseeable future." He noticed the austere look in her eyes. "Don't worry! I got him an ambulance." He stood up. "You know? You ought to be nice to me. I've been shot at tonight and I'm *very* traumatized."

"Oh, shut the fuck up with that shit," Brianna said.

"Well god*damn*!" Luke exclaimed, pretending to be offended.

Brianna rolled her eyes. "*Are* you alright?"

"Not so much after your boys took my gun."

"Sorry, man!" an officer shouted from within the crowd.

"Standard procedure," Brianna said. "Not like you don't have ten other revolvers."

"Yeah, but that was my favorite one," Luke said.

"You'll get it back," Brianna said. "Where are the other bodies?"

"Sunbathing with your buddy Norton." Luke led her to the shoreline. Detective Norton was kneeling by a body with a spear shaft sticking out of its shoulder.

"Good evening, Captain," he said. He looked at Luke and smirked. "How'd you manage to do this?"

"That one wasn't me. That was the witness' work."

"A spear with a tranquilizer dart? Wonder how high a dose…" Norton said.

"Actually, it's loaded with pesticide," Luke said.

"She tell you that?"

"No. The pesticide bottle on the boat did." Luke pointed up to the deck. Norton raised his palms, conceding defeat. Luke pulled the tarp from the dead British gunman. "This guy was in charge of the little fireteam. I've got people running his fingerprints."

"Seems we've got a lot of Englishmen visiting Amadea today," Brianna said.

"It's California, Captain," Norton said. "You're gonna run into people with foreign accents."

"Oh, quit with the white-knighting," Luke muttered. "You're distracting from the most interesting part."

Brianna rubbed her aching temple. She thought of the stress she felt when this case was nothing more than a shark attack. Such good times. "Which is?"

Luke paused, noticing Elise watching them from a couple dozen meters off. Close enough to overhear. She was at the pier, and she knew exactly what he was going to say.

"The one still alive: you're already acquainted with him. He was one of the crew that brought in the great white."

"What? That fisherman Beau Mott?"

"No, not him. One of the guys that was with him. Don't know his name, but we'll find out soon."

"He's in critical condition. Probably won't get a chance to speak with him for a while," Norton said.

"Not if I have anything to say about it," Luke said. "Guess what, Norton? This is *my* case. Go cry in a pillow."

"As long as you don't overblow it. From what it sounds, your witness probably saw a drug deal go down. They spotted her and tried to chase her down."

"It wasn't a drug deal," Elise interrupted.

"She saw something, and whatever it was, they felt it was worth killing her over to keep it quiet," Luke said. "Whatever it is, it's connected to these shark attacks we've been experiencing."

"The shark's dead," Norton said.

"*A* shark is dead," Luke said.

"There were bodies inside," Brianna replied. "The shark's record size. I don't get it. Why would they fake this?"

"To keep us from finding the real shark," Luke said. "Get some DNA run on those victims. Accelerated test. I don't think those are the same people attacked on the beach."

Norton started to laugh.

"What's so funny?" Elise said. Norton cleared his throat and erased that smile. For a moment, he forgot this was the same woman whose nephew was killed.

"It just seems odd. None of this matches up. A decoy shark to cover up another? You think this 'guilty' shark is somebody's beloved pet or something? I can't line the dots up."

"Hence the oh-so-fun detective work," Luke said. "To start, we learn more about these guys. They're mostly foreign. This dead guy in particular is English, as is the survivor. They like their German-made firearms. Interesting the models they've chosen are popular with the British SAS. And the best part," he reached into the dead man's shirt pocket, "he has a great taste in cigars."

"Great. I'm sure you and he would be great friends," Brianna said.

"If I'd known he had a lead on these, probably so!" Luke held the cigar up. "Arturo Fuente Opus X. They sell for about thirty-grand a box. I hear they're the best tasting cigars ever made. Looks like Christmas came early for me this year."

Brianna pointed a finger at him. "Ah-ah! That's evidence!"

"I'll hang on to it then," Luke said.

"What's gonna happen with the witness?" Norton asked.

"She'll be kept overnight in the hospital," Brianna said. "People as determined as these guys might try and seek her out. We need to keep her protected."

"I agree," Luke said. Brianna almost laughed.

Luke Jansen agreeing with ME?! What world am I living in?

"Listen, I don't need to be watched over…" Elise said.

"You don't get a say," Luke said. "First of all, you've been shot."

"It's just a graze…"

"You're spending the night in the hospital, and probably in the police station until this case is solved," Luke said.

Elise stood quietly. Not only was she not going to win this fight, but she realized she actually wanted to be in that hospital. As long as a certain criteria was met.

"Is that the same hospital where the gunman is being taken to?" she asked.

"We can move you to a different facility," Elise said.

"No. Please don't," she said. "I wanna be where *he* is." They thought she was referring to the shooter until she pointed at Luke.

"Lovely," Luke muttered. "Fine. Let me guess; you'd like me to ride in the ambulance with you too."

"Don't flatter yourself," Elise said.

Luke tucked the cigar into his shirt. "I might do it just to piss you off." He walked past her as forensics personnel arrived to collect the weapon and bullet casings.

Elise walked alongside a very tired-looking Brianna.

"You feeling alright?" the Captain asked.

Elise's hands were still a little jittery. Despite her brief time in the military, she never experienced having a gun pointed at her, let alone had to actually evade enemy fire.

"I'll be fine," she said. "What about him, though?"

"Nothing he isn't used to, unfortunately," Brianna said.

"I see. He almost seems spry."

Brianna sighed. "He's not in pain right now."

Elise looked over at her, unsure of what she meant, but decided it was better not to ask.

CHAPTER 31

Kirk Raye usually began his day grumbling over his alarm clock. He loved what he did, but it didn't mean he enjoyed getting up at the ass-crack of dawn to do it. This Monday morning, however, he knew better. His wife had been out much of the night. As usual, she didn't state much, but the news got out fast that there was a major shooting involving one of her detectives. Whatever was happening, it was more excitement than Amadea was used to.

She was up at the same time as him, with only three hours sleep. Kirk knew better than to say anything other than 'I love you' and 'coffee's fresh'. He was thoughtful enough to make it extra strong. Then again, on Monday mornings, he needed it that way anyway.

By six-thirty, he was in the shop. Every time he took in that sawdust smell, it was like the first time. His hardware store was no *Home Depot* or *Lowes,* but it was beloved on this corner of town. In front of him were ten aisles, ranging from gardening supplies to power tools, with a garage area in the back for the ATVs and *John Deere* tractors. Unfortunately, he had seen repeated delays in his stock shipments over the past few months. Many shelves and racks in those ten aisles were empty. Today, that would change. His past two shipments were due to arrive by nine-o'clock.

Just like with home, first thing he did was go to his office and get the coffee going. Nine o'clock came, and so did the trucks. The drivers unloaded the product and stored them on pallets outside the garage. At nine-thirty, they departed, and Kirk was left waiting for his assistants whom Brianna had recommended for him.

It was a quarter-to-ten, yet still no sign of Glenn. Twelve minutes from home, and yet the kid was still late. Managed to join his buddy at the docks with no problem. But something for Dad? Nope, gotta drag ass.

He pulled his phone out and dialed his son. Near the fourth ring, he answered.

"Hey, we're on our way."

"Was starting to think you weren't coming," Kirk said.

"Sorry," Glenn said. *"Went to pick up Malcolm. Got held up a little bit. He's kind of..."* His voice trailed off. Kirk could hear some kind of commotion in the background. He couldn't make it out, but it almost seemed like Malcolm was trying to keep Glenn from stating something.

"Something wrong?"

"Malcolm's a little under the weather, but he says he's well enough to work."

"Uh-oh. Poor guy. Let him know there's no pressure. Doesn't need to make himself worse on my behalf."

"He's adamant that he's fine. We'll be there in five minutes."

"Alright. See ya soon." Kirk hung up, then stared across the room in deep thought. He felt kind of bad putting a sick kid through manual labor. Some of the equipment he'd be carrying around was pretty heavy. Then again, with enough perseverance, they'd be done in three hours. Not so bad. And the way Glenn was talking, it sounded like Malcolm was dealing with a little bit of flu.

Nothing that'll kill him, I'm sure.

****

Glenn tossed the phone into the cup holder. The light turned green, leaving him no choice but to go through. The one after that was also green, faltering his attempt to stall and talk Malcolm into letting him take him back home.

"Dude, you *really* don't look well at all."

"I'm fine." Following those words came a heavy cough. "I tend to get sick near the start of September for some reason. So, this bug is right on time. Almost."

"That was because of school. Kids from all over the neighborhood, who spent the summer doing God knows what, all getting confined in that building. *That's* why you got sick—and that was only for a DAY! You're a vitamin freak, so your immune system's more buff than Dwayne Johnson."

"Thanks."

"I said your immune system's buff, not *you're* buffed. Idiot. And I should state that it 'used to be'. It's not doing shit for you right now."

Malcolm leaned his head against the window. He could feel himself starting to sweat. When he woke up at one, he took his temperature. No fever, but he had a feeling he was on the brink of one. He was up again at four. Normally a solid sleeper, he could not stay asleep. His stomach wasn't doing him any favors. What little was in there was cleared out by five. He felt better for the next couple of hours. With a little bit of green tea and another wave of Vitamin C, he still felt crappy, but believed he'd be able to tough out the day. Then again, the only thing that sounded worse than being sick was the series of lectures from his dad regarding the boat.

Just need to tough it out a couple of hours, then I'll have it off my shoulders.

"You didn't catch anything from that sick guy, did you?" Glenn asked.

"Hmm?"

"That sick guy from the boat. You don't have what he had, right?"

"Oh, him?" Malcolm faked a smile and shook his head. "No. He had something else going on. Not me. Just a little bug. Probably from messing with that bait. I'll be fine. It's not like I'm being subjected to ten hours in a labor camp in the blazing heat."

"I suppose that's true," Glenn said. A minute later, he took a left turn, then found his dad's shop. They could see the pallets outside. There were a couple of cars in the parking lot. Monday mornings weren't particularly busy. Not until the late afternoon, at least.

Malcolm got out of the car as soon as he parked. "Alright!" He clapped his hands. "Let's get this done."

Glenn watched his friend walk to the shop, rubbing his forehead with the edge of his sleeve. That alone wouldn't have bothered him too much had he not noticed the redness in Malcom's eyes. He felt stupid now. He'd just spent eight minutes in the confined space of the car, breathing the same oxygen as him. Hopefully, whatever he had, it wasn't too serious.

He got out and followed Malcolm into the shop.

"Probably just some stomach flu."

CHAPTER 32

It was an odd feeling for Luke to sleep in the hospital room of a woman who spent the previous afternoon tracking him down. Except she didn't sleep much. He could hear her shifting in the bed. In fairness, hospital beds were never comfortable to begin with. The few times she did fall asleep, she'd wake up shortly after, seemingly out of breath. He pulled the curtain, claiming it was for her privacy, when in actuality it was for his. Sharing this confined room was a chore to begin with. To have to watch her sleep only added to that inner turmoil.

Morning couldn't come soon enough for him. And when it did, Elise had to grace him with the local news. Of course, Anthony Zach got the morning spot, shooting his mouth off about last night's shooting.

He checked his watch. It was twenty minutes to seven. The next shift would soon begin for the ER doctors. Maybe he'd be able to coax his way into the hospital room and have a word with the suspect. Last night's doctors wouldn't let him anywhere near him, stating it had taken hours to stabilize the patient, and that he was in no condition for interrogation. 'Do-no-harm bullshit' is how Luke would describe it. All they would allow were for two officers to stand guard outside his room.

He opened the door to leave.

"Where are you going?" Elise said. She got up and pulled back the curtain. Luke looked at the floor, contemplated numerous responses, but settled on something more polite. For his standards, at least.

"I'll be right back. Gotta make a coffee run. You know us cops. Coffee and donuts are our thing."

Elise looked at the TV then back at him. "You believe me now?"

"I know those guys wanted you dead. Badly. Maybe you annoyed them as much as you are me, and they had shorter tempers. I'm still waiting on the fingerprints. Apparently, our assholes weren't even American. Had to run it by the FBI to see if they had any files."

"Any other news?" Elise said.

Luke shook his head. "No."

"You're lying."

"What? Me?! No way!"

Elise cracked a grin. His efforts to piss her off, oddly enough, seemed more effective in amusing her this time.

"Spit it out. Did the Coast Guard find the boat?"

Luke cleared his throat. "Yes."

"Is that a lie?"

"No." It wasn't. It was actually something that made it hard for *him* to sleep last night. At two-thirty, he received the call from the station, relaying the message from the Coast Guard. Knowing Elise's determination to pester him, and the fact that it was illegal to shoot someone for being annoying, the quickest cure to this headache was to spit it out. "They found it heading south toward San Francisco. It was abandoned as far as they could tell."

"But you can go through that ship for evidence…"

"Yeah, they torched it. All two-hundred feet of that yacht. From bow to stern. Takes a hell of a lot of gas to get that kind of fire going. But they did it. Obviously, they knew they were going to be found, so they used their own boat as a decoy."

"And what happened to them?"

"Probably transferred to another boat," Luke said. "They could be anywhere now."

"That doesn't seem strange to you?"

"I never said that. Then again, the whole world's a strange and ugly place," Luke said. He opened the door to leave.

"So, what do we do from here?" Elise said with heightened urgency.

Once again, Luke was stopped halfway out the door. He turned around. "We?"

"Yes, *we*."

"Do we need to undergo the cliché exchange of 'there is no *we*'?"

"Listen, Detective, I just want to get to the bottom of this. There's something going on beyond a killer shark swimming around."

"As you stated, *I'm* the Detective. Not you. There's not much for you to offer right now. Except Tylenol." He looked at his watch again. "Time to go. Got a date. See ya later." He shut the door before Elise could say anything else.

Luke stepped to the floor lobby where a few patrolmen were standing guard with coffee. One of them pointed to the detective. "There he is, right there." Luke realized he was talking to the forensic technician.

Pete Chow, a skinny eighteen-year veteran of the Amadea Police Department, greeted the detective. He had a thick tan folder in his hand. Finally, someone Luke Jansen actually wanted to talk to.

"FBI finally got back to me."

"Good. Walk with me. Heading to Critical Care. Gonna demonstrate some physical therapy techniques for a patient."

"That's…lovely," Pete said. He opened the folder as they made their way down the hallways. "Well, sir, you've done a real number last night."

"That's my job. Start with the piece of sewage I'm about to visit."

"Uh, last name Wells, first name Greig. His alias is Vick. Served in the Royal Navy from Oh-seven to Ten, got discharged after smuggling drugs into London."

"So he's not a U.S. citizen."

"Nope."

"Wonder what he's doing over here, then."

"We've got one from South Africa named Arno. Used to fight in a freedom fighter militia. Lost his way and decided to get paid for his labors. Smuggled diamonds from across the continent, using slave labor in a couple of cases. You might've done the world a favor on that one."

"Just him."

Pete shrugged. "You may have a point there. We've got one from New Zealand. Joined the French Foreign Legion. Went AWOL. Wanted by France on two murder charges. The one chopped up in the propellor…well, we never found his hands. Waiting on the dental records, but I have a feeling he's not much better than his friends." He shuffled through some papers while trying to keep up with the detective. "The other one killed by your witness is John Cullen. Irish crewman who worked on cargo ships until he tried smuggling drugs from Africa. Fled the country. Disappeared. Until last night, at least."

"What you're telling me is that this crew is full of no-gooders."

"Precisely."

"They're hard hitters, but not to the extent where they can call the shots. They need the cash and the security. They can be controlled. Whoever hired them is aware of this. They're controllable and disposable if they cause issues." They found an elevator and took it to the first floor. Luke stared at the floor number, not seeing it, but past it, envisioning the cruel world beyond this hospital. He spoke as though deep in thought. "Now why would this employer want *these* guys? Clearly, he can afford them, and he has the means to reach out to such types. To have such risk, there's got to be some sort of financial gain. But what? And what are they doing *here*?"

"Maybe they're shipping heroin," Pete said. "Criminal organizations make shipments from foreign sources all the time."

Luke didn't seem to hear him. He was still in a kind of trance as he struggled to put all the pieces together. "All around the time of a freakish shark attack. Then I have a witness telling me she's seen a prehistoric species…"

Pete cocked his head back. "Pardon?"

Luke snapped into reality, then shook his head. "Nothing." Finally, the elevator started moving. "What about the last one? The guy who was clearly in charge."

Pete puffed his cheeks out and released an exasperated sigh. "These other ones are cheese puffs compared to this guy." He pulled the file and a series of photos. "Trace Dixon Henry. Former British SAS. Took part in Operation Telic. Deployed to Basra during Operation Row. During which, he was part of a unit which captured two air bases and a highway. Remained in the SAS, conducting raids in Kenya and Libya. Was part of the hunt for Gaddafi after the Battle of Tripoli. In 2012, his military file goes blank."

"Meaning he went AWOL," Luke said.

"Correct."

"A man with a distinguished military career such as his tends to throw it all away for two reasons. Either they become disillusioned with the motherland, or they figured if they're gonna get shot at, might as well do it for something better than a government pension," Luke said.

Pete pulled out a couple of photographs. "And he was likely paid a fortune by God-knows-who." He handed the photos to Luke. The pictures were grainy, but there was no mistaking the man in the center. Dixon was in full tactical gear, in some sort of large field. By the looks of the people working in ragged clothing, he had a decent guess.

"Colombia?"

"Yes," Pete said.

Luke shuffled through the next image. His eye widened at the sight of partially buried bodies. The next photo, while not showing the mass grave, was definitely a similar area. Two men were in front and center in the photograph, one with a cigar in his hand while talking to Dixon.

"Where was this taken?"

"A village in Africa called Marikana," Pete said. "We're not sure what the operation was, or what his involvement was, exactly. But we don't believe he was part of any response team sent in to weed out extremists."

Luke kept his eye on the photo, not at the man named Dixon, but the man sharing the frame with him. Like recognizing an old acquaintance, except this was a new one—they'd met the previous day. Even if had been years, Luke would have no problem recognizing him. He never forgot an asshole. In the photo, the SAS man had a cigar in hand. He wore the same gear as Dixon. It didn't take detective skills to know they were part of the same unit.

"That's all I've got for you so far," Pete said.

"What about this guy?" Luke said, pointing at the other man. Pete took a look, then shook his head.

"Nothing on him yet."

Luke studied the photograph, burning the image into his brain. He looked at the British man standing beside Dixon. He wasn't the only thing he recognized in the photo. The cigar—Luke couldn't make out the label, but its color was the same as the Arturo Fuente Opus X.

Got an expensive taste in cigars, don't ya?

"Um, excuse me?"

Luke looked up. In his trance-like state, he didn't notice the doors open. Outside were a few staff waiting to get in. "Isn't there a staff elevator?" He and Pete stepped out into the hallway.

"Do me a favor. Check for any aliases for Beau Mott. See if he's wanted by anybody. Start with the FBI, then go further. Somebody knows something about this guy."

"Is it really that important?" Pete said.

"Yes. Check with *everybody.* Interpol, FBI, CIA, MI6, KGB, DNC, MLB, NCAA…anybody and everybody. I don't care who, as long as we figure something out."

They proceeded into the main lobby. Before they entered, they heard shouts of "Get out of the way! Let us through, please!" followed by a few gasps. There were the sound of stretchers rolling across the tile, and intense coughing. Luke and Pete hurried into the lobby just in time to see a team of paramedics transfer some very sickly patients to some doctors.

"Some morning, huh?"

Luke turned around to the sound of his Captain's voice. She was tired, her hair damp from a quick shower, and knowing her, this was her second coffee.

"Getting more interesting by the moment," Luke said. He watched the doors shut.

"Sooner it's behind us, the better," Brianna said. "Pete, I see you've made it here."

"Morning, Captain."

"Just got word on the yacht. They seriously *torched* it?!"

"That's what I'm told."

"That's an expensive piece of equipment to waste. And in that manner? It'd make more sense to sink the boat if they wanted to hide the evidence."

"Unless they wanted it found," Luke said.

"You think misdirection was the plan?"

"No bodies on the yacht. Sounds like the weapons and major equipment was taken. I think they met up with somebody, abandoned ship, steered it south, and lit it up like a beacon to attract attention. And I can't help but find it interesting that the fishing boat was never found."

"Hell, they could've sunk that." Brianna sighed. "But then, why do that, yet leave the yacht to be found? If it is misdirection, it's logical they went in the opposite direction. Damn it! Since we don't know what kind of boat they transferred to, there's no way we'll find them. They could be anywhere." She kicked the leg of a lobby chair. "All we have is the suspect. He's our only clue of figuring out who these people are."

"We can make an educated guess based on these files." Luke handed her Pete's findings. "Here. Get yourself caught up on last night's bozos. I've got stuff to do."

"Like what?" Brianna said.

"I need an opinion on British beer. Who better to ask than someone who's actually from there?!"

"Luke!"

Ah, first names.

Luke waited for the doors to open back up, then breezed past the nurses. "Pardon me."

"Hey!" one of them exclaimed. He ignored the protest and made a straight line toward the two patrollers standing guard.

"Detective?" one of them said. It was Corporal Randy Shane. As usual, he looked as displeased as ever to see Luke approach.

"Doctors give any update?"

"Still in critical condition," Shane replied.

"Aw. Well, maybe I'll make him feel better with chicken soup." He moved to step past the officers.

"Detective! We've been given explicit instructions *not* to let you in here," Shane said. He almost looked happy to defy Luke.

"By who?"

"By Raye, who got her orders from the Chief, who is acting on recommendation by the doctors here."

"The hell is Pino doing in this case?"

"Um, he is the Chief of *Police*, after all," Shane remarked.

Luke turned around as another stretcher was wheeled in. Again, the doctors were delivering a very sick person. They were getting blood pressure and heart readings as they took him into an examination room.

He faced the Corporal. "How many of those have they wheeled in?"

"Fourth one since I've been here, and I only started fifteen minutes ago. Zielinski here is working a double, though."

"I started at eleven. I say they brought in at least five people overnight," the other patroller said. "Seems like something's going around. Whatever it is, I don't want it."

"Any fatalities?"

Officer Zielinski nodded. "Overheard two had died. Whatever it is, seems like people with preexisting conditions suffer the most. One guy had a heart issue, so he didn't last long. Another had some sort of respiratory issue. It started with a couple cases yesterday. Nobody really thought anything of it. Now, the hospital administration is considering getting help from the State Government."

Luke listened to the echo of vomiting from one of the rooms. "Speak with the doctors. Find out if these people have been near the water within the last twenty-four hours."

The Corporal scoffed. "You serious, Detective?"

"As serious as a heart attack. Or whatever it is these guys are suffering from."

"Detective, I don't answer to you—"

"Hey, Randy, how 'bout you quit whining and actually do some real police work," Luke said. "I'm not looking for personal histories. I just want to know if these people have been in or near the water in any way. If they had handled fish or crabs, or had otherwise touched or consumed anything from the ocean."

Shane softened a bit. "You think there's something in the water causing this?"

"I think there *was* something in the water causing this," Luke said. Shane nodded. He wasn't sure what the Detective was getting at, but it didn't seem like it would hurt to gather some info.

Luke stepped back into the lobby. Brianna was in conversation with one of the Intensive Care doctors. Her expression was one of concern.

"You're kidding me! In less than a day?"

The doctor nodded. "His heart failed. Couldn't take it."

"So, an infection?"

"Of sorts. We're waiting on the autopsy to figure out what exactly went wrong," the doctor said.

"He seemed healthy when I met with him. I was right there with the paramedics. Heart rate was a little off, but obviously because he was ill. He gave his medical records to the paramedics. No history of major heart condition."

The doctor groaned. "What do you want me to say, Chief?"

Interesting.

Luke crossed his arms and waited for the conversation to end. In that time, he noticed Pete watching the television intently. "Something good on?"

The forensic technician looked back at him. "I wouldn't call it good." Luke watched the live broadcast. To his surprise, they weren't talking about last night's shooting. Instead, the reporter was on a beach north of the harbor, giving details on the phenomenon sweeping across Amadea's shores.

"As you can see, there are at least a hundred dead fish washed up on the beach. Some appear to have some sort of odd growth. We've seen crustaceans wash up further to the south, a couple of dead dolphins and sharks. Our sources tell us that the EPA's been alerted and will be looking into it. There's not enough detail on this situation yet, but some are speculating that there might be a hazardous spill somewhere along the nearby coast."

"What an unfortunate event. After the shark attack, this is the last thing that the city of Amadea needs," the news anchor replied.

"Alright, I gotta go. Thanks for letting me know, Doctor."

Hearing her conversation conclude, Luke turned around and saw Brianna approach. "What's going on? Kid run off again?"

Brianna shook her head. "Just checking up on a patient."

"The sick guy you found on the boat yesterday?"

Brianna squinted. "How'd you know about that?"

"Paramedics mentioned it when they were picking up 'Crab Guy'."

"Oh. Yeah, we were on our way back, then we see this guy leaning over the side of his boat. Malcolm and I boarded, checked on him, then took his boat to port. Transferred him to an ambulance there."

"Ah, I see." Luke continued to watch the footage of dead fish on the beach. "Quite the fascinating chain of events we've got going on. First, we have a mass murdering shark; a crew of guys who bring it in, who then are caught using deadly force on a witness; a bunch of dead things washing up on shore; an outbreak of sorts; and to top it off, a witness who states she's seen a prehistoric shark."

"Not to mention a record-sized great white with two people found in its stomach…brought to us by those gunmen," Brianna said.

Luke spun to face her. "Where is that great white?"

"I believe it's kept in a refrigerated trailer near evidence. I already spoke with the Chief, and he stated we're to give it to the local fishermen. Might as well use it for bait, because it doesn't serve much purpose once the researchers are done taking measurements and everything."

"Get blood samples and tissue samples from it. STAT."

"Last time I checked, *I'm* the one who gives the orders," Brianna said. She closed her eyes and sighed. Despite her reservations, she knew Luke's intuition was sound. "What's on your mind?"

"I want to run some tests. Just curious about a couple of factors."

"The researchers are already doing that…"

"What do we know about these researchers?"

"Oh, for chrissake, Jansen. Not everyone's a suspect."

"I'll ask again…"

Brianna groaned. "They're from a couple of different institutions. I don't know much about the scientists themselves…"

"My point exactly. This criminal organization—we don't know who they are, but we know they know something about sharks. And that they have a long reach. I don't want some nameless idiot giving us reports. I want my own person working on this."

"We have lab techs."

"To hell with that. Wouldn't trust those idiots to make me an egg salad sandwich," Luke said.

"I wouldn't trust *you* to make it," Brianna retorted.

Luke thought for a second, then nodded. "Fair enough. I should've used t-boned steak as an analogy. The point remains the same: I'm using my own expert to examine these samples. Someone who has a dog in this fight."

Brianna's gaze turned inquisitive. She knew who he was referring to. The professional side of her wanted to argue that Elise Sheldon was a witness and not a consultant. But it was Luke Jansen she was dealing with. Her condoning of this action meant nothing. In fact, nothing short of termination would stop the detective. And frankly, this case was already spiraling out of control. To get answers, someone would have to skip the red tape and bureaucratical nonsense.

"You think she'll be up to it?" she asked.

"She spent all day yesterday tracking me down. What do you think?"

"That seeing her nephew killed *really* screwed with her mind." She facepalmed her forehead. "Jesus, I'm turning into you."

Luke slapped her shoulder before walking away. "You'll never be that good looking."

CHAPTER 33

The aroma of fresh coffee was welcoming. It was the first time in forty-eight hours that Elise could stand the taste of anything. Not that her appetite had returned, but her sleeplessness was taking its toll. She was low-energy, in need of a boost. At least the jitters had ceased...for the most part. There was still an anxiousness about going to sleep.

Elise had taken a couple of bites of the eggs the server brought in for her. She watched the door intently, hoping for Detective Jansen to make his return. In that time, she had gotten dressed. Being in that hospital gown was driving her even more insane. Her leg was freshly bandaged and feeling fine for the most part. A few days of painkillers, and she'd be back to normal. Physically, at least.

She stripped off her shirt and dug for her clothes.

The door opened.

"Whoa!" Luke spun back toward the door. "I suppose that's why we're supposed to knock when coming into hospital rooms."

Elise ducked behind the curtain and closed it all the way. "That tends to be customary." She heard him take a seat on the sofa. The curtains were somewhat see-through if one tried really hard. "You better not be watching."

"I can't. You're on my blind side."

Lovely. She got into her shirt and jeans, then stepped back out. "What's going on? Did you interrogate the guy?"

"The docs all say he's in too critical shape to have a chit-chat," he said.

Elise leaned against the bed. "So, what now? We wait?"

"For a little while. During that waiting, I've thought of something else to investigate."

It struck Elise's mind that this was the most garrulous Luke had been since she first encountered him. He didn't simply warm up to her; he had a use for her. "I suppose you need my help with whatever it is."

"You're a PhD in marine biology. I don't know what actual skills you have, but I'm assuming you can perform dissections and test for toxins and other substances in blood samples. Correct?"

"Piece of cake. What are you looking for, exactly?"

"Anything that doesn't belong," Luke replied. "I need answers and I need them pronto. I need you to examine tissue samples from the great white. Also, we're going to collect specimens that are washing up on the shore. Whatever's going on, it's related to recent events."

"I'd ask again if you believe me about the Helicoprion, but I guess I should know better," Elise said.

Luke looked away for a moment, then looked back at her. She saw it in his eye; the suspicion that whatever was going on, it defied logic and practicality. When that happened, he'd have to consider what would normally be regarded as illogical and impractical for answers. Then again, logic and practicality were relative.

"I'll entertain that idea for the sake of this conversation. *If* there was such a thing swimming around out there, I'd first want to know why and how. How could it have survived all this time? And why did it come here of all places?"

Elise sat on the edge of the bed. "Your guess is as good as mine."

Luke stood up. "No it's not. You're the expert. Your guess is *better* than mine. If you don't think so, then I'll consult with somebody more driven." He turned and went for the door.

Elise followed him. "It is possible it simply went undiscovered." Luke stopped and turned around, waiting for her to continue. "It's a big ocean. We're talking about the damn Pacific. There's always speculation of what kind of things lurk beneath the surface. We've only explored seven percent of the ocean. It's seven miles deepest at its deepest and twelve thousand miles from Colombia to Indonesia. Over sixty-three million square miles of ocean all around. That's a lot of ocean for something to hide in. Also, there's the fact that it's not unheard of for species believed to be extinct to be discovered again. That was the case for the goblin shark."

"We're talking about a forty-foot shark which, according to you, has some very recognizable features," Luke said. "Not to mention this fish has no problem with making itself well-known. It attacked numerous people in broad daylight in a single day. Even for a prehistoric shark, that can't be normal."

"No, it's not," Elise admitted. "Detective, I can only speculate as to how and why it's here. It probably chose this location for the abundance of prey. Though, it seemed more interested in killing for the sake of killing, rather than sustenance. As to where it came from, our mutual friend in Critical Care likely has an answer to that."

"Which brings me to another question," Luke said. "Whoever these people are, they have a vested interest in the shark. But what do they have to gain from it? Is there fame and fortune to be made from discovering it?"

"Ha! People think that, but it doesn't work that way. For something to make money, it has to have a market value. Also, when something is discovered, it's often a year, if not a few years, for it to make the news. There's all kinds of research that has to be done before such an announcement is made. The only exception would be if the thing was genetically engineered from DNA."

Luke slowly paced around the hospital room as he tried to put the pieces together in his mind. "You know, had you suggested that yesterday, I would've sent you packing."

"You *did* send me packing."

"Fair enough. Point is, we know more now. This group that tried to kill you are well financed. Whoever's paying the bill would probably have the means to conduct such research. But again, I have to ask why? What's to gain from genetically engineering a prehistoric shark? They planning on opening a zoo?"

Elise chuckled. "I doubt it. There's been talk about de-extinction. Reasons include conservation efforts to help protect currently endangered species. There are some species that have been wiped out by man, and some people have proposed to bring them back through genetic engineering. Some have proposed that new vaccines could be discovered through de-extinction."

"Or diseases."

Elise perked up, realizing what he was getting at. "I still have lab access. We can study the samples there."

"Good. You have hazmat gear?"

"I do. I know where we can get supplies to transport the specimens."

"Good. Let's get started then. Sooner we figure this out, sooner I can go back to my peace and quiet."

CHAPTER 34

The man stepped out of his 2020 Chevy Equinox, then straightened his shirt and tie. His shoes were freshly shined and his slacks ironed. He was a professional, and had to look the part. He took one last minute to gaze across the long parking lot at the hospital entrance. He lifted his suitcase from the passenger seat, stepped out, and locked the vehicle. It was still early, with several staff currently arriving to work, while some of the night staff were heading out.

He double-checked the employee tag on his car. Last thing he needed was for hospital security to flag him for wrongfully using employee parking. There were two patients he needed to see. One in critical care, the other in Med/Surge. The latter was simply an overnight observation stay. Thus, time was limited. He would see her first, then visit the more critical patient.

With his hospital badge on a lanyard, he entered the building. As he expected, there were a few cops in the main lobby. Two patrollers, one that looked like a detective, in addition to the two he was informed were guarding the injured suspect.

The detective, a female in her later forties, saw him come in and greeted him with a police nod before looking away.

"Morning," he said, pretending to be surprised by the sight of officers. He found an elevator and took it up to 5A-B. The nurse sharing the elevator with him seemed to be lost in her thoughts. Just the way he wanted it. The last job he performed in a hospital, he got bogged down with chitchat from staff who just so happened to have nothing to do that day. So far, nobody here seemed to take real notice of him.

The elevator arrived at the fifth floor. He followed the signs to 5A Med/Surge unit. Immediately, he was taken by surprise. There were no cops here. He had been informed that there were at least three standing guard in the lobby, but there were none. He checked his watch. It was only a few minutes after seven.

He placed his badge to the card reader. The red light turned green and the door popped open. The charge nurse looked up and saw him walk in. She looked at his name tag. Dr. Carl Harker.

"Good morning, Doctor," she said. By her expression, she wasn't familiar with his name. But his badge worked, so what was there to question? The man named Dr. Harker approached the desk.

"Good morning to you." He opened his tan folder. "I'm here to see Elise Sheldon for possible infection in her injury. My file didn't state her room number. Can you direct me, please?"

"The marine biologist?"

"That's the one," he said, smiling.

"She's already gone, sir."

"Gone? This early?"

"Yes. They've checked out. The detective with her seemed to be in some kind of hurry. We instructed that it would be best to stay for another couple of hours, but apparently, whatever they needed to do was more important. Since she was just an overnight observation, there wasn't much we could do."

"I see."

The nurse reached for the phone. "If you'd like, I can call Dr. Arton. He's the physician in charge of her case. If there's a concern, he'll probably want to talk to you. I don't believe he's left yet…"

"No, no, it's fine. If she's not here, there isn't much we can do," Harker said. He looked at his watch. "There's another patient I need to see anyway. Thank you for your help."

"No problem, Doctor. Sorry you came up here for nothing."

"Ha. You know these patients. Think they know best until they get sick," he quipped.

The nurse laughed. "I know that's right."

"Have a good day." He waved goodbye and stepped out into the lobby. As soon as that door clicked, his smile vanished. Poor intel, always the root of fuckups. Elise Sheldon was out of the hospital, and he had no way of determining her whereabouts at the moment.

Now wasn't the time to dwell on it. He had another patient he needed to meet, and this one was a more urgent case. First, he needed to lay low for a couple of hours until he was scheduled to see this case. Getting there too early wouldn't do any good.

He tucked the badge into his pocket, took the elevator back downstairs, then exited the building. Being a professional, he took his car off site, then made a phone call.

"Yeah. Number one's a no-go… don't ask me, I arrived right on time… When are they coming?... No, too soon. I can't be seen waiting around doing nothing. Plus, I need to change outfits anyway... Yes, I know you want this taken care of, but it has to be done properly… Yes, you'll get paid what you've been promised. That's up to the client… Just do your part… Ten o'clock. Marked. Make sure you hold up your end, or you won't get paid. Don't fuck with me on this. Our deal is on record… I know the client. Once a deal is made, he expects it to be held up… Glad to hear it… I'll be back at ten. Wait until I'm in the building."

He hung up the phone, drove a little further, then chucked it as soon as he came to a street corner where nobody was around. The phone shattered on impact. Its owner pulled a replacement from the glove compartment. All the contacts were already installed.

The man named Carl Harker found heavier traffic and disappeared into the population. Before long, he would change outfits and vehicles. He double-checked his logs. Flight-time at eleven-fifteen. Plenty of time to complete his task and disappear.

Those plans would not falter. He made them himself. If the professional trusted anybody, it was himself.

CHAPTER 35

"You sure you're alright, dude?"

Malcolm Barnhiser could sense the relief in Glenn's voice as they pulled into his driveway. Somehow, he had mustered the strength to get the job done. He even managed to keep his coughing down to a minimum. The Tylenol was starting to wear off, releasing the fever he so desperately hoped would not surface.

I made it through the day. Now for some soup and to lay in bed.

"Yeah, I'm good. Might be getting a little bug," he said.

"Well, if you gave it to me, I know where you live!" Glenn joked.

Malcolm mustered a laugh. Truth was, he was as relieved as Glenn was. And judging by the tightening in his stomach, sitting around chitchatting was not in his best interest.

"Alright. Thanks for the ride," he said. He got out, smiled, and waved goodbye as Glenn backed out of the driveway. That was the last of the false impressions. He calmly walked to the door and opened it, then once inside it turned to a dash. He made it to the bathroom just in time to empty his insides.

There he remained, huddled against the toilet bowl. In that time, he praised God for not humiliating him at the shop. In his pocket was a hundred-and-fifty dollars, more than enough to get his dad off his back. Considering how crummy he felt all morning, he figured he deserved three hundred.

"What a way to wrap up the summer," he muttered. He was feeling a little better at the moment, but still extremely lackluster. Carrying around heavy supplies probably didn't help.

Malcolm could feel that fever return like a raging river that just burst through a dam. He tried to stand up, but couldn't. It was as though all his energy had been vacuumed out of him. All concept of time was gone. Malcolm had no clue how long he was in there before his dad knocked on the door.

"Hey, whatcha doin' in there? Mr. Raye feed you an entire pizza or something?"

Malcolm squeezed his eyes shut. Go figure classes didn't start until Friday. Then again, maybe it was a good thing. This was no simple stomach flu. Something was seriously wrong, because Malcolm *never* had problems with his breathing.

"I—" he couldn't get any words out without coughing. His dad tried twisting the door handle to get in.

"Malcolm? You alright?" Malcolm tried to answer, but couldn't. His dad tried wrestling to get the door open. "Unlock the door, bud." When his dad called him by a nickname, it was always out of genuine concern.

"I—" Again, he couldn't speak. He stood up, fell against the door, barely twisting the lock back before crashing to the floor.

His dad had to push hard against his weight to get the door open. Malcolm's feet were visible near the frame. "Oh, God. Malcolm, what's wrong?" He squeezed through and knelt by his son.

"I—barely—breathe," Malcolm muttered.

His father scooped his son in his arms and carried him out to the car. "Hang on, bud. I'm taking you to the hospital. You'll be fine. Probably just ate some bad takeout."

Malcolm was half-conscious at this point. "I got…money… pay you… back…"

"Shit, kid. You should've stayed in if you were feeling like crap." He kicked the door open and carried Malcolm to the lot.

"I owed."

Mr. Barnhiser felt his soul grow a little heavy as he put his son into the backseat of his car. Maybe he truly did push the kid a little too hard.

"Don't worry about that, Malcolm. You'll be fine. I promise." It was intended as a comfort to himself as much for his son. Malcolm's veins were pronounced, his eyes red, his breathing raspy. Whatever infection he had, it was attacking fast.

He had no sooner clipped his seatbelt before he was speeding onto the road.

CHAPTER 36

Like with everything else in her life, it was odd for Elise to be in the lab without Chad. He didn't always accompany her, but he did on several occasions to learn the ins and outs of lab testing and data analysis. His presence was by far favorable compared to that of Luke Jansen.

The other lab techs in the facility seemed unnerved, both by the fact that Elise came into the office despite everything that had happened, and by the one-eyed detective that accompanied her. Already, there were a couple of 'What are you looking at?' remarks thrown by him.

During their stop at the beach, they collected a small bluefin tuna, a Pacific salmon, a small hammerhead shark, and a few crabs. The specimens were handled with great caution. Elise had warned the police officials on site *not* to touch anything with their bare hands. The EPA was yet to show up and take care of the situation, which worked for them, as it meant they got to avoid explaining their actions, as well as the argument about stepping on the agency's toes.

He was on his phone, keeping a distance from the specimens while Elise performed the autopsies. One thing both of them noticed immediately was the odd growth on the gills.

Luke nodded as he listened to Corporal Randy Shane give his report. He put the phone on speaker and set it down on one of the lab tables.

"You said there's now fifteen patients?"

"That's right, with more of them likely to come in."

"So we have a potential contagion outbreak on our hands," Luke said.

"I'm getting nervous that that's the case," Shane said. *"Sir, I should probably get this information to the EPA."*

"You will, but I want it first."

"But Detective—"

"But nothing, Corporal. This is connected to my case. You wanna help or not?"

Shane sighed through the speaker, then continued. *'Eight of the patients have reported being in or near the water since yesterday morning."*

"Alright. And what about the others?"

"The ones who could give a history stated to the doctors that they were NOT in fact anywhere near the ocean in our allotted timeframe. That blows our connection, sir."

"Not unless the ocean came to them," Luke said.

"I don't recall any tsunamis in the last few days," Shane retorted.

"Ha-ha-ha, very funny. What I mean is that they've probably been in contact with something or some*one* who had been in the water. Dig harder. Figure out everyone and everything these people have been near. We're gonna need to know anyway, because if this is some sort of outbreak, we're obligated to figure out how far it's spread before it gets worse."

Another sigh from Shane. This one sounded less frustrated and a little more genuinely concerned. The weight of the situation was dawning on him. *"Oh my God."*

"If you believe in Him, I'd start asking for his help. Because something tells me we're only seeing the start of a real big headache. Now get those histories pronto!"

"Yes, sir."

Probably the first time Shane regarded Luke with something more than the obligatory level of respect. He put it out of his mind immediately. *Not here to make friends with others.* Luke hung up the phone and read a text message he received during the conversation.

"The Captain's having the great white tissue samples delivered directly over here." Elise acknowledged with a nod, then hung up the X-rays she took of the specimens. Luke stepped beside her and gazed at the images. "So this is what it's like to have eyes like *Superman.*"

"Funny," Elise said.

"What are we looking at. Looks like a fish skeleton to me," he said.

"See these little blots here, here, and here?" Elise said, pointing to various areas in the image. "That's growth."

"Tumors? You telling me these fish died of cancer?"

"No. These aren't tumor growths, these are infections. Whatever's killing them, it tends to attack the respiratory system and digestive tract. The shark, for instance, has more growth in the stomach than along its gill slits. I think it ate infected prey. Same with the crab specimen."

"Give me the fundamentals," Luke said. "How does a virus work, exactly? I'm like the rest of the dumb population: I get sick, I take medicine, fix myself a bowl of soup and a glass of orange juice, and watch reruns of *Breaking Bad* until it goes away. But I don't actually know the ins and outs of how a virus actually works."

"Why do I have a feeling it'd be chilly cheese steak and bourbon instead of chicken soup and orange juice for you?" Elise said.

"First you stalk me and claim you desperately need my help. Now that you've gotten it, you proceed to throw insults at me. *After* I saved your life, no less."

"I'm not that stupid, Detective. This has nothing to do with you helping me. You're eager to solve a case. Why? I don't know. Maybe you're bored and this is your only hobby. Maybe you're an adrenaline junkie—which would make sense considering the fact that you don't seem the least bit fazed from last night's shootout. OR, maybe you're trying to make up for that Laskey case from L.A. Whatever the reason is, you're not helping me. You're helping *yourself.* I'm just a tool for you to use to connect the pieces."

They stood in silence. The detective's blind side wrinkled, much in the way a person did when one eye was wincing. But there was no eye there; just a black patch surrounded by gravelly skin.

Elise exhaled through her nose. Now that she had let off steam, that stupid sense of regret started kicking in. She wasn't so arrogant to not comprehend that she would indeed be dead right now if not for him.

She opened her mouth to say 'sorry', but the word never came out. Why waste more time? A guy like Luke Jansen would probably see it as weakness anyway. Best to just answer his question.

"Viruses are small pieces of ribonucleic acid or deoxyribonucleic acid—commonly referred to as RNA and DNA—wrapped in a layer of proteins. Those proteins act like an armor to protect the genetic material. Because of that suit of armor, they cannot replicate on their own, so they require a host to survive. They can adapt to whatever environment and any host, which is how they mutate and create other variants.

"They enter the body through the mouth, eyes, nose, genitals, and open wounds. Often, they're spread through direct contact. Clearly you understand that much, considering the instructions you gave to the police officer a minute ago. When they enter the body, they adhere to the cell surface. What part of the body they seek depends on the virus. Some go for the respiratory system, some attack the liver, blood, and so forth. The virus attaches itself to the healthy cell and enters it, like a freaking parasite.

"Once inside the cell, it opens that suit of armor I told you about, and goes straight for the nucleus. There, it makes copies of itself. Those copies eventually come out of the nucleus, get a suit of protein armor to protect their RNA and DNA, then leave the infected cell to attack other cells. Then the process continues as the virus multiplies.

"That brings us to the growth we see here. When a virus infects a human or animal, it doesn't always end up as a disease. The infection happens when the virus multiplies. That infection turns into a disease when several cells are damaged. That's when you typically see symptoms and illnesses appear. What we see here are areas where the virus has duplicated itself out of control—an infectious disease. And these sea creatures are somehow spreading it to each other, and now to us."

"Is it safe to assume they're all suffering from the same infection?"

"Yes," she answered.

"And you can get it by eating them?"

Elise scowled at the thought. "Oh yeah."

"Explains what happened to Crab Guy," Luke said. "Crabs ate some infected food, Crab Guy goes crabbing, eats some infected crab, now he's in the hospital groaning about missing his first day on the job... So, what's going on? This had to start from somewhere. Did a Chinese bat drop dead into the water or something?"

Elise chuckled. "I don't think so." Her grin quickly disappeared. This wasn't a laughing matter. She heard the policeman's report on Luke's speakerphone. The number of cases was escalating rapidly, and at this rate, there was no sign of slowing down. By the end of the day, it would be breaking news broadcast across the country. "You bring up a valid point. For something to cause this, it would need to be a variant not native to the environment."

"Like a wandering shark," Luke said.

"You said it. Not me," she replied.

Luke watched the images as though about to interrogate them. "A shark that very powerful people do not want the public to know about." He thought of the images he saw in the folder. South America, the mass grave, the ex-SAS specialists. "I wonder what they were covering up there?"

Elise raised an eyebrow. "Pardon?"

Luke shook his head. "Nothing. Thinking out loud." He looked again at all the specimens. Lab techs were loading them into thick containers, treating them as they would radioactive material. After the specimens were removed, Elise got to work sanitizing the lab. "What are the odds of this spreading beyond our coast?"

"Luckily, anything that gets infected tends to die quickly, making them easy to identify. If the Coast Guard and EPA can scoop up the dead bodies before something else can consume them, we can limit the spread."

"And if they can't?"

Elise took off her gloves and threw them into a hazmat bin. "Then we could be looking at a pandemic on a worldwide scale. The fishing industry could be forever changed, not to mention the ease in which this can be spread person-to-person. Vaccine creation takes time..."

They got out of their protective gear and washed up. Even though Luke hadn't been anywhere near the specimens, he made sure to sanitize. He vividly remembered the infected man he helped last night, and was thankful he had the good judgement to not touch him. He even ran a sanitizing cloth over his phone before picking it up with his bare hands.

"All units, respond to—" Luke looked down at his radio and smacked it like an unruly child. Damn lab was garbling the signal. He heard the tone in the dispatcher's voice. Something urgent was happening. Another voice followed. Then another. He recognized Detective Norton's voice.

"He's out in the—" It cut out again.

"The hell?"

Elise perked up. "You hear that?" She pointed to the door. There was heavy commotion and running footsteps in the hallway outside. They tossed their suits in a bin and hurried out of the lab. They saw lab employees rushing toward the lunch lounge. Cries of "Oh my God" filled their ears. Something was happening and it had everyone's attention.

Luke and Elise followed the crowd into the lounge and gazed at the television. On the screen was a reporter. In the background was the Amadea Hospital, with flashing cop lights near the lot entrance.

"We know multiple shots have been fired so far at Amadea Hospital. We're not sure if it's one gunman or multiple. Police on site are engaging the suspect as we speak..."

"Son of a—" Luke hurried to the door. Elise followed him into the hall.

"Stay here! Do NOT leave this building, and don't let anyone know you're here."

Elise nodded. It wasn't hard to put the pieces together in her mind. Another shooting? At the hospital she just recently discharged from after escaping several gunmen? She couldn't know for sure whether this was a separate incident or if there was a connection, but Luke couldn't respond and protect her at the same time.

"Good lord! What is wrong with the world?" a tech said from inside the lounge.

"More than we know," Elise said.

CHAPTER 37

9:53 a.m. Amadea General

In his high school days, Harvey Clin was referred to as the San Francisco Spartan. Majoring in sports, he was voted most likely to be rich and famous of his class. With a football scholarship, he attended the University of California, and scored twenty-four touchdowns in his first year. Talk of an NFL draft quickly spread.

Then came the tackle that ended it all. There was no malice in the hit. Just the risks of the game coming to fruition. To this day, Harvey remembered the *crunch* of his knee twisting violently. He was on his way to the endzone. The ball was in the air, angling toward him. But it was high. To catch it, he needed to jump. As he leapt, so did the equally determined defensive lineman who was on his tail. The catching of the ball and the grabbing of his legs were simultaneous. Time slowed down. Harvey was just a couple of steps from the endzone. The tackler's grip was weak. He just needed to twist and free himself.

In a split-second, Harvey's world changed. The tackler resisted his struggle, shifting their weight further. Both men plummeted to the earth like meteors, putting a combination of four hundred pounds on Harvey's outstretched leg.

Harvey had never screamed in pain before in his life. But when that shinbone popped out through his skin, his odds of getting drafted ended as swiftly as his involvement in the game. One bad twist, one reckless decision—knowing this was worse than pain. Pain of the mind wasn't simply cured with drugs, just suppressed.

Over the years, that's what Harvey attempted. In the two decades that followed, he walked with a limp. Being a physical guy, he gravitated toward manual labor jobs. At home, he'd cure the pain with pills and booze. For four years he coasted by. Autumn was the worst. Everyone talked about football, which was now a subject he tried desperately to avoid. Then came arthritis and a slipped disc, as though his mangled leg wasn't enough. The manual labor jobs were impossible. Waking up in the morning became a chore, let alone the task of lifting heavy objects and moving them from point A to point B. The icing on the cake was being denied for disability.

Harvey was stuck with no plan and no skills. He hated computers, yet office jobs seemed to be all that remained. Then, at the age of twenty-nine, he met Kristen. For once, a ray of sunshine came into his world. Love brought marriage and a beautiful daughter. Driven by purpose, Harvey mustered the strength to work whatever jobs he could.

Unfortunately, even something as beautiful as sunshine can burn.

It was in their ninth year of marriage when Harvey came home from work early. Sitting down was now agonizing, thanks to his lower back pain. He had put on fifty-pounds and his fatigue was at an all-time high. But none of this matched the mental torture of walking in on his wife in bed with another man—a football player, no less. Their activity was so intense, they didn't even hear him come in, nor did they notice him standing there for several minutes. Never in the decade he had known her had Harvey heard Kristin howl in such pleasure.

Pain and anger were two elements that, when combined, had explosive potential. When his outburst ended, the bedroom looked as though an explosion had occurred. Kristin's lover suffered a fractured neck and internal bleeding. During the rage-fueled assault, she tried to pull Harvey away. Blinded by his momentary hatred, Harvey did something he never thought he would do—something he was staunchly against. The blow across her face nearly sent her across the room. A crown was knocked free completely, leading to bleeding and swelling. A neighbor, having heard the ruckus, phoned the police, who came in full force. Seeing the injured people sprawled out, and a hulking man with a baseball bat in hand, it wasn't hard to determine what occurred.

His next year was spent in criminal and divorce proceedings. Kristin's lawyer managed to push it past the ten year anniversary mark, forcing Harvey to pay alimony for life. Following a two year prison sentence, Harvey was frequently hounded by the court to make child support and alimony payments, with no consideration for his ailments or ability to find work. What little money he had went to booze and a few grams of cocaine.

Every morning, he woke up angrier than the last. He was a volcano, shaking with immense pressure that was dying to get released. Failure was his legacy. Misery and hopelessness were his only friends. The final straw was desperation.

Harvey's heart was racing faster than it ever did on the field. He was no longer a man. He was a machine. Uncaring, unfeeling, almost unaware that the people walking in the hospital lot were even sentient. His only sense of affection was for the now-thirteen-year-old in the five-by-eight photograph on his dashboard. He watched the image, as though about to plead with the child for forgiveness.

In his lap was another gram of cocaine. He snorted it, then leaned back as it took effect. In those few seconds, he downed what remained in his whiskey bottle. The tiny bit of humanity he now felt was gone. Now, all he had was primal rage, and a twelve-gauge shotgun and pistol. He could barely remember where he obtained these weapons. The serial numbers were scratched off, and the muzzle and grips showed signs of wear.

Harvey didn't care at this point. He stepped out of his rusty vehicle, tucked the pistol into his pants, then marched toward the hospital. The pump of the shotgun drew a few eyes toward him. Recognition of the weapon and the attitude sparked a few shrieks. The first discharge ignited panic.

****

Detective Norton had arrived at the hospital around nine. The Captain was still in the lobby, waiting to personally interrogate the suspect when given the go-ahead by the doctors. During their wait, they witnessed more patients get wheeled in through the ER.

"Jeez. Another one?" Norton said.

"I'm afraid so," Brianna replied.

"No wonder Jansen was eager to get out of here. Where the hell did he go, anyway?"

"He's chasing some other crazy lead," she replied.

"What, exactly?" Norton asked.

"He thinks there's a connection between these gunmen and this outbreak that's going on."

"You sound like you believe it yourself," Norton said.

"I don't know what I believe," she replied.

His phone rang. "Detective Norton... uh-huh... no shit... what about the other files?... Right... alright, keep at it." He hung up then turned his attention to the Captain. "All computer data on that yacht has been deleted. All charting is missing. There's no record of who the ship even belonged to. There's not even a serial number to go by."

"Maybe we could get with the manufacturer and get their sales records," Brianna said. "Maybe we'll find somebody with a history of criminal association."

"If they say no, we'd need a warrant, and I doubt a judge would grant us one," Norton said. Brianna crushed her coffee cup. He was right.

"Guess all we can look forward to is for this Vick guy to wake up and—" The crack of a gunshot drew their attention to the front doors. Everyone seated in the lobby jumped to their feet and darted for the back. More shots rang out, followed by deafening screams from both inside and outside the hospital.

Norton and Brianna drew their sidearms and moved toward the doors, backed up by the patrol units accompanying them.

"All units, we have an active shooter in Amadea General. North Lot. Unknown number of shooters. All units converge on Amadea Hospital at once," Norton barked through the radio.

It was almost impossible to get through the front door, as there was a reverse flow of civilians racing into the building. More shots rang out.

"Out of the way! Come on!" Norton said, shoving through moving bodies to get into the sunlight. Brianna and the other officers followed him. Once outside, they could see the suspect moving between the cars. He shot a windshield out. There didn't appear to be any rhyme or reason to his attack. He was simply shooting blindly.

"Norton, go to the left. I'll take the right. Set up a crossfire," Brianna said. She looked to the patrollers. "You go with him, you come with me, you stay by the entrance and keep people coming in."

The group split.

Norton and his fellow officer moved to the west side of the lot. They crouched by a car to observe the shooter. The gunman was a male in his mid-forties, overweight, unshaven, and almost unbalanced. The way he moved indicated he was intoxicated.

Norton emerged from cover and pointed his weapon. "Police! Drop the damn shotgun!" He saw the muzzle swing in his direction. Norton ducked, then felt the reverberation of a shot hitting the car. He got on his radio. "Shane! Get your asses out here now."

****

"Son of a bitch," Corporal Shane muttered. He pulled his Glock and took a breath. Every officer was always warned a moment like this could happen in their career, but how many actually *expected* it to? He looked to his fellow officer, then back at the room they were guarding. Vick would just have to wait unguarded. There were more pressing concerns at the moment.

The two officers rushed through the door and shut them, nearly knocking over a physician in a white coat as they hurried into the lobby.

"Doors are locked, sir."

"It's okay." The man proceeded to pull out a badge and let himself in. Shane didn't pay him a second thought as he and his partner raced outside. They immediately saw the shooter firing his weapon to the west. Glass flew apart from the windshield of a car. Behind that car was Detective Norton and another officer.

The patrolman waiting by the door pointed to the right of the shooter. "Raye's over there somewhere, closing in on the guy."

"We'll converge from here," Shane said. They rushed the lot and ducked behind an abandoned shuttle. Several nine-millimeter rounds struck the vehicle. The bastard saw them coming and switched to his sidearm.

More gunshots echoed from the right and left. Shane peeked from around the back and saw the gunman ducking for cover as the other units opened fire on him. The three patrolmen took aim and fired into the lot. Bullets struck the tightly packed group of cars which provided cover for the gunman. He emerged briefly, fired a few rounds in the direction of the Captain before a bullet from Norton struck him in the back.

The gunman fell forward. With the distance, confusion, adrenaline, and fleeing bystanders, it was difficult for the officers to determine what the suspect was doing. He was still alive, though gushing blood through his shirt.

A police helicopter hovered several hundred feet above them. *"He's on the pavement. He's going for his dropped pistol."*

More police vehicles swarmed into the lot. Leading the group was a SWAT van with a dozen well-trained men armed with high-powered rifles.

The gunman leaned up, as though to observe the situation. He raised his pistol, pressed the muzzle under his chin, and squeezed the trigger one final time.

"He's down!" the spotter announced.

The SWAT team moved into the lot, secured the weapons, and confirmed that the suspect was neutralized.

"Secure the lot. Make sure there's no other shooters," the Lieutenant ordered.

****

The haziness brought about by the drugs did little to cloud Vick's judgement. When he awoke to the sound of distant gunfire and screams, he knew exactly what was happening. He understood the kind of man his client was. More importantly, he knew what kind of man *Barton* was. Being here in this hospital, on life support, he was a liability.

Liabilities didn't last.

When he saw the figure standing in his doorway, he knew his time had come. He didn't bother fighting against it. Not that he wanted to die, but he understood his predicament. Plus, despite the drugs, his body was in hell. He had tubes and wires attached to him. The respirator had an annoying droning sound to it.

"Sorry to disturb you," the man said. Vick's eyes went to the badge. *Dr. Carl Harker*. Vick wasn't stupid. That wasn't his real name, nor was he a doctor. But he had the expertise to perform this basic medical procedure. The man reached into his coat pocket, pulled out a syringe, and stabbed it into the IV line. "Sorry. Your next of kin will be well compensated." He removed the needle and shut the door on his way out.

CHAPTER 38

When Luke Jansen left Amadea General that morning, the lot was half empty, the air smelling of an odd mix of coffee and gasoline. When he returned three-and-a-half hours later, there was the smell of gunpowder, oil, and canines. Crowds had formed around the outer perimeter, slowing Luke's arrival. More than once, he was tempted to floor the accelerator through the gathering. These curious bystanders were doing no good. Then there were the cop-haters shouting vile insults at the patrollers for the sin of being cops.

One had the audacity to get in front of Luke's vehicle and place his hands on the hood. He leaned forward. "This is the result of social injustice!" Luke put the Dodge in reverse and floored the accelerator. All of a sudden, the idiot was leaning on nothing. He stumbled and fell onto the pavement, much to the amusement of some of the other bystanders. A couple of officers goaded the man off of the road.

"Blue-haired whales," Luke groaned. He continued into the lot. SWAT was still on site. Canine units were searching the vehicles for drugs, weapons, and explosives. News was all over the place, including Anthony Zach. As soon as Luke arrived, the reporter did an about-face and marched straight for his window.

Does the guy have radar or something letting him know when I'm near? Luke drove past him, parked near an island in the lot, then located Brianna. She was standing in the round-a-bout for the buses, speaking with the Chief. Detective Norton was standing next to her, looking somewhat perplexed.

"Nice to see you made it."

"Sorry. I forgot we had a mass shooting scheduled for today," Luke said. "How many was it? Just the one?"

"Yeah. So it seems," Norton said. He looked around. "Where the hell is your witness?"

"Like I was going to bring her to the scene of a shooting," Luke retorted.

"Where is she, though?"

"Safe." Luke watched the officers as they combed between the vehicles. "We have an ID on the guy?"

"Just some lunatic," Norton said.

"Right! 'Just some lunatic' who happens to shoot up the same hospital treating a witness and a susp—" Luke's voice trailed off as he recognized Corporal Shane and Zielinski through the lobby window. He pushed past Norton then between Brianna and Chief Pino, much to the latter's irritation.

"Hey!" the Chief shouted. Luke ignored him and rushed into the lobby. Both Officers turned to face him, alarmed by the agitation emitted by his face.

"What the hell are you doing out here?!"

Zielinski scoffed. "Uh, not sure where you've been, but there was a shooting—"

"Who's guarding the suspect?"

"The double doors are locked. Nobody's been in there except staff—"
Luke marched to the lobby desk, the clerk gasping as he pointed a finger at him. "Open the doors right now."

"Uh, sir, we're on lockdown. I can't."

"Threat's neutralized. Open the doors."

"I have instructions to keep them locked," the clerk said.

"I'm with the police. I need to get in there. Open. The. Doors."

Pino approached the desk, his patience wearing thin. "Detective, I swear to Christ I'm gonna have your badge." Luke kept his eye on the clerk. In a blur of motion, he snatched the badge from the man's shirt and raced to the electronic lock. "Detective!"

Luke let himself in and pushed past several people until he got to Vick's room.

Immediately, he noticed there was no sound from the monitor. The pulse reader was on the floor. Above it was a limp hand, partly closed. Vick's eyes were open, his face blank, staring at the corner of the ceiling. Luke ran to his side and checked his pulse. There was none.

"Shit!"

He went to work doing compressions. By the third, Pino and Brianna hurried into the room. Their intent to chastise him shifted when they realized the suspect was not responding.

Brianna leaned out the door. "We need a doctor in here, stat!"

"Doesn't matter. He's gone," Luke said. He kicked the leg of the bed. "*This* is why we had a shooting today. Draw the guards away and allow these people to close their loose end."

"Calm down, Jansen," the Chief said. "His injury was severe. He was still listed as critical. It's possible he might have succumbed to his wounds."

Luke picked up the pulse reader. "Give me a break. You think this simply fell off?" He tossed it on the body then examined the IV line. "Here. You can barely see it, but there's a hole in the line. Somebody injected something into him. Toxicology report will show it. Whoever it is, they had access."

"You think it was a staff member?" Brianna asked.

"Or somebody posing as a staff member," Luke said. "Where's the security office?"

****

It took a little bit of arguing with hospital security to get the badge files, as their policy required a warrant to release such information. Normally, Brianna wouldn't stand for Luke's assertive methods of obtaining information. However, this wasn't a normal situation, and she offered no help when the security dispatcher looked past the scary one-eyed detective at her.

"I want names of *everyone* who went in Critical Care."

The dispatcher relented and scrolled through the files. The printer went hard at work, producing four pages of names from that morning. Most were the same, with doctors and nurses going in and out. It actually made it easy to narrow down possible suspects.

"Who's Bob Grass?"

"Janitor," the dispatcher said. "He's worked here for years."

"Where's he now?"

"You think he's a suspect?"

"Let me ask the questions. Where can I find him?"

The dispatcher pulled up the video feed of the janitor's office, then pulled up the log. "He went to the office around the time the shooting occurred."

"Any way out of there?"

"No. No doors or windows. Only way out is through there."

"Then it's not him," Luke said. "The person we're looking for will want to get out of dodge as quickly as possible." He combed through the list. "What about Amanda Don?"

"Nurse. I think she's in the ER hall..." the dispatcher pulled up the video feed. "Yeah, that's her right there." He pointed to a pudgy woman in scrubs standing in the corner.

Luke shook his head. *Not her.* His eye returned to the list. "Carl Harker?"

"Carl? I didn't know he was in today." The dispatcher looked over the list himself. "He works in Critical Care. Usually, I see him arrive on camera."

"You didn't notice him today?" Luke asked.

"I assumed I missed him but then... wait a sec." He brought up access files for Med/Surge. "That's right. I noticed his name here, in 5—"

"A," Luke completed his sentence. "Where Elise was staying."

"Where is she now?" an alarmed Brianna asked.

"She's at the lab performing tests on fish samples," Luke said.

"Then stop wasting time here," Brianna said. "If they're willing to go this far to eliminate her, they'll track her down at the lab."

"Interesting to know where exactly she was staying to begin with..." Luke said.

"Pardon?" Brianna said.

Luke didn't answer. "Get as much background on our shooter as we can."

"You do realize *I* am the superior rank, right?" Brianna replied. She then sighed. "Already on it."

Luke turned his attention back to the dispatcher. "Where can I get information on Dr. Carl Harker?"

"I can pull it up for you. Might lose my job by doing that, but..."

"Just say I threatened to hit you," Luke said.

"Why do I have a feeling that I wouldn't be lying by saying that?" the dispatcher asked.

"You're catching on quick," Luke said.

The dispatcher printed the info out and handed it to him.

"We need someone to pick up Elise. She has to be under police protection until this is straightened out."

"Yeah, sure. You do that," Luke said. The Captain picked up on the reluctance in his voice.

"You have a problem with police protection?" she asked. Luke had the face of someone on the verge of taking an assignment he really didn't want, but knew he had to do.

"How do you think these people knew exactly where to look? The hospital doesn't give out this information. The news didn't even know. Yet, this Dr. Harker guy knew Elise was in 5A."

"What are you suggesting?"

"You don't want me to answer that," Luke said.

"No, something tells me I don't," Brianna replied. "What I *do* want is for you to pick up Elise before you do anything else."

"I'm going to investigate a potential crime scene," Luke said.

"She'll be safer with you than with anyone else," Brianna said.

"Don't need her hindering me."

"*Luke*!"

"Fine." He was out the door in an instant.

As he stepped outside, he took another moment to study the area. He saw several damaged vehicles, a couple of ambulances and Fire/Rescue personnel. He heard shouting in the middle of it all. Not from a wounded or grieving person, but from Detective Norton.

"That son of a bitch shot up my car. Got holes in the windows, door, one in the hood. Agh! That crooked piece of shit."

Luke smiled. *Looks like there's at least ONE casualty.* He glanced about. Nobody was getting treated. All those bullets had been fired, yet he saw no indication that anyone was dead or severely injured.

He snapped his fingers at a fireman to get his attention.

"What can I do for you, Detective?"

"How many casualties came from this, not counting the shooter?" Luke asked.

The fireman shook his head. "None, actually. There were a few close calls and a couple of people caught a few nicks from spread shot, but overall, nothing serious. Thank God he was a bad shot."

"Yeah…thank God," Luke said.

CHAPTER 39

It took forever for Luke to get out of that parking lot and even longer to get through the huge crowds of people assembling outside the hospital grounds. In his frustration, he questioned whether these people had jobs or hobbies, which in turn, led to a few remarks about the welfare system.

At least the Schmidt lab parking lot was fairly sparse, which brought a sense of relief. The hallways were quiet except for the murmurings of the staff. All worries were centered around the events circulating the news cycle. One of the techs recognized Luke and agreed to take him to Elise's office.

Nobody answered when they knocked on the door. Luke was about to kick it off its hinges when someone came around the corner and stated she was doing tests in the lab. He let himself in and found her wearing a facemask and gloves, peering into a microscope.

"I told you to wait in your office," he said.

She looked over at him. "I told *you* not to come in here without a mask and goggles."

"You never said that."

"I printed that sign," she said, pointing at the door behind him. He glanced at the warning, then back at her.

"Listen, cupcake, my sense of humor is the only one that matters while we're paired together."

She looked up from the microscope. "Paired together?"

"Don't flatter yourself. It's protective custody."

"What happened at the hospital?"

"You heard the story. 'Crazed gunman opened fire at a crowd.'"

Elise peered back into the microscope. "Something tells me you don't believe it."

"I believe the actions. Not sure about the 'crazed' part," Luke said. "The suspect is dead."

Elise looked up again. "What?!"

"Someone injected something in his IV. That's what the shooting was about—to get the cops away from his door. Whoever that person was, they intended to pay you a visit as well, judging by the log readings from the badge they likely used." He held the door open with his back and held a hand to the hall. "Come on. We've got places to be."

"You brought me here to work," Elise said.

"I did, but there's something else I need to do, and I can't leave you by yourself."

"Then why don't you assign someone else to me in the meantime?" she asked. Luke didn't answer, yet, it wasn't due to his usual distain for conversation. He was looking away, deep in thought—the kind when someone can't come up with a convincing lie.

Elise waited, the impatience making her hands jitter. "Answer me!"

"They want you with an experienced cop…"

"Give me a break," she said. She stepped forward. "You think someone in the department is in on it?"

"You said it, not me."

For several seconds, Elise kept her eyes on him. Voices of Anthony Zach and the bait shop owner at the harbor echoed like spirits in her mind.

"According to the reports, his old buddy in L.A. got a bunch of money. One-Eye accused him of getting paid off by a human trafficking operation, which turned out to be bogus. Some think he was trying to get the cash for himself. Whatever the motivation, it all got out of hand, and a few vigilantes ambushed the partner, believing the scoop of him being a criminal. Heh, didn't surprise me at all that he was gunning for that fifty-grand reward today."

"How'd that injury happen?" Elise asked, pointing to her left eye.

"I believe it happened during the attack. I guess the guy deserves a tiny morsel of credit: he tried to save the partner, whatever his name was. Got cooked in the process. Guess he just wanted to blackmail him, not kill him. Everyone has the line they aren't willing to cross, I suppose. Still, serves him right for the false accusation. Takes a real dick to do that to his own partner."

Elise turned around. She never had a good poker face, and there was no other way of hiding her newfound doubt in him.

Her mind went into a civil war, as though controlled by two opposing entities.

He saved your ass. He's the one who asked questions when nobody else wanted to dig further.

Of course he saved your ass: he's a cop. He'd certainly get kicked off the force if he stood by idly while those assholes killed ya. And he's known for digging into cases for his own gratification. He hates the department, the department hates him—this could be another potential blackmailing case. He seems to enjoy making money…

Would he really put himself out there like that for mere gratification? He was raising questions about the shark attack even when the white was brought in.

"Hey!"

Luke's voice snapped her from the trance. Elise turned around. "Sorry. Was thinking about…something—" *Get back on topic!* "Let's say you're right. How could they corrupt someone in your department so quickly?"

"This group has deep pockets. And who's to say there isn't anyone in our department not already corrupt? Or in financial distress? These idiots are easy to weed out."

"Are they?"

Luke noticed the way she was looking at him, and it wasn't flattering.

"Yes. They are."

"What evidence do you have that suggests a fellow cop is feeding information to these guys?" she asked.

"The fact that they knew where you were," Luke said.

"They could've gotten that from the hospital staff."

"It was off-record for the short term," Luke said. "We're capable of working out those deals with the local hospitals if we have a person in protective custody. Only person who knew your location was in our department."

Elise nodded. At least that made a little bit of sense. Still, it didn't quell the storm raging within her. "I don't want anything to do with this police conspiracy! I just want the damn shark dead."

"Like I said before, you need a shrink," Luke said.

"Like you're one to talk," she replied. Her finger pointed at his face as though it had a conscience of its own.

"You sought *me* out, lady," he said.

"Because I wanted the fish dead and I figured you were the only one who wouldn't think I was insane."

"You really don't know me then, do ya?"

"No. I don't," Elise replied. "Perhaps I can forgive myself for having shitty judgement. You don't know what it's like to have someone you love slaughtered right before your very eyes. And to know it was all your fault."

Luke stood quiet to let Elise regain control of herself. In that time, he felt that all-too-familiar nerve flare-up. He winced briefly, his eyepatch obscuring the squinting of his left eye.

Elise exhaled sharply. "Sorry."

"You done?"

"When we find and kill the shark—the *right* shark, I will be." She took a breath, then fixed her posture. "You want the criminals arrested. I want the shark dead. Luckily, they're one and the same. Sooner we solve this case, the better."

"Took the words right out of my mouth," Luke said. "Works for me. I hate conversations."

Elise held her hand to the microscope. "Then let me spare you by letting you have a look for yourself." Luke took a look. All he saw was a glob of blue, red, and green, and oddly shaped cells.

He looked up at her. "Ha-ha, very funny. What the hell am I looking at?"

"Some of the tissue samples from the white," Elise said. "The thing is *loaded* with steroids and GMOs. I'm running some tests to be sure, but I'm quite certain the shark was not record-size by nature's will."

Luke stood up straight, but still gazed at the sample as though about to interrogate it. "To make a shark that big artificially takes time, so it's not like they ballooned the bastard up to cover their tracks—they *already* had it on standby. Why? What the hell did they have to gain with loading a great white with growth hormones?" He looked at Elise. "Are great whites a delicacy or something?"

"No. They actually have very little nutritional content."

"Then what's the point?"

"*You're* the detective."

The desire to smoke crept into Luke's throat. Plus the need for whiskey. Looking at Elise, those desires were only to intensify the longer he was stuck with her. Sooner he finished this case, the better.

"You're right. Time to seek out some clues. Come on."

CHAPTER 40

The house was a two-story brick building with a three-thousand square-foot backyard. The front door was shut as were the windows. In its driveway was an SUV. In the thirty minutes Luke and Elise observed the property, they saw no movement.

During that wait, Luke repeatedly checked the address to make sure it matched that on the printed paper. There was no mistake—this was indeed Dr. Carl Harker's address.

Elise, who was anxious at the start of the stakeout, was now growing bored. "So, are we gonna wait all day and hope someone shows?"

"Forgive me for playing it a little safe," Luke said. "It's not typical police procedure to bring a civilian to investigate a possible crime scene."

Elise stopped herself from asking 'Why not just have someone else investigate?' The answer was clear: Luke didn't trust anyone else on the department and, knowing hospital procedure, he likely didn't get this personal info through legal means.

Luke checked the cylinder on his revolver, then holstered it. Before stepping out, he reached under the car and pulled out a metal case locked with a padlock. He opened it, revealing a Bersa Thunder 380.

"I'm assuming you know how to shoot a pistol," he said, extending the weapon to her.

Elise took it. "Let's go to the range right now. I'll go toe-to-toe with you any day of the week." She checked the mag and chambered a round, then shot him a glare. "I've handled more impressive weapons than this little thing."

"Express your girl-power to someone that cares," Luke said. "Besides, it's loaded with hydra-shock hollow points. If you know anything about guns, you know they'll do the trick." Elise bit her lip, checked the bullets in the spare mag, then nodded. Luke stepped out of the vehicle. "Stay here."

"What? You expect me to wait?"

"Yes. I do. I'm stupid enough to bring you here, but not stupid enough to have you investigate the house with me."

"Right…and if someone comes up to the car?"

Luke made a finger pistol, made a 'bang' sound, then slammed the door shut.

He approached the house, cautiously watching the windows, as well as those in the neighboring houses. The next door neighbors seemed to be off to work. There were no vehicles in their driveways. The neighborhood was quiet, typical for the middle of a Monday.

A knock on the front door brought no results.

Luke peered through the living room window. The lights were off. He had to put his face up to the glass for a good look. He could see what appeared to be an entertainment center on the right side. There was no television. However, there were some items scattered on the floor. He recognized a lamp and some picture frames.

Luke's hand was on his revolver now. He tried the door. As he figured, it was locked. He moved around the side and hopped the backyard fence. Walking along the back of the house, he spotted a broken window near the kitchen.

"Totally called it."

He made sure to snap a photo of the window with his phone before scraping away the shards of glass on the frame.

"Hello? Amadea Police Department. Anyone inside?" He heard a muffled groan from somewhere within. Luke had heard enough gagged and bound individuals in his career to know this person had duct-tape over his mouth. He crawled through the window and pointed his revolver into the empty room. Household items were scattered on the floor. At the edge of the kitchen was the family room.

A man in his mid-forties squirmed on the floor. His hands were tied behind his back, his ankles tied together, and his mouth covered in duct-tape. His forehead was bruised and swollen.

Luke knelt by him and ripped the tape off. "Howdy, partner. Let me guess: your name's Carl?"

"Yes. Carl Harker. I'm a—"

"—Doctor, I know." Luke cut through the bindings with a pocketknife. Dr. Harker sat up and pressed a hand to his forehead. "Don't get up. I'll get someone to have a look at you."

"I've been on the floor all day," Dr. Harker said. He stood up, put a hand on the counter to help balance himself, then gazed at his house. "Jesus! Those jackasses wrecked the place."

Luke combed through the house, then opened the front door. He waved at Elise, who exited the Dodge Journey and stepped into the house.

"Call 9-1-1," he said. "Use the landline. Tell them to send an ambulance. Possible head trauma." Elise went to the phone and dialed. Luke continued searching the house. Two televisions were missing, one from the living room, the other from the bedroom. Laundry drawers and closets were open, their contents spilled out. "Tell me what happened, Doc."

"Not much to tell. I was up at four. I was getting some reading in when I heard the glass break. I went to investigate, then *boom*. Took a hit to the head and the rest is hazy after that. I just remember seeing a masked figure." He grimaced. "Forty-six years old, I've *never* experienced a break-in in my life. Like you can't buy a television for cheap these days…"

"Don't take it too personal, Doctor," Luke said. "You work at Amadea General. You mind telling me where you keep your work badge?"

Harker led him down a hall. "In my dresser… aww, you've got to be kidding me!" He looked at all of his belongings tossed about the bedroom. "The hell did they gain from this?! You'd think my house was a big pepper shaker!"

Elise stepped into the hall. "Dispatch is sending units over. So, what happened?" She and Luke watched Dr. Harker check his drawer, unable to locate his work items.

"Just as I suspected," Luke said. "They broke in, made it look like a simple B&E so it wasn't obvious what their intent was. They came here for his badge."

"Who came here?" Dr. Harker said.

"Not sure, Doc."

"Why'd they want my badge?"

"To get access to a patient."

Elise followed him to the front yard. "You think they were counting on you putting the pieces together?"

"I think they knew they were on a clock and had to come up with something fast," Luke said. "When you have to come up with a solution on the fly, you're willing to get a little messy, as long as you don't leave clues to your identity. The cops will dust for prints, but knowing the kind of people we're dealing with, they had gloves on. And now our only lead is dead."

Two cop cars and an ambulance arrived. Luke directed them to the house, then proceeded to walk to his vehicle.

"There's gotta be another lead," Elise said. "What about the hospital cameras? Surely you'll be able to track down the guy who killed the gunman."

"We might get his face, but we won't get an ID," Luke said. "That guy was a professional contractor. Unless we have him tied to a chair with electric rods embedded in his thighs, he's probably not the type to talk. Let alone be caught alive."

"You're making a lot of assumptions."

"I'm merely stating facts based on experience."

"Sounds more like you're giving up."

Luke got in his vehicle. "I didn't say that. Not yet, at least."

"There's gotta be a way we can track these people down HAS to be a way!" Elise said.

"Lady, you need to come to grips with the fact that you may never get retribution on that fish."

"Helicoprion," she said.

"Whatever. Doesn't change a thing. You're mad that your nephew's dead. I get it. Even if you do kill the fish, he'll still be dead. I say it s time you work on *that.*"

"Yeah? Well, I say it's time for you to think harder. What other breadcrumbs have these people left?"

"None. We can't track the bullets or the weapons, which could've come from anywhere. The bodies identified aren't currently connected with any organization. The yacht's destroyed. The fishing boat's gone. There's no record of who bought it. I don't even have a photograph to reference."

Elise perked up. "Photographs…" She thought of the previous day when she left the harbor after the great white was brought in. "Anthony Zach."

"Lovely. You had to bring up that asshole," Luke said.

"I saw him take a picture of my plate when I left the pier."

"Yeah, he does that. That's how he knew where to tell you where to find me," Luke said. "He does that with everybody. Has a few ex-cops who know how to look up people's data, and he's savvy enough to cover his tracks. That's how he digs up dirt on so many people."

"He was there at the pier. When the boat came in," Elise said. "The boat has a serial number…"

Luke leaned his head back against his seat. "Oh, great."

"'Oh great'? Isn't this a good thing? We might have a lead!"

"It means me talking to dipshit. I'd rather slam my left nut in a car door."

"Luke, start the damn car!"

CHAPTER 41

It was around noon when Glenn's throat started feeling scratchy. He didn't pay much attention to it—it felt like a typical mild flu. It wasn't enough to distract him from the important task of playing *Xbox*.

By two-o'clock, he was coughing more frequently. No longer did the flu feel mild. The fatigue was starting to set in. Though not quite nauseous, he had lost all appetite. Then came the headache.

"Malcolm, if you got me sick, I'm gonna kill you," he said. As the afternoon went on, the headache and fatigue worsened It wasn't any worse than the typical stomach flu. Glenn was more annoyed than concerned. This was *not* how he wanted to spend his last few days of summer break. If anything, couldn't this have waited until school was back in session? Could've extended the break a bit.

He thought about texting his parents. Mom was still at work. He didn't understand what was going on, but apparently it was a very serious case, which meant she'd likely be working late. And today was Monday, meaning Dad was going to work late at the shop. Most days in the week, he had an employee watch the shop from five-to-nine, but they weren't available on Monday nights. Not wanting to hire another employee, Dad simply accepted that Monday was his sixteen-hour day.

Glenn didn't want to bother them. If there was anything he understood about his parents, it was to not bother them when they were busy at work unless it was an emergency. A stomach flu was not an emergency, though it was damn annoying. Even more annoying would be the questions he'd then receive from Mom and Dad. "Why didn't you say anything?" "Don't forget to take your medicine." "You need me to run to the store?"

The teenager tried to put the illness from his mind. Maybe it would just run its course and be gone by morning. He only had a slight fever so far. A little Tylenol should do the trick. If nothing else, it'd at least grant him the excuse to play on the *Xbox* all day without his parents commenting on how he wasted a fine day indoors.

Maybe this is a blessing in disguise.

His stomach tightened, and Glenn rushed to the bathroom. That sentiment was lost as quickly as his lunch.

CHAPTER 42

"Well color me shocked. If Jesus Himself told me the day would come when Detective Luke Jansen would come begging *me* for help, I would've told Him to fuck off. And I consider myself a Christian!"

Coming here to the Channel 8 News office physically hurt Luke.

What am I doing talking to this schmuck?

"Well, keep waiting. Keep in mind; I don't beg."

Elise was standing beside him. She was watching the room as the conversation took place. Some of the news staff took the liberty to snap photos of the exchange. It was obvious they planned on concocting some sort of story from this visit.

She put a hand on Luke's shoulder. "Maybe it's better *I* do the talking. You're more likely to give these people enough material to draw up a hundred stories about you."

"Trust me, they don't need material," Luke said.

Elise shook her head and faced Anthony. "Listen, Mr. Zach. Can we please speak privately in your office?"

He leaned back in the cubicle seat. "Why? Afraid of everyone overhearing your request?"

"Don't worry. We know you'll make it known to the world," Luke said.

Elise sneered at him. "Shh!" Turning back to Anthony, she took a breath to keep her own blood pressure down. "Please, this is very important."

"Since when do you work for the police?" Anthony said. "I never knew Detective Jansen to rely on outside help! You're a marine biologist, so is he investigating the strange events of fish washing up dead? Clearly, you can't still be working on the shark attack case. It's dead! It's been proven that it's the shark." He looked at Luke. "Despite someone telling them they caught the wrong fish."

"Wouldn't you like to know?" Luke remarked.

"Yes. I'll admit it for him," Elise said. "We *are*. Or rather, the people who brought the shark in. You heard about the shooting, right?"

"Which one?" Anthony said.

Oh, right. "Last night's shooting. On the beach."

"I heard something went down. Possible drug deal gone wrong," Anthony said.

"Where'd you hear that narrative?" Luke said.

Anthony smirked at him. "I'm not at liberty to say. We protect our sources."

"Listen, listen, listen..." Elise raised her palms to deescalate the rising tempers. "We're asking for *one* thing. Just one. You were at the pier yesterday. I know there's a ton of footage left on the cutting room floor. We just want to look at it."

"Why? What do these fishermen have to do with last night's shooting?"

"One of the gunmen was in that crew," Elise said. Anthony's grin faded. He studied her with his eyes, determining whether or not she was bullshitting him. "I was the one they were shooting at." Anthony was even more interested.

"Why the hell were they shooting at you?"

"Because—" She stopped herself from telling the truth. "I might have witnessed criminal activity. I can't say what exactly, it's part of the case." She pointed her thumb at Luke. "He saved my ass. So, if nothing else, please give him a little respect."

"I was aware of that part," Anthony said. "A shooting last night. A shooting this morning. It's been a busy couple of days for you, Detective."

Luke leaned toward him. "Listen, weasel, we lost our main lead. We have nothing left. I need to see the footage of that boat." Now, cameras were clicking across the room. It was the only reason Luke didn't grab Anthony by the shirt collar and strangle him until he got the footage.

"You know what the boat looks like? What good would the footage do you?"

"I need the serial number," Luke said.

"Was the boat owner part of the gang of shooters?"

"Yes, obviously."

Anthony put his hands behind his head, maintaining his relaxed posture. "I mean, did you *see* him? Or the boat at the scene of the crime, for that matter."

"Of course we did," Luke said.

Anthony looked at Elise. She had broken eye contact. "I'm calling bullshit on that one."

"No, we didn't see the boat captain. It was a different group entirely," she said.

"Then I can't be giving out personal information on non-suspects," Anthony said. "Such things are—illegal, some would say." He chuckled. "Maybe that's your plan, Mr. Jansen. Get me to commit a crime? You'd love nothing more than to arrest me."

"That last sentence might be right," Luke said. "Like you care about standards. You think I don't know how she found my address?"

"Ah-ah!" Anthony rose his hands. "I did not provide your address."

Elise sighed. "He's right…technically."

"Technically is all that matters," Anthony said. "Besides, shouldn't your department have that guy's name and information?"

"It's fake," Luke said.

"How do you know that? I heard the city's check cleared," Anthony said.

"It's a fake alias, made by people with deep connections."

Anthony's grin was frozen on his face. "This keeps getting better and better! What makes you believe that? You admitted the guy was not part of the group of gunmen."

Luke turned around, swore under his breath, then spun toward Anthony. "Are you gonna give me what I want or not? Or am I going to have to beat it out of you?"

Anthony reached for the phone. "Maybe I should call the Mayor's Office."

"Wait! Please," Elise said. She took Luke by the arm and led him out of the room. He shook her loose as they entered the hall. "For the love of God! Is this how you usually work?"

"Like you know the first thing about police work. Dealing with morons is not the same as peering into a microscope, Doc."

"No, it's not. But treating Anthony like he's aiding and abetting a crime is not going to get anything done."

"Oh? What would you have me do? Buy him chocolates? Take him out to lunch? Get him an *Amazon* gift card."

"Might get you further than acting like 'Mr. Tough Guy'. He might be a jerk, but he's not a criminal."

"He's a reporter. Not much better."

"Why? Because of how they portray you? Can't imagine why anyone would think you're anything less than an angel."

"Can't imagine it myself," he muttered. He paused as someone came down the hallway with a coffee carrier in hand. She stopped after taking notice of the bizarre conversation. "What are you looking at?!"

The employee darted into the cubicle system.

Elise turned red. "Case and point!"

"She's a nosy reporter."

"She was the *coffee girl*!"

Luke shrugged. "She should've brought me some."

"Is this what you do? Alienate yourself from the world, then hide behind a sense of humor?"

"Trust me, kid. The world's worth alienating yourself from."

"First of all, don't call me kid. I'm only a few years younger than you. Second, there *is* good in the world. There's no reason to isolate yourself."

"Yeah? Then why are you with me?"

Elise stammered momentarily. "I—your captain assigned me to you."

"Yeah, after you decided to stick your nose in where it didn't belong. Almost got yourself killed in the process. Wouldn't be the case if you turned to the oh-so-good world for help," Luke said. "Yet, you chased after *me*. Surely, you have friends and family. Shouldn't you be hanging with *them* instead of playing detective?"

They stood in silence.

Elise seemed incapable of replying. She looked like someone who was completely alone and bitter about it. The look on her face said it all. *Who am I to make these comments? I've been so busy with my career, the only real friend I had was my nephew.*

Luke, on the other hand, knew he jabbed a sensitive area by bringing him up. "Look, my bad for mentioning Chase…"

"Chad."

Luke looked at the ceiling and gave his blood pressure a moment to settle. "Point is, you shouldn't have put yourself in this situation to begin with."

"Someone had to figure out what's going on."

"You couldn't give a seal's fart about this weird outbreak that's occurring. You just care about killing some prehistoric fish!"

Another moment of silence passed between them. This one seemed to have no end in sight.

They heard the sound of a clearing throat, then noticed Anthony poking his head out the door. His eyes were wide and unblinking, beneath them was a grin simultaneously demonstrating fascination and shock.

"Prehistoric shark?"

Luke closed his eye. *Great!*

"Give us another minute, will ya?" Elise said.

Anthony hesitated. He was still taking in what he just overheard. "Meet me in my office." He disappeared back into the cubicle system.

Luke waved a hand at the door. "See what you did there?"

"Yes. I got the meeting with Anthony to proceed. You ought to be thanking me."

"As much as I thank the ants that show up in my kitchen sink."

"Probably because you don't wash it." Now, it was Elise pausing to control her blood pressure. "You know? It's not that you don't make the right calls. It's the *way* you conduct yourself."

"Gets results."

"Not all the time. Not here. You came to this place READY to pick a fight with Anthony. Yes, yes, I get it. He can be a nosey dick. And it sounds like the two of you have quite the history. But can you attempt to reach across the aisle?" She waited for him to make another sarcastic remark, and was surprised when he didn't make one.

"What do you expect me to do? Ask nice?"

"YES, actually," Elise said. She took a deep breath. "Please."

Luke let the slightest hint of a laugh slip. *Demonstrating.* What he wanted to deny was its effectiveness. "Fine. I'll play nice—ish."

"I guess I'll take it. When all you've gotten is mule piss, even light beer tastes good."

Luke tried to make sense of that comparison as he followed her to Anthony's office.

When they got there, he was waiting in his chair with a pen in hand. "Let's get right to it."

"You planning to take this on air? Or you planning to write another article?" Luke said. He noticed the wrinkles in Elise's face as she struggled to withhold a scowl.

Nice—ish.

"Mr. Zach…this is an extremely important and time sensitive matter. If you could help, I'd…greatly appreciate it." Those words made him want to vomit, as did the look on Anthony's face.

"I want to hear this news of a prehistoric shark," Anthony Zach said.

"I can't confirm whether we're dealing with a prehistoric shark, but I can promise you that you're in for the best story of your life if you help out," Luke said. "This will make headlines across the nation."

"I've already got the lead scoop on plenty of stuff," Anthony said.

"Nothing like this," Luke said. "There's a connection between the gunmen at the beach, the attack at the hospital, our now-dead suspect—who died *during* that shooting…" That got Anthony's attention. "And now, we've got some kind of viral outbreak. Dead fish washing ashore. A doctor whose house was broken into, made to look like a burglary…yet, it was *his* badge that allowed someone access to our injured suspect. *During* the shooting. Not a coincidence."

"Tell him about the white," Elise said.

Anthony was tapping his pen to his chin. "What about it?"

"The fish was loaded with growth hormones and steroids. Why? We don't know. But it didn't get that big simply from eating tuna. Somebody did that to the fish, and whatever the reason is, it's connected to what's happening here."

"I did x-rays on various specimens collected from the beach," Elise said. "They have died of an infection—the same infection that's spreading across this city. At least, that's what I believe."

"We need answers ASAP. People are dying from this thing, Anthony. This is bigger than me solving a case or you breaking a huge story." It felt odd to speak with the reporter without burying him in a hail of insults. By the look on Anthony's face, it was equally odd for him.

"Has anyone that's been infected recovered so far?"

"Not to my knowledge," Luke said.

"Has there been any word from the federal government?"

"Not yet. It's still only a local issue, but it's accelerating quickly. Besides, do you *really* want the feds in charge of this?"

"That would give me more material." Anthony chuckled. His smile quickly faded. He stood up and went for the door. "Come with me."

He led them to the fourth floor, where the bulk of the video editing took place. It was a large room with dozens of computers and editing staff. Anthony moved to the back row and beckoned to the editor stationed there to leave.

"Mr. Zach? I gotta get this done. We have a show at five and—"

"Take a hike, Tim! I need to do something. Are the files from yesterday still on here?"

"Yes…"

"Alright. Give us a few minutes."

Anthony took a seat, then gestured for his visitors to sit down on the adjacent chairs. He clicked on a few files, combed through the dates and locations, then clicked on the one for the harbor. A long line of unedited footage started playing.

Right away, they saw Anthony's face on the screen. It was B-roll footage.

"The whales on the bus go 'round the town! 'Round the town! 'Round the town. The whales on the bus go 'round the town! All day long!"

Anthony quickly killed the audio and fast forwarded the video. Noticing the looks on his visitors' faces, he laughed nervously. "I have a two-year old nephew. He likes me to sing—never mind."

They continued watching the footage play out. Luke leaned closer to the screen, watching accelerated footage of the reporter attempting to do a karate kick, only to fall on his ass.

"The hell were you trying to do there?"

"Alright, sometimes when we're on site, we have time to kill before we can actually work. We get bored!" Anthony said. "We're people too. We do stupid shit sometimes."

"Gosh, I need to sneak in here one of these days," Luke said. "Switch the files right before you go on air… 'we're gonna go to footage of the president's speech from this morning… *Wheels on the bus…*'"

Elise turned to laugh.

Even Anthony smirked. "For your information…it's *whales*. It's a different version…ah, finally!" He stopped the footage after the boat arrived. *Namesake*. He used the mouse to skip the unnecessary footage, then slowed it after the fishermen arrived at the pier. "Which one did you encounter last night?"

Luke pointed to the one on the boat. "That one. He's dead now, and not by my gunshot wound."

"Hang on a sec…" Anthony located the snippet where the cameraman got the serial number of the vessel. "Here we are. BEA 53719 B6 06."

"Good. I need another favor from you," Luke said.

"I had a feeling you would."

"I know you have access to databases. Look up who this boat belongs to for me."

Anthony rotated in his seat. "Can't you do that yourself at the station?"

"I'd rather not."

"Mind if I ask why?"

"I do, in fact." That got him nowhere. Accepting he had to give a little to take a little, he groaned. "I think there's someone in the department who's covering for this group. Probably with financial gain."

"You *know* this?"

"I suspect it." Luke knew how he sounded. "Listen, I'm not accusing anyone specifically. But I need answers fast." It came time for the word he absolutely hated. "Please."

Anthony stood up. "I'll deny ever helping you if any bullshit is flung my way. Back to my office."

Once there, he pulled out a separate laptop. "Got this from an old police buddy. Bribed him a hefty fee to grant me access to the state's databases. I can look up license plates, boat serial numbers…and I'll delete this in a heartbeat if you decide to get smart."

"Why you helping, then?" Elise asked.

"You said people are dying. I'm not completely heartless. You are telling the truth? Yes?"

"Yes."

Anthony typed the serial code in, then perked up when he saw the file. "Gary Starch."

"Gary Starch? You sound like you know that name," Luke said.

"I do. He's a doctor—an immunologist. Owns a medical research firm: Starch Industries. They develop pharmaceuticals and—"

"Vaccines?"

The reporter looked at the detective. "Yes. His firm was the first American organization to develop an Ebola vaccine. He developed a successful vaccine for the African Zika virus. Some say he's had a hand in halting other serious outbreaks. I don't know too much more than that."

"That's more than enough for me." Luke went for the door. "Tell you what; if I find anything big, you'll be one of the first to know."

Anthony smiled. It was the closest to a 'thank you' he'd ever get from Luke Jansen. "Good luck."

The staff in the cubicle system were surprised that the meeting had gone so smoothly. Luke assumed Anthony would spin the conversation to make it more dramatic, but he didn't care. He got what he needed.

At the parking lot, Elise finally broke the silence. "What's next?"

Luke boarded his Dodge. "I'm thinking."

She got in the passenger seat. "We have a new lead."

"We? What we? I'm the cop. You're just tagging along for the ride."

"Right. Like you would've gotten any results without my help." She was triumphant in making that statement. "The boat belongs to Gary Starch. An immunologist? Vaccine manufacturer? Happens to own a boat…which happens to show up around the time a weird outbreak is occurring? One hell of a coincidence if you ask me."

"And someone with deep pockets," Luke said. Elise understood the reason for his apprehension.

"Is that serial number enough to get a warrant on him?"

"Maybe. But the judge will need more convincing. For me to be able to do that, I need more information on this guy."

"Where can we get that? The internet? Can't authenticate that in a short period of time."

"No. We need someone with knowledge of medical firms." Luke's face tensed.

"What?" Elise said. "Have to talk to somebody else you don't like?" He glared at her, then started the ignition.

"Buckle your damn seatbelt. Or don't. I really don't care."

She sniggered. "Got a headache? I've got ibuprofen for that."

"Unless you got beer, don't offer me anything."

He steered out of the driveway and sped to the coroner's office.

CHAPTER 43

"What do you want, Luke?"

Rupert McGibbeny looked as happy to see the detective as a rottweiler was to see the vet.

"Doc. Mind if we come in?"

McGibbeny looked past him. "Who's the lady?"

"Consultant," Luke said.

"She's definitely not a corpse. That's all I deal with around here, Detective." McGibbeny didn't budge from his office door. "Again, I'll ask: what do you want, Luke?"

"Knowledge."

"Won't find any here. Unless you've killed another dope-head."

"Maybe. The day's still young enough." He saw Elise's piercing gaze in his peripheral vision. *Don't go in guns-blazing.* "I'm looking for certain medical advice."

"What medical info would you possibly be interested in? Got a stomach ulcer? Quit drinking that damn whiskey. Especially on an empty stomach."

"What the hell is the deal with you two?" Elise said.

McGibbeny pointed a finger at Luke. "You realize who you're tagging along with, right?"

"Yes. He's a real saint, I know, but we really do need your help, sir."

"Ha! Real saint indeed! You knew he almost got me terminated? Claimed I covered up evidence during an examination procedure."

Elise aimed a disgusted look at Luke.

"Oh, don't fall for that crap," Luke said. "I didn't say he 'covered-up' evidence. I said he was looking for the wrong thing. It was a suicide case. I believed otherwise, based on the alcohol in the victim's house. What I discovered was that he kept his grocery receipts, and there was no record of alcoholic items."

"There was booze in his system, Luke."

"Oh, come on! Like someone couldn't have forced that down his pipe."

"There were no signs of strangulation."

"Financial records don't lie."

"They can by omission. Perhaps he filled his canteen at a different watering hole. Plenty of liquor stores around here, Luke. You know this—better than anyone."

Luke tilted his head like a predator ready to pounce. "Hey, Doc? You didn't happen to sew any personal items to your patients today, did you? Didn't stich the edge of your jacket to some guy's leg by any chance?"

"I never—alright, I've got a busy schedule. Up until now, I was dreading it, but maybe it's a blessing in disguise. Have a nice day." McGibbeny slammed the door.

"Fantastic police work," Elise said. "I can only imagine how you act in court."

"Jury loves my ass," Luke said, turning around to leave.

"I'm sure they gush all over you. Haven't we been over this at Local 8?"

"Hey, *you're* the one who brought up old wounds and made him lose his shit. Christ! You've known me for twenty-four hours, and suddenly you're my mother?"

"No, I—" Elise froze, looked away, then closed her eyes. "I'm sorry. You're right, I don't have the right to cast judgement. I've never done this, and maybe I'm still a little shaky after last night. I've killed two people, and I've never done that before. It's not a natural feeling. You, on the other hand, seem used to it."

Luke munched on a piece of jerky. "As long as the right people end up dead."

Elise looked at the scarring on his face then dwelled on his words.

"I just *really* want to get to the bottom of this case. And these feuds are getting in the way of that."

After a moment of internal resistance, Luke faced the door again and knocked. "Doc? This is a serious matter and you might be the only one that might help me find answers."

They could hear McGibbeny groaning on the other side. He opened the door a crack. "What serious matter? I'm a coroner."

"Yeah, *now* you are. In the two decades leading up to your position here, you worked in medical tourism. You've spent time in Asia, Africa, South America…bunch of other places I don't have time to name."

"How do you know that?" McGibbeny said.

"I always check the background of anyone I work with," Luke said. "What can I say? I'm a busybody."

"Damn right you are," McGibbeny said.

"I need your help, Doc. I'll even say please—but only because *she's* making me." Luke pointed at Elise. That drew a smirk from McGibbeny.

"Fine. Can't be long. I've got appointments with very important patients."

Elise stepped in behind Luke. "Many appointments? Do people die that frequently?"

"They do today."

"From the outbreak?"

"Unfortunately, that's what it's looking like." He sat on his side of the desk. "I've taken four showers today already. My hands have had so much sanitizer that they feel like they might burn off."

"This disease—have you seen anything like it before?" Luke asked.

"It's a virus, that's for sure. Seems to vary mildly in its attack, depending on the victim. But it attacks the respiratory and circulatory system. Builds up masses in the lungs like a cancer. Attacks the throat, specifically the airway. Heart gets infected. Travels through the blood. It's fatal. It's bad. It's spreading. Watch what you touch."

"Has there been any word of anyone catching this thing and surviving it?" Luke asked.

"No. Antibiotics and a very high dose of vitamin C and D seem to slow it down a bit. But so far, nobody's recovered." McGibbeny leaned back and crossed one leg over the other. "You seem pretty interested in this pandemic for a detective. Planning to arrest the virus?"

"I'm working on that special power," Luke retorted.

McGibbeny chuckled. "If only it were that easy to get rid of it."

"How easy is it?" Luke asked. "What if a fella, say, Gary Starch were to swoop in and develop a vaccine? How quickly could he pull something like that off?" Luke noticed the shift in his eyes. That name had McGibbeny's attention.

"Haven't heard that name in a few years."

"You ever worked with him?" Elise asked.

McGibbeny pointed to the bookshelf. "See that book there? Brown spine with the crack near the top corner? Pull that out for me, would ya, Miss?" Elise grabbed the book and opened it. "Flip it to the...I think fifth page... Yep! That's him."

Luke and Elise gazed at the picture of a very tall man dressed in button shirt and trousers. He was a balding individual, wore glasses, standing near a hut with several medical personnel. The area was definitely Third World with a very hot climate.

"Where was this?" Luke asked.

"Sudan, during the yellow fever outbreak. Roughly a hundred-and-sixty-four people died. There was a shortage of medical personnel and supplies in that region, so my firm went over to assist. Turns out Starch Industries decided to do some charitable work."

"Is that sarcasm I hear?" Luke asked.

McGibbeny clenched his jaw, carefully choosing his words. "We received instructions to use their vaccine supply. And *only* theirs."

"Does this guy make a habit of showing up where outbreaks are occurring?" Luke asked.

McGibbeny nodded. "The measles outbreak in Vietnam; Western African Ebola; his firm did work to contain the Nipah virus in Kerala."

"What about an African village called Marikana?" Luke asked.

McGibbeny hesitated. "What's your interest in Marikana?"

"Just curious."

"Well, there's nothing official. Definitely nothing I was a part of. Though, in one case, I was supposed to be. There was a viral outbreak, though I'm not sure of the strain. Hundreds of people were reported dead. *Reported*."

"How long did it take to get contained?" Elise asked.

"Two months? Not sure exactly. The news from that area was sparse at best. Word is a lot of people died."

"Sounds like a pretty bad virus," Luke said. "Interesting it didn't expand from that region."

"Especially since no other clinics were allowed. Officially, at least. And that order was from the South African government." McGibbeny checked his watch.

"A clinic doctor I worked with in Sudan had mentioned something about going to Marikana. He was under employment by Starch. Interestingly, no official records turned up from that operation."

"What happened to that friend of yours?" Luke asked.

"Turned up dead in his home two weeks after the outbreak. Police report stated trauma from falling down steps. No wife, no kids to mourn him. Good guy though."

"Good guy—good enough to sound an alarm on a company's wrongdoing?" Luke asked.

"Maybe. We kept in touch, but it wasn't like we were neighbors."

Luke noticed that McGibbeny didn't challenge the notion of Starch Industries potentially doing shady business. "Starch Industries develops vaccines and medicine, right?"

"That's right."

"And such a thing takes a while, right?"

"Right. And mainly because of red tape."

"If you wanted to develop one quick, one might pay off a government who didn't give a shit about its citizens for the privilege of, say, test a new drug. And if things went wrong, hire a few guys to…" Luke made a finger pistol and 'fired'. He then chuckled. "But, of course, that's just silly, right?"

McGibbeny smiled. "About as silly as Operation Whitecoat, where the government injected infectious agents into soldiers so that they could study the effects on human anatomy. Or Chester M. Southam, who injected cancer cells into healthy individuals without their knowledge. Or how about Project MKUltra, run by our very own CIA? Or meningitis drugs that disabled two-hundred kids in Kano?"

Luke craved a cigar and a drink. He noticed Elise looking at the photographs in McGibbeny's book. Like him, she took notice of the fact that the doctor didn't seem bothered by the idea that they were making such wild claims surrounding Gary Starch, even if they were hypothetical.

"You worked with this man. What do you know about his character?"

"Deep voice. Really friendly face-to-face, at least he was with me. Doesn't dress too extravagantly—you wouldn't tell he was rich by looking at him. He enjoys the usual stuff rich guys like. Yachts, planes, girls. A few private islands along the west coast."

"Sounds like he's living the dream," Luke said. "When you were in Sudan, what kind of people were in his firm?"

"You asking if he's an affirmative action kind-of-guy?"

"I'm more interested about character."

McGibbeny shrugged. "He's got connections, and not only in medical fields. Hires his own security. Manages to make contracts with governments. Sponsors other research programs, including geographical ones."

"Geography?" Elise said.

"Yeah. Digs. Someone else I kept in touch with mentioned something about construction equipment being hauled to some place in South America. Word is Starch is digging up loads of limestone."

Luke smirked. "What the hell would he want with limestone?"

McGibbeny held his hands up. "Like I would know! I don't work for the guy."

"Any word on that other doctor you kept in touch with?"

"Haven't spoken to him in a year. Dropped off social media. Last I heard, he was on a trip to an outpost in Antarctica. Ice samples. Fits into that geographical fascination of Starch's. That's all I know on that guy. Hope I satisfied ya." McGibbeny checked his watch again. "Unless you have any other questions, I really do have to get going."

"Just one more," Luke said.

"Had a feeling you did."

"Yeah. Say if there was a mass outbreak of a deadly virus, how much money would result for the firm that develops an effective vaccine?"

The doctor thought for a moment. "It'd be paid through tax dollars, but for something really widespread... I'd say billions." McGibbeny looked out the window. "This is quickly becoming a serious outbreak. This'll be all over the nation by evening. You need anything from the grocery store, get it as soon as you leave here, because the panic buying is nearing."

Luke nodded. "The news...interesting how it seems we've already forgotten about these shark attacks, haven't we?"

"The population has a short memory, young man. Plus, not to minimize the victims of that shark attack—I did the autopsy on the ones from the Stuckey's beach after all—but this matter is a hell of a lot more serious."

Elise perked up. "You inspected some of the victims?"

"Yes, ma'am."

"Did those look like normal shark bites to you?"

McGibbeny shook his head. "Never seen anything like it. But there was bacterial evidence that it was a shark. Combine that with the numerous eyewitness sightings, not to mention the footage taken at South Beach. And, of course, the body that was brought in yesterday."

"Have those bodies been officially identified?" Luke asked.

"I'm not in charge of that. Detective Norton had them shipped to a lab in San Francisco where tests are being run. I do find it interesting that the dental structure got completely mangled, though."

"You and me both, Doc," Luke said.

McGibbeny stood up. "That's not my department, though." He went for the door, stopping just a few inches from the knob. He looked back at Luke. "Between us—it *is* odd that this happened following a bizarre series of shark attacks..." his gaze moved to Elise, "...which resulted in mutilation inconsistent with a great white. Even one as large as the specimen brought in." He twisted the knob and let them out. "Gary Starch has a main office in Seattle, though there are other facilities. Be careful. You asked about the people he hires—I don't think his security is from your typical firm. I think he hires specific people willing to do specific things, *particularly* if plans go wrong. Marikana wasn't the only site...as far as the rumors go. BE. CAREFUL."

"Thanks, Doc." Luke shook McGibbeny's hand then walked with Elise to the lot. The sunshine was only mildly refreshing, as the grim details of what they suspected made both of them sick to their stomachs.

"What's next?" Elise said.

"We do a little more hunting. Luckily, this can be done in my office. I just need to research private islands in the nearby region."

In the two hours following the meeting, Luke located a half dozen private islands on the coast of northern California and southern Oregon. What followed were a series of phone calls digging into the ownership of the nearest ones.

"Bingo." He spun in his seat and looked at Elise. "Son of a bitch has an island a hundred-and-twenty-five miles northwest of here." He picked his personal phone up again. "Captain. Meet me at the office."

CHAPTER 44

By late afternoon, Luke felt he had explained the details so much, he may as well write a book on it. There was a little pushback by Brianna Raye and Detective Norton, particularly regarding the probable cause.

"Everything you've stated about this Gary Starch guy is hearsay," Norton said. "So what if Dr. McGibbeny heard rumors from someone he used to work with?"

"Who ended up dead when he was about to blow the whistle," Luke said.

"Again, hearsay."

"Then how 'bout some evidence that hits a little harder? Like the tissue samples we took from the great white?"

"What about them?" Norton asked.

Luke glanced at Elise, allowing her to take center stage. She stood up from her seat and provided a faxed printout from the lab.

"These are the results from the analysis on the shark's blood and tissue that was sent to me. There are large traces of growth hormones and steroids in its system. I can't even recognize the signatures of these GMOs. It's like they're new. Experimental, even. But they *are* man-made, and they *are* the reason that shark was so damn big."

"Sounds like something a medical research facility might experiment with," Luke said.

"Gary Starch does medicine. Not food production," Brianna said.

"There's talk about the effects on humans that consume GMOs in food," Elise said. "Maybe he's trying to figure something out to counteract that."

"Interesting theory. Unfortunately, it's nothing a judge will listen to. We can't make warrants based on rumors and circumstantial evidence."

"Yeah, but we do have the serial number for the boat used by our dead suspect. It traces back to Starch. That right there is just cause for getting a warrant signed off." Luke looked at the captain for validation.

She had a smirk on her face. "Since when have you been buddies with McGibbeny?"

"Never said I was. I just was very persuasive," Luke said.

"He worked on his manners," Elise quipped.

Norton laughed. "Trying to impress the witness, are we, Luke?"

"No. Just trying to spare myself the nagging." The remark was successful in sparking a grimace from the marine biologist.

Norton sat at his desk with a box of junk. "Son of a bitch."

"What's the matter? Wife kick you out of the house?" Luke said.

"No, not yet. Had to clean out my car. It's being sent for repairs since that dipshit at the hospital shot it up."

"Glad you brought that up," Luke said. "What info do we have on our lone gunman?"

Norton opened up a tan folder and read from the notes. "Harvey Clin. Born 1974. Attended University of California. Football scholarship that went to hell. Bounced around from job-to-job. Divorced. One kid. No real criminal record until 2016 when he was sentenced to three years for aggravated assault and battery. Guy went from zero-to-a-hundred. Served two years, three months. Trouble with alcohol. Did small jailtime for possessing drugs in 2019. Unemployed. No record on the firearm used." He pulled the next sheet of paper out and held it to Luke. "This is a photo of the suicide letter he wrote just before coming to the hospital. 'My life's a shit-show. I've failed at everything I've ever done. My ex-wife and kid hate me. The world's out to get me. Screw this place. Blah-blah-blah.' That's the abbreviated version of it."

"Oh, right. Sure. And you knuckleheads are buying into it?"

Brianna shook her head. "We're still looking into it. But, Detective, as of right now, it's looking like an unrelated incident."

Luke stood up. "It's NOT unrelated."

"Whoa!" Norton raised his hands. "I'm totally convinced now."

"Knock it off, Norton," Brianna said. She looked over at Luke. "We're still digging into it. So far, nothing's been found to connect Harvey Clin with the shooting at the beach."

"Except for the fact that he showed up at the same hospital as Vick, who remarkably ended up dead *right after* the officers guarding his door were lured out into the lot."

"Maybe we should look for any financial connections between Clin and Gary Starch," Norton said.

Luke held back a remark which would've expressed his shock that Norton would suggest something useful. "It's worth a look, but I doubt you'll find anything. The payment would've been under the table."

"Let's not forget he was strung out on cocaine," Brianna said.

"Violent history. Drugs. Suicide letter."

"Yeah, like nobody could've penned that for him," Luke said. He sank back into his chair, resigned. "Unfortunately, regardless of whether the letter was true, the guy *did* know he was going to die this morning. He had to know. I don't care how much cocaine you've snorted—you don't go shooting up a hospital with a bunch of cop cars on site and expect to walk out. Hell, he blew his own head off for chrissake."

Brianna considered the information presented. "We can't accuse this guy of starting a viral outbreak. The judge will laugh us out of the courtroom. But we *can* have him investigated as an accessory for attempted murder, since his boat has a connection to Vick. I'll get the warrant."

Luke snapped his fingers. "Sounds like a win for me."

Brianna chuckled. "Partial win. You won't get to do the arrest. His main residence is in Washington. Thus, the troopers there will get the action."

"Let me also clarify that it's not even an arrest yet. Just an investigation," Norton said. He took a few crumbled paper bags from his box. "Son of a bitch. No wonder my wife calls me a slob."

"No shit, Norton," Luke said. "You live in your vehicle? Seems that's where you eat most of your meals."

"Like you're one to judge," Elise said. She looked at the other detectives. "You guys see the inside of his house? And he's calling the other guy a slob?!"

They shared a laugh.

Luke put his feet on the desk and allowed them a moment to have their fun. "To be fair, Norton called *himself* a slob and I agreed."

"No, I said my WIFE calls me a slob."

"That why you're dumping your trash here?"

"Yes, as a matter of fact," Norton said. "She's forbidden me from eating *Burger King* and *Taco Bell*, and I'm not willing to give it up."

"Damn, Norton. Hiding stuff from your wife. Not a good look," Luke said.

"It's fast food," Norton retorted.

"That's how it starts," Luke said, his shit-eating grin growing larger. "First it's fast food. Then it—"

"Alright! Alright!" Brianna said. "Knock it off before this conversation goes too far."

Norton chuckled then pointed at the captain. "Probably doesn't want the topic gravitating toward her house."

"My house is very clean, thank you very much!" she replied. She cleared her throat. "My *desk* is the issue."

"It's because you're never there. Instead, you're always out on the road," Luke said. "You're the captain. You're supposed to be calling the shots, while eating donuts and sipping coffee. Perks of the job. Not out playing detective—leave that to me. Send him out too if you want it to look like you've got two functional employees."

Norton snorted then proceeded to go through his box. "Thanks, Jansen."

"You want me to give assignments?" Brianna said. "You've got it. Your job is to keep Dr. Sheldon safe during the night until we're sure she's out of danger." She glanced at Elise. "You gonna be okay with that?"

"Yes. He's the only one I trust," Elise said.

Norton raised an eyebrow at that open admission. "Only one you trust? What's the implication there?"

Elise's smile only further revealed her nervousness. "Nothing. I'm just tired. It's been a long few days."

"Get her out of here," Brianna said to Luke. "Get her something to eat. Find her someplace safe to stay. I don't want her staying at her own house. If someone is looking for her, they'll know to look there."

"I know just the place," Luke said.

"Why not just keep her here?" Norton asked. He watched Luke stand up and walk with Elise toward the exit. The lack of an answer was an answer in itself. "Luke…this is the safest place she can be."

"Is it?" Luke replied.

He closed the door behind him. Brianna could handle the mess. That's why she was paid the big bucks.

CHAPTER 45

"You know? On second thought, maybe it would be better if we stayed at my place," Elise said. She felt a tad regretful for being so blunt toward Luke's house. Even worse was the phrasing—made it sound like they were hooking up.

Luke's response only enhanced that effect. He looked at the grocery bags, then at her. "First you whine about the clothes I picked out for you. Now you're complaining about the house."

"Well, *of course* I had an issue with the clothes. You grabbed the first goddamn things you saw. You wouldn't even check the sizes."

"I have a good eye."

"The hell you do! The fact that you thought I'd fit into those freakishly skinny jeans should be a crime in its own right. And don't even get me started on that skimpy outfit you were eyeballing." She opened her door and sighed. "You know, we could've simply stopped at my place to grab some clothes. I think we would've survived."

"No. You would've been tempted to stay. There's less chance trouble will show its ugly face here.

"I'll neaten up a spot for you to sleep," Luke said.

"I'd appreciate that," she said. They got out of his Dodge and approached the house. "Why is this the safer option again? I mean, if someone is tracking me, wouldn't they know to come check your home?"

Luke opened the door. "They're willing to get sloppy, but only as long as they can cover it up. Coming here, invading a cop's house—let alone actually *killing* me to get to you, would only muddy the waters even more."

"Wouldn't the same thing result at the police station?" Elise asked.

"Whoever's out to get you, if they're working with someone in the department, they would've found some way to get to you. Slip something into your coffee or sandwich. Something that would result in a heart attack—make it look like you've had some kind of underlying medical condition." He dusted off the couch and the chair then studied Elise's facial expression. "What? That sound too paranoid of a theory regarding gunmen who you believe were capturing a prehistoric shark?"

"No…I'm looking at—" she paused, unsure if it was appropriate to point out the barbeque stains on the arm of the sofa. Luke followed her eyes, then rolled his.

"I'll get a few wet towels. Not like I was gonna make you sleep here anyway. There's a spare bedroom down the hall."

"Can't wait to get a look at that…"

"I've hardly set foot in there," Luke said. "Trust me, it's clean. I'll neaten my place up to your liking. Go ahead and make yourself at home." He walked into the kitchen and wettened a few towels. He looked at the ants crawling in his kitchen sink, then with silent glee, washed them away. *Maybe I should have a little more dignity in my living space.* He returned to the living room and found

Elise making herself at home as instructed. She had the TV remote in hand, her thumb on the power button. *Oh, shit.*

"Oh!" She almost jumped when she saw the crude activity taking place on the screen between two females.

"Ah, crap. Here, let me see that." Luke took the remote from her hand and changed the channel. A guilty smile creased his face as he went to work scrubbing the furniture. "Don't know how that got on my TV."

"You're pathetic," Elise said. She carried her belongings into the spare room.

Luke shook his head, muttering under his breath. "*I'm* pathetic? You're the one who came knocking at my door." *Except she turned out to be right that something weird was going on.*

"Oh, look at this."

Luke saw Elise holding an all-too-familiar apron. "Asking me to put that on?"

"Yeah—no thanks. Once was enough. More than enough. My psyche can only handle—"

"Good God, woman! Gee whiz!" He proceeded to scrub the sofa. Elise went to the kitchen sink, groaned at the mess, then went to work cleaning it up. Luke looked back. "What? You my maid now? Why don't *you* wear the apron?"
"Not after where it's been."

"I had just gotten out of the bath. That apron couldn't have touched a cleaner surface."

"Aw, you're a bath guy." Elise giggled.

"Nothing wrong with soaking. What? Were you the high school bully when you were a kid?"

"No. Other way around, actually. I was the one always drawing whales and sharks during class."

"Ah. Overcompensating, I see."

"Overcompensating, but only because I'm doing this."

"Nobody asked you."

"*I* asked me. Jesus-Mary…how could you stand living like this, man?"

Luke stared into the living room, deliberately looking away from her. "I work all the time."

"Oh, right. Because Amadea has such a high murder rate. We're not L.A., you know." She scrubbed the sink and drowned it in soap and disinfectant. "Got my hands full on this one."

This time, Luke turned around. "I already said you don't have to worry about it."

Elise smiled. "It's alright. I'm just giving you a hard time. I could use something constructive to do anyway. Not like you're the first guy I've ever had to clean up after."

The splashing of water ceased. Luke looked back again. Elise hadn't moved from the sink, but was as still as a statue. He knew the deer-in-headlights body language from recurring memories better than anyone. The worst ones were the memories you try and suppress, as they fight the hardest to remind you of who you once were.

Both of them resumed their chores without saying much. Soon, dusk came over the city. As nightfall neared, the living room and kitchen looked the best they had since he first settled in.

After Elise finished with the kitchen, she went to work on cleaning the bathroom. Luckily, it wasn't quite as bad as the rest of the house.

"Well, now you can bring girls here again and not have them run off as soon as they see the inside of your house. You're welcome." Luke gave an unenthusiastic thumbs-up. "So much for humor. I thought you were a jokester."

"A jokester *makes* the jokes," Luke said.

"Well, excuuuuse me." Elise turned toward the hall. "Mind if I take a shower? Haven't had one in two days."

"Explains the flies buzzing around."

"OH, I see! Mr. Jokester! By the way, I think there's a better explanation for any insects in your house." She waved her hand around the kitchen. "Up until now, that is."

The slightest hint of a grin took form on Luke's face. "Go get cleaned up."

"Thanks." She disappeared into the bathroom. A moment later, the shower came on.

Luke took a moment to admire the freshly cleaned living room. It felt good not to be surrounded by clutter, grease, and dust. He wondered if he'd have the motivation to maintain the cleanliness in the future.

More important matters flooded his mind. He sat on the sofa and opened a tan folder he'd brought with him from the office. At the top of the file was the mugshot of Harvey Clin. He flipped through the profile and read through the personal history. He found the details of Clin's divorce and the police report of the battery incident.

The next page included testimony from friends and family regarding the incident, as well as photos of the victims.

"Kristen Wallis, previously known as Kristin Clin." He looked at the name of the male victim. "Dwight Henry, the prick she was cheating with. Can't say I feel bad for that broken nose, Dwight."

He leaned back and thought about the shooting. *Suicide note. No affiliation with Starch Industries or any other organization. Drugs and alcohol in system. Yet, he didn't kill anybody. Was he that bad of a shot?* The thought of alcohol made him crave a drink.

"Fuck it, I'm in my own house. As long as I don't get blackout drunk." He heard Elise complaining to herself about the shampoo. "On second thought…"

He went into the kitchen, found the bottles of bourbon and whiskey, settled on the *Southern Comfort* and returned to the living room. He took a slug as he sat down.

No way was this shooting unrelated. Yet, what was in it for this guy? He knew he was gonna die, so it wasn't cash. So what? And why this guy? In the limited time they've had, how'd they know to find this guy of all people?

Too many questions spawned a headache. Luke took another drink and gazed mindlessly across the room. His eye eventually went to the one piece of clutter he didn't touch.

Every day, he tried to convince himself to get rid of that snippet of Morgan Laskey. Yet, he couldn't bring himself to touch it. The damn reporters used a picture of Morgan that Luke himself took. It was at a barbeque celebrating the Fourth of July. Luke recalled how his partner nearly blew up his own back yard when the fountain he lit accidentally fell over and spat flames toward the propane tank. Almost right above it was the picture of Chad which Elise had placed there when she first pleaded her case. Pictures that haunted the two of them. Pictures which initially represented love and friendship now only brought pain.

"Pictures…"

Several patrolmen were checking the gunman's car. One held up a little square object.

"A picture of some kid."

"Daughter, maybe?"

"Probably. It was propped up on the dashboard. Sweet looking kid. God, you'd think the sight of her would maybe persuade the jerk from going postal."

Luke moved to his computer. "Why were you looking at little missy, huh, Harvey? Somehow, I think there's something more to it than you saying goodbye."

He got on *Facebook* and looked up Kristen Wallis' name. As usual, he received a list of people with that name.

"No, too fat. No, not a redhead." He compared each one to the photo until finally he found one that resembled her. He clicked on the name. "There you are."

"Oh! So you're *Facebook* stalking people now?!"

Luke turned around and saw Elise with a towel strung over her shoulders. "Feel refreshed?"

"Yes, actually." She nodded at the computer. "What's going on? Lady friend?"

"Not mine. Ex-wife of the gunman."

"She's a smart gal," Elise said.

"Depends on what you mean by 'smart'." Luke clicked on *photos* and scrolled through. It didn't take long to find what he was looking for. "Bingo, you bimbo bitch."

"Excuse me?"

"Not you. *Her*." He pointed at a photo of Kristin Wallis posing with Dwight Henry. "That's what ended their marriage. Wifey was getting some on the side, then acted shocked when hubby walked in on them and went a little crazy. Yeah, he should've kept his cool and not *Hulked* out. But I'm not gonna pretend Ex-Clin was an innocent little angel as her lawyers portrayed her. Especially not after she drags the proceedings out, makes the husband pay alimony for life, then takes the kid and moves in with the guy she was cheating with."

"How'd you know they're living together?"

Luke scrolled down. "Most of these are in the same property. And if I were a betting man—" He searched Dwight's profile and went through the photos. "Same property. Doesn't take a genius to find out they've shacked up without tying the knot."

"Wow." Elise glanced at the photos. "Someone should tell them to put their shit on private."

"Hell, half of people on social media leave their profiles open for the world to see. This Kristin woman is the type to scam her husband into paying her and avoid getting married to keep getting a free paycheck. Someone like that is usually the type that would boast her personal life on *Facebook*."

"You seem to know a lot about people."

"I know how shitty they can be."

"She may be a bitch, but it doesn't justify shooting up a hospital," Elise said.

Luke sat quietly. *The type to boast about her personal life on Facebook...* He returned to Kristin's page and scrolled down to see her recent posts.

"Good news!" It was posted an hour ago.

"Damn. She really is a bimbo bitch," Elise said. "Good news? Today of all days? Takes a real sick person to post their joy of an ex's death, even if he was an asshole."

"That doesn't make sense though? He was the gravy train, or was supposed to be."

"He wasn't making any money though. It was probably intended to torture him until he snapped," Elise said.

"Possibly." Luke scrolled down. "But it doesn't add up when you see this."

"I am in complete shock. This really breaks my heart. No, for anyone wondering, no I never saw any signs of this. After everything that's happened in the past few months, turning on the news and seeing this was the last thing I needed." The post came at eleven-thirty and was attached to a CBS article regarding the incident.

"Hmm, 'with everything that's happened in the past few months'... what's been happening to make your life so miserable, Ms. Wallis-Henry?" He scrolled down further. After several miscellaneous postings, he found something about a GoFundMe for Marsha Wallis. The next was a post about finally finding an appropriate hospital for Marsha. An earlier posting was a hysterical update stating the lymphoma was at Stage 3.

Luke clicked the GoFundMe. The goal was a hundred-thousand dollars, with only twelve-thousand raised. He then clicked on the hospital link and looked up the contact information. He got on his phone, checking the time before dialing the number. It was a quarter to eight, leaving him fifteen minutes before the billing office closed.

He called and was placed on hold. He watched the clock anxiously. "Hi, I'm calling to make a payment for a patient. Marsha Wallis...might be under Kristin Wallis... No, I'm not aware of the case number... Her date of birth? I, uh..."

Elise scrolled through the page, then whispered, "Mom or kid's?"

"Mom's."

Elise went to the *about* page. "Ten-thirteen-eighty-four."

"Ten-thirteen-eighty-four... uh-huh... yeah, pediatric lymphoma... oh really? All of it? Just curious, mind if I ask when this happened? This morning, huh... I guess that GoFundMe worked out well... Anonymous? Really? They paid for the whole procedure and everything? Wow, that's really generous... Yeah, the world is full of generous people... Like me? Well, yes of course like me! Hell, I would've donated MORE! Actually, not really—I'm really a dick who was gonna hang up as soon as I heard what the bill amounted to. See ya!" Luke hung up. "There's *always* an incentive."

"So, let me make sure I understand this: Harvey Clin's kid was diagnosed with lymphoma, and some anonymous person paid their medical bills?" Elise asked.

"One hundred percent," Luke said. "It takes a very rich guy to simply toss out that kind of money like loose change."

Elise nodded. "Like someone who owns a medical research firm. Very generous indeed..."

"What nice people there are in this world. Man, imagine if some rich prick found a down-on-their-luck ex-con on the brink of suicide and bribed him with paying off his kid's medical debt in exchange he perform a violent criminal act. But that just sounds silly."

He stepped away from the computer in search of his *Southern Comfort.* Elise glanced over the files, then looked over her shoulder at him.

"Let's say our suspicion is true—how would they know to get *this* guy?"

"They've got long reach. Hence they were able to hire former S.A.S. That guy leading the charge wasn't some street thug. If they could hire him, they can hire anyone."

"But it seems like a rather specific choice in the limited span of time," Elise said.

Luke muttered something and took another drink. "Maybe there's a newsletter. *Expendable Ex-cons R Us.* I don't know."

"Aren't you supposed to be the world's greatest detective?"

"Do I look like *Batman*?"

"More like *Darkman*."

"Oh, gee. Thanks!" He took another swig. "I'm amazed you're enough of a geek to even understand that reference."

Elise smiled. "Only because of Chad. He was quite the comic book nerd."

Luke watched that smile slowly fade. *Oh, great. Please don't cry on my shoulder.* He checked his watch. "Oh, look at that! Dinner time!" He hurried into the kitchen. "Hope you're not too picky."

"I figured you were the type to order a pizza rather than cook," Elise said.

"Nope. No visitors. You're under the witness protection program."

Elise laughed. "Okay, the entity behind these events has a lot of reach, but you really think he's got people in every pizza parlor in town...because he *knows* you'll order one on this very night?"

Luke opened the fridge and gazed at the contents, or lack thereof, inside. "It's possible. Technically." He continued staring into the fridge. Most of the produce was turning purple. The lunchmeat was a couple of weeks old. He was out of bread and the chips were stale. He glanced at the *Jim Beam* on the counter. *Oh, right. The last grocery trip ended a little prematurely.* "What do you like on your pizza?"

"I was just messing around. I'm not really hungry."

I am. He dialed the number for the local *Marcos.* When he looked at her, he noticed her eyes were fixed on the *Jim Beam.* "Thirsty, rather?"

"A little."

A hint of possessiveness took over. How dare anyone covet his bourbon! Then he thought of the restless night she had in the hospital. It wasn't a matter of being uncomfortable, not with the way she woke up. He heard the suppressing of tears behind that curtain.

As Luke made the order, he opened a cabinet and pulled out a shot glass. "Don't go too overboard. And don't tell the captain. Then again… eh, it doesn't really matter. She'll find something to be pissed at me about anyway."

CHAPTER 46

After the day she'd had, the sight of home was practically Heaven.

Brianna got out of her vehicle and approached her front door. Kirk wasn't home yet. *Oh, right. It's Monday* It was only a little after eight. *Hopefully his day wasn't as chaotic as mine.*

Glenn was home, however. She could see the television flickering through his window. Probably on his fifteenth *Call of Duty* campaign. Then again, he could've been playing anything. With the money his dad gave him, he probably went to the nearest used game store and blew it all.

She stepped inside and went straight for the refrigerator. There was a glassful of margarita left in the bottle on the lower shelf. She filled a glass, downed half of it, then searched the pantry.

As she munched on a few crackers, she listened to the audio coming from Glenn's bedroom. Whatever she was hearing, it repeated over and over again. A DVD menu?

Is the kid asleep already? She went to his room. The door was shut. She gently knocked, heard no response. *Must've fallen asleep watching some flick and now it's back to the menu screen.*

She let herself in. "Oh, Jesus! Glenn!" He was face-down on the floor near a wastebasket. She pulled him onto her lap and checked his vitals. He had a pulse, but his face was flushed. She tapped his face. "Glenn? Glenn, honey? Wake up."

He stirred.

"What happened?"

"I feel like crap. Hard to breathe." Right away, he started coughing uncontrollably. Saliva and hot breath flooded his mother's arms. He mustered the energy to throw himself toward the wastebasket. As he heaved, Brianna got on her phone.

"9-1-1, what's your emergency?"

"I need an ambulance." As she stated the address, she noticed the redness in Glenn's eyes and the scabby buildup on his face. "He's showing symptoms of this new disease. Tell the crew to wear protective gear."

CHAPTER 47

After a few drinks, Elise finally mustered the will to eat a little bit of the pizza. She wasn't hungry, rather she didn't want to tear up her empty stomach too much with the bourbon.

Luke watched her gradually slope along the couch as though she owned it. The booze made her feel completely at home indeed.

"Might wanna take it easy on that stuff," he said.

Elise raised a hand to her mouth and took a deep breath. "Can you move the pic?"

Luke realized she was looking away from Chad's photo on the arm of his chair. He flipped it over. "That better?"

"Not really," Elise said. She slapped her slice of pizza back on the paper plate. In her other hand was the bottle of *Jim Beam*. She wasn't even bothering with the shot glass at this point. "I'll pay you back for this."

Luke shook his head. "Nah. I probably should be cutting back anyway."

Elise stared at the bottle. "It'll get better once we make this right. It has to. Right?"

"Yep. Sure." Luke continued looking over printouts of files and notes regarding Gary Starch and the history of his company.

"You planning on writing a doctoral thesis on that guy or something?"

"Gotta know your enemy." Luke skimmed the next couple of pages. "That company accrued over eleven-billion dollars in revenue last year alone. Talk about big business."

"Lot of money in medicine." Elise rested her head in her palm.

"It's one of the fastest growing medical firms ever," Luke said. He closed the folder. "I suppose human testing in Third World countries might help accelerate the development of product. Just allow a time for patenting, make it appear like it went through the proper channels, and voila, you've got a new money-maker."

"Doesn't it bother you?"

"Does what bother me?"

"Knowing there's so much injustice in the world?"

"Not really."

"How?"

"I don't know. Just used to it, I guess. I've simply accepted it as part of human nature," Luke said. He looked over at the pizza box. "Except in the case of those assholes, skimping on the sauce like that."

Elise's eyes were half shut as she massaged her face. The exhaustion had officially caught up with her. She was beat, yet fighting off sleep.

"Why'd you become a cop, then?"

"Heard girls liked the uniform."

Elise glowered at the ceiling. "No such thing as a straight answer with you, is there?"

"You should know better than to ask me questions by now." Luke stuffed half a slice in his mouth. "Because I was a naïve idiot who thought I could stop bad things from happening."

"I assumed it was because of your parents."

Luke swallowed, his face creasing as he stared at her. "How'd you know about my parents? What has the Captain been spilling? Or was it Anthony Zach?"

Elise felt a second wind take hold. "What? No! I don't know what you're getting at. I meant that I thought your dad or mom was a cop, so you followed in their footsteps."

"Oh…" Luke's expression softened. "No, they weren't. *Definitely* not her."

"I take it Mom's not a fan of the police."

"You can put it that way." Luke leaned back in his chair. *Not the least bit sleepy myself yet, and she's fighting it like a freaking six month old. Looks like I'm stuck chatting.* "What about you? Mommy and Daddy so proud of you for playing *Captain Nemo*?"

She shook her head. "They never saw me get my doctorate."

"Dead?"

"Jobsite accident for Dad, and six months before that, Mom died in a car wreck. It was a trip they were supposed to go on together, but he wasn't feeling up to it. I guess the guilt led to prescription meds, which caused him to lose balance at work...You get the story." She chuckled. Not a happy chuckle, but out of dark realization. Car crash killed Mom, led to Dad's death in a way, then Jaqueline and Mick were killed in a crash a few years later. Then there was Chad's death. "I guess I understand now how Dad felt." She downed more bourbon.

"You've got nothing to feel bad about," Luke said.

Elise nearly choked on the drink. "Wow! You actually said something nice?"

"Just trying to lower the alcohol intake. Don't feel like cleaning your filth off my bathroom floor in the morning."

She chuckled. "Like you would actually do that."

"I would. I have *some* standards."

"That why you don't work in L.A. anymore?" The words seemed to come out on their own. Elise thought about the question, then looked at the bottle. *Shit.*

Luke avoided eye contact. "What's so bad about this place?"

"Nothing *bad*. Just rather low-key for someone like you."

"Not really by choice."

"Oh! I figured it was, since you hate people so much."

"I do. I'm currently being reminded why."

"I'm not trying to pry. It's just that I'm shocked you don't simply move out into the country and become one of those small-town cops. Less people. Plenty of donuts."

"That *does* sound appealing."

Elise noticed how he avoided the question. Had she not drowned her sorrows in half a bottle of bourbon, she'd have the restraint to not pursue. "But you like cases. Not simple cases, but complex ones. Like a jigsaw puzzle. That's why you pursued this case. It's a distraction—not just a distraction, but salvation. Or, uh, redemption. For the Laskey incident."

Now, Luke was looking at her. These weren't questions, but statements. "So word really does get around fast."

Elise looked at the bottle and realized that she had gone down a rabbit hole that she never intended.

"I think I'm done." She put the bottle on the tray table.

"Good, because it's not working, what you're trying to do. The alcohol, which you hoped would block your misery, only makes you dwell on it further. You talk about distractions—which is why you're now dissecting me. Don't pour your guilt onto me, lady. Your kid was killed by a crazy shark. You didn't put him in a situation that could've been prevented. It was simply wrong place, wrong time. Ease up on yourself."

Elise watched him stand up. "Except it *could* have been prevented." She stood up. As she did, the pain in her leg flared. It wasn't from the gun wound, but the spot where the coral pierced her. "We heard the vibrations. It was killing a whale. We didn't know it was a Helicoprion, but there were clear signs of danger. But I lost my balance. I hurt myself and couldn't muster the energy to swim. All that time it took for him to get that line so I could return to the boat—we could've escaped *twice.* And he'd still be here. Then, to top it off, I forced him to ignore the safety stops once we finally did realize what was happening. The nitrogen buildup—he lost his bearings, because of what I told him to do. He tried to reach for me but couldn't find my hand." She collapsed back onto the couch. "That's how the shark got him. He should've been on that boat."

"Like the safety stops would've saved you from the shark," Luke said.

"If we remained perfectly still…"

"Uh, did you forget the fact that you were bleeding?" Luke said. Elise looked at the floor. "Yeah, that's what I thought. Stop beating yourself up, Doc."

"Is that what you did with the Laskey incident?" Now, it was intoxication, grief, and projection—three storms combining into a massive whirlwind in her mind. "I need to know how you got past it."

"Move forward with time."

Elise looked at the bottle on the tray table. "Moving forward. That why you're here?"

Luke started for the dining room. "I'm here because nobody else will hire me." He took a few more steps and stopped. He opened a cabinet over the dining room counter, grabbed a bottle, then tossed it to her. "These'll help."

Elise looked at the bottle of melatonin. Ten milligrams a dose. "Surprised you didn't toss me pills."

"Like I'd be stupid enough to supply someone with God-knows-how-many pints of bourbon in her with sleeping pills. Trust me, turn out the lights, and those'll do the trick. Take 'em and sleep. I don't feel like dragging around your drowsy ass all day tomorrow."

He found his bedroom, stopping momentarily to listen for the pop of the bottle. It took a few seconds before he heard it and the sound of rattling tablets. *Waking her up will be a pain in the ass. Oh well. Better to let her sleep it off.* He entered his bedroom and stretched out onto the bed.

It took a half hour before he heard Elise turn in for the night. He waited another fifteen minutes, then stepped back out and peeked at her door. There were no lights creeping through the frame. No sound. She was out.

He returned to the living room, leaned back in the chair, and opened the tan folder back up. He realized he had Harvey Clin's file instead of Gary Starch's. *Aggravated assault and battery. State police responded to scene and arrested him. Divorce, alimony, prison. Blah. Blah, blah. Already got your case figured out.* He tossed the file aside and started looking at the Starch file.

"Donated two-million dollars to archeological dig in Antarctica… why the hell is a medical guy interested in Antarctica? Ice dig, limestone dig… Mr. Starch, you've got some weird hobbies." He stuffed another piece of pizza between his teeth. "Wonder what other interests you have. I guess we'll find out once that warrant is served."

CHAPTER 48

The screams were sharp as a blade, piercing her very soul. Elise felt pain shooting through her. There was no detecting where it originated from. It was everywhere, like a river that had breached a dam. And like debris, that pain carried panic.

One minute, Chad was right there. His fingertips were close to hers. So close, she could feel the slightest graze from his fingernails.

"I got you! Just reach!"

Out of the water came the mouth. On its lower jaw was the devil's power tool, an instrument of death and misery. The mastermind of her suffering, the beast closed in on Chad. He disappeared from view, yet she still knew where he was, thanks to the cloud of blood.

Through that cloud came an angular snout. Black eyes stared back at her. Huge fins stretched to the side, the tail thrashing the water behind it. The creature was airborne, shooting straight for the deck. Clenched in its jaws was the dreadful reminder of the pain it had caused. Her nephew lay limp, motionless, his pale eyes expressing the betrayal he felt in his last moments.

With a gasp, Elise shot up from the pillow. She was in a world of darkness. Not death. She felt a mild wave of disappointment. Living with this guilt seemed like an impossible task. It had only been a few days, and the weight of the tragedy made her feel like she was in high gravity. How could she go on for years, a *lifetime*, like this?

Then came the intense thirst. She was paying the price for drinking that bourbon. That, along with the high melatonin dose, succeeded in keeping her asleep. The downside was that the nightmares were far more lucid. Rest was now a thing of the past, it seemed. Either she couldn't sleep at all, or when she could sleep, her mind would torment her with her new ugly reality.

This is hell.

She searched for her phone to check the time. The light was starting to seep into the window—something she was grateful for. Morning was here. Freedom from her nightmares. Then she remembered that ugly reality.

The nightmare was her life.

I have to make it right.

She could hear chatter from somewhere else in the room. Luke was talking to somebody. The lack of another voice made it obvious that he was on the phone. Elise went through the typical morning routine of cleaning herself up, then got dressed, and went to the living room.

Luke was wearing the same outfit as yesterday. Leather jacket, blue jeans—now with a small pizza stain on the right knee. *Did he sleep in his clothes? Or was he up all night?*

He didn't seem tired. Rather, he looked like a man in his element.

"Uh-huh... What date?... Gotcha... Do a search for any known associate who's been busted for—anything. Business partners, employees, contractors, *anyone.* I want any dirt on this guy we can get... yeah, I'm on my way to the office... Cool. See ya." He hung up and turned toward her. "Oh, there she is. Feeling better?"

She considered a few insolent replies before ignoring the question altogether. "New information?" She nodded toward his phone.

"Been doing some digging around Dr. Starch's island of paradise."

"And?"

"You know, rich people buy private islands all the time. Usually, it's a place of luxury, to enjoy the sea, and to be away from everybody. Then they sell them. Islands, like houses, always see new owners over the years. It's the previous owner of this island that I find most interesting."

"Who?"

"The United States Government, specifically the U.S. Navy. It was a submarine base used during World War 2. At least, that's what they called it. It was actually a testing facility. Turns out, before Vietnam and Agent Orange, we were playing with the idea of chemical warfare while we were fighting Japan."

"Starch purchased a Navy research base?"

"That's the news."

"A place like that, with submarine ports, interior pools, labs... just the thing someone would need if he was going to store a prehistoric shark."

"Or engineer a virus. But sure, we'll go along with the prehistoric shark thing."

"I saw them raise it out of the water," Elise said. "How many times do I have to explain this?"

"Fine. We'll have our answer shortly. Good thing you're already dressed. Get some breakfast in you. We're gonna head over to the station. I wanna be there to speak with the Seattle Police when they ransack Starch's offices."

"You say that as though there's anything edible in this house."

"Last grocery trip didn't go so well. Sue me."

CHAPTER 49

"Interesting. Where the hell is the Captain?"

Luke glanced around the lot. Brianna *always* beat him to the office. If she called in sick, she'd send him a text, usually stating something like 'I'm out today, don't do anything that'll cause me more grief.'

"Maybe she stopped for donuts," Elise said.

"If that's the case, then I'm gonna regret picking this shit up." Luke tapped the sack of breakfast burritos in Elise's lap. He then shook his head. "No. Even if she did, she'd still beat us all here. Captain Professional. Oh well. Let's go inside."

They entered the building and made their way up to the Homicide floor. Several desk cops were glued to the television screens. The news was on each one, focusing on the cases filling the local hospitals. State and Federal resources were now being sent to Amadea.

"I'm standing in the front lot of St. Peter Mercy Hospital in North Amadea. As you can see, hospital security are only allowing sick patients and hospital staff into the facility. Health officials are urging the public to monitor your temperature and check for any symptoms. If you spike a fever and have difficulty breathing, please report to the nearest hospital." The footage cut to a view of inside one of the corridors. *"This was footage taken during the night before the new order was put into effect. As you can see, all patients are being separated. Those infected are being isolated to prevent further spread. Non-critical appointments are being cancelled left and right, as doctors are being reassigned to the ER and Intensive Care. Please do not try and enter these hospitals unless you are exhibiting these symptoms, or are otherwise having a medical emergency."*

The view cut to a list of symptoms and guidelines while the reporter continued. *"As the number of cases continues to climb, so does the death toll. Doctors from all hospitals have reported zero recoveries. So far, they have managed to slow the effects of the virus down with a high dosage of antibiotics, but have had no success in stopping it. It has been reported that those with compromised immune systems have been succumbing to it much faster than those in good health. Please, follow the instructions from your health officials, and do not hesitate to get a doctor if you experience the symptoms listed on your screen."*

The footage cut to the news anchor. *"We appreciate you staying on it, Stephanie. The California Governor is expected to visit Amadea later today, after two cases were reported outside of Amadea. One in Red Bluff, another in Yreka. Both patients reported to local authorities that they had visited Amadea within the last two days."*

Elise was feeling sick. "This is getting scary. I didn't think this thing could escalate so quickly."

Luke pulled up a spare chair for Elise to sit on, then pushed some loose papers and folders aside—right towards her end of the desk, to make room to work. Elise groaned, placed the takeout bag on the floor, then proceeded to stack the papers.

"How can you stand being such a clutter-bug?"

"I keep things just the way I like 'em."

"Uh-huh. Sure."

Luke picked up his phone. As he dialed, Norton walked in and sat at his own desk. "I see you guys survived the night."

"That was the plan," Luke said. "Where the hell is Raye?"

"Haven't heard from her."

Luke gave up his initial phone call to dial her cell. It rang four times before going to voicemail. "Hey! Don't know what the holdup is, but bring coffee when you get in."

"We've *got* coffee!" Elise said, holding up her cup.

"We're cops, lady. We *live* on coffee." Luke hung up the phone and started calling another number.

"Who are you calling?"

"I'm trying to see the status on that warrant."

"Warrant's been declined."

Luke spun in his seat to face the office entrance. Chief Pino walked in, visibly displeased to see Luke. Nothing surprising there. What was new was his statement.

"The hell do you mean the warrant's been declined?" Luke said.

"Dr. Starch has reported his vessel stolen from his oceanfront property in San Diego. Here's the report." He handed a sheet of paper to Luke, who promptly looked it over.

"He reported this at eight p.m. last night."

"Yeah? So?"

"Those guys had to have his boat for at least a couple of days. Why the hell did he wait so long to report it?"

"He stated he isn't always at that property. He's the CEO of a very large firm. He travels quite a lot. Didn't find out until yesterday."

"Bullshit." Luke stood up. "*We* found out yesterday."

"Your point?"

"You don't think it's a little convenient that he happened to phone it in just *last night*?"

"Stop with the riddles. What are you implying?" Pino said.

"I'm dying to hear this," Norton said.

Luke snorted. "You guys don't have to like it, but facts are facts. Somebody tipped that bastard off."

Pino closed his eyes, inhaled deeply through his nose, then looked the Detective in the eye. He made sure not to lose his temper in front of the civilian. "Detective, in my office please."

"Not yet," Luke said. "I need to get ahold of Raye. Don't know what the hell she's doing, but she can explain—"

"Captain Raye is out on a personal matter."

"Is she alright?" Norton asked.

"I don't know the details, she just said it was a personal emergency." Pino turned his focus back to Luke. "I'm not standing for this. Not without sufficient evidence. You've been through this once already, Detective Jansen. You know how that turned out. You left your L.A. department in a mess, both behind the scenes *and* in the eyes of the media. Such a thing really sours the public's trust in their police department. The same is *not* going to be the case here in Amadea. Am I clear?"

"You need to go over all phone records, personal and office—assuming they were stupid enough to tip Starch off from here," Luke said.

"Jesus, you're not giving up! What evidence do you have? I'll bust crooked cops, but you need to give me something to chew on!"

"The incident at the hospital. We have records of the ID badge being used in Critical Care right around the time of the shooting. That same badge was used to get into Med/Surge, where Elise was being kept. Nobody knew her location except select hospital staff, and a few of our own. That ID was the same used by a physician whose house was broken into the night before. He was knocked unconscious and tied up, his hospital badge stolen. The guy who took it used it to get to Elise and the suspect, whom he killed before we could get any information out of him. Then there's the case of the shooter!"

"What about the shooter?"

"He was paid to attack the hospital."

"*Paid*?" Pino tilted his head. "To get himself killed?"

"His daughter had been diagnosed with lymphoma. Costing hundreds of thousands of dollars, which the family couldn't afford. I did some digging. Somebody, conveniently listed as anonymous, paid all the hospital bills, current and future. I think they got to Mr. Clin, knew he was in a desperate state, and used this as leverage to distract the cops from Vick's hospital room. All so we couldn't talk to him."

"What does this have to do with Gary Starch?"

"It's his boat that Sunday night's gunmen were using. Don't give me this crap about him not knowing it was stolen. He was tipped, both about the suspect's location, and about the warrant."

"The judge turned it down," Pino said. "It's not my call. If you can find more serious evidence linking Starch to what happened, then I'm all ears. But everything you've just stated is speculation. It doesn't point to anyone."

"It absolutely does. Especially when you see what's been happening all around here."

"The hell are you implying?" Pino said.

"Dr. Starch has been front-and-center in several epidemics lately. Think it's coincidental his boat is spotted at the exact site a new outbreak is occurring?"

"I'm gonna stop you right there, Jansen. Don't come to me with this speculative nonsense. Find some real evidence." He checked his watch, then looked at Norton. "Detective. You ready to face the press?"

"That time already?" Norton said.

"Yeah, the usual routine bullshit of giving them answers they already know."

"What answers?" Luke asked.

"We're meeting *Channel 8* downstairs," Pino said. "They want our perspective on the hospital shooting that occurred yesterday. I guess there's concern around the locals regarding going to the hospital, not because of the virus, but because they're afraid other crazies might be lurking."

"Tell them not to worry—there's no more witnesses that need to be killed."

Pino twitched, contemplated a response, then decided his time was better spent elsewhere. "Come on, Norton."

"Coming."

The two cops exited the office and proceeded downstairs. Luke looked at the TV, located the remote, then changed the channel to *8*.

"It's gonna be live?" Elise asked.

"I believe so."

"Surprised you're going to watch."

"I could use a good laugh. Norton will play himself up as a big hero for shooting his gun off. Never mind the fact that he can't hit the broad side of a barn." He picked up the phone again and tried calling Brianna. Again, voicemail. "Damn it! Probably jerking off."

"The Chief said it was a personal emergency."

"Yeah-yeah." Luke waved a hand dismissively. "Stupid ass judge. As usual, the Chief's going along with it. We're screwed."

"What are we going to do now?"

Luke shrugged, then dug into the breakfast bag. "Eat. Got nothing else to do."

"We can't quit."

"Yeah-yeah, I know. Gotta kill that shark."

Elise bit her lip. "We just need to counterpunch. There's gotta be something we can find on Dr. Starch to show that he's involved with everything that's going on."

"Yeah? How? Every lead tends to turn up dead or simply disappear. Unless we snap photos of him in the act, we've got nothing."

Elise put her elbow on the corner of the table and rested her chin on her palm. A moment later, she perked up again. "We know where that island is."

Luke paused from unwrapping his burrito. He looked at her with caution, as though she carried a contagious disease. "Yes…"

"We can go ourselves! Take my boat, travel toward that island, snap a few photos. Maybe, if that fishing boat is there, we can prove Gary Starch's involvement."

"Your boat got shot to shit."

"It's been in the repair shop the last two days. I got an email. The damage was thankfully minimal. They just needed to repair the hull, replace the windows and a few parts of the engine, and it's good as new. Beats using your little boat."

"What's wrong with *my* boat?"

"It's not as fast and it's *small.* Not customary for a hundred-twenty-mile nautical trip."

Luke looked away. "No."

Elise leaned forward. "*No*?!"

"A: You're not a cop. B: I don't work with partners, anyway. I'll go myself."

"Oh, so you admit it's a decent idea." She gave Luke a chance to respond, but received silence. "You do realize it would take an experienced boater to go out that far, right?"

"I can operate a boat."

"Oh, give me a break. Yeah, you can steer a helm, but you've never been more than a few miles away from the shore. You're no seaman, Detective."

"Isn't the politically correct term sea-*person*?"

"In the words of your captain, shut up with that nonsense."

He unwrapped a breakfast burrito. "No. I work alone."

Elise looked to the ceiling and laughed. "Make sure you film the trip because I'll get a good laugh out of it. You'd run out of fuel before you even got there."

He crumpled the wrapper, then tossed it onto the cleared space on his desk.

Elise glared at it, then at him. "Why am I surprised?"

"Now you're up in arms about *that*?! Why do you care? You don't even work here." Luke put his feet up on the edge of the desk and leaned back.

"I'm just giving you a hard time." She proceeded to organize the junk on his desk.

"You don't need to do that," he said.

She laughed again. "Been practicing in the mirror to perfect giving the impression that you give a shit?"

Luke shrugged. "Didn't work, huh?"

"Not in the slightest." She lifted some old notes from the desk, glancing at the dates. "These are from six years ago."

Luke took them, crumpled them up, then tossed them beside the wrapper. He proceeded to eat the burrito, then winced. "My god, this tastes like ass." He tossed it into his wastebasket, only for it to hit the garbage pile bulging out of it, and rolled onto the floor.

Elise didn't know why she was surprised. Luke saw the look on her face. "Hey, there's a janitor that's supposed to come in here and empty that."

"And knowing you, he was probably warned not to come anywhere near your shit."

The seven o'clock news came on. There were a few moments of regular updates before they cut to the live interview taking place downstairs. Norton stood in position of attention while the reporter spoke into the camera.

"There he is, looking pretty. Guy looks like he just entered the State Police Academy."

"Uh-huh. Appearances are overrated, right?"

"It's California. Appearances are all anyone is ever concerned with nowadays," Luke said.

Elise looked at the burrito and wrappers. "So, you're a 'what you see is what you get' kind of guy?"

"At least it's honest," Luke said. Elise smiled, unfolded a napkin and started to reach under the desk. Luke groaned. "For Chrissake, gimme that." Luke took it from her then scooped up the mess. He walked around his desk to Norton's. "Might as well make him useful for something." He pulled out Norton's wastebasket, then looked back at Elise. "I see you're not judging *his* garbage can."

"Something tells me he doesn't make it a habit."

"A habit? The guy *admitted* his car was a pigsty, since he's buying stuff he wants to hide from his wife." He pointed at the neat, clean, well-spoken guy on the screen. "Appearances. They're—"

His eye turned to the wastebasket. In the upper right corner, barely protruding from behind a series of crumpled paper bags and fast food containers was a clear, narrow piece of plastic. On its end, barely visible, was the edge of a red label. Luke reached down. His hand was slow, as though he was reaching into the mouth of a toothed predator that would clamp down on him at any moment. Just as slowly, he pulled the label into view. It was red with a golden X in its center.

Arturo Fuente Opus X

"—everything…"

Elise stood up. "What's wrong?"

Luke was lost in thought. *State police…* his mind flashed to the report. *State Police responded to assault and battery and arrested Harvey Clin.*

He rushed to his desk and got on the phone to patrol dispatch. "This is Jansen from Homicide. Get in touch with Corporal Randy Shane and have him TX my office phone ASAP." He hung up then got on his computer. He pulled up Harvey Clin's file. While it included the man's arrest, the State Police report was not on file.

With his personal phone, he dialed the State Police office in San Francisco. "This is Detective Luke Jansen with Amadea Police Department, Homicide. Badge number Double-Three, Zero, Five, Ten. I'm calling to see if I can have you fax me a copy of a police report from 2016. The arrest of Harvey Clin… Yeah, he was just in the news recently." He gave them the fax number, then looked up at the TV screen. The footage had jumped back to the anchor, who was talking about current events. He glanced at Elise, who read his mind.

"They haven't started yet."

After verifying his badge, the dispatcher got back on the line. *"We'll get it sent."*

"Make it fast." Luke hung up. Right then, his office phone rang. "Detective Jansen, Homicide."

"Hi, this is Corporal Shane. You rang, Detective?"

"Shane, listen up. Yesterday, during the shooting, I want to know your side of what happened *exactly*."

"The shooting?"

"I want to hear your account. Tell me precisely what happened." *"Ooookay. It happened really fast. Shots were fired in the lot. My partner and I went out to assist…"*

"Slow down. HOW did you know there was a shooter?"

"Um, I was at the hospital when it happened. You alright, Detective?"

"Be specific. Did you hear the shots? Did someone say something?"

"A combination of both. Staff came retreating in, terrified. Then we were called to assist with the response."

"Who ordered you?"

"Norton."

The fax machine buzzed.

"Thanks, Corporal." Luke hung up and pulled the paper from the machine. He looked over the State Police report, written by Trooper Scott Conner who was first to arrive on scene.

At five-forty-two P.M., Dispatch alerted me to a 9-1-1 call regarding possible assault. I arrived at the Clin property at five-forty-seven to find suspect Harvey M. Clin violently striking another adult male. Troopers Drake, Boyles, and Norton arrived and assisted me in breaking up the incident. His wife, Kristin Clin, exhibited bruises to the face...

The paper crumpled in Luke's fists. His eye went back to the television. The interview had begun. Chief Pino had taken a few questions and was now stepping aside to allow Norton to take center stage.

"Detective, you were at the hospital during the shooting, correct?"

"Yes, ma'am."

"Can you give your account of what happened?"

"Absolutely. I was on standby at the hospital, regarding a separate matter. I was in the main lobby when shots suddenly rang out in the lot. We heard screams and saw people rushing for cover. My Captain and I, along with a few other officers went outside to engage the threat..."

Elise watched Luke's expression grow increasingly livid. He was like a madman, his brow creasing, his eyebrow angled, the veins from his neck starting to protrude. The paper dropped to the floor. Before it touched the tile, Luke was out the door, leaving a very confused Elise standing by his desk.

When they saw him marching through the hallways, all personnel hugged the wall. It was as though the slightest touch would lead to obliteration. Like a red hot asteroid slicing through space, Luke Jansen marched through the lower floors. His temper was evident in his fiery eye. Nobody questioned him—they wouldn't dare.

He reached the first floor. Those in the booking area, upon laying eyes on him, cleared a path. Luke was notorious to begin with, but never had this department truly seen his dark side until now.

Only one desk cop dared to call out to him, not to stop him, but warn him. "Uh, Detective. They're live right now. Detective?" His words were nothing more than wasted breath.

Luke entered the lobby, pausing briefly to identify his target in the crowd. Norton was standing twelve feet right of the entrance, answering questions from the reporter. The chief was standing next to him, his facial expression shifting when he saw Luke march into view.

"No, this was an isolated incident. In terms of violent behavior, there's no need for the public to be afr—holy fuck!"

The whole room erupted with alarm as Luke grabbed the detective by the shirt. Nobody was more surprised than Norton himself, who was lifted off his feet and slammed into the wall.

"You son of a BITCH! You lowly scum!"

"Get off me!" Norton tried to wrestle Luke's arm away, only to be surprised by his rage-fueled strength.

Cameras flashed, the newsfeed still rolling. The reporter stammered, then realized it was best to let the scenario play out without her commentary.

Chief Pino grabbed Luke by the shoulder. "For the love of God, Detective! What the hell are you doing?! Let him go right now."

His words might as well have been lost in high wind. Luke's attention was completely on Norton. He saw and heard nothing else. It was all black. Deaf. Nonexistent.

"Now I know how Starch knew to report his boat stolen! Not to mention how he knew to bribe Harvey Clin! How much did he pay ya, asshole? Had to be quite the payday to spit on your own department!"

"Luke, you better let me go—"

"Let him go. Now!" Pino said.

"You called the cops away from Vick's room. *You* arranged the hospital shooting so the bastards could get to him. You were up to date with the Clin case—you *knew* his situation and that he was at rock bottom and desperate. And you *recommended* him to your employer to create a diversion. Now you're covering up for Starch! What else have you been doing for him?"

"Detective!" Realizing Luke was deliberately ignoring him, Pino waved to a couple of uniformed officers to wrestle him off Norton. The cops shared a glance in hesitation. Neither wanted to get anywhere near the crazed one-eyed detective. But orders were orders, and the bills didn't pay themselves.

They closed in. One grabbed Luke by the arm. "Hands behind your back, sir." He yelped as his arm was twisted behind *his* back. A foot struck the back of his knee, wrecking his balance. Luke shoved the cop into the other. Heads clunked together and both officers fell to the floor.

Luke faced the Chief and pointed at Norton. "He's the rat."

Pino collected his composure. He already had a public relations disaster on his hands. Blowing up in front of the cameras would only add to the mix. The physical aggressiveness seemed to have subsided, though Norton appeared to be holding back by a thread. He was fixing his jacket, his eyes fixed on Jansen. Had they been anywhere else, he'd already be tackling his foe to the ground and throwing fists.

Pino turned to the cameras. "This meeting is over." Another breath. "Jansen, my office. Now."

CHAPTER 50

Coffee splattered as Pino slammed his mug onto the desk. "Do you realize what you've done?!"

Luke was standing, despite instructions to sit. "Don't give me this shit about the press."

"Oh yes I fucking will! It's all over the news already! The media's gonna be on it just as much if not *more* than this viral outbreak! Damn you, Jansen! We didn't need this shit."

"Sorry I've ruined the image of your cushy desk job, but there's a larger picture you need to get concerned with. Norton's been collaborating with Gary Starch. When in the State Police, he arrested Clin."

"That doesn't prove anything. He arrested a lot of people."

"Goddamnit, Chief! He's the reason Starch knew to bribe Clin with his daughter's medical bills! HE drove the officers away from Vick's hospital room so the hitman could get to him."

"Norton was involved in the shootout. He was shot *at* by Clin. Doesn't add up."

"Sure it does, considering Clin didn't kill *anybody*. Either the guy was the most incompetent mass shooter in history, or he didn't want to actually kill anybody. At the very least, he was probably instructed to not kill Norton."

Pino leaned back and put his hands over his face. "My God! THIS was EXACTLY what I warned Raye about when she hired you. Even then, though I was afraid of this, I didn't think it would actually happen. L.A. all over again, only it's *worse*."

"Yeah, it's worse, because I'm right this time."

"You thought you were right last time. We know how that turned out, don't we?"

Luke leaned over the visitor chair. "Call Raye. Tell her to get her ass in here."

"No can do. I told you, she's *out*."

"Don't care. Get her in here now."

"You don't get to order me around! That privilege comes with rank. With rank also comes headaches, but I'll be damned if they were to come from my own people."

"You're ignoring the wider issue, Chief."

"No, Luke. I'm afraid *you* are." Pino leaned forward and pointed a finger. "First, you interfered with the shark attack investigation. You set a media craze by suggesting the Stuckey family murdered their own people. You then made a scene at the pier when the great white was brought in."

"Yeah, there's info about that you're casting aside…"

"Shut up. I was willing to tolerate your antics, only because I respect Captain Raye and she vouched for you. But she's not here to protect your sorry ass today. You crossed the line today, Jansen. And I'm not having any more of it. The damage you caused, at *this* time of urgency—it'll take years to repair."

"Why don't you look into it yourself?" Luke said.

"Because Norton, despite a somewhat annoying personality, has a distinct record of being an honorable police officer with zero violations or reprimands, as opposed to you. Allegations of police brutality, shootout after shootout, property damage, questionable interrogation methods which have lost you a number of cases."

"Was never about that, Chief. If I, say—twisted someone's arm a little, it was to find the whereabouts to a missing person. Not set a case in court."

"Except lawyers and juries don't look at it that way."

Luke scoffed. "Right. Like they'd understand real police work by watching *COPS*—"

"You've already gotten one partner killed. Now you may have placed a target on Norton's back. Nobody died, but some people were injured in that firefight at the hospital. Who knows what could've happened if there hadn't been such a quick response."

"Nothing, because Clin had no intention of killing anybody."

"I've had it." Pino stood up. "Shield. On my desk. This instant."

Luke tilted his head. He knew there was no point in arguing. The Chief's mind was made up when they walked into the office. Luke removed his badge, then tossed it in the coffee cup. The intended reaction only lasted a moment, as Pino was enjoying the relief and satisfaction of having Luke off the force. That relief was as momentary as the coffee splash, as there was one other instruction he had to make.

"Sidearm too."

"Ah-ah. Gun's mine. The department-issued one is in my desk. You keep it."

"Fine. Get out of here. Don't come back."

Luke's hand was on the door handle before the words were spoken. "Enjoy your pandemic. Too bad you're more concerned about appearances than getting to the bottom of it." He opened the door and gave a two-finger salute. "Later, Chief Penis."

CHAPTER 51

When Elise arrived in the main lobby, she found a tense atmosphere. Staff, both cops, clerks, civilians and other general staff, were still in a state of shock after the recent altercation.

She watched it occur live on the television screen in the Homicide Division's office. Her heart had practically leapt through her chest when she witnessed Luke grab Norton and pin him against the wall. Now, it had been twenty minutes since she heard from him. And with the understanding that Norton was the one collaborating with Starch, she did not want to wait in the office in hopes that Luke would return before he did.

"Where is he?" she asked the desk clerk.

"Ma'am, he's with the Chief. Frankly, I don't think it's in your best interest to concern yourself with him."

"I'll be the judge of what's in my best interest," Elise said. Several more minutes passed. She knew Luke was in the room when the crowd's murmuring went silent. It was like in the military when a high-ranking officer was announced on deck, only this wasn't out of respect, but fear.

Fear and curiosity.

Luke said nothing as he walked directly for the door. She knew he saw her—she was standing on his good side. She waved but received no acknowledgement.

"Luke?" She ran after him. By the time she caught up, he was out the doors and walking into the lot. After clearing the steps, she stepped in front of him, forcing him to stop. The look on his face was, oddly, one of relief. A shade of irritation swept over him after being halted. "Luke?! What the hell happened?"

"I've been canned. Apparently, I overreacted."

"Well—" *Yeah, probably would've been best to wait till the cameras were off. Then again, I've never experienced such betrayal.* "What about the case?"

"Pino thinks I'm chasing ghosts."

"You can't convince him otherwise?"

"He's been wanting to can me since I first got here. Now that he did, I actually feel pretty good!"

"Good?"

"Damn right. Don't have to put up with this shit anymore."

Elise stepped back. Now, it was *her* who felt the sting of betrayal. "You're giving up?"

"I'm not a cop anymore, kid."

"Stop calling me a kid."

"Alright, Doc." He walked past her to his vehicle.

Elise walked beside him. "We can still get to the bottom of this. That thing we were talking about in the office. We can take a boat to Starch's island. If we can find even the slightest bit of evidence, we can have the Coast Guard swarming that place. What do you say?"

Luke unlocked his vehicle with his fob. "I think you need to return to real life."

"But Detective—"

"Ah-ah! Not a cop anymore. I'm just a guy on extended vacation. I figured this day was coming, so I stacked a bunch of money away. Might not be good at much, but I'm good at saving. Between that and the unemployment, I should be good for a while." He got in the Dodge. "Should've let one of those bastards on the beach shoot my ass. Between that and the eye, maybe I could collect disability."

Elise tried to speak, but nothing would come out. Every word was a stammer. Luke looked at her as though she was having a stroke. "You'll be fine. They'll assign you to someone else for protective custody."

"To hell with that!"

"Suit yourself." He started the engine.

"You can't quit, Luke!" She grabbed the edge of the door, preventing him from pulling it shut.

"I didn't quit. I was fired."

"You *are* quitting. You know there's something sinister going on, and you know Gary Starch is at the bottom of it. If we don't solve this, more people will die!" She jumped back as Luke rose from his seat. The look on his face was similar to how it was when he learned the truth about Norton, only this time it was directed at her.

"Listen, Doc, you're not pulling the wool over my eye. You couldn't care less about this stupid pandemic. You just wanna get revenge on a fish! Guess what? You're gonna have to live with it. You're a marine biologist. You should know that it's a predator and thinks like one. It's not evil. It's not seeking people out for its own gratification. If it is, I'm willing to bet it's due to its handling. Yeah it sucks that your kid's dead, but you're not the only one who lost someone due to the shark. I don't see any of these other families leading campaigns to kill it."

"That's because they're buying into the story about the white." Elise shut her eyes and looked down. Just by saying that, she proved Luke's point. Her mind was on the shark. Everything else was just a means to an end.

Luke returned to his seat. "Arrange the funeral, Doc. Then move on. You don't get to use me anymore." He shut the door and drove off.

"Luke!" She reached out, as though her fingers would somehow pull him back. But they didn't. Luke disappeared out of the lot. Now, he was just one of many vehicles speeding along the road.

She was alone now. She had no friends, no family, and was seen as crazy by everyone else. She looked back at the police station. They wouldn't do her any good. Just provide more protective custody which would be useless.

All she had was her phone. With no other option, she called a taxi. Time to go home. An empty home which would haunt her forever.

CHAPTER 52

"As we can see here, authorities are quarantining the beach area. The chief of police has warned the public that nobody is to come past the caution tape barrier, which has been stretched out for miles along with orange cones. The Governor is expected to arrive later this afternoon to meet with the mayor and discuss further course of action."

As soon as the words were spoken, Anthony Zach noticed two officials approach. They wore facemasks and hazmat gear. Behind them were pallets full of dead fish which had been collected from the shore.

"Apparently, we're too close." He waved for the cameraman to back up. "It may seem inconsequential, but for everyone at home or in the office watching, the death toll has hit thirty-one, with many others being quarantined. So far, not a single person has recovered from this new virus. Locals are referring to it as the 'Sea Virus' while experts have not yet released an official name for it. However, with how quickly the new label has caught on, it's likely 'Sea Virus' might be what this pandemic will be known as.

"We have Coast Guard Cutters now in the area, stringing long nets about two miles out in hopes of containing the spread of infected wildlife. Some say it's a wasted effort, that traffic control for sea life simply doesn't exist. Other skeptics have stated that even if this effort was useful, it's far too late to do anything about it. But the EPA has reported that the inflow of dead sea life has decreased significantly in the past twelve hours. With no reports of dead fish washing up in other areas of the coast, experts are clinging to the hope that maybe the virus has run its course, and was strictly limited to this area. Unfortunately, the landward spread seems to show no signs of stopping. But nor do the medical heroes, who are working tirelessly to extend the amount of time patients have, and hopefully invent a cure."

****

"Here we are at St. Peters Mercy Hospital. Security has placed barriers thirty feet from the hospital entrances, with a single port of entry for patients and another for staff. Both are manned with security, who are wearing protective gear, and are equipped with radios to alert staff inside when a patient exhibiting symptoms needs transferring into the building."

Anthony walked along the yellow tape, stopping a couple of yards from a doctor wearing a face mask, goggles, gloves and a thick suit that hung over his white coat.

"Here we have with us Dr. Winzeler. Doctor, you typically work in the ER Department, correct?"

"That's correct."

"How many years have you been doing this?"

"Fifteen."

"In those fifteen years, have you ever experienced such an inflow of patients?"

"Never. This has truly been the test of my career. Up till now, it's mainly been car crashes, work accidents, the occasional gunshot or assault. This though? Completely different. Please—" he faced directly at the camera, "everyone, monitor yourselves. We don't even have a way of *testing* for this thing. That's how limited our knowledge is of this particular disease."

"So, this is *brand new*?" Anthony asked.

"Yes. It has characteristics of other viruses, but it doesn't respond the same way to treatment. We've managed to slow down the effects, but so far—I hate to sound negative—but we haven't issued a clean bill of health for anyone who's come in with it."

"With help from the federal government, do you think we might see come positive change?"

"Only in politicians' careers, maybe." The doctor looked at his pager, then started for the employee entrance. "Gotta go."

The cameraman focused on Anthony. "It has been a tense few days for Amadea. What can you do to help? Stay away from the water. Do not go to the hospital unless you are experiencing a medical emergency. Monitor your symptoms. If you are experiencing sudden shortness of breath, nausea, fever, and fatigue, isolate yourself. Do not have another person transport you to the hospital—sharing that space might infect the other person. Call 9-1-1 or one of the numbers on your screen to have a medical professional pick you up. From *Channel 8*, this is Anthony Zach."

"Cut."

Anthony lowered the mic. "Gosh, I need coffee."

"You and me both," the cameraman said. "That sentiment will probably last a while. Especially for the guys working here."

"Yeah, no shit. Glad I didn't pursue nursing school like my folks wanted me to." Anthony checked the time on his phone, then watched the building. The next broadcast wouldn't be until ten o'clock, and he'd be covering the same general material. "Got almost two hours to kill."

"Couldn't boot Austin from his nine a.m. spot, huh?"

Anthony sighed. "No."

"What's next? Try to catch another doctor? Try and interview him for another perspective?"

"Maybe. Somebody. Anything to add some spice to my next appearance. Unfortunately, all the doctors are busy." Anthony looked at the main port of entry. Two security guards stood, their body language that of bored individuals. "Wonder if these guys have anything to add." He waved the cameraman on. "Record. Maybe we'll get something we can send to the editing room."

They approached the guards, stopping at the painted yellow line. "Hey, gentlemen. Mind if we have a chat with you?"

Both men shrugged. "Probably won't get much info from us."

"I'm just curious at the number of people you've seen come in for treatment," Anthony said.

“Too many,” one of the guards said.

“What about your staff? Or any hospital workers? Doctors, nurses—is there any infection rate spreading among care workers?”

“We’ve got two people in our department under observation,” the female guard said.

“I’m checking my temperature every ten minutes it seems. I’m getting paranoid,” the male said.

“The people you see come in, what are their symptoms upon arrival? Are they simply coughing? Or something more severe? Skin welts? Blisters? I’ve heard there’s a multitude of symptoms.”

“Some are able to walk in just fine,” the female said. “Others need to be brought in on a stretcher. I’m working a double right now. I’ve been seeing them come in all night. The scariest is when it’s people I recognize.”

“Oh, I’m so sorry. Friends?”

“Not so much, thank goodness. Just people I’ve seen in passing. The manager from *Aldi*—he came in last night. Another was a patient who’s been in and out for Chemo. That was heartbreaking to see her come in. The worst was probably that detective and her kid…”

“Detective?”

“Yeah, saw her on TV yesterday with the coverage of that shooting. Recognized her right at the start of my shift last night. ER brought them in.”

Anthony put the pieces together in his mind. “Detective?... The Captain? Brianna Raye?”

“I don’t know her name, but—”

The male raised his hand. “Yeah, I think that’s who she was. Happened around shift change last night. I was just on my way out.” He sighed. “Seems nobody is safe.”

“No indeed,” Anthony said, now suddenly disinterested in anything else they had to say. “Thanks for your help, guys. Stay safe.” He waved for the cameraman to follow him to the van.

“Where are we going?”

“We’re gonna go to the police station. I’m curious what Detective Jansen might have uncovered regarding his little investigation.”

“You saw what happened earlier, right?”

“I did. Which makes me all the more interested.” They got into the van and drove off onto a road which was eerily serene for a Tuesday morning. People were staying home, valuing their lives over their employment. For the first time, Anthony Zach felt the thrill of pursuing the story starting to wane. Instead, there was a desire to solve the ongoing problem. Oddly, it wasn’t a medical professional who seemed to be nearing the answers, but a homicide detective.

CHAPTER 53

The dopamine hit of not caring about anything happening around him served as a natural painkiller. The nerves in his face had been throbbing earlier, but since his termination, Luke decided to treat himself to a little retail therapy. Chili dogs for breakfast? Who was to judge? Certainly not him. And what went better with chili dogs than a couple of pints of whiskey?

He slammed a twenty and a ten on the checkout counter and went straight for the door. "Keep the change."

"Uh…" the cashier raised a hand. "Won't be hard, because the bill comes to thirty-eight-twenty-one." Luke stopped, dug into his wallet, then tossed another ten…which, of course, fell a little short. The cashier reached over the counter, then glared at him. "Really?!"

"Oh, like a little walk around will kill ya!" Luke chuckled and exited the building. It was vacation time. No more nonsense with Chief Pino. No more dealing with stupid people. At least, not on a regular basis. Better yet, he was able to speed home, since the roads were much clearer than normal. Considering what he knew of this epidemic, his next concern would be moving. Even if this outbreak didn't spread too far beyond Amadea, if his prediction on Gary Starch's intentions were correct, there was going to be a much more widespread one in the future. As far as Luke was concerned, nobody was going to believe his warnings. So, all there was to do was look after himself. Best place to be during a pandemic was somewhere isolated.

"Well, Dr. Sheldon, that suggestion of moving somewhere in the country was probably the most useful thing you've ever said…"

As soon as he arrived home, he was on the computer hunting for properties in the Midwest. The money he'd get from selling his boat would cover the down payment. He'd have to act fast though. Considering the way things were going, nobody would be in the market for one soon. Then, naturally, he'd have to worry about new employment in the meantime. There was the option of cashing out his contributions to his pension, which in principle he wasn't against, but the taxes were a pain in the ass.

He'd have to figure out something. Unfortunately, even a small town police job was a longshot at this point. If anything, he was probably going to be blacklisted after this morning's events.

Who cares? There's nothing more thankless these days than a police career, anyway.

One property he found was a cabin near a river. No electricity. No propane. Just man and nature. A simple porch, charcoal grill, fireplace. No internet. Likely no television.

A few months ago, Luke would have balked at the idea. Now? Something about going to a simpler way of life sounded…fun. Relaxing even. Even the thought of having no real technology. The cabin itself wasn't particularly expensive either. Nice woods all around. There was a river for fishing and plenty to hunt. Luke had plenty of bullets on hand.

He laughed. "Wow! Never thought I'd consider the life of a hermit, but now it sounds really appealing." *Inexpensive, too.* Hell, he might even consider getting a horse. Less overall maintenance than a vehicle. Then again, there was the vet bills, hay, grain, and sometimes horses could misbehave like any other pet. Still, the thought was appealing. At least it would serve as a natural lawnmower for the yard. He'd live on this property like the cowboys of the old westerns he grew up watching.

The idea of trying a lifestyle so new and absurd added another much-needed dopamine boost. He flipped through the posted images of the landscape, river, and forest. Nature—maybe it offered something he craved. He couldn't deny it was one of the reasons he got his boat, to be on the water. Away from the thankless people surrounding him.

He looked over the seller's info. 'Email me for offer.'

Luke checked the contact info, clicked the link, and began to type. 'Good morning. I'm emailing to express my interest in…'

A knock on the door broke his focus. Luke sneered. *Case and point.*

"Go away. Doormat isn't just for show."

"Taking a vacation day, Mr. Jansen?"

Luke knew that voice. Did that bastard Anthony Zach seriously come to his house? Luke went to the door. Sure enough, as soon as he opened it, he saw the pesky reporter standing with a cameraman, who was smart enough *not* to be recording right now.

"The hell do you want?"

"My gosh, Detective! No need for that attitude. Didn't we make some degree of amends yesterday?"

"Amends does not constitute an invitation," Luke replied. "The hell are you doing here?"

"I was actually gonna ask you the same question."

"Easy. I live here."

"I figured you were at the police station, but they're now restricting access due to the outbreak, and we didn't see your vehicle."

"You should go back and make a fuss, considering they let your co-workers in earlier to interview Pinto Bean and Dipshit."

"Something tells me they're using the current issue as an excuse to avoid having more reporters flooding the office with questions. You've already hit five-hundred thousand clicks on *YouTube.*"

"Do I get any of that monetization?"

"You'd have a case if you didn't willingly barge into a live feed to brawl with your fellow police officers. You're lucky no charges are being filed."

"The Chief simply wanted me off the department. He was satisfied with that."

Anthony leaned back. "Wow. So they *did* fire you! That was fast."

"Damn straight. I'm not a cop anymore."

"I bet that stings."

"Not really."

"It's got to."

"Again, not really. My troubles are over. I don't have to solve the world's problems."

"What are you going to do from here?"

"That's what I'm figuring out right now. Time for a change of scenery—which involves not talking to you. See ya." He slammed the door shut. Anthony, being the persistent reporter that he was, proceeded to knock again.

"That's not what I was asking!" No response. Anthony knocked again. "What about the case? You were investigating Gary Starch! What came of that?"

"Maybe we should just leave," the cameraman said.

"No. We're going to stay here till he talks."

"But he has a gun."

"Shh!" Anthony knocked again. "Jansen! I'm not done here. You were the only one in the ballpark of getting to the bottom of this situation. You know the feds aren't gonna find any answers. At least, not before many more people are dead. Including Captain Raye." The door opened again. Luke studied the reporter's face, scanning for any physical hints that he was lying. Instead, he saw shock. "You don't know, do ya?"

"Know what? What's happened to the Captain?"

"She's in the hospital. St. Peter's Mercy. She's caught the virus. She—"

Luke pushed him aside and raced to his vehicle. With Anthony's van parked right behind him, he sped over the grass in a tight U-turn, tripling his speed as soon as he was on the road.

****

"No, no. SIR! You can't enter here!"

The male guard placed his palm on Luke's shoulder. It retracted, only to break his fall after a blow to the gut doubled him over. To Luke's relief, the female guard was smart enough to stand aside. She spouted commands, none of which registered in his mind. He hurried to the front entrance, where two other security guards met him.

"Stop right there!"

Luke pushed past them and went straight for the desk. "A patient came in recently. Captain Brianna Raye."

The desk clerk stammered. His eyes went past Luke, inadvertently alerting him to the advance of the two guards behind him. As soon as the hand touched his shoulder, Luke cocked his elbow back into the first guard's jaw. He pivoted left to face the other. The guard had his baton in hand. Clearly, he had forgotten any skills he learned in the typical four-hour training course, judging by the wide swing he used. Luke closed the distance, grabbed the arm, and with a twist of his hips, he flung the guard over his shoulder.

The first one, though not quite recovered from getting hit in the jaw, still tried coming at him. Again, the guy attempted a grab. He screamed as his arm was twisted, his wrist locked back, and within the next heartbeat, that scream turned to a "WHOA!" as he was thrown head over heels into the lobby.

Luke faced the clerk. "Raye. R-A-Y-E. Is she here?"

"Y-yes." The clerk tapped a few keys. "Back in Intensive Care. Second floor, room 243B."

Luke snatched the badge from one of the guards and hurried for the back doors. Better to take the stairs than the elevators. He let himself through, dodging flabbergasted hospital staff as he rushed through the hallways.

"Hey!" a guard shouted from further down. He was on his radio, alerting his dispatch to the intruder's location. Luke was already in the stairwell moving up. He arrived, took a left and followed the room numbers until locating *Intensive Care B Unit.*

He heard running feet. Realizing that guard was not going to let up, Luke stopped to engage him. Apparently, the meager training these guards were given focused on Jiu-Jitsu, because they all attempted to grab him by the jacket. And it was obvious that most of them hadn't practiced since their mandatory course, because they were very unprepared when he countered their technique. After a twist of the wrist and a sweep of the leg, he had the guard face down, then cuffed him with his own handcuffs.

At the end of the hall, he encountered another. This one had a can of mace handy. Unfortunately for her, Luke had taken the can off the last guard. Like two cowboys, it was down to who had the faster draw. Luke's arm was extended as soon as she was around the corner. She cried out, spraying wildly, unintentionally increasing the cloud that she was now trapped in. Luke, having been exposed to the chemical dozens of times in his life, simply walked through.

Doctors and nurses stepped aside, hands up, not sure what this crazed man's intent was. With the badge, Luke let himself through the double doors. The charge nurse stood up, alarmed, with a phone in hand. "He's here." She looked at him. "Police have been called. You better get out."

Luke followed the room numbers, dodging a couple more staff until he found 243B. A janitor raised a broom handle like a baseball bat, then swung it as Luke approached the door. It cracked in half over his forearm.

The janitor looked at the broken handle, then at the unfazed intruder who stared back at him. Hearing the unspoken warning, the man dropped the stick and took off running.

Luke opened the door. Sitting up in her bed was an exhausted Brianna Raye. Her hair was down, her eyes baggy. In her hand was a tissue, just another in a series that would end up in a wastebasket beside her bed.

"Jansen! What are you doing here?"

Luke couldn't answer. He stood at the door, jaw partly agape, taking in the reality of this new threat. Though he had never denied its existence, this virus had now become truly real.

Not since he saved her life in L.A. had he seen Brianna so helpless. She was a broken woman, alone in a hospital room, facing an enemy that was yet to lose a single battle. Those tissues were not strictly used for her cough. Her face was red, the kind of red that came after tears.

"How?"

"From Glenn. He got it from Malcolm, who I think got it from that fisherman we helped. I would've picked up on it sooner, but with everything going on—"

"Not your fault." Luke looked away. "What about your boy and husband?"

"Kirk's not showing symptoms, so he's been ordered to stay home. He's not allowed to see us."

"What about Glenn?"

"Not good. They're pumping us full of antibiotics. Slowing this thing down. But—" Her face welled up and she looked away as well. "Malcolm didn't make it."

It wasn't often Luke felt the sting of learning of someone's death, especially someone he hardly knew. But Malcolm's death came with a heavy weight. It was as though the virus was taunting its victims. It was a demonic spirit, slowly killing its victims from the inside out, and would not leave until it was finished…

…or driven out.

Brianna was clutching the bedsheets. "You never think something like this will happen to you. Until it does…"

"Have the doctors indicated how long?"

"Two days. Three at most." She took a breath, though only to keep her composure. "Unless a miracle happens."

Luke could hear approaching steps near the hallway. Despite this, he couldn't take his eye off Brianna. This *couldn't* be his new reality. The ONE person who had ever truly cared for him in any way, gone in a few days' time. Reduced to a statistic.

The EPA and CDC would not save her in time—they didn't know the shortcuts. Alerting them would simply result in him being blown off as a crazed, violent ex-cop. His arrival at this hospital didn't improve on that perception.

Brianna was going to die. Unless a vaccine already existed. If it did, there was only one location within traveling distance where it would be.

"I'll be back to visit."

He expected Brianna, usually a stickler for the rules, to respond with 'You aren't allowed.' Instead, her eyes were hopeful. *Please come back.* He answered that with a thumbs up, then hurried for the exit.

The way out was a journey of dodging security guards. Despite efforts to alert them that he was leaving, the idiots *still* tried to restrain him. Like their co-workers, Luke had little difficulty putting them onto the floor. He had been in close combat with hardened, murderous criminals. He had experienced knife wounds, broken bones, gunshots, and third-degree burns. There was truth to that famous quote regarding what didn't kill you.

He could hear police sirens as he ran out into the lot. The same two entrance guards were there. As soon as they saw him, they took off running. *That was easy.* He ran to his vehicle and got in. As soon as the door slammed shut, the cops arrived. After parking in front of the entrance, they hurried into the building. His gamble had paid off—they hadn't been notified that he exited, sparing him an on-road pursuit. As soon as they entered the building, he steered out of the lot.

****

Elise shook hands with the mechanic. Standing on her deck, she gazed at her vessel.

"It's as good as I could do in the limited time I had. But she's fit for travel," he said.

"Works for me."

"Don't know why you're in such a hurry to get it back. I think the authorities are gonna restrict boats from going out."

"Just fishing boats at the moment," she replied. "I appreciate your help."

The mechanic handed her the bill, then boarded his tugboat. He gave a final wave as they steered away from her dock.

Once again alone, Elise examined her research vessel. *Barracuda.* There were a few patches in the lower sections of the hull. She wasn't concerned that it didn't look particularly pretty. She was still debating herself on the next course of action.

She'd be going out all alone, with no weapons, and nobody to rescue her if things went wrong. If only she could just receive a bit of evidence, she could persuade the authorities to investigate the island.

The next several minutes were spent collecting her items. She had food stored away in a cooler. A whole case of water. More importantly, she had long ranged cameras. The scuba gear was stowed in the carbo hold. It made enough sense to bring those along, along with the underwater camera.

She heard an ambulance in the distance, then thought of her last exchange with Luke. The words had hit hard, but whether he meant to be or not, he was right. She blamed an animal for being an animal. No, it didn't mean Chad's death was any less tragic. But the shark, while hyper-violent and probably in need to be put down, was a product of the people who captured it. It did not experience pleasure. If anything, if there was a desire other than hunger, it was a taste for freedom. If it was held captive for months, *years*, against its will, then no wonder it was so aggressive towards people.

But the main issue was the disease that appeared with it. There was a connection, and it was being guarded by evil men who would kill to keep their secret hidden.

She looked at the patches where bullets had made their mark. "Shit, this is crazy. I'm gonna get myself killed doing this."

"Damn straight you are."

Elise turned around. She had been so deep in thought, she never heard Luke pull into her driveway. She smiled. His intentions were obvious. Why else would he show up at her place with two high-powered rifles, four handguns, and his own set of long-range cameras?

"I trust you know how to shoot?" he said.

"Slightly rusty, but I'll adjust pretty quick."

"Good. Hopefully we can avoid it, but we're going into some hot territory. And nobody's gonna help either of us. That is, unless we give them proper incentive." He looked at her boat. She already had a drum of extra fuel on hand and supplies ready to be loaded. "Good thing you got a head start. We're gonna want to leave quick—they're probably gonna be looking for me."

"What'd you do this time?" she said.

"Tell you on the way."

The two of them loaded the remaining supplies, removed the moorings, and cast off. They were headed northwest. Into the lion's den. Where answers lay.

CHAPTER 54

By the end of the first hour, the Dramamine had kicked in. During that time, Luke thought about Brianna, and how she would take great pleasure in seeing him nauseous after the hell she went through during their Sunday trip to find Glenn. Being the fighter that he was, he was able to keep control—though his main motivation was to avoid Elise poking fun at him.

It didn't matter in the end.

"Awww! You feeling better? You need me to get you some Tums? Or a Gatorade? Or a blankie?" Luke glared up at the fly deck. His expression said it all, and it was everything Elise could hope for. She laughed. "Don't worry. It's only a sixteen-hour round trip."

"Fantastic." Luke groaned. "You can't push this thing any faster?"

"Maybe a little. It's a hundred twenty miles of ocean we have to cross. Don't want to stress the engines too much. Something goes wrong, there's nothing but four thousand feet of depth to look forward to." She shook her head. "Thank God you didn't end up going alone. You'd probably get halfway there before blowing your own boat up."

"Ha-ha-ha. Have your fun." He stood up from his chair and watched the ocean. The mainland was completely out of sight. They were completely at the mercy of the Pacific. So far, they only saw a couple of sailing yachts far out in the distance, and one Coast Guard cutter. Luke wondered if it was called to be on standby, or if was part of an effort to contain contaminated sea life. "What's the likelihood of this thing spreading further into the ocean?"

Elise pondered the question. "There's been no reports in other areas. If we're lucky, it's just limited to the Amadea coastline. The virus needs a living host. Once the host dies, the virus doesn't have fresh cells to infect. Unless the contaminated tissue is consumed in a matter of time, the virus can't spread. On land, it can live outside the body temporarily on surfaces. This is evident in how fast it managed to spread on land. Hence, we wipe down tables, wash our hands, etc. But usually, viruses can't be transmitted through water. Especially not saltwater. No, as long as the outbreak is limited to our local area, I think everything will be fine."

"And if there are more carriers?"

"Then God help this planet." Any remnant of joy disappeared. Who was to say that the Helicoprion was the only one? Or even the only infected *species* swimming in the ocean? It all brought to mind the allegations of human testing that has occurred throughout human history. Was that all this was? A test? Or was the creature released by accident? Did the shark inadvertently bring to light a more sinister plot?

Could Gary Starch, assuming they were right about him, be so evil?

Now Elise was the nauseous one. She thought of the question she asked Luke last night. "Does it bother you knowing there's so much injustice in the world?" His answer— "No. You just accept it as part of human nature." She hated hearing that. It felt so wrong, probably because it was wrong in principle. But wrong didn't mean untrue. Anyone who studies human history understood that. Human history, an endless bloodbath with little bits of hopeful progress sprinkled within. Many people quote the Third Reich as the most horrid event to occur in the Twentieth Century. Most people, especially the younger generations, considered the atrocities of the Soviet Union. The mass starvation; the theft of food from farmers without compensation; The Great Purge, where a reported six-hundred thousand to possibly over a million wealthy peasants were eradicated in the name of social revolution. Most people with an inkling of understanding of the Soviet government understood that the numbers were far greater than that. That didn't account for standard executions that resulted from defying the totalitarian government or attempting escape.

Elise thought of Mao Zedong. Sixty-million people dead at *minimum*. Many believe the number of people killed during that communist reign extended far above a hundred-million. How did people not quote that maniac? Hitler was a monster, sure, but he could only dream to be the mass murderer that Mao was. The Great Leap Forward, from 1958 to 1962, resulting in forty-five million deaths in those years alone.

Then there was Pol Pot the Cambodian Genocide, resulting in over two million deaths, as well of the Serbian Genocide in 1945, which went overlooked in history due to the much larger scale of the Holocaust. There was Burma, South Africa, the Darfur Genocide in Sudan, and too many others to consider. Millions upon millions of deaths, all at the hands of man.

Sure, these were government genocides—governments run by man. Such men craved power, whether in terms of political office, or a position to influence. Money usually bought such positions. Money and resources. Those who supplied advanced weaponry, technology, oil… medicine.

Elise thought of all the people dead and dying in those hospitals in her home city. All dead, not from the jaws of a fish, but the virus that it brought. In the world of science, Elise had read about the debate surrounding cloning of prehistoric species. The arguments in opposition usually centered around the aspect of man playing God and how prehistoric species could adapt to present day. Until now, Elise never considered the fact that prehistoric creatures could carry diseases that present day lifeforms had no immunity against.

Every aspect of this presented its own set of questions. Was cloning of long extinct organisms truly possible? If so, could a virus be replicated along with its physiology?

That would probably depend on the source of the original DNA.

"God Almighty."

"What's wrong?"

Elise glanced down at a puzzled Luke. "Sorry. Nothing. Just thinking." She watched the ocean break against the bow. The boat was on autopilot. The nice thing about driving on the Pacific was that she didn't have to worry about potholes. After a while, she climbed down to the main deck. "I should've packed beer."

"Damn right you should've." Luke sat down and put his feet up on the gunwale.

She smirked. *Yeah, you'd probably be three bottles in by now.* She felt guilty for making that judgement. She knew what was on his mind. After castoff, she asked him of Captain Raye's opinion of his termination, only to learn that she was in the hospital fighting for her life.

"I'm sure she'll be just fine."

Luke kept his eyes on the horizon. He said nothing. What was there to say? Should he point out that the virus had killed everyone it had come into contact with? He had enough grim in his life.

That only motivated Elise to press further. "I know she'll be okay."

"That's good to hear."

Normally, his monotone voice indicated a lack of interest. This time, Elise knew it was a method for controlling emotion.

"I didn't realize the two of you were really close."

Luke turned his head. "Huh?"

"No! No! I wasn't implying anything like *that*. But there clearly is a connection between you two that extends beyond a work relationship. I've seen the way you interact."

"We fight like siblings."

"That's exactly what I mean," Elise said. "You're at each other's throats, drive each other insane. Despite that, it's obvious you care about one another."

"Here we go. Psycho babble."

"It's not psycho babble! I'm just being nice and assuring you that she'll be okay. I have faith in what we're doing. And you do too, otherwise you wouldn't be here. Above all, *she* has faith in you. Always had."

Luke dug into the cooler and pulled out a bottle of water. He put some on his palm and washed his face, particularly the burnt side.

"You in pain?"

"No, I'm fine. Just a nerve flare up."

"Nerve pain? Does water help soothe it?"

"Not really. Just feels like I'm still on fire sometimes and I follow my natural instinct."

"Does that happen often?"

"Every damn day since the fire."

Elise nodded. It was the first time the Laskey case was brought up by him, even if not specifically by name. All this time, she had her concerns about that, until this morning when Norton's involvement was discovered. "Seems you have a rough habit of being betrayed by partners."

"Not really," Luke said.

"No?"

Luke stood up and walked to the starboard side. He crossed his arms over the gunwale and watched the water. "First time, actually."

"Oh..." A few moments of silence passed, during which Elise was unclear of what to say next. Pursue the conversation? Don't pursue it? Knowing Luke wasn't the chatty type, she almost went with the latter. But the awkward silence quickly proved too much, and they had many hours to kill. "I figured you got screwed just like you did today. I thought that's why Captain Raye hired you in the first place."

"She hired me because she thinks she owed me a favor."

"A favor?"

"A bad standoff in L.A. She was just a patroller at the time. In a nutshell: There was a shootout, she got hit, was about to be finished off, I saved her ass. Fast-forward a decade and some change, the Morgan Laskey situation happened. No need for me to explain that. I know you've been told the story."

Elise shook her head. "I've been given the passed-around consolidated version of you betraying your partner, and the speculation surrounding it."

Luke snickered. "People love to do that."

Elise unfolded a chair and sat down. "Mind if I ask what happened?"

Luke looked at her, then back to the horizon. "Long story."

The marine biologist laughed, then held a hand to exhibit their surroundings. "Does it look like we have anything other than time?"

"No. It doesn't. Should've packed a damn TV."

"Well, gee! Sorry. Wanna turn back and pick one up?"

"Very funny. Well, I know one thing I have that'll help kill the time." Luke dug into his pants pocket and pulled out a cigar. Elise leaned forward to catch the label.

"That's the cigar from the dead gunman."

"Damn right. Worth a few hundred bucks." Luke pulled it from the plastic tube, smelled it, then dug into his pocket for a lighter."

"You're gonna smoke that?!"

"Damn right I am!"

"That belonged to a freaking terrorist. You should get rid of it."

Luke scowled at her, then held up the stogie. "Get rid of it? The cigar didn't do anything wrong! And now that I'm no longer a cop, I don't have to worry about Brianna whining about evidence."

Elise stood up and leaned on the port gunwale. "I know what you're doing."

"Firing one up."

"I guess I'm like you in a way—meaning, I can be a little nosey. Curious, is probably the better word. But if you don't wanna talk about sensitive issues, I'll back off."

Luke stared at the cigar and lighter. After a moment of consideration, he put the cigar back into its plastic tube, and tucked it back into his pocket. "I'll fire it up when the time is right. Sure as hell not wasting it, though! Cigar like that deserves to be put to good use." In the following moments of silence, Luke realized he was done stalling. He contemplated the option to say no, but the word never came out.

"Morgan was my partner in L.A. We'd known each other since we were in grade school. Went to the academy together, I was best man at his wedding, yadda-yadda. Eventually, we climbed the ranks, managed to vouch for each other when it came to promotions. I spent almost every weekend at his house.

Practically became an uncle to his kids. Always annoyed the hell out of him with jokes that his wife was secretly attracted to me.

"Eventually we made detective. In downtown L.A., there's no shortage of homicide cases. Year after year we'd bust some scumbag, learn his connections to other crime organizations, and pursue a case against them. Then came the Krasnewski Case, in which we intercepted a human trafficker after he murdered one of his goods—goods meaning victims. To those fucks, people are a commodity, like tomatoes or avocados. In digging, I learned that this group Krasnewski worked for used a bank as a front. Used for tax reports for their shipping operations.

"It wasn't long before shit went downhill. Over time, I noticed Morgan getting extravagant with his spending. It started with smaller things, like more trips to restaurants in his off time, to eventually buying a new house and car. Nice ones too! And even then, he was spending as though he was a movie star. He hardly talked about it, though. In fact, he seemed to avoid the topic when it was brought up.

"Me, being the nosey prick that I am, started digging after he dodged the question. I combed through his records, using backdoor channels of course. He was given a shit ton of money—I'm talking almost a million. That money was funneled to him using that same bank that the traffickers were using. When I put that together along with his behavior and avoidance of the topic, I *knew* he took money from them assholes. It all added up."

Elise watched Luke's knuckles turn white as he recalled the memories.

"What happened?"

"I confronted him about it. He denied it. I started an internal investigation. The press got ahold of it. Made a big scoop about the homicide detective that received an enormous bribe from a human trafficking ring. That enraged the public, particularly family members of the girl that was killed during the Krasnewski Case.

"Then came the truth, something *I* didn't even know while growing up with him. Morgan's 'dad' was actually his stepdad. His biological father took off before he was born. Guy never mentioned it, nor did his folks. Kept it skin-tight to the chest all them years. Turns out his biological dad ran a very successful company. That year, he got terminal cancer, and I guess started reflecting on his life. Maybe he felt guilty for being a deadbeat dad. Regardless, he had a trust fund set up for Morgan. That's how he came into sudden wealth, and also why he wanted to keep it to himself. Unfortunately, that information came a little too late."

Elise put a hand over her mouth. "The family members of the victims?"

Luke nodded. *She catches on quick.*

"I intercepted one doing a stakeout near his old home—it was still up for sale and he'd return every so often to check up on it. Found out this person was related to the Krasnewski victim, and using 'unconventional methods' I learned that he was part of a larger group, and that they learned of Morgan's whereabouts. Morgan wasn't speaking to me at the time, so he ignored my phone calls. The fuckers managed to intercept him at his vehicle as he was leaving. They boxed him in and hit him with a barrage of Molotov cocktails. Car went up like it was made of paper."

"Oh my God. You got him out. That's how you got burned," Elise said.

"He died that night. Family despised me and the whole department despised me. They don't take kindly to their own being investigated, *especially* if it turns out to be false. Press got wind of it and released articles speculating that I was trying to extort him for a cut of the cash. I was fired. Blacklisted.

"Then came Brianna Raye. She was working in Amadea at the time. Convinced the department to take me in after all my medical bullshit was done with. Kept me on as a detective in a relatively low-crime area, keeping with Pino's wishes to keep me off the streets as much as possible."

"And you blame yourself for that?"

Luke looked at the cooler, instinctively craving a drink even though none existed on this boat. "There's no alternative facts, Doc. Not only was I wrong, but it was my judgment that led to Morgan's death. Now his kids are without a dad, his wife without a husband, his parents forced to bury their only son. Closed casket. There's a heavy price for failure."

More silence followed. Elise wanted to follow the natural instinct to offer comfort, but knew it wouldn't do much good. She was talking to a man who believed he got his partner killed. In a sense, it was the truth, though it was not intentional or malicious as people made it out to be.

It all came together: his bitterness, his hatred towards the press, his desire to work alone, the constant pain—which she suspected was more psychological than physical. It all stemmed from a desire to punish himself for the harm he caused.

It opened up the pain in her heart like a fresh cut. The memory of Chad's death, the knowledge that he'd be alive if she acted faster. Like the nerves in Luke's face, her leg throbbed. A dreaded reminder of the turmoil within her.

The world seemed like a dark and violent place. The sunlight and beautiful clear water failed to relieve that intense weight she felt. That last sentence spoken by Luke hit hard, especially while seeing him reliving the misery that had defined his legacy.

Here we are, two people weighed by guilt, embarking on a seemingly impossible mission, based solely on judgement and limited evidence, in an effort to save hundreds of lives. Assuming we make it out alive, would either of us be able to live with it if we failed?

With that thought, the reality of the situation was finally seeping in. They were going up against a billionaire with a vicious group of former military associates who had no qualms over exterminating loose ends. What did she and Luke have? A few guns, a camera, and no backup.

Then came the spurt of water. Elise looked out fifteen degrees off the port bow. The water had separated into a thin mist. A whale! She saw the fluke, and a few moments later, a flipper. It was a humpback.

"Look at that!" Luke stepped across the deck, took a glance, then shrugged. Elise climbed up to the fly deck.

"What are you doing?"

"Mind if we take a moment?"

"We have places to be! This trip's long enough. We don't need to waste time whale watching."

"Is ten minutes really going to affect the outcome?" Elise said.

"They're whales! You're a marine biologist! You see them all the time!"

"Please. I *need* to do this."

"I—" Luke watched the whale's fluke rise and fall, gently lapping the water. He looked up at Elise. He saw the desperation in her eyes. This wasn't a simple sightseeing. What the importance was exactly, he wasn't sure, but it was indeed important. "Make it fast."

She appreciated the gentleness in his voice, even if his words were intended to be strict. She brought the boat near the whales, then went below. A couple of minutes later, she reemerged in her diving suit and scuba tank. Luke didn't bother questioning her actions.

"You wanna come?"

Luke was taken aback by the question. "No. Not really in the habit of swimming with sixty-ton whales."

"They're harmless."

"I'm good."

"You sure?"

"Yes, I'm sure. I can see them from here. Don't need to play mermaid with them."

"It's…it's something you'll never forget."

Luke groaned. *Why are we doing this?!* He watched the whale emerge along the surface. A few yards behind it, a smaller shape splashed the water. A youngster! The mother swam beside the boat, inspecting the humans aboard. Elise moved to the back.

"Alright. I'll just be a minute."

Luke slapped his forehead. "Fine. Assuming you have a wetsuit that fits me."

"You'll fit into Chad's spare suit. Down below. Can't miss it. Oh—I should've thought to check if you knew how to dive."

"Yes. No worries," Luke said.

"Great!"

CHAPTER 55

Elise didn't bother waiting for Luke to gear up before taking a dive. The mother whale was roughly the same size as Silver. The youngster, however, was much younger than Silver's late offspring. The two whales were ten meters below the surface now, slowly gliding in unison. Both of them had trackers on their back. Attached using suction cups, they were shaped like raindrops. Elise had seen this particular model before. They were used to monitor heart rates and stress levels.

The marine biologist followed the same routine as before, moving her feet up and down like a dolphin. The whales saw her but didn't move away. Instead, they turned and moved closer.

The mother cocked her head to the side, allowing the swimmer to look into her left eye. For an animal that couldn't make facial gestures, there was a lot of emotion in that eye. There was no sense of hate, bitterness, or entitlement to this space in the ocean.

"You have a name?" Elise wondered if the mother understood the gesture of a smile. "No? Let me fix that." Elise studied the mother's features. She swam over her back, then shivered when beholding the sight of various scars along her back. One was near her dorsal fin, another not too far from her blowhole. Each scar was rounded, with a small, coma-like tail extending to the back. This whale had been hit with harpoons, which were used in an attempt to pull her backward. A whaling attempt.

Now it made sense why those particular tracking devices had been installed. Looking closer, she saw the logo for CCS (Center for Coastal Studies). Since 1976, they'd been heavily involved in emergency rescue operations, mainly focused on freeing whales from net entanglements. Elise suspected they came across this whale after it had been injured and were using the tracking monitor not only to monitor her movements, but to be ready for a rescue effort should she come into danger again.

"Oh my goodness. You poor thing."

The whale sang her chorus. It was not a sound of contempt but one of harmony. A rockabye for her child and a melody for her new friend. It was a melody that warmed the heart and lifted the spirit.

Melody. That's her name.

"Good to meet you."

Melody answered with a low hum. She gently stroked her flippers and waved her fluke, not to maneuver her body, but as though performing a ritual. It was ceremonial—a *dance*. It was as though she was on stage, the sun's rays streaming past her like studio lights.

Elise sniffled. It took everything to keep the tears in. Definitely didn't want to cry with this mask on. What she was witnessing was that impactful. Swimming in front of her was a gentle giant who had seen the worst of humanity. She had been attacked, impaled, likely survived by the narrowest of margins. Yet, she held no grudge. Melody did not treat humans like the predators they were. She could've easily fled when the boat came near. Instead, she put on this beautiful display which brought warmth and calm to Elise's soul.

"Thank you. I think I understand now."

"You guys talking about me?"

Elise looked back and saw Luke approach. She was impressed with his swimming technique. Turns out he *did* have diving experience. The comm did nothing to obscure the gruffness in his voice. In fact, it *enhanced* it. Elise couldn't help but laugh at that.

"Yes, in fact, we were! They were asking about the smell. I told them it wasn't me."

"Glad you're having fun while we've got more important things to do."

"Just admire them for a sec. Please?"

Luke approached. By the way he slowed, he was a little nervous. She couldn't blame him. It wasn't natural getting so close to such a huge animal.

"She's talking to you."

"How do you know it's a she?"

Elise pointed down at the infant. "Um. Duh!"

"Doesn't necessarily mean it's a she. Mom could've skipped town. You might be looking at a single dad right here."

"Alright, smartass. That's enough." The whale descended, then came back up with a graceful arch, lining her underside with the divers. Elise gasped as the flippers extended. She shoved Luke forward. "Go. She's inviting you."

"The hell are you talking about?"

"She wants to dance."

"Alright, where did you hide the beer? You must have some on board, because you're either insane, or you've got a buzz going on."

"Just do it. This is rare! You don't understand what you're missing."

Luke watched the whale. "Oh, you've got to be kidding me. If I was gonna die on this trip, I figured I'd get shot or blown up. Not crushed by freaking *Moby Dick*." He inched forward, then looked back at Elise, who gestured for him to keep going.

"She's waiting. Reach out."

"Reach out like…" he pointed at the flipper. She nodded. Luke watched the huge titan. Her fluke waved back and forth, keeping her in place. Despite his caution, he gently took a hold of the flipper.

In the following moments, they glided together. A creature of the land in motion with that of the sea, in mutual harmony. Keeping in that vertical position, the whale took him on a slow spin, singing her chorus all the way.

Meanwhile, it grew even more difficult for their spectator to hold back her tears. *One was lucky to see such a display by these animals once in a lifetime. I've been fortunate to see it twice in a matter of days.*

"I'm getting dizzy," Luke said.

"You're lying."

The ritual continued with them swimming near the surface, with the infant following a few meters back. After a couple of minutes, the baby swam close to Luke and nudged him with its snout.

Elise heard a sound she wasn't used to. It wasn't a hum or a chorus beat. In fact, this came through the comm. Luke chuckled. It was slightly audible, but real. She resisted the urge to point it out, as that would cheapen the moment. Instead, she watched the hardened man take genuine pleasure in interacting with the angels of the Pacific.

"Want your mommy back?" he said to the youngster. He finally broke away. "Hate to cut this short. But we've got places to be. Thanks for the dance."

Luke swam back. To Elise's surprise, he stopped every so often to look back at the whales. He even offered a wave goodbye before climbing back aboard the *Barracuda*.

Up on deck, they gave a final glance to the mammals as they took another breath. Luke watched, his facemask in hand, his eye containing a little more of a glimmer than usual.

"Fun." His attempt to sound unfazed did nothing to convince Elise. After the whales submerged, he went below to dry off and get back into his regular clothes. It was then that Elise allowed a couple of tears. They were not ones of sadness but of joy.

The whales emerged for one final appearance, then continued on their journey. A mother and her child. Angels of the Pacific, warming her soul. Above them, she imagined Jaqueline and Chad. Angels in Heaven. Not in pain, not feeling despair, but in Paradise. Together.

"Thank you."

CHAPTER 56

Hours passed, though they felt like moments.

Elise never felt herself drift off to sleep. She was resting on the main deck when all of a sudden she was in a world of bliss. She couldn't remember the dreams, or if there even was one. What she immediately took notice of was how rested she felt. Sleep was no longer an agonizing torture for her nightmares to haunt her.

For the first time, she believed things would be okay going forward.

She looked around, spotting Luke standing up on the fly deck. He kept an eye on the helm while the autopilot continued taking them northwest. He was looking over his weapons, filling the magazines, and cleaning the muzzles. Not that they needed it, but it was something to kill the time.

"How you feel?"

Elise smiled. "Good, actually." She stood up and stretched. "Sorry. I didn't mean to doze off!"

"It's fine. Not much else to do."

Elise looked around. "How long was I out?"

"A while. I'm bummed you woke up, actually. I had an elaborate plan in place to wake you up. It involved the bullhorn. But, of course, you HAD to ruin it."

She looked away and laughed. "Sorry I ruined your day. How far out are we?"

"We're almost there, in fact. Hence I was about to wake you up."

"Alright. Give me a sec. I'll take the helm." Elise went below, freshened up, then climbed up to the pilothouse. When she arrived, Luke was opening up a small metal case. Inside was a long scope. Elise cocked her head back. "That for a sniper rifle?"

Luke held it to his eye and scanned the ocean. "Damn right. Works better for me than a pair of binoculars. Range is about fifteen-hundred yards, which makes it appear to the viewer at roughly a-hundred-fifty feet away. If we stay out at two thousand yards and some change, we might be able to remain fairly inconspicuous, while getting a look at the island."

"They'll just think we're cruising by," Elise said.

"Exactly."

"And if we don't see anything peculiar?"

"One thing at a time." Luke lowered the scope.

"Might be a good idea to plan," Elise said.

Luke groaned. "We just need to get close enough to identify the fishing boat. Then we might be able to get an actual investigative team over."

"And if not?"

Luke rolled his shoulders, as though warming up for exercise. "Then we get closer."

"We get any closer, they'll get suspicious."

"Not if they don't see us."

Elise laughed. "Sorry, I left my submarine in my other pants."

"First of all, sarcastic humor is *my* thing. Second, there's an alternative option. How long do those cannisters last?"

"About three hours." Elise shook her head. "That's quite the distance, though."

"You have a better idea?"

She shook her head again. Luke was right. They had limited resources, options, and time. Also, there was the diver propulsion device, which would help with the physical exertion.

That feeling of rest quickly dissipated. Elise knew the scale of what they were attempting when they first cast off. But now the reality of it was *really* dawning on her. She prayed it would be a simple matter of identifying the boat, radioing the proper authorities, providing the facts and evidence, and allow someone else to do the rest.

Unfortunately, if these past few days proved anything, NOTHING surrounding this strange scenario was simple.

"With our luck, he probably sank the boat like he did the yacht," she said.

"Maybe. Maybe not. Now that the police are officially no longer interested in him, he may see a reason not to. Keep in mind, that yacht stuck out like a sore thumb. The Coast Guard would've eventually found it, so he had to get rid of it. Not to mention, get us looking in the wrong direction."

"True." Elise went over the chart. They were close. *Very* close. She watched the horizon and double checked the radio channels to know which one was the Coast Guard's.

Luke pointed twelve degrees off the starboard bow. "Land ahoy."

Elise squinted, then raised her standard binoculars. The shape was so far away, it almost seemed transparent. But there was no doubt it was land. The only land in this region was Gary Starch's island.

"Finally here." A wave of anxiety passed through her. Then she snapped back to her Army self, listening to the drill sergeant yell in her ear.

"What you so damn nervous about, little girl? Snap out of it or go home!"

Home to what? A disease stricken city? A virus that had now become national news. Likely international within a couple of days.

She kept the boat pointed at the island. The cruise forward was like the dreaded climb of a roller coaster up that first slope. Only she didn't know what she'd see beyond that bend.

Luke stood on the starboard side, watching the island through his scope. "Proceed another five hundred yards then angle fifteen degrees port. Take us straight west. Let 'em think we're passing by, if they even see us. Let's see what we can see with this first pass."

"Aye-aye."

There was no going back now. They were committed.

CHAPTER 57

"Sir. Please report to the station. Tango arrived on screen."

Barton smiled. The moment he was waiting for had finally arrived. He walked through the long metal corridor, paying no mind to the men in white coats as he made his way to the antenna station.

Several men were stationed at computer desks, each with headphones equipped with microphones. The one at the sonar monitor raised his hand. Barton approached and gazed at the screen. There was a blip on the southeast side of the island.

"Looks like our source's warning was correct. They're coming *themselves.* Took 'em long enough. Must've stopped off for beer along the way. How far out are they?"

"Just over a mile, sir. Coming in at ten knots. They've slowed in the last few minutes."

"They don't want to raise alarm." Barton chuckled. "They don't realize they're being monitored. Stupid idiots."

He left the station then got on his radio. "Alpha Two to One."

"One here."

By the tone, it was clear his employer knew why Barton was radioing him.

"They're here."

"You certain there's no other alternative?"

"Negative. I've seen this guy. I know the type. He's not one to quit. He's a dog chewing on the rug. He won't stop unless we put him down."

"What a shame. I suppose maybe I should've assigned Kent to the case."

Barton was glad he didn't. Now, he would get to kill the prick who killed Dixon. His brother-in-arms, Dixon had saved his life on multiple occasions.

"We've already discussed it. That *would* have increased police suspicions—to the point where we wouldn't be able to buy them off. Plus, Kent's on the other side of the country by now, and has long forgotten about us."

"Fair enough. Alright. Don't make too much of a spectacle. I'd hate to see the animals disturbed."

"Will do. I'll keep you informed. Alpha Two out." He lowered the radio and started walking to the flight deck. "Christ, the guy's fine with killing millions to make a few bucks, but blowing up two hotheads is apparently a 'shame'." He switched to the security frequency. "Alright. I need two flight teams stat. This is a Code Five. Got pests in the perimeter and it's time to hit 'em with some spray."

Minutes later, Barton met the teams on the flight deck. Two choppers were being prepped for flight. The crew loaded the weapons, including a fifty-caliber machine gun for each chopper, multiple automatic rifles, and an M32A1 Grenade Launcher.

"That's mine." Barton took the launcher, boarded Razor One, then strapped himself to the machine gun unit. "Razor Two, you provide backup support. The cop is mine. Anyone else kills him, you won't make it back to the island. Am I clear?"

A series of "yes sir" followed.

"Alright. Let's get to it."

CHAPTER 58

As the *Barracuda* slowed to five knots on its western course, Luke kept his eye fixed on the island. Through the scope, he saw a bit of the island interior. There was elevation rising to a few hundred yards. There wasn't much vegetation on this side of the island, which allowed him to spot the man-made structures within. Some of the facilities had been reconstructed since their initial purpose in the 1940s, while others still contained remnants of those who previously occupied the island. There was a rusted steel structure on the southeast end. It stood twenty-feet high and maybe thirty feet wide.

"I'm willing to bet there's an elevator unit that leads somewhere beneath that."

Elise opened the window. "You think the lab is underground?"

"Yep." Luke gazed at the other facilities. One appeared to be a barracks of sorts, the others he couldn't quite identify. However, one building that caught his eye was a tower further into the interior. A radar unit was installed at the top. Where there was radar, there probably was sonar. "Well, shit."

"What's wrong?"

"Let's hope they don't suspect anything, because I can guarantee they know we're here."

"Great. What should we do?"

"Keep going west. Pretend we're just curious sightseers." Panning between the shorelines, he estimated the island to be three-quarters of a mile in diameter. He spotted a few personnel patrolling the shores. They seemed like standard sentries. To the untrained eye, they would look like nothing more than typical private security. It wouldn't be enough to arouse suspicion from the authorities. 'Gary Starch is a billionaire. Of course he would hire private security wherever he goes,' they would say.

The patrollers didn't carry rifles, though it did appear each one had a sidearm on their thigh. *Probably an armory in one of these surface structures where they have access to bigger and badder toys.* Gazing further left, he noticed more structures. There was a small peninsula extending from the west shore containing what appeared to be a guardhouse. There were a few more men moving about over there. They didn't resemble guards. From what Luke could make out, their attire ranged from jumpsuits to ragged maintenance clothing. "Keep taking us around. I think the docks are around the corner."

He passed the scope to Elise, who took a look. "They'll probably see us."

"Yachters gaze at islands all the time. I'm sure we're not the first boat that ever passed by. They'll just think we're sightseers."

"Yeah, but this isn't a yacht."

"It's not like we're operating a gunship. Relax. As long as we stay far enough out, they won't give a rat's ass." *As long as we don't do this for too long. They're definitely monitoring us.*

Elise maintained course. It took several minutes to get two thousand yards west of the island where she could turn northward without arousing suspicion. "See anything?"

"We've got a bunch of boats," Luke said.

"What kind?"

"Standard patrol vessels. All docked at the moment. There's a watch tower overlooking the pier. Got a couple dozen guys moving about. There's a two-story structure behind them. A work shed of some kind. This isn't a little private resort. Gary Starch is running some kind of operation." As the *Barracuda* continued north, Luke was able to get a glance at a cove in the northwest corner. There was some sort of metal structure along the waterline.

"What about the fishing boat?" Elise said.

"Hang on."

"Can't hang on too long. We can't keep doing this. If we remain in sonar range, and they're watching, they'll get a little antsy."

"Will you be quiet for a sec?" Luke leaned over the guardrail, as if those extra few inches would put the object closer into view It was a structure of some kind. Whatever it was, it was built into the island and went below sea level.

He remembered the info he uncovered when researching the island's military history.

Submarine port, maybe? He thought about it. *Submarine berth—perfect place* to store a large marine animal.

"Luke!"

"Right, right, right! I'm looking." He panned back to the boats. As he had stated to Elise, most were patrol vessels—Interceptor models, capable of speeding to thirty-four knots. Docked further to the north were a pair of maintenance vessels. No fishing vessel. "Shit."

Elise knew what that meant. "Nobody said this was going to be easy."

Luke gave his eye a moment to rest. He gave the dock area another glance. One particular detail stood out. It wasn't something he saw—it was what he *didn't* see. "Keep taking us around."

"Alright. But if that boat's not docked, I don't know if we're gonna see anything worth reporting…"

"There's no loading bay on this end. There's gotta be a port for shipments. There's no sign of an airfield, so deliveries have to come by sea."

"They could just dock with the staff boats," Elise said.

"Would you quit arguing and just take us around. Gosh, and you complain that *I'm* too negative."

Elise couldn't argue that one. After a few additional moments of thought, she realized he had a point. A yacht as big as the one she saw would need special docking, especially if it was delivering a near forty-foot shark. And since the fishing boat was part of that operation…

She steered her vessel to starboard.

Luke put his eye to the scope. After a few seconds, a smile came over his face. "Bullseye."

Elise felt her heart rate rise. "You see something?"

"Seems like Mr. Starch got himself a towing vessel. And plans to do a little fishing."

Elise came out on deck. Luke handed her the scope. She gazed at the sixty-foot tugboat docked nearby in a large cove. Next to it was a fishing boat. Its size and features were exact to the one she had encountered.

"Can't read the serial number." She handed the scope back to Luke. "I'll get us closer. Get the long-range camera ready. I can digitize the file and alert the Coast Guard and your chief."

"Sounds good to me. Mr. Starch might've shot himself in the foot by not getting rid of the boat. The Coast Guard might find it interesting that his boat magically turned up on his property after being reported stolen."

As they drew closer, he examined the loading bay. The entire section was man-made, the pier constructed from metal that was newer than the 1940s engineering. The rest of the shoreline on the north side appeared to be made from granite. For such a structure to be flat and level would have required major construction. This cove was man-made. *Gosh, I can only imagine how much explosives and drilling was required to carve this out.*

Slowly, they edged closer to the island without making it too obvious they were adjusting course. Then again, simply by circling the island, they knew they were drawing suspicion. That serial number better match, otherwise they'd have to move further out and continue with Plan B.

Luke winced and leaned as far out as he could. "Come on. Almost in view." They were just far enough away that the numbers blended together. After closing in another dozen yards, Luke could finally identity the digits.

BEA 53719 B6 06.

Luke smiled. "Oh, Mr. Starch. Even you billionaires get a little careless. Didn't think somebody would actually stop by to check on your story, did ya?!" He grabbed the camera and zoomed in. Before snapping the images, he glanced through the window at Elise. "Get on the horn with the Coast Guard. Inform them we have a positive ID on a vessel connected to the Amadea beach shooting. Reference the Amadea PD report number 21-1928. Boat number included in the supplement."

"You got it." Elise grabbed the speaker mic. Before pressing the transmitter, she noticed a faint droning sound in the distance. Turning to face the window, she saw that Luke had lowered the camera lens. His grin had vanished, his body language now filled with tension. He wasn't looking at the island, but *above* the island. She leaned toward the window and looked to the sky. Two choppers had just ascended over the island and were speeding directly toward them. As they grew closer, their features became more distinct to the naked eye. These were CH-146 Griffins. Canadian model. She knew gunships when she saw them, and the C6 GPMG protruding from the starboard mounts. "Ohhhh crap. They're on to us."

"Get us out of here." Luke said. Despite the advancing threat, he zoomed in and snapped several pictures of the boat. In a single leap, he descended to the main deck, secured the camera in a metal case to protect it from water exposure, then grabbed one of the carbines.

Elise angled the boat away from the island and gunned the throttle. Its speed was no match for its pursuers, who had now closed in to five hundred yards. As they got within three hundred yards, the choppers separated. At two hundred yards, the one near the starboard quarter angled to port, exposing the starboard-side gun toward the boat.

Even at this distance, Luke recognized the features of the man operating the weapon. "Yeah, I see you."

He dove for the hatch. In the following split-second, the weapon opened fire. The deck splintered, the weapon acting like a power tool sawing through the skin of the vessel.

There was no mercy. No sense of compassion. The gunner had the advantage and was more than happy to exploit it. The only thing that brought him pause was the return fire. Not from the police officer, but from the fly deck.

Elise stepped outside, grabbed one of the rifles stored up top by Luke, and blasted away at the chopper. Lead rounds clanged against the reinforced armored hull. The chopper ascended and banked to port.

She ejected the empty mag and loaded a fresh one. There was no time to take aim. Pieces of the deck and pilothouse exploded nearby, followed by the drumming of machine gun fire. Bullets whistled by her head. Elise dove for the starboard side, using the entirety of the pilothouse as cover. That cover was quickly breaking into small pieces. Both choppers were now pounding the vessel. Bits of metal and glass rained all around. Bullets punched through the structure, flying inches above her head.

For several seconds, she kept face down on the deck. It felt as though the slightest movement would put her in the path of one of those wild bullets. After those seconds, which felt like an eternity, she looked over her shoulder. The pilothouse was barely recognizable. The glass was completely gone. Large chunks of the structure were missing entirely. She could see through the now-empty windows that parts of the overhead were dangling.

The helm and radio were destroyed. As though to torture her psyche, she heard the engine clank repeatedly before shutting down.

They were dead in the water.

Above that ravaged pilothouse, she saw the second chopper approach. It banked to port, positioning a few yards past the bow. Its gunner centered her in his iron sights.

Gunshots rang out.

Bullets struck metal. The next burst caught flesh. There was a scream.

When Elise opened her eyes, she saw the gunner reel backwards, his jumpsuit now red with his own blood. The chopper shot forward, with sparks shooting from various areas along its hull.

She looked back to the main deck. Luke was still shooting at the chopper, stopping only when his magazine ran dry.

More machine gun fire struck the boat. Luke dove near the ladder then worked his way around the side. The gunner—the man who called himself 'Beau'—continued his assault.

Luke watched the second chopper circle back. The crew pulled the dead gunner away, allowing for another to take position.

The vessel vibrated with the nonstop impacts.

Luke opened fire on the approaching chopper, which angled off toward the stern. As it did, the other began circling around the bow. Right then, the machine gun fire stopped. That didn't bring relief to Luke's mind—quite the opposite. His fears were justified when he saw the fuselage. That gunman unharnessed himself to take possession of a different weapon. Luke recognized the large canisters.

Great. Just great. A goddamn grenade launcher.

He looked up at Elise. She was on her feet now. In one hand was the empty rifle, the other holding a full mag. She slammed it home and pointed the muzzle at the chopper.

"Forget it! Dive! Abandon ship!"

"We go in the water, we're dead!"

"We stay on the boat, we're dead!"

Elise gave one last glance at the chopper, saw the man take aim with the grenade launcher, then cut her losses. Luke was right. Diving probably meant certain death, but at this stage, it would grant those last few precious moments of life.

She flung herself over the guardrail and dove into the water. As she did, the first grenade hit the pilothouse. The gunner launched a second and a third, decimating the whole structure.

Luke sprayed bullets, hoping to land a lucky shot. His attempt was cut short as the second chopper closed in from behind. Bullets struck near his feet. He sprang for the hatch, popping off rounds blindly in the hopes of throwing off his opponents' aim.

He descended into the cargo hold. Sunlight peered through the bullet holes in the hull. The machine gun fire had ceased momentarily, indicating that 'Beau' was getting ready to finish him off with the grenade launcher.

Luke was trapped with nowhere to go. He tossed the carbine aside—it wouldn't do him any good at this point. All he could do was find something to absorb the blast and hope for the best. He looked around for anything he could use as a shield.

Storage tubs? No good.

Lab testing equipment? He might as well stick a piece of glass in his eye right now and spare 'Beau' the effort.

Think of something fast, you moron.

Across the room was a duffle bag. It was stuffed tight, as though its owner was planning a huge trip. Luke didn't care, it would suffice. Among the scattered equipment were some metal sheets, trays, a large suitcase stuffed with rubber gloves and other medical supplies, and an inflatable raft. He peeked through one of the bullet holes, saw the chopper taking position on the starboard side, then dove for the opposite corner. In the next two seconds, he packed the supplies against himself, finishing with pulling ripcord to inflate the raft.

He ducked down on his knees and put his palms to his ears.

****

"Hope you enjoyed your visit."

With a smile on his face, Barton emptied all six cylinders, each resulting in explosions which sent shockwaves through the ocean. Debris rained out as though from a volcanic eruption. The fuel tank ruptured, sparking flames, adding to the apocalyptic imagery. The boat split in half and the ocean surged inside. Each half angled into the ocean and began to sink.

Barton lowered the weapon and watched the ship break apart. Satisfaction took hold. It was a shame he couldn't personally witness the cop blow apart, but it was enough to know he was dead.

It would've taken a miracle for anyone to survive that.

The wreckage would drift apart, with most of the fragments washing ashore at the island. The rest, if ever found, would never be traced back to this location. His job was finished.

One of the crew members pointed to the right. "Got a swimmer! The female!"

Barton looked. Sure enough, she was still alive.

"Well, goddamn." He tilted the machine gun on its swivel. "I'll fix that."

The radio crackled. *"Alpha One to Two. I see the smoke. What's the status on our visitors?"*

Barton groaned. Figures the guy would radio at this moment.

"The cop is dead. No longer a problem. Nobody will come looking for them."

"And the scientist?"

If Barton was alone, he would've lied. But there were too many people listening in. "She's in the water. Alive."

"Good. Bring her in."

Barton shook his head then tightened his grip on the radio. "Sir, I'm not sure that's a good idea..."

"If she becomes too much of a problem, I'll leave her to you. But for now... Bring. Her. In."

A seething exhale, hot as engine exhaust, escaped Barton's nostrils. "Roger." He killed the frequency and snapped his fingers to the pilot. "You heard the boss. Bring us down."

Like a Coast Guard rescue operation, the chopper descended. One of the men went into the water with a harness, secured it around Dr. Sheldon's torso, then hauled her aboard.

They slammed the fuselage doors shut and set course back to base.

CHAPTER 59

It was the third time in his life that Luke Jansen truly felt weightless. The first was in his mid-twenties during a high-speed chase. In getting the suspect vehicle off the road, they hit a construction ramp and flipped. To the rest of the world, it happened in the blink of an eye. For Luke, it felt like forever. The second occasion was when he and Morgan were nearly caught in a gas explosion. It was a trap set for them when they were investigating a lead to a murder case. Two steps closer and they both would've been cooked. Still, the blast was strong enough to knock them off their feet.

This time, it was during his descent to the seafloor. There were flashes of light followed by moments of complete darkness. He felt light as a feather and heavy at the same time. It was a slow sensation of falling, while simultaneously being lightly tugged in all different directions.

An unpleasant sensation intruded this strange bliss. Mild pain. A sting—like salt being rubbed into his pupil.

As though hit with a defibrillator, Luke snapped into full consciousness. He was falling, but only in the slightest sense. He was *sinking*.

Debris descended along with him. The boat had broken apart entirely. Some of the fragments were above him, blotting out the natural sunlight.

The burning sensation in his lungs alerted him to his dwindling air supply. He ditched his jacket, then shot for the surface, watching that bright glow get ever brighter. Almost there—right to that sweet supply of air.

A shadow came over him.

Luke froze. Memories reactivated his brain. The natural instinct to swim for air had nearly killed him. The choppers were still up there. A search for survivors? Regardless, if he surfaced, he'd be gunned down.

Then again, if he remained here, he'd drown. Time was not on his side.

Fabulous. Never thought I'd die by willingly drowning.

He could feel his lungs make their demands. Fatigue was setting in, not to mention the narcosis from rising too quickly.

Think, Luke. Staying here is not an option. You're either going up, or down…then up after you bloat.

Up and down…

He didn't take time to consider the specifics of his new idea. He had no choice, or time. Were those air tanks damaged? Only one way to find out.

He reached the wreck. By now, it felt like his body was on fire. His vision was starting to blur. Combined with the darkness and duress from lack of oxygen, it was almost impossible to focus. Luckily, there was just enough sunlight streaming down for him to locate the wreck without a flashlight.

Forward section—straight ahead.

He closed the distance, the bow section of the *Barracuda* looking like a hollowed out section of a canoe. The pilothouse was gone, the supports pointing upward like medieval pikes. He entered the severed region where it previously connected with the rest of the boat, then entered a corridor. The diving supplies were further up.

He continued another few feet.

His eye started to droop, his hand slowing to a stop. Luke's knees gave out. He was battling against himself now. His body was ready to force him to suck in whatever he could, despite the fact that doing so would kill him. He clenched his teeth, falling forward.

There was a smooth, cold sensation against his fingertips. Metal. A cannister. Full of air!

The will to live granted him those precious few extra moments' worth of energy. The canister was right there, the same one he used to interact with the whales. The regulator and mask were still hooked up, as he was too lazy to take it apart earlier.

Never thought laziness would actually benefit me.

He shoved the regulator into his mouth and inhaled. Like an extinguisher to a raging flame, the inflow of oxygen calmed his lungs. For the second time, Luke sank to the deck, completely spent. Had he not been underwater, he could have fallen asleep right there. He allowed himself a few breaths before strapping the harness on. He fixed the mask over his face. There was water splashing around inside, which was more annoying than it was a hindrance. Unfortunately, the flippers had drifted off somewhere, and he didn't have time to look. After all, he had almost three hundred feet of ocean to ascend, and several safety stops to make.

Before doing so, he took a moment to check the surprisingly intact compartment. Elise's air tank was there. Good, he might need it. Go figure, the diver propulsion device had drifted away, forcing him to rely on good old-fashioned swimming to get to safety.

Better to get started now. Yes, he had air, and thus—time. But both were still limited and he didn't want to be stuck down here when they ran out.

CHAPTER 60

His presence was like that of a Roman emperor. His subordinates avoided looking him in the eye, even though many of them contained the combative skills and experience to kill him many times over. Their employer may not have been a soldier, but he did wield power. With wealth came opportunities, which trickled down to benefit those around him.

Each employee on the island had been carefully selected. They were on the run, off the grid, easily controlled. They had nothing on their employer to blackmail him. Even if they did, they would disappear. Those who tried were never heard from again.

Even without military experience, the wealthy man knew how to command. The first secret was to have loyalists at the top. That's where Barton came in. The man was a pure mercenary, willing to sacrifice his own mother if the price was right. And being the billionaire, he knew it was almost impossible to outbid him. Truly impossible, once his plan came to fruition.

Standing near the helipad, he waited the arrival of the island's newest occupant. There was a mild sense of remorse. He usually smiled. Though not distraught, there was a mild indicator of sadness in his eyes.

The radioman didn't notice. Like the rest of the crew, he didn't look his employer in the eyes. He did, however, sense the grave tone in the man's voice when he spoke.

"Instruct housekeeping to prep room S-201. Have two guards on standby to keep an eye on her."

"Aye-aye." The radioman relayed the message, all the while finding the hint of remorse a bit of a paradox, considering the operation they were leading.

Moments later, the choppers came within view. Like twin hummingbirds, they hovered in the sky, then slowly descended to the helipad.

A smile finally appeared. "She's here."

****

Elise leaned forward in her seat, dripping wet. The men in the chopper didn't bother restraining her. What would she do? Disarm them all? Seize control of the chopper?

Her mind went back and forth between her predicament and Luke. His loss was soul-crushing. She didn't think this mission would be easy, but she certainly didn't expect such a drastic defeat right out the door. Part of her wondered if he somehow survived. The mercenaries had hovered over the water for several minutes, during which he never surfaced.

She tried to focus on the fact that she was still alive, but it brought little comfort. Instead, she felt apprehension. She was a prisoner who may as well be in a foreign country. Nobody was coming to rescue her, least of all the government.

These people wanted her for a reason. Not as a hostage—there was no desire for ransom. Nor did it add up with everything they'd learned about Starch. She looked at the men around her. Hard men with hard pasts. Murderers. Thieves. She wondered if any of them were involved in the chase at the beach.

Elise was quiet during the trip. There was nothing to gain from speaking to these people. Nor did she care to speak with them, no more than she would the inmates in a maximum security prison.

The chopper lowered onto the pad. A half dozen crewmen waved flags and barked on radios. Most wore jumpsuits or military-style outfits of some sort. Tactical pants and black short-sleeve shirts. One figure stood out in the crowd. He wore grey slacks, a white shirt, and a blue tie. He was like any average Joe stepping outside after a long day in the office.

There was no mistaking the balding head, the tall figure—he towered over the guards—glasses, and scrawny figure. Gary Starch. She was about to meet the man himself.

She was pushed outside as soon as the fuselage door opened.

Starch raised his hands. "Easy now. Our guest has been through enough already." He looked down at her. "Dr. Sheldon. A pleasure to meet you."

Elise stood straight and looked him in the eye. It came with no surprise he knew her name. "Dr. Starch." She looked around. Why waste time with formalities? "Where is it?"

"I beg your pardon?"

"Quit playing dumb. I've seen the Helicoprion. It got loose. You're hiding it on this island. And somehow, it's connected with everything going on at home."

Starch chuckled. *Coming out the gate swinging, I see.* "I saw the reports from Amadea. 'Marine Biologist reports seeing prehistoric shark.' Seems nobody believed your story, especially after the shark responsible for those horrific attacks was caught and killed."

Elise wiped beads of sweat from her forehead. "As far as the public is aware. I know different. I saw it *twice*. And your goons tried to make sure I didn't live long enough to speak of it."

"An unfortunate turn of events," Starch said.

"Not as unfortunate as what your shark has done."

Gary Starch's face turned somber. "Dr. Sheldon, it brought me extreme displeasure to learn the harm my creation has brought to you. It was never my intention."

'Creation.' Elise was more taken by the use of that specific word than the odd display of remorse. *Is it true? True genetic engineering?* Elise was lost in thought, missing whatever followed Starch's statement. It genuinely made more sense that the Helicoprion was simply undiscovered all this time. The ocean, as big as it is, was the perfect hiding place.

"—then to hear how it killed your nephew, words can't express my feelings."

"Your actions do. Rather, the actions of your men. They tried to kill me. *Twice*, if you count the attempt at the hospital."

Starch removed his glasses and used his shirt to clean the lenses. "Our source may have gotten a bit overzealous on that job. The main priority was Vick. Poor Vick. He was a good soldier. Unfortunately, I had no choice. As for the beach, it was a spur of the moment mistake."

"Yeah, sure." Elise raised her hands and looked at the guards. "So, let's get this over with, shall we?"

Starch tilted his head. "I'm sorry?"

"There's no getting away for me this time. You won. You're finally gonna eliminate your loose end. So, let's quit wasting time."

Starch smiled. "You misunderstand, Dr. Sheldon. I would prefer *not* to kill you."

Elise stepped back. "Why? There's nothing for you to gain by keeping me on this island."

"On the contrary, there is," Gary said. He glanced about. "Men of combat, men of low-level skills, men and women to do the utilities and general upkeep—those I can find. Medical professionals, harder, but doable. But people with your skill and knowledge, not so much. Marine biologists, as I've learned, tend to stay on the straight-and-narrow more-so than people of other professions. Maybe it's the animal conservationist side of you all. I'm not sure. All I do know is that the man I had on staff died when the Helicoprion escaped. Brutal scene, sliced him right in two as though he were a blade of grass. Fact of the matter is, I'm short a specialist, and I *need* someone to monitor these creatures. And then you arrive on my shores."

Elise scoffed. "You're offering me a *job*?!"

"A very generous job with generous pay."

"Blood money."

"I tend not to think of that aspect. I believe in creation, Dr. Sheldon. Creation and discovery. I've read your files. I know all about you."

"You know *nothing* about me."

"I know you had aspirations beyond being a little microplastic sampler on the California coast. You wanted to explore, be on research vessels, discover new species—have your name be known. Well, I can't give you the pleasure of actually discovering our specimens, but you will be doing something significant. These animals need studying and documentation. That's something that can't be faked, even by PhDs in other fields. I need a marine biologist, not just some animal handler. At first glance, you knew what the shark truly was, despite the evidence we forged."

"You actually think I would work for you? Even after what you did to Luke? After what your pet did to Chad? After your attempts to kill me?"

"Again, my apologies, Doctor. But keep in mind, would the recently disbarred Detective Jansen really have allowed himself to be taken captive?" He paused to allow an answer, only for none to be offered. "I didn't think so, either. He's got more principle than you'd expect from looking at him."

Elise did nod for that statement. "I'm not gonna be a prisoner on this island for the rest of my life, Dr. Starch. I have nothing to gain from you. I know what happens if I say no." She tilted her head to the nearest rifle-baring guard.

Starch shook his head. "I'd rather it not come to that. However, I have to prioritize the security of this operation. If you won't join my organization, you'll simply be a liability." Elise nearly smirked. At least the guy was up front about her fate should she not comply. "Personally, I think it's in your best interest to work for me. You'll be given first class lodging—private quarters, the best food, access to medication and treatment should you need it. There's no point in refusing. We've monitored your radio transmissions—we're aware that you were unable to alert the authorities on any findings you had while surveying my island. Yes, I know that's what you and Mr. Jansen were doing. And *no*, you wouldn't be a prisoner. You'd be a revolutionary scientist."

"How?"

"First of all, you'll be on the front lines of studying creatures that this planet hasn't seen for hundreds of millions of years. Second, you'll be regarded as a hero by the world when it is revealed that *you*, after working with me, helped to develop the vaccine that saved thousands of lives. See, you saw the shark. That's already on record, even if it's been dismissed by the mainstream. After the events at Amadea, you teamed up with my firm to locate and capture the shark. During our research, we've learned that this Helicoprion was in fact carrying a disease that is fatal to other organisms. And through our teamwork, we've developed a vaccine to save peoples' lives."

Elise crossed her arms. A marine biologist and a cover story all in one. At least now she knew why he was keeping her alive. Made sense, to develop a virus, he would need an explanation for where that virus came from. Hiding the presence of a prehistoric shark would be impossible by that point. So, what better option than to pretend he discovered it and engineered a cure from the disease in its blood?

"So, it is true. You've created this shark in an attempt to create a pandemic, that way you could come out as the hero in the end."

"There's a lot of money in medicine, Dr. Sheldon. At least I'm getting ahead of a very important issue in the world of science, even if it's one that's hardly being discussed."

"What's that? How to extort?"

"Ha! No, ma'am. Something like this was eventually going to happen. Maybe in our lifetimes, maybe in the next. But it *would* absolutely happen. You see, there's been much talk in using fossilized DNA to resurrect extinct species. It's been a debate that's lasted for decades, perpetuated by pop culture. Slowly but truly, man would've gotten to the point of genetically cloning prehistoric animals, with or without my involvement. What always interested me about the topic, however, was the fact that we'd be bringing something from a different era and putting it in ours. You might as well bring a lifeform from a different planet and bring it here.

"Remember the lesson from *War of the Worlds*? How the Martians couldn't handle Earth's diseases? In my opinion, it also would've worked the other way around—they would've brought diseases that would've wiped *us* out. Just as the Europeans did with the Native Americans. Bringing prehistoric species back to life would also bring their natural viruses to life—viruses our bodies are *not* used to. It'd be a disaster unlike anything we've seen in generations. As proven by the little mishap of our shark escaping."

Had there not been several armed men surrounding her, Elise would have struck him across the jaw. "Wasn't a *little* mishap."

"My apologies, again. Poor choice of words. However, I can make it up to you should you agree to join my operation."

"I don't get it. Why not go ahead with your master plan? Why not just let the shark roam? You already are unleashing your plague."

"It's a simple matter of producing the vaccine, Dr. Sheldon. We've only just recently had our breakthrough on the formula. Though we have the technology to produce it fairly rapidly, it still takes time to generate the quantity required for our operation to be a success. Keep in mind, we're talking about a supply for a world-wide outbreak, as opposed to a few hundred cases along the California coast. With a little luck, the incident in Amadea will be contained, and after another year or so, we'll be ready." Starch crossed his arms. "This is happening whether you like it or not. In my humble opinion, it's in your best interest to accept my offer. However, I don't expect you to answer on the spot. I see you've had a long day. We've got your quarters prepared for you. Barton here will escort you down."

Elise looked over at the former SAS operative. "Barton, huh? Not Beau?"

"Had to think on the fly," he said. He was just about to light up one of his expensive cigars. Now, he would have to wait until after escorting her. No way would Starch allow smoking indoors. "If nothing else, there's wine and coffee waiting for you. One thing we can agree on is that Dr. Starch treats his staff well. Provided you do your job."

Elise closed her eyes and started to laugh. The mercenary was talking to her as though he didn't tried to kill her just minutes ago. *Not like you didn't shoot at me, blow up my boat, kill my friend—potentially kill my friend.* She wasn't sure if it was woman's intuition, or just hopefulness gone mad, but something inside her was screaming that Luke was still alive.

Reality hit her. The odds were not in her favor, but the only way to lose was to quit. *Stay alive and figure something out later.*

"Fine."

Starch grinned. "Fine? Does this mean you accept my offer?"

The thought of saying 'yes' made Elise want to throw herself into a spiraling propellor. She shrugged. "Do I really have a choice?"

"Technically, you do, Dr. Sheldon."

"Right. Get the paycheck or get the bullet. Terrific options."

"At least one is far more generous than the other. As our Security Commander has stated, I treat my staff well."

Elise turned around, looking at the surrounding island. She was taking a hell of a gamble. Her world would consist of less than a mile of land. What time wouldn't be spent in the sunshine would be underground in steel corridors. And how long would she keep up the act? If nobody showed up in a couple weeks, then it'd be clear nobody would stop the mad doctor. Elise would not allow herself to take part in the useless killings of innocent civilians.

It's not over. This can change.

"That pay better be *damn* good." She was sickened by how convincing she sounded.

Starch clasped his hands together in excitement. "Believe me, you'll wish I hired you sooner."

"When do we get started?"

"We'll get you acquainted with the staff and work locations tomorrow. It's getting late and I understand you probably want to clean up. So, my men will escort you to your quarters. Just be aware, there will be guards posted near your door. Just a precaution, but don't worry, they won't be prying. You'll have one-hundred percent privacy. Get some rest. We'll have a meeting first thing in the morning." He started down a paved trail going around the other side of the building. He slowed as he took one last glance at her. "I'm very much looking forward to what we'll accomplish together, Dr. Sheldon."

After his employer disappeared, Barton took a step toward the nearest entrance. "Please come with me, Doctor."

CHAPTER 61

The ascent took over an hour. Last thing Luke needed at this moment was to risk nitrogen buildup in his veins. Nobody was coming to rescue him. Hell, it was curious that the *first* course of action was to send two chopper units to shoot him into oblivion.

The answer was obvious. They were alerted by their rat in the Amadea Police Department.

Luke was tempted to speed through the last thirty feet of ocean, but managed to restrain himself. When he finally did, the first thing he did was tear off his mask and inhale some pure fresh air. Until now, he never appreciated being above water. It was something taken for granted by any land-dwelling organism. Luke had experienced plenty of unfortunate situations, but this was the first time he'd nearly drowned. He would see to it that it was the last.

The first step was finding a piece of floating wreckage capable of holding him up. Luke threw his shaky arms around the decking. There he rested, maintaining a hold on his spare cannister.

"Shit, I think I discovered a new exercise routine. I should tell the Doc that—" He perked up and looked around. *Elise*... She was nowhere to be seen. Was she dead? Her body wasn't floating anywhere. He didn't see her sink, but then again there was so much debris down there, he was lucky enough to find the front of the *Barracuda*.

He thought of when he saw the choppers upon initially swimming to the surface. They had been low to the water, so low that their rotors were generating vibrations. If they were searching for survivors, they'd ascend and use the greater vantage point. All they had to do was wait.

To be as low as they were meant they needed to be close to the water. The only logical reason was to lift somebody out. The only person other than him in the ocean was Elise.

"She's alive." It was a declaration of hope rather than pure fact, but there was enough logic supporting it.

The sky was darkening. He looked to the west and watched the sun slowly sink into the horizon. It was both a blessing and a curse. Swimming across almost two thousand yards of ocean in the dead of night was not going to be a fun venture. On the other hand, it would provide some much needed cover once he finally reached the shore.

Luke watched the island, which seemed to be getting smaller and smaller by the moment. Damn wreckage had to drift *away* from it, as though nature itself was having a laugh at his expense.

"Sooner I start, sooner I'll get there."

He switched air cannisters, as the first was near empty. He wasn't worried about supply, as the first half or more of the journey would be along the surface. Once coming within sight, he would travel underwater to avoid being spotted.

After a few additional moments of rest, he placed his feet against the wreckage and kicked off like a competitive swimmer. By the end of this journey, he would put any swimming athlete to shame.

CHAPTER 62

If there was an issue Luke wasn't experiencing, it was keeping warm. The endless stroking of water made his muscles feel as though they were on fire. He envisioned his joints as twigs being rubbed together to spark a flame. Still, better to be in moderate pain than dead.

There was an advantage in the enemy believing he was a corpse. By the look of the shoreline, there didn't appear to be an extensive lookout. Just standard patrols moving along the shorelines.

As he drew closer to the island, he realized that he must have drifted further east while clinging to the *Barracuda* wreckage. The cove was further to the right, the area dead ahead being a rocky peninsula. There were a few scattered lights, nothing that would prevent him from sneaking aboard. It didn't seem that Gary Starch was particularly concerned with secret operatives sneaking onto his island. Aside from the trouble Luke stirred, there was no suspicion levied in his direction. Still, there was a degree of caution.

At eight-hundred yards, Luke resorted to using his rebreather. It was actually a relief to let himself sink and give his body momentary rest. He thought about kicking his boots off to lessen the weight and allow for better movement. The thought of walking on those shores without footwear made him reconsider.

It was nightfall by the time he reached the island. Despite the physical exertion, Luke carefully explored the shallows before coming ashore. There were two guards patrolling the northern shore, both wearing semiautomatic pistols on their thighs. The two men were in conversation with each other, barely glancing at their surroundings. They had done this walk a thousand times before. Nightly walks with no trouble, water on all sides, nobody to escort away from the facility. All they had was the braindead patrol. Reporting a burnt out light bult was probably a highlight to their shift.

They were average sized men. Fairly fit, but nothing Luke hadn't faced before. If he encountered them on the street, he'd have no concerns about engaging them. Especially not in his current mood. The problem was the radios they carried. Should Luke be spotted, he'd have the whole island converging on him in minutes. So much for surviving the aerial assault.

He dove again, opting to explore the east shore again. Right away, he made a new discovery. Another wall of steel—a submarine port. *Two* enormous berths made for containing submarines over three hundred feet in length. What the hell were they using these for if not for storing weapons of war?

It was around eleven at night when Luke finally scaled the west shoreline. The time was an estimate—he had heard one of the patrollers complain that it was only a quarter after ten during one of their passes. The amount of time exploring the water had to be nearly an hour. Regardless, he couldn't wait any longer. He ditched the scuba tank, then slowly moved into the shallows.

He crouched low, shielding himself in three feet of water. There was a guard posted a dozen yards south. There was a small light in his post, illuminating his figure. He was smoking a cigarette while staring in the opposite direction out to sea. Luke moved inland, careful not to splash the water with his feet. In the dead of night, each sound he made, no matter how minimal, was practically a siren.

There was a slap, followed by a grunt. "Son of a bitch!"

Luke crouched and gripped his revolver. There was no way to tell if the bullets were any good at this point. The other two guards emerged from the darkness and approached their companion.

"Trouble?"

The guard looked at his hand. "Damn mosquito."

"Look at that. You've *finally* made a friend!"

The two guards shared a laugh, while the third groaned at being the butt of the joke. The commotion served Luke well. He moved further to the right, using some of the vegetation to obscure him from view. Aside from a few light posts, he didn't see any engineering on this corner of the island. Further west was the loading dock. There were more lights that way. He predicted it was a quarter-mile ahead.

The commotion behind him stopped. A few minutes later, he heard approaching footsteps. Luke found some thick bushes and ducked behind them. The two guards passed by, oblivious to his presence. They were chatting, one with a New Zealand accent, the other sounding American. The Yank did most of the talking, the Zealander chuckling at the bad jokes.

Luke studied them as they walked further west. Both were roughly his size. They wore standard tactical gear with a radio mic clipped to their shirt collar. The Yank wore a ball cap and appeared to have a tobacco tin in hand.

After they gained some distance, Luke stood up. He glanced around at the trees, particularly those near the spotlights, in search of security cameras. Obviously, he hadn't been seen yet. The guards would've been on high alert otherwise. If there were cameras, he couldn't imagine the guard monitoring them was well disciplined. Aside from today's events, there probably hadn't been much action, if any, on this island. The dispatcher was probably slumped in his chair, suffering from boredom. Staring at the same patches of vegetation and rock would put even the most disciplined soldiers to sleep. This wasn't a warzone with an unseen enemy lurking over the horizon. This was an operation that the world at large was ignorant to. There was no threat. If there was any kind of concern, it would be for Coast Guard vessels in the unlikely scenario the intruders alerted the authorities before being neutralized by the chopper units. By now, there'd be at least one ship on the horizon.

Still, he couldn't risk being spotted.

Luke wringed the water out of his shirt. He checked the bullets in his revolver. After that long in the water, the powder was probably wet. Even so, he didn't have enough bullets to take on the whole island. And conflict was inevitable. He couldn't live in the jungle forever like *Tarzan*. His best bet was to steal a boat and take off.

Doing so would leave Elise stranded on this island. She'd be alone with these nutjobs.

Is she even alive?

The attempted rationale didn't work. He had to make sure. In order to do so, he'd have to explore the interior of the island. So far, he hadn't been seen by any cameras, and that luck would run out if he continued venturing further. He needed to hide in plain sight.

He had seen those guards pass by twice so far. No doubt they would cross by again. In this instance, Luke didn't mind the wait. He needed to take a breather.

Luke double-checked his surroundings, then lowered himself to the grass. He winced as he withheld a groan. Every muscle in his body was protesting.

They don't pay me enough for this shit—worse! They don't pay me at all now.

CHAPTER 63

When Elise arrived at her quarters, she was surprised to see that the room was fairly luxurious. There was a private bathroom, a small wheel tray of food made ready, a living room area with a flat screen television, a work desk, and a bed made out of the best memory foam. Lying on it was like being on a cloud. Starch was truly trying to win her over. He probably figured giving her a taste of the luxuries he provided would work better than stating the obvious fact of 'If you refuse to work, I'll have no choice but to terminate you.'

There were clothes on standby, all of which were her size. She probably wasn't the only female on this island, or else it was an odd coincidence that Starch had all this stuff handy.

Despite her reservations, she took advantage of the private shower. She rinsed herself of the ocean then checked out the assortment of clothing. There was a nightie made available. Considering the circumstances, she hated the idea of being in such thin and revealing clothing. With that in mind, she chose the jeans and tank top. The shoes they supplied worked just fine.

She lay down. There was no denying the bed was remarkably comfortable. Had the scenario been different, she'd drift off to sleep right then. But how could one sleep after what occurred in the previous hours? She stared at the ceiling. Her fingers still jittered. The explosions that ravaged her boat echoed in her mind. Only during grenade training did she experience the shockwave of a blast, and hand grenades were nothing compared to those fired from that chopper.

"Luke, if you survived that, you re the luckiest son of a bitch to set foot on this Earth. Or, you're just really fast on your feet.. "

Her attempts to deviate her mind from him failed. She thought of her fellow Army buddies who had actually been in combat. Up until now, she thought she knew how they felt after losing a friend in action. As it turned out, she was more naïve than she thought.

Crying would do no good—Luke wouldn't want that. She already could hear his voice in her mind.

"Oh God. You're not gonna shed some tears, are you?" With those words, she imagined that scowl. She hated it when she first met him. Now, it was oddly charming, something that would only be picked up by those who knew him and understood his thought process. It was probably best he wasn't captured. He'd be executed for sure, and it'd be a miserable way for a man like him to go out. What did it matter in the end? Death was death. Except there was that odd feeling in her mind. It was like someone was speaking to her, letting her know that Luke was still alive.

It was the same feeling she had when she encountered the whales, the peace she felt knowing that Chad was in a better place and he was united with his parents in Heaven. While Elise didn't feel particularly at peace now, she didn't feel hopeless either.

She was still alive. While she was alive, she wasn't beaten yet. She needed a plan. In order to do that, she would have to play Starch's game. She would accept his offer. Knowledge was the key to winning battles, and here she was, on the verge of being given access to the entire operation.

It was nearly one in the morning when she finally drifted off. She had already set the alarm clock for five-thirty. Guys like Starch were usually early birds. He'd better be, because she'd be paging him early.

CHAPTER 64

"By the way, did you hear that thing last night?"

"I did. It's been getting more riled up lately. Marco said it's been ramming the walls. Shook the entire facility. Either it's trying to commit suicide, or it's eager to get out again. I'm told it woke up all of crew quarters Section C the other night."

Smith fixed his hat, then looked at his partner, Parsons. "All of 'em?"

"That's right. Happened while we were up top. Us night guys don't usually have to listen to that thing while we sleep."

"No. Just the racket everyone else makes during the day. Jackasses. When's the next rotation?"

"Who says there's going to be one?" Parsons said. "No Union here. Just whatever the boss chooses."

"Just my luck he would choose *us* for this." As they passed the east guard post, they noticed the guard on duty leaning to the side. Whether he had drifted off, they weren't sure. Best not to know. Orders were to report such failures to Barton, who didn't take well to such negligence. Instead, he bumped the seat with his boot.

The guard snapped to life then stood up. He turned around, then relaxed when he saw it wasn't the boss inspecting him.

"Need some coffee?" Parsons asked.

"Nope. I was just, uh…"

"Another mosquito, right?" Smith tilted his head and raised an eyebrow, making sure their fellow guard understood the hint.

"Oh, yeah. Damn bugs. Can't stand 'em."

"Good luck with that. Maybe coffee might solve the issue."

The guard turned to a pot in his little guardhouse "Sounds like a good idea."

Smith and Parsons carried on. As they continued toward the northeast peninsula, they glanced back. They could see the guy returning to his chair. Smith groaned. *The idiot will be back asleep by the next pass.*

As they followed the bend, his lenses began to fog. He removed his glasses and used a cloth to clear them. "Damn humidity. Always fogging 'em up."

"Should go for that eye treatment Starch offers," Parsons said.

"Maybe. I'm getting tired of this," Smith said, putting his glasses back on. They followed the trail, eyeing the lights further west. There was a couple of night crew working in the maintenance department. Mostly machine repair. There was going to be more deforestation in the coming week to create more lab space.

The lights illuminated an annoying speck that he missed on his glasses. "You know," he took them off, "I think you're right on that eye treatment. These things are more trouble than they're worth. I'll speak with—"

As soon as the lenses returned to his eyes and the gift of corrected sight returned to his senses, he saw the figure in blue emerge from the vegetation. His eyes only registered the eyepatch, black shirt, jeans, and the white knuckles before they connected with his nose.

Smith fell back, his world spinning. All he registered were the sounds of punches landing and Parson grunting. Smith leaned up, saw a haymaker strike the New Zealander across the jaw, knocking him out. He reached for his pistol, but the one-eyed man had already turned toward him.

A kick struck him square in the face. Then all Smith saw was darkness.

****

Immediately upon waking up, Smith registered the sensation of cool, yet humid air against his skin. There were no layers shielding him from the elements. The next thing he realized was the tightening around his wrists and the crick in both elbows. His arms were tied around his back, linked behind a tree. He couldn't breathe through his mouth, as his rag had been stuffed in it, held in place by some other piece of fabric.

Staring straight ahead, he noticed the one-eyed man standing before him. He was wearing black clothes. Security clothes! Including his hat! Smith looked down at his own bare skin. He had been stripped down to his boxers and socks.

"Ah, finally." The intruder fixed his shirt, then turned to face him. "Looks good on me, don't ya think?" He spoke low. Not a whisper, but not loud enough to alert nearby posts.

Smith's blood raced when he saw the pistol in the man's hand. He checked the magazine before reinserting it, then holstered the weapon. Then he pulled out his standard issue combat knife.

Then the guy knelt down and pressed his palm to Smith's mouth. The reason was made evident a moment later when the blade plunged into Smith's left leg. His scream was barely audible through the muffling. The man yanked the knife out, muffling a second scream.

He eased up just enough to let his victim see the blood flowing from his leg.

"Sorry, but I don't feel like wasting time with a back-and-forth of threats, then you calling my bluff, ya-dee-da." He looked at the knife, then pointed it to Smith's left. "And just in case I haven't made my intent perfectly clear…"

Smith looked over, then shook when he saw Parsons tied to a similar tree. He was equally bare, his head slack. It wasn't the similar gash in the leg that had Smith's attention—it was the thin red line across the throat and the blood that rained down from it.

The one-eyed man shrugged. "Yeah, he thought it'd be best *not* to tell me what I want to know. Well, his body, his choice. Although, I've had a little time to think since our chat. I didn't provide enough incentive. Luckily, I believe in second chances. So, I'm going to offer *you* the proper incentive…"

Smith shuddered as the knife came toward him. The man lowered it between his legs, prodding the flap in his boxers to expose his genitals. He shivered as the tip of the blade pressed against the soft skin of his package. His eye were wide and not from his leg pain.

"You know, I've seen a lot while investigating gang activity. When those guys smell a rat in their ranks, it's barbaric to think the lengths they'll go to, to find out what the informant exposed to the police. Truly, medieval tendencies remain in our species. I investigated a case where a guy was strung up, much like you are now. Only, they didn't use a knife. They used an ice pick. They slooooowly pressed it in, twisting it repeatedly..." he twisted the knife, making his point clear. Smith shook. "Shh, I wouldn't. I'd hate to have you skewer these yourself. Which leads to my point: I heard, once they are ruptured, it's like a water balloon splattering. I tell ya, it's gross. Then again, 'gross' was not what the informant was worried about by that point. Man, it was a hell of a way to go out."

The one-eyed man looked Smith in the eye. He shook his head. "Nah. Who am I kidding? You're a dedicated soldier. You're not gonna talk. I suppose I'll just get right to it—" He started to push in with the knife.

Smith screamed, his voice drowned out by the rag. The man put his fingers to the cloth. "You yell for help, you do *anything* stupid, you will experience what that informant felt. Understand?" Smith nodded. The cloth was slowly pulled down, freeing his lips.

The man leaned forward. "Listen carefully. Is Doctor Sheldon on this island? Yes or no." He added the slightest bit of pressure with the knife, eradicating any second thoughts.

"Yes."

"Where did they take her?"

"Sublevel-2. Room One. It's staff quarters for the scientists."

The man covered his mouth again. "Good. Keep it up, you're doing great. I have another question: You guys brought a shark to this island a couple of nights ago. I imagine it's being kept in one of these pens. Which one?"

"Number two."

"Which one is that. Northwest or northeast?"

"West."

"How many security staff are on duty? And if I even suspect you're lying—" Another twist of the knife.

"Three on post. Four on patrol, including us, so two others, and one in operations."

"And that is?"

"Sublevel-1. Room twelve."

"What corridors in the sublevels do I take to get to the pens?"

"Uh..." Smith's hesitation cost him. A scrap of the knife resulted in a small laceration. Nothing deep, but enough to motivate him. Nerves lit up like fireworks. He tried shrieking, though nothing got past the gag. After squirming, he spoke. "They're listed by letters. Sublevel-3, Bravo tunnel leads straight to the west one. Charlie leads to the east one."

"Okay, good. We're almost there. Last but not least: I'm aware this operation has used explosives in the past. So don't play dumb, or your tongue will be the next to go. Then you'll experience the real thing. So answer—where are the explosives being stored?"

Smith couldn't believe the position he was in. Barton would absolutely kill him if he found out he relinquished this information. On the other hand, Barton wasn't the one who stabbed him in the leg, executed Parsons, and was on the verge of castrating him. And this psycho wasn't playing.

"Armory. Southwest side. Two-story structure. First floor. It's mostly monitored by the construction crews—"

"What kind of explosives?"

"Mostly dynamite. There's C4 also. Barton keeps that closely monitored."

"Barton? That the boss?" Smith nodded. "British guy? Likes cigars?" Smith nodded again."

The one-eyed man retracted the knife and stuffed the rag back into Smith's mouth. "See how easy that was?" He wiped the blood off the blade, then raised it like a gavel. "I'd like to continue chatting, but I've got places to be." The hilt of the handle came down on Smith's head. Once again, he was lost in darkness.

****

Luke sheathed the knife. *Man, when you don't have to worry about police procedure and a court of law, this shit is pretty easy!* He took the shirt from the other guard, tore a section free, then wrapped it tightly around the leg wound. The *other* injury would just have to heal by itself.

He made sure the restraints and gag were secured, then turned to the other guard. He allowed himself a chuckle as he reached for the 'incision' in his neck. In the dark of night, to a hazy person just coming out of unconsciousness while also suffering the trauma of a severe stabbing, the thin blade of grass, wettened by human blood looked like a laceration. Of course, the New Zealander's leg injury was real. Luke couldn't fake everything and he was on a clock.

He peeled the blade of grass, which had darkened from the globs of blood, which also served as a glue to stick to the guard's neck. Knowing the kinds of people Starch hired, this asshole was probably worthy of the real thing. Let someone else decide that. As long as these goons remained out of sight and didn't raise any alarm, they could live to see another day.

Luke went over the supplies they carried. Radios, nine-millimeter Berettas, six-inch double edged knife, taser. The Yank had a tobacco tin. Luke wasn't a chewer, but it might help him to blend in. The hat would certainly come in handy, as would the sunglasses the New Zealander carried.

He checked the Yank's prescription glasses. They were only slightly bent from the fight. Easily fixable. He put them on. The altered vision was a little blurry, but nothing Luke couldn't work with. As long as it helped obscure his most defining feature…

Luke rarely removed his eyepatch. It was practically a part of him. He despised the scar underneath, the dull dried up thing inside the socket. However, even with glasses and from afar, that black patch would stick out like a sore thumb. Yeah, he had the facial scarring around it, but as long as he angled his head the right way and tucked his cap down, he could get away with it.

Carrying two guns would look suspicious, but he could take all the magazines. There were enough pouches in his shirt to store them. He took the badges, and clipped one to his shirt. He was now 'Reggie Smith, security guard.'

He checked his own discarded clothes for anything he wanted to keep. Unfortunately, the revolver would stand out. He had no choice but to leave it behind. That irritated him, but with a little luck—*a lot* of luck—he would get it back. All he did take was the cigar and lighter.

"*Not* letting this bad boy go to waste."

After tucking them in a shirt pocket, he stepped onto the outer perimeter. The two guards were obscured from view, their hands and feet tied. They'd likely be found once the next shift came up top, but until then they wouldn't cause any problems.

Luke tucked the cap down, angled it slightly to the left, then walked the beat.

The two-story building was further south. *Just keep walking, avoid other people as best as possible, and monitor your surroundings. Time to ruin Gary Starch's day.*

CHAPTER 65

Luke kept a watchful ear on the radio. He'd kept a gradual pace since starting the patrol. So far, there were no alarms raised.

There was movement and commotion up at the loading dock. Luke rested a hand on his belt, keeping a casual appearance, while putting himself in position to draw quickly. He saw three figures grouped near the fishing boat. One had his hands up.

"I don't understand this! This is just ridiculous!"

Luke slowed, analyzing his surroundings in search of cover. Were these guys armed? What was the tension about?

The nightshift supervisor slapped his hands to his legs and continued his tirade. "What the hell do they expect us to do with these chainsaws?! They want us to trim some of the overreaching branches on the western ledge, yet they don't give us the proper equipment to do it. Stupid sons of bitches."

"What do you want us to do then, boss?"

"Ugh. No freaking choice now. Load 'em on the tugboat. We'll use the lift to get you where you need to be."

Irritation, but not alarm. Luke kept going. Better to not draw attention to himself since there were supposed to be *two* men on patrol. It would be his luck that they would ask where the other guard was. Luke had a few answers in mind. That wasn't the problem—the fact that he didn't sound like Reggie Smith was.

He followed a bend in the path that led north. The next several minutes was nothing but power lines and vegetation. The island flora was an odd blend of mainland trees and Hawaiian species, as though the environment itself was some kind of genetic experiment.

Two-story structure, Smith had said. Luke thought about the buildings he saw when surveying the island through the sniper scope. There was a structure near the docks, close to the southwest corner. He also remembered the vast number of crewmen he witnessed. Hopefully most had turned in for the night. It was likely, though there might be some more night staff on duty. There were also the remaining security patrollers to watch for.

As he followed the trail south, he saw lights in the interior of the island. There was a clearing further in. Curious, he broke off the path to investigate. He stayed within the trees, while simultaneously being conscientious of his role as 'security guard'. Didn't want to appear as though he was sneaking around.

Look as though you're investigating something.

Luke passed through thirty meters of wooded area before arriving at the clearing. Stationed in the middle were the two choppers. There was a guard on site, walking circles around them, listening to a radio program to stay awake. The choppers were still equipped with their machine guns, and by the status of the surrounding equipment, had recently undergone refueling.

It was clear that Starch's 'rationale' for owning these, if ever questioned about it, was that they were rescue units. Hence the lack of explosive armaments installed.

The guard completed his pass, then took a seat near a small garage several yards behind the choppers. The open overhead doors allowed the porchlight to reflect off the windshields of Jeeps and a pickup truck. It made sense, even for an island this small, to give staff vehicles to get from point A to point B more quickly. Those vehicles spelled trouble though. If he had to make a run for it, they'd easily run him down. He'd have to make his getaway through the trees.

Hence why silence was so important.

Luke stepped away, taking each step carefully. Last thing he needed was to step on a branch and draw the guard's attention.

He returned to the trail and proceeded south.

Several minutes later, he arrived at the docks. As he determined during the survey, the island had five high-speed interceptors and two maintenance vessels. There were a couple of staff on duty, though they didn't appear to be doing much. One was seated at the pier smoking a cigarette. Another was cranking a tool on the flybridge of one of the utility boats. Deck repair, possibly. As long as their attention wasn't on him.

There were a couple of maintenance sheds. One was a single-story facility—*not* what was described by Smith—the other a small two-story structure. Luke went straight for it, and casually checked his surroundings before checking the door. There was a security camera on a twelve-foot post nearby. He tucked his head accordingly to keep his features hidden, then examined the entrance.

There was an electronic scanner near the handle. Luke lowered his badge. The red light turned green. With a *click*, the door opened. Nothing but tools inside and an office upstairs, all empty.

Luke stepped out. "That little bastard. If he lied to me, I might have to go back and make good on my promise."

He looked around for any other structures, spotting another further south. It all came back to him—he had seen the men moving in and out of the building when surveying.

As expected, he needed to use his badge to get in. This building contained high-powered tools and repair equipment. It was practically the *Lowes* of Gary Starch's private island. There was siding, lumber, windows, spare tires, wiring and so much more.

He took the stairs to the second floor. There was more equipment here and a locked door to the left. A red banner was taped across the door, with black letters reading '*Authorized personnel only'*.

"Ah-ha!"

Luke's enthusiasm quickly evaporated when he noticed something missing. This door had no electronic lock. It was key lock only. He dug for the keys in Smith's pants and tried each one. None would fit. "Oh, that's just great..."

"Reggie!"

Luke started to spin, stopping himself mid-way. More importantly, he kept himself from drawing his pistol.

The maintenance guy raised his hands and stepped back, chuckling nervously. "Whoa! Didn't mean to scare ya!"

Luke eased up, keeping the left side of his face angled away from the guy. He hesitated, knowing his voice was nothing like Smith's.

"What's going on? Whatcha doin up here?"

Luke always hated chit-chat to begin with. Now he was faced with chit-chat that would get him killed!

There was only one out he could think of. He grabbed the tobacco tin, stuffed some chew into his mouth to mask his voice. "Sorry. I was in la-la-land. Didn't know you were there."

"Oh."

Luke cleared his throat and pretended to cough.

"You alright there? Your voice sounds a little hoarse."

"I think I might be catching something."

"Oh, I see. Hope you feel better. Where's Leo?"

"Leo...?" *Parsons!* "Oh, yeah! Uh, he went off to take a dump. Dumbass has been on the can for twenty minutes. I'm starting to wonder what else might be going on in there."

The maintenance guy laughed, then glanced at the door. "Having trouble? Why you trying to get into the explosives?"

Gosh, I'm improvising so much, I ought to pursue theater acting.

"Barton is getting extra strict on us night guys. He's ordered an hourly check of the C4 and armory every night. And I don't seem to have the damn key."

"You haven't been checking up till now?"

"The other guys were supposed to be doing so."

"Oh. Haven't been seeing them make the checks. Lazy bastards."

"Damn right!" A part of Luke was starting to like this guy. He gave another peek in hopes that the guy was wearing his tag. *Hobert Dawson.* "Hobert, I'm having a brain fart on where the keys are located."

"You lost them?"

"No."

"Wait…have you not checked with your dispatch office? You guys store it."

"Oh…" He got the info he needed, but needed a good excuse as to *why* he didn't already know. "Sorry, I have a headache. I meant the other guys have it, but I can never seem to find them. They tend to keep their radio volume down to the point they can't really hear me when I call them. I was hoping I'd catch them up here." A stupid lie, but hopefully the headache and flu angle would give him a pass. He was simply a guard who was a little under the weather.

"Man, you need some sleep," Hobert said with a chuckle.

"Damn right." *No acting there.*

"I thought I saw them over by the guard shack over there." Hobert pointed southwest.

"Appreciate it." Luke turned around, raising a hand to his face, pretending to soothe a headache while obscuring himself from view as he walked by Hobert. "See ya later."

"Sure thing. Feel better."

Luke exited the building. 'Sublevel one, room twelve,' Smith had said. Luke remembered seeing a large structure not too far inland. He proceeded south in the direction of the guard shack, spitting his tobacco after distancing himself from the maintenance shed. Cigars, good. Chew, not quite his thing.

CHAPTER 66

Lights to the east gave away the position of a large building. Judging by his current position near the southwest peninsula, it was the building he spotted when observing the guardhouse.

He took a left and went for the building. So far, the other guards were nowhere in sight. He could see the guardhouse on the peninsula, its occupant inside. Probably struggling to stay awake.

The building looked like an administrative building. The walls were made of brick, much of it cracked on the left side. There were all kinds of repair equipment all around. Luke believed this building had been built in the 1940s and was still in the process of renovations. Piping and structural aspects had to be replaced without tearing down the entire structure.

Still, there were some present day additions, such as an electronic lock.

He entered a hallway of rusted steel. There wasn't much to this facility other than medical supplies. It almost looked as though Starch was setting up a hospital. Isolation rooms—Intensive Care!

Hmm, in case your virus spreads to your staff, Gary?

The room full of body bags and stretchers reinforced that suspicion. It brought to mind the question: how many people did Starch sacrifice to make this virus? Clearly, he needed test subjects.

The corridor led to a juncture. To the right was the elevator. It was out of order. Fortunately, there was a set of stairs nearby.

Two dozen steps lay between him and Sublevel One. There was a metallic smell down here. The tunnel seemed to go on forever. There were overhead lights, some of which needed replacing. This entire island was a mishmash of old and new technology, and it was clear they didn't mesh together. Old units required bulbs and components that were no longer produced today. The conduits stood out, being shinier than the dull, almost green metal on the bulkheads.

Luke looked at the nearest room. *1-03*. He followed them down the hall, the count ending at *1-11*. To the left was a long hall with a single room.

1-12.

A swipe of Smith's badge to the scanner unlocked the door. It popped open, revealing a room with a large horseshoe-shaped desk, equipped with six separate computers. Countless monitors were positioned on the walls, putting the entire island on display.

In the middle was a half-awake guard. The guy perked up as soon as the door clicked, then spun around to face his visitor. "Smith, what the hell are you doing—" He stood up when he realized it wasn't Smith in the doorway.

Luke cocked a smile. "No. Not Reggie." A kick to the jaw knocked the guard back into his chair. He slid to the floor, unconscious. Luke removed his equipment, cuffed him with his own zip ties, then covered his mouth with duct tape.

After scooting the unconscious guard to the side, he proceeded to loot the key cabinet. Going over the poorly handwritten labels was an excruciating task, but he eventually found a key ring labeled 'authorized use only'. He checked the label on the four keys on it. *Prophylaxis; Operations; Chemical Storage; Maintenance 2nd floor.*

"Bingo."

There was more good fortune: the guard had logged into the computer files, granting Luke virtual access to the entire facility. The misfortune came with the realization that he could not contact the outside world from here. He checked the radio frequencies, only to find they were all limited specifically to this island.

Starch was thorough. If for any reason the Coast Guard needed to be notified, it would be done by either Barton or himself. The rest of this island, as far as he was concerned, was closed off to the rest of the world. It made sense after Luke remembered the type of people he preferred to hire. Didn't want a suspected terrorist interacting with the government.

Luke proceeded to familiarize himself with the controls. It functioned similarly to dispatch stations in the jails, prisons, and police stations. making it easy to learn. He was able to pull up a schematic of the facility, which also displayed the various camera locations.

Sublevel One was primarily the main offices, lounge areas, galley, the infirmary, a few conference areas, and had tunnels linking to surface structures labeled water treatment and chemical storage. Sublevel Two was primarily crew quarters, with a few janitorial and maintenance offices.

He went over the schematic to identify the room numbers. *Sublevel Two Room One. Easy enough.* He combed through the camera feeds until he found one located near the end of that corridor. The room was easy to identify thanks to the two guards.

On the upper right corner was a volume control button. He clicked on it.

"...Right. I don't know. It's best we keep away from each other. If Patrice mouths off to me again, there might be something of a staff shortage."

"Careful, man. He's a chopper pilot. You know how the boss favors them over grunts like us."

Audio monitoring. Gary Starch really was paranoid. In all likeliness, he had audio recorders in all crew quarters, maybe without their knowledge. If staff conspired against him, they would be identified.

It was Sublevel Three that contained the most interesting stuff. Corridors led to laboratories on the north side of the island There were two main labs according to the map. Luke clicked on the camera unit for the lab marked *Prophylaxis*. The lab appeared on the central monitor. With a few clicks of the mouse, Luke expanded the image to take over the entire wall screen, giving him full view of the lab and what was developing inside of it.

What he saw was a brightly lit room, full of test tubes, microscopes, protective gear, medical beds, strange technology he didn't recognize—like advanced supercomputers from the future. They were the size of the desk he was currently sitting at, a complete contrast to the old 1940s technology that made up the facility.

Luke panned the camera.

There were large coffin-shaped units on the south wall. From what he could see, they looked like refrigerator units.

He zoomed in on a label on one of the units. There were two words. He couldn't make out the first one—it looked Latin. The second word, however, was definitely storage.

His eye went to the name of the lab. *Prophylaxis.* Disease treatment!

"The vaccine's in those fridge things."

He went over the tunnel route to get to that lab, memorized it, then returned to the schematic for that sublevel. He went to the other lab, which was simply labeled *H-10 Development,* and clicked on the camera link.

This particular lab was a little dirtier. As soon as the image came into view, Luke noticed the abundance of protective gear. Disposal areas for gloves, masks, and safety glasses were lined throughout the walls along with numerous hazmat suits. There was a glass door on the far side with a changing room. There was a doctor in the room. At least, Luke assumed it was a doctor. There was hardly any way to identify the man through the thick mask and hazmat suit, but the way he was peering through the microscope, then jotting notes into a computer, essentially screamed scientist.

Again, there were storage compartments similar to the one in *Prophylaxis.* Considering the uncleanliness of the lab, despite obvious efforts to keep it sanitary, the incubation equipment, chemical processing technology, heavy emphasis on hazmat gear and disposal, it wasn't hard for Luke to put two-and-two together.

He squeezed the mouse, cracking the plastic shell. "I see the plan, Mr. Starch. Develop the vaccine, disperse it in various regions across the globe, create public hysteria—not to mention a large death toll. Let politicians make fools of themselves. Then 'Hey! I discovered the cause! Better yet, I have the cure! Just pay me hundreds of billions and you'll get it.' By then, the world at large will be so desperate for a solution, nobody will question it."

Luke panned the camera left. "The hell?" There were six enormous glass cannisters stationed against the wall. Each were hooked up with wires and tubes, with electronic monitors hooked up. They were all powered down and stored for future used. Whatever they were, they were medical in their intention. They brought to mind incubation tubes he had read about in conspiracy articles on how the government was going to clone human beings. Only these were the real thing! Whatever they were, they didn't seem to have any role in developing the virus.

After looking over the layout, he returned to the overall schematic. Right then, he noticed there was a button for Sublevel Four.

How deep does this place go?

He clicked on it. It was smaller than the other three levels. There were no measurements, but Luke guessed based on the map and the overall size of the island that this area was only eight-thousand square feet. Like bedrooms to a house, it was divided up into sections, each given their very own camera unit.

He clicked on the northernmost one. What he saw was a dull chamber with what appeared to be a glass aquarium. It was full of branches, logs, a small pond—reminding Luke of aquariums used for housing pet lizards. Only this one was as large as the wall itself. It was equipped with an atrium on the left for handlers to feed, medicate, and otherwise handle whatever was inside.

And there was indeed something inside.

"The hell is that?" Luke zoomed in. Something emerged from behind that log. At first glance, he thought he was looking at a Komodo dragon. Except Komodo dragons didn't have a large fin on their backs. It was almost as tall as a man, brownish in color. The creature crawled toward its pond, scratched its neck with one of its forelegs, then drank.

Luke was consumed with shock. He remembered looking at magazines featuring prehistoric reptiles as a kid, and he remembered seeing something like this named *Dimetrodon.*

I'm looking at a goddamn dinosaur... are those things considered dinosaurs? Who freaking cares? It's not from this timeline!

The first question to pop up in his mind was 'how'?

He remembered the incubation tanks in the development lab. Then it hit—the son of a bitch actually brought this thing back from the dead. That lab, before it was repurposed into developing viruses, was used to grow prehistoric animals. The specifics on how Starch did it were probably details Luke couldn't comprehend. But the guy did it, and he was using it to his advantage.

The next question was 'what else did Starch resurrect?'

He clicked on the various other cameras. One featured a two-legged dinosaur. A velociraptor, maybe? It wasn't much bigger than a chicken. Another was a bird of some kind. It resembled a vulture, though its head was as red as blood. Another creature was some kind of prehistoric crocodile. He could see its snout protruding from its pool, the right eye facing the camera, as though it knew it was being watched.

Luke leaned back in his seat. "He actually cloned extinct animals. All so he could engineer new viruses." *Hell, he might have designed a different virus and vaccine for each one! He could engineer all sorts of pandemics then offer solutions, for a 'few' bucks, that is. Hell, if that shark hadn't gotten out—*

The shark...

Luke returned to the schematics for Sublevel Three. Using the mouse, he followed Bravo Tunnel all the way to Pen Two. There were two camera units in there. Luke clicked on one.

He saw the inside of a concrete bunker. In its center was the pen itself, a huge rectangular pool filled with thousands of gallons of ocean water. The backside was a mechanical door, built into the steel exterior of the pen by Starch's crew. The other three sides of the pen had metal barriers over the ledges. They looked fairly new. *Brand new,* as if they were a reactionary measure to an accident that may have occurred.

The same accident that started this whole scenario, I'm willing to bet.

There were two people in the lab. They were dressed in plain clothes, chatting with their feet up on a semi-circular table. Watchmen. They had no role tonight other than to have eyes on the specimen at all times, and alert the necessary personnel if needed.

Luke enhanced the image as a dorsal fin came into view. There it was, the shark that started everything. It was swimming in circles, its snout occasionally protruding over the water. As he watched it swim, he noticed a peculiarity. He knew that the length of a shark's tailfin and dorsal fin indicated half its length. The distance for the fins on screen, compared to the humans in frame, it had to be eighteen-to-twenty feet!

Making the sucker anywhere from thirty-six-to-forty feet in length.

The fish splashed water with a swing of its fin. In the blink of an eye, it came to infuriated life. The two watchmen stood up as the creature launched itself into the steel door.

Under his feet, Luke could feel a slight reverberation.

On screen, he watched waves of water lap over the ledges. The creature hit the wall again, its head rising over the water as it changed course.

Luke leaned forward. That circular row of teeth that made up its lower jaw…

Elise had been right all along! It wasn't her imagination—she truly witnessed a prehistoric shark.

It all made sense now. The smooth cuts on the disemboweled jet skier, the abdominal laceration on the Stuckey victim, the strange cut in the anti-shark net. Elise had told him. Despite all the irregularities and strange occurrences, even with the suspicion that the great white at the dock wasn't the right one, it still seemed impossible that a prehistoric shark was swimming off the coast of Amadea. It was too much! Too ridiculous. Except it wasn't. This creature was *real*. More importantly, it was carrying disease. Even while in captivity, the fish was killing people in his hometown. Including Brianna and her kid.

The beast hit the wall a third time before quitting. It was a creature yearning to have its freedom returned. All of its life, it had lived in this dull pen, its killing instincts suppressed by imprisonment. Worse, it had finally experienced the freedom it was meant to endure, only to be pulled back into this dungeon. It *knew* it needed to be out in the open ocean.

Luke took no pleasure in killing a captive animal, especially one that was a scientific miracle. This creature was the only one of its species on the planet. Cloned or not, it was a marvel to behold. Unfortunately, it was a killer, not just in its instinct but in its biology. That virus could not be allowed to return to the ocean.

There was no choice. Luke had to destroy it and everything else on this island. There wasn't time to worry about evidence, due process, and letting the authorities find proof of misconduct. This was about saving the lives of thousands. Millions.

He checked the time. It was after three in the morning. At best, he had three hours before the staff would be out and about. Three hours to get the explosives, find the lab, set the explosives, figure out the location of the antivirus—assuming there was one—find Elise, and steal a boat.

"Before I go—" He glanced at the monitors one last time. His gut instinct warned him that he wouldn't likely make it back here before the shit hit the fan. If anything went wrong—anything at all—they'd be on him like white on rice. Someone would come into this office and track his movements, then direct the entire island to his location.

Unless the equipment didn't work.

Luke got under the table and cut every wire he could find that didn't look like it would set off an alarm. Monitors went fuzzy and the computer lights went dark.

After double-checking the restraints on the unconscious guard, Luke exited the dispatch office and hurried for the surface.

"Time to get crack'n."

CHAPTER 67

Elise woke up to the sound of chatter outside her room. She sprang out of bed, fists clenched, ready to tackle anyone thinking of barging in. Her senses quickly returned. She recognized the voices as those of the guards stationed in the corridor. Her first reaction was mild relief, followed by surprise that she slept so silently. Relatively speaking, at least. It was twenty minutes after three. Thanks to the adrenaline rush, she was wide awake.

With nothing else to do, she put her ear to the door to eavesdrop on the conversation. The guards weren't frantic, but they weren't at ease either. One was repeating the same phrase into his radio with no response.

"Dispatch, you copy?" No answer. "What the hell? Curtis isn't one to sleep on the job."

"What's going on? You guys alright?" Transmission from somewhere else on the island.

There was a scoff, then a remark toward his partner in the hall. "Damn idiot on West Watch probably dozed off again."

"Must have. If he was actually listening in on the traffic, you'd think he'd know what was going on."

The first one cleared his throat. "Unit Two, have you been able to get ahold of dispatch?"

"Negative."

"Unit Three? How 'bout you?"

"Negative."

"This is Patrol Team Bravo to post units, either of you seen Alpha Team?"

"This is Three. Not in a while."

"Two here. That's a negative."

"That's true, they haven't checked-in in a while," one guard said.

"What's going on? Everyone asleep up there?"

"I don't like it."

"Oh, they're probably just screwing around."

"Even when they do, they remember their check-ins. You know how strict the boss is on that."

"You think there's a problem?"

"Normally? Not so much. Tonight? The *same* night we blew up a boat with a guy who was investigating the boss? Pardon me for being a little nervous."

"You think we should wake up the boss?"

"Hmm…let's do a little more digging first." There was a twist of the knob. "Security to M-One?"

"M-One here. What's up?"

"Not much. Sorry to bother you, but have you or your crew seen Reggie Smith or Leo Parsons walking around?"

"M-Two here, Security. I saw Reggie up in High Service second floor doing the new routine security checks."

Elise noticed the pause, and the muttering of "What the—?" by both guards.

"New routine checks? Of the maintenance building?"

"Yeah. For the explosives."

"We don't do—standby a sec, will ya?"

"There's cameras on that room, aren't there?" the other guard asked.

"Not just that, but there's all kinds of alarms on that door. If someone tries breaking in without a key, it won't matter if the dispatcher is passed out. Those alarms will wake the dead. No way would Barton have the single key constantly be out of the office unless there was scheduled use for the explosives."

"Okay, now I'm getting nervous."

"Yeah same here… M-Two, was Leo Parsons with Reggie?"

"No. He was alone. Claims Leo was using the facilities."

"You have any clue where Reggie went?"

"I think he went to dispatch to get the key."

"Wait—he was planning to check *inside* the room?"

"Correct."

"Christ!" The knob clicked as the guard returned to the security frequency. "Bravo Patrol, I've received word from maintenance that Smith was up in High Service performing so-called routine checks on the C4. They said he went to get the keys to check *inside* the room."

"Uh, Alpha Two would kill us if we went in there unauthorized."

"You're catching my drift. Get over there asap. I'm heading over to dispatch." There was the sound of boots against the floor. "You stay here."

"Hold on a sec. The maintenance guy said he saw Reggie."

"Someone who *looks* like Reggie."

"Wait. You think there's someone going around dressed up as Reggie?"

"I don't know. But you know as well as I do that those guys are inseparable. Also, I really don't like these irregularities and radio silences. Especially not tonight. Something's off. I'm starting to think Barton might not have killed that guy."

"I was in the chopper with Barton. We hovered for a good long while after we sank the boat. The guy never surfaced. Even if the beast didn't kill him, he can't breathe underwater. Plus, it's a decent swim from there to the island."

"Not impossible. Let me check it out."

"Should we notify Barton?"

"Let me figure out what's going on in dispatch. Once I'm there, I'll wake him up."

Elise backed away from the door. Now she was *really* awake. Fear and excitement struck at once. Either these occurrences were a big coincidence…OR Luke was alive and on this island.

"I knew it. I knew he was alive."

And knowing him, he was PISSED and ready for some payback.

CHAPTER 68

"Well, shit," Luke muttered after listening to the radio traffic. His cover wasn't completely blown, but the guards were on to the fact that something was off. Luckily, he was alerted to the fact that they would be closing in on the maintenance building. He had a minute at best.

He packed as much C4 as possible into a carrying case for lugging maintenance tools around. He stuffed triggering devices and detonators into the pockets, then went for the door, shutting the door behind him. On the radio were repeated calls for Patrol Team Alpha. At this rate, it wouldn't be long before Barton and the other security forces were called into action.

Luke took a peek out the front entrance. The maintenance guys were doing their own thing. They weren't on guard, seeing as the alerts were on the security channel. Once they checked dispatch, they would *really* know something was wrong.

Gotta go!

Luke crossed the dirt trail into the interior of the island. Peeking to his right, he noticed two figures coming toward him from the guardhouse. *Shit!*

"Hey! Reggie?"

"Hey guys! Long night, huh?" Luke replied, pretending to be chewing tobacco. They probably couldn't see the case in his left hand. Unfortunately, they weren't letting up.

"Hey, wait a sec, Reggie."

Luke quickened his pace. Not a run, but fast enough to keep ahead of them. "Hang on. Be right back. Gotta take a leak." He disappeared into the vegetation. A few meters, he heard the bushes rustling behind him. He listened to the pace of the footsteps. They had quickened their pace as well. They weren't buying his act.

Luke coughed. "Just a sec, guys. I'm feeling like shit."

Flashlights beamed into the wooded area. "Let us get a look at you, Reggie."

"The fuck you need to look at me for?"

"Stop!"

Suddenly, another flashlight struck him, this one coming from up ahead. Luke stopped, momentarily blinded. The other guards approached from behind. As his eye adjusted, Luke looked at the guard ahead. It was the one who was guarding the choppers.

"What's in the bag?" The guard raised his light. As he did, Luke removed the glasses. The guard gazed in shock at the deformity that was his face. "Jesus—"

"Take a look for yourself!" Luke launched the case like a softball. It struck the guard in the nose. His light flickered high into the trees as he fell backward.

Luke heard the draw of a pistol leaving its holster. He pivoted to the right, identified the guard standing a yard away from him, weapon half-raised. He cocked his knee then launched a kick into the guard's chest. As the opponent fell back, Luke turned toward the other, blocking his draw by pinning his wrist, then striking him in the nose with an elbow.

A kick to the shin dropped the guard to his knee, making him easy prey for the next kick, which hit him square in the face. Before his opponent hit the ground, Luke was already turning to face the other, who was getting up and fumbling for his dropped pistol. Unable to obtain it, he tried to draw his taser. A knife-hand strike to the throat sealed his airway momentarily before a right hook to the temple put him to sleep.

Luke turned to face the third guard, who was scrambling to his feet. With one hand, the guy was going for his pistol, while grasping the speaker mic with the other.

"All units, we—"

Luke closed the distance and blew his air out with a punch to the midsection. A blow to the face bent the guard's nose to the left, a strike to the right wrist knocked the pistol away, and an elbow to the jaw put him back on the grass. The guard was still conscious. Luke mounted his back, took a handful of his shirt collar, and twisted. The guard fought for a moment, then went limp from passing out.

After confirming the threat was neutralized, Luke stood up.

"Ohhhh, shit."

He turned around and saw the maintenance man, Hobert, standing in the woods. As soon as the intruder locked eyes with him, he took off running.

"Great." Luke snatched the unconscious guard's taser and ran after him. Hobert was on his radio. "Security! Security!"

"This is M-One. You're on the wrong channel. What's the problem?"

"That guy! I—"

Luke fired the prongs into his back, stiffening him with a charge. The radio flung from Hobert's grip as he fell.

"M-Two? Hobert?"

Luke cuffed the guards and Hobert, tossed their radios, then hurried off into the direction of the main building. He had lost his sense of direction during the fight, forcing him to make his best guess. He could see lights up ahead.

Gotta be it.

As he proceeded, he heard more traffic on the radio. *"M-Two to Security?"*

"Go ahead." It was the guard who had alerted the patrollers to investigate High Service.

"I'm not sure what's going on. I lost contact with one of my men. I think something's going on up here."

"Order your men to the docks. I think we've got an intruder... Patrol Team Bravo?" He called for them twice more before quitting. *"All remaining units, switch to the alternate frequency."*

"Lovely," Luke muttered. Now he was on the verge of having the entire island bearing down on him. Worse yet, he wouldn't be able to monitor their radio traffic.

He gripped his sidearm as he arrived at the clearing, ready to draw on anyone moving about. What he thought was the main building was actually the airfield. The two choppers were right there, unattended. When he tried to evade the guards, he must've gone further north than he thought.

There was a facility nearby. He had seen it on the schematics. There was a stairwell leading to the sublevels.

Luke moved for the doorway, only to stop. He glanced back at the two choppers. An idea came to mind, one that brought a grin to his face.

He'd head below in just a few moments. There was just something else he wanted to take care of first…

CHAPTER 69

The guard arrived at the dispatch office. It was standard procedure for the door to be locked at all times. It *wasn't* standard procedure for the electronic system to be disabled.

"Good Christ!" He banged on the door. No answer. All doubt had been removed now: There was an intruder in the premises and he had the technical knowledge how to bypass security systems. If he had been here, he had access to weapons, schematics…the keys to the explosives. On top of that, with the electronic swipe disabled, there was no getting inside without a key. Thus, they wouldn't be able to monitor the intruder's movements.

There were only two keys. One in the office, the other in Barton's possession.

He switched to Barton's frequency. "Alpha Two. Come in."

Luckily, the security commander was quick to reply. He was good like that. *"What's the problem?"*

"We need to pull an alarm. We have an intruder on the base."

"Intruder? Any vessels off our coast?"

"Negative. Nothing the guard posts have reported. But we're losing contact with the patrols and dispatch. I'm locked out of the office—I think someone's been inside. The electronic swipe is disabled. Maintenance lost contact with one of their guys. And boss—they said someone was tinkering around the explosives."

"I'm on my way. What about our guest?"

"Still asleep, as far as I know. Walley's still at her door. I've instructed the men to go to the backup frequency."

"Good. Instruct Walley not to move. I'll meet you at the dispatch office."

"Aye-aye, sir."

****

Barton swung himself from his bunk. He threw on his battered black tactical pants and a black t-shirt, tucked it in so he could properly string the clips to his duty belt around his regular one, then hurried for the phone. He dialed the number to Gary Starch's room.

"Yes?"

"Sorry to wake you sir, but we have a situation."

"What situation?"

"We might have someone sneaking around on this island."

"How many?"

"I'm figuring it out, but we're losing contact with personnel left and right, and someone disabled the lock to our dispatch office."

"Damn it. I thought you killed him!"

“We monitored those waters. He never surfaced. If it *is* Jansen, then all I can assume is that he had access to a scuba tank and remained underwater.”

“Maybe I should’ve hired HIM to lead my security team.”

Barton refrained from making his desired response. “I’m heading out there right now. I’ll keep you updated.” He hung up the phone, grabbed a radio and a rifle, then headed out the door.

“Alpha Two to all units. We have a Code Orange alert. Report to Conference Room Two on the double. Surface units, remain on post.”

CHAPTER 70

Elise recognized Barton's voice through the radio call. All units on alert? Something was definitely going down.

No way am I sitting in here the entire time.

She clutched the handle, and took a breath to settle her nerves. In that moment, she went back to close-quarters training in the Army days. Such techniques had been drilled into her so thoroughly, it was almost impossible to forget.

Elise opened the door and stepped out into the hallway. The guard on duty spun toward her.

"Ma'am! Uh, Doctor! It's best if you remain in your quarters."

"What the hell's going on?" she said, playing the role of the self-important high-level staff member she technically was. "You guys are trying to win me over, and now I can't sleep because your damn radios keep blasting off. You and your buddy keep talking loud, as though the rest of the world doesn't sleep."

"My apologies, Doctor. We have a situation."

"A situation? What situation?"

"We're taking care of it," he said. "Just return to your room."

"Is there danger involved?"

"Potentially. Please—"

"If there is, then why aren't both you guards here to provide protection like you were instructed? Where's the other guy?"

The guard groaned. "He'll be back. He had to check on something in our dispatch station."

"Guard station? Which way is that?"

"Upstairs."

Elise pointed at a stairwell further down the corridor. "Is that him coming through those doors now?"

The guard turned to look. He shook his head. "I don't hear anyone com—" He gasped as Elise threw an arm around his neck, stomped on the back of his knee, then arched him backward. The guard, caught by surprise, struggled to breathe through a closed airway, while clawing at her arm. She had him in the perfect position. Had he stood up straight, he'd have the leverage to throw her over his shoulder. But his back was arched and he had no balance.

Elise twisted slowly and dug her arm in deeper. Finally, the guard's hands dropped and he hung limp from her grasp. Stunned at her own effectiveness, she let him go, shuddering at the sound of his head hitting the floor. If he wasn't unconscious before, he certainly was now.

It was shocking, yet somehow remarkable how easy it was to subdue a man. Elise took in several deep breaths and took control of her jittery hands, while contemplating her next move. Would she head up to the surface? Or would she take her chances and try to find the Helicoprion? Would a nine-millimeter even be enough to kill it? Maybe there was a radio station where she could alert the Coast Guard…

"Holy goddamn!"

Elise pivoted to the right. In her peripheral vision, she saw the man in the guard uniform approaching from behind. Relying on instinct, she threw a haymaker, clocking the asshole across the face.

"Hey! What the hell?!" The glasses and hat flew off. The guard staggered back, rubbed his cheek, then glared at her. "You'd actually hit a guy with glasses on?! How rude!"

Elise recognized the scarred face of Luke Jansen. "Oh my God! You're alive!" She threw herself on him, nearly choking him out with her hug.

"Alright, alright, alright! I appreciate the gesture." He tapped her arms to get her to loosen up.

"I'm so sorry, I thought you were a guard."

"Well, it's good to know my cosplay is top grade." He grabbed his eyepatch and fixed it over his damaged eye.

"Luke, they know you're on the island."

"Yeah, I know."

"I heard Barton on the radio. He's ordering all guards to duty. I don't know how many of them there are, but before long, these tunnels are gonna be crawling with them."

"I know. I need to—you said you *heard* Barton on the radio?"

"Yeah." Elise pointed to the unconscious guard. Luke's eye lit up. He snatched it off the floor.

"Excellent. They're on the alternate channel."

"Doesn't change our predicament."

"Yeah, but I can have a little fun. First, let's take care of him." They opened the door to her room and dragged the guard inside, cuffed him, and gagged his mouth.

After checking the name on the badge, Luke went outside with the radio, then suddenly started running down the corridor. He held the radio to his mouth with one hand, while cupping his other hand around his lips to obscure his voice.

"All units! I've located the intruder. He's in stairwell-C. Ascending…he's heading up top, heading for the choppers. I'm in pursuit."

He doubled back and rushed toward Elise's quarters. As he entered, Barton's voice came through the radio. *"Charlie and Delta teams, get up there and intercept. Fire on sight."*

Luke dragged the unconscious guard behind the bed, out of sight from the door. He then pointed at Elise. "Turn off those lights and get those clothes off."

"Excuse me?!"

"Sorry, poor wording. Change into your pajamas or whatever sleepwear they provided. They're bound to check on you in the next minute or so, and it might look a tad suspicious if they see you dressed and ready to go. Pretend you've just woken up."

He turned his back.

Elise quickly got changed, hit the light switch, then threw herself in bed. "This better work."

"Don't worry. I've got something to help convince them." Luke pulled out one of his detonators and depressed the triggering mechanism. They heard an explosion above them, then felt the tremor. Luke adjusted the radio volume so he could hear it.

"Alpha One to Two. What the hell's going on?"

"Bastard's setting off explosives. Alpha Two to Teams. What's going on up there?"

"He hit the garage!" a guard replied.

"Are the choppers damaged?"

"Doesn't appear so."

"What's the location on the target?"

"No visual."

If his little radio stunt didn't drive them to the surface, the explosion certainly did. A few moments later, they heard running feet in the corridors. Luke switched off the radio and ducked out of sight, while Elise pretended to be asleep.

There was the sound of a card swipe followed by the click of a door handle. The lights flashed on as a guard stepped inside. Elise flung herself out of bed, fixing her nightie to keep too much cleavage from revealing itself.

"What?! What's going on?"

The guard did a brief glance of the room, then looked at the drowsy, scared, and simultaneously angry marine biologist.

"Apologies, ma'am. Just checking to make sure you're alright. We have an intruder on the premises. Just making sure you were intact, was all."

"Intruder?"

"We're taking care of it. Remain in here." He shut the door behind him and rejoined the response effort. Elise took the opportunity to get dressed again.

"Alright, good thinking," she said to Luke. "What do we do now?"

He handed her a pistol and holster "I disabled the camera system, so they won't be able to track us. But make no mistake; Barton's not stupid. He's probably got men roaming the corridors. We don't have much time."

"To do what?"

He revealed the blocks of C4. "You on board for destroying that virus?"

Elise checked the Beretta to make sure a round was chambered. "Damn right I am."

"You sure? There's gonna be gunfire. And if you're seen with me, you'll be a target. If you want, you can stay here and I'll come back for you…"

"You want me to deck you again?" Elise said. "I'm well aware of the risks and what I'll have to do when trouble shows its ugly face."

Luke nodded. "Alright then."

"What about the labs and the shark? How do we find them?"

"I studied the schematics. I know the way."

"You remember them?"

"Doc…" Luke pointed at himself. "Detective, remember? Details are my thing." They started for the door. Before he opened it, he faced her again. "By the way…that shark…"

"Yeah?"

"Yeah… I saw it. It's real alright. I'm sorry I didn't believe you."

CHAPTER 71

With his personal key, Barton opened the dispatch door. He and his subordinate found the dispatcher on the floor, hands and feet tied together. That wasn't nearly as alarming as the fuzzy monitors.

"That son of a bitch killed the feed." He knelt down and pulled the gag from the subdued officer's mouth. "What time did he show up?"

"Before three, I think. I thought it was Reggie Smith. Used his badge to get in. Don't remember anything after that. I woke up right as Emile," he tilted his head to the security officer, "tried opening the door."

Barton rose to the computer, tapped a few keys, but could not bring the camera feeds back up. "He's still down here, that bastard."

"Walley said he spotted him," Emile said.

Barton lifted his radio. "Fireteams. Status report."

"Team One here. Searching west side of island. Nothing."

"Team Two reporting. Still near choppers. No sign of him."

"Where's Walley?"

"Haven't seen him, sir."

Barton sneered, then looked at Emile. "That blast was a diversion."

"We should call the fireteams back," Emile said.

"No. If my suspicion is true, he's now monitoring our transmissions. If I bring everyone down here, he'll just evade. Now that we can't monitor the badge readings, he can hide anywhere in the facility and we wouldn't know it. Not without a thorough sweep of every single room."

"What do we do then?"

Barton was back on the radio "Teams Three and Four, meet me near the main entrance to Operations. I'm heading up." He lowered the radio and looked back at Emile. "Let's make him think we're buying into his bullshit. First, let's get to my office. My computer can access the monitors. I need you to be our eyes. Go through the camera feeds and find the prick. Unfortunately, my private computer isn't as efficient as this setup here—you'll only see three camera feeds at a time. But you can scan through them and find where he is."

"How will I communicate if we don't want the intruder monitoring our frequencies?"

"I have a pair of backup two-way radios, not connected to the security channel. You'll guide me through those if you see anything. Clear?"

"Aye-aye, sir."

****

Elise gazed in stunned silence as she watched the prehistoric reptile moving about in its prison made from reinforced glass. It seemed to take a curious interest in the humans as they placed a block-shaped object on each side of the aquarium. She felt tremendous guilt in that moment. The lizard had probably never harmed a soul in its life. Hell, it wasn't even meant to be in this life. Yet, like the Helicoprion, it was a living bag of diseases of which present-day organisms had no immunity.

Had Elise not seen the warning signs on the door, she would've considered talking Luke out of killing these animals. But those warnings, designed for the staff, made it perfectly clear that these resurrected creatures were deadly to the touch.

"Damn you Gary Starch for making us do this."

"What?" Luke said, looking up from the block of C4.

"Nothing." She looked at a few preserved glass containers on the wall. It was like the room was also intended to be used as an exhibit. In one of those glasses was a piece of limestone. "Now we know why he was investing in digs in South America. He was looking for specimens to clone."

Luke stood up and goaded her toward the door. "Hopefully he can get a good tax write-off, because the money spent on that is about to go to waste."

They continued to the other containment chambers and set some C4 to explode.

"My God, he actually brought a velociraptor to life," Elise said.

"You surprised at this point?" Luke asked. He jumped back as the dinosaur leapt at him and bounced off the glass. It rolled over, sprang back to its feet, then leaned forward. It shook its feathery body, then took another aggressive stance. Luke finished setting the charge. "Let's hurry up before this little prick alerts the whole facility."

As soon as those words came out, he heard the door open behind him. A lab tech stepped in, wiping his eyes. "What the hell's going on—" He staggered back as he realized the security guard was not, in fact, a security guard.

Luke sprang at the scientist, twisted his arm behind his back, then rammed his head into the doorframe. The scientist collapsed, unconscious. Luke checked the hall to make sure nobody else was nearby, then faced Elise, who had a flabbergasted look on her face.

"You alright?"

"Yeah. I'm just nervous about who we might hurt by doing this. If we set off all these charges—"

Luke knelt by the scientist and pulled back on the shirt collar, revealing a tattoo he noticed during the brief clash. It was a black comet going down his neck.

"You know what that is? It's a symbol from a death squad in Ukraine. Responsible for executing maybe three-hundred civilians." He stood up. "Starch doesn't hire people with good moral foundations. Everyone here has some sort of black mark on their record."

"Not me," she said. "He was going to hire me. I'm not like these people."

"And if you refused?"

Elise nodded. His point was clear, most if not all of Gary Starch's crew were recruited. Elise was the odd duck where it was more useful to keep her alive rather than be exterminated. "Let's finish this before someone else shows up."

They planted an explosive near the holding pen for a prehistoric bird called Physornis Fortis, a species native to Argentina that went extinct twenty-six million years ago. The next one was a prehistoric crocodile called Diplocynodon. It was only about five feet in length, discovered in Europe in the nineteenth century. The reptilian raised its head out of the water in protest, as though it knew what the human was doing.

"Sorry buddy. For what it's worth, it'll be painless," Luke said to it. He and Elise went for the door. The job in Sublevel Four was complete. They went for the one entrance—the reason they started in this sublevel first. With a dwindling window of opportunity to sabotage Starch's plan, this area would be impossible to escape should security detect them.

They picked up the unconscious scientist and carried him upstairs to Sublevel Three. Enough space to protect him from the blasts downstairs. Might have lung issues from the smoke—but he'd live. Whether he deserved it was a different matter.

Luke peeked his head around the stairwell entrance. There were two security guards in the hall, facing the opposite direction. He looked the other way, seeing a juncture that would take them to tunnel B.

"Shh. This way to the labs."

Quietly, they snuck across the pathway and made the turn.

****

Emile shuffled through the camera feeds, starting with the submarine pens. The Helicoprion staff were still at their desks, clearly on alert—not just from the intruders but the activities of the shark. He had heard the damn thing ramming the doors. Was it going to bust through these ones as well? The damn thing seemed unfazed by the looks of it.

The sight of the thing ramming the door again gave him a headache. He flipped through the next set of images, shifting to Sublevel Four. The animals were all awake. He wasn't sure whether that was normal or not, as he hardly went down there. But the important thing was the intruders were not there. He studied the creatures for a moment, particularly the velociraptor. It seemed agitated though he couldn't understand why. It was hard to see every little detail on this smaller screen, but it seemed to be digging at something in the corner of its enclosure. Emile wished he could balloon the image so he could get a better look, but right now there were more important things to do.

"Any updates?" Barton asked through the receiver.

"Negative. Nothing in Sublevel Four. Nothing in shark enclosure. Standby."

"Hurry it up. We're descending into Sublevel One and initiating our sweep of the corridors."

"Copy." Emile hastily shifted through the various feeds. One of the feeds gave him a view of a dark room. *Stairwell 3-4C.* He saw the white coat of a scientist who was on the ground with his hands behind his back. "I've got a trace. Got a lab tech on the floor in Sublevel Three, Charlie Stairwell. No video sign of them in lower level. I think they're in Three."

"Have the guards call you directly at four-nine-one-eight. If that prick is on that level, he's probably going for the labs. Direct them there. The rest of us are on the way."

"Copy." Emile switched radios. "One-Thirteen and Twelve, call me at four-nine-one-eight. Use the landline down the hall. Hurry."

****

"Damn, that doesn't sound good," Luke muttered.

"What's wrong?" Elise asked.

"Landlines…they don't want me to hear what's being said. I think they're on to us again. We'd better hurry." They turned the corner and found a single door on the left side of the hall. There was a small square window looking into a compartment filled with protective gear, overhead sprays, and a door on the opposite side which led into the lab.

"This is where they make the virus," Elise said.

Luke moved to the door and swiped his card. A red light flashed, followed by a dull beep. "Son of a bitch. Only lab staff must be authorized for this entrance."

"You've got to be kidding." Elise peered through the manual keylock. "I don't suppose you have any keys that work with this?"

"I don't—wait a sec…" Luke pulled out the keyring attached to the maintenance shed key. There were three other keys attached. One didn't work. Luke tried the second. Same result. He was down to one more. *Oh boy.* To his relief, the key disappeared into the slot. The latch retracted.

They heard running feet behind them. "Oh, shit. We've got company." They disappeared into the decontamination chamber. There was no point bothering with the suits.

Through the window, Luke saw the lab worker at a table. Night staff, oblivious to everything going on in the facility. He knocked frantically on the door, then flashed the badge through the window when the worker looked over.

The lab worker approached and opened the door slightly. "What the hell are you doing in here? Security's not authorized unless—"

Luke kicked the door open the rest of the way, crashing the edge against the tech's face. The tech fell on his rear, tried to stand up, only to be knocked out by a kick to the nose.

"Whoa…" Elise muttered. She hadn't been in many fights, but she knew it wasn't as simple to knock a person out as the movies made it look. Unless you were Luke Jansen, apparently. "You fight in the UFC or something?"

"Kenpo. Put it to a lot of use in the last fifteen years." He nodded toward the big refrigerator-looking units. "I think they're storing the virus in there."

Elise went to the nearest one and yanked the door open. Clouds of vapor billowed around her, dissipating in the warm air. She swallowed hard as she gazed at four shelves packed with vials of red fluid. Fluid of death, drawn from the Helicoprion's blood.

"He's really trying to do it. He *actually* plans to kill millions in the name of the almighty dollar."

"That's where we come into play." Luke approached the containment units and armed a few blocks of C4. "What's your opinion, Doc? This is thirty feet below ground. Would a cave-in seal this virus?"

"That along with the heat from the explosion might be enough to do the job. We just need to—oh no."

The sound of running footsteps outside drew their attention to the door. Over a dozen security personnel had gathered, each one armed with automatic rifles.

Luke looked up at the camera in the ceiling. *Damn it. I should've known they'd access the feed from another monitor.* He drew his Beretta and fired a round, shattering the unit. Elise jumped, her ears ringing. She knew that was the least of her problems right now.

They were boxed in with nowhere to go. All they needed was another minute to set the charges.

"Shit. I knew I should've taken one of the M4s when I had the chance," Luke muttered.

The mercenaries started hammering at the outer door. They weren't bothering with negotiations. They were going to break in, kill the intruders, and clean up the mess afterward.

"If that's how they want to play—" Luke armed the charges and placed two in each of the units. They pulled one of them out for Elise to use as cover. With a hull made of two-inch steel, the container would suffice for protecting her against enemy gunfire.

She took position and readied her sidearm. The time for playing nice was over. Now there was no choice but to use live rounds with irreversible consequences.

Luke took the last of his two C4 blocks and moved toward the door. "They wanna blast their way in, huh? Let me help them…"

****

"Lost visual. They know you're out there. Probably prepping a last stand."

"Good. Let 'em think they've got a chance," Barton said. "Well done, Emile. Report to the main office and monitor radio traffic."

He directed his security guards to take breaching position while two of them set explosives in the outer door.

"Clear!"

With the press of a button, the charges blew the hinges. The huge metal door fell like a slab, the latch protruding to the side like a spike.

Barton glimpsed through the window. He saw the biologist ducking behind one of the containment units with the pistol in hand. "Ha. They actually think they have a chance."

"Sir, it'll be difficult to smoke them out without damaging the product," one of the explosive technicians said.

"Not a problem. We'll smoke them out with gas. Prep the charges and prepare for breach."

The men completed their task and moved out into the hall. They detonated the charges, flinging the door into the lab.

Two lines of security officers flooded the atrium. The leads took cover behind the frame and prepped their gas grenades. There was something under the fallen door. Something black and plastic in appearance, with a small metal rod protruding from its center.

"Oh, sh—"

The C4 burst, the shockwave consuming the atrium. Half a dozen men fell backward, four of which were killed instantly by the blast. Gunfire immediately followed, striking the confused horde behind them. The men broke ranks, some deaf and unable to register what was happening.

"Stop moving out into the open, you stupid idiots!" Barton said. He grabbed one by the shoulder and shoved him toward the opening. "Return fire." That guard peeked around the corner to take aim, only to catch a round in the neck. He spun on his heel and fell at Barton's feet. He shook his head, rolled the body off his boot, then approached the entrance, keeping to the right to avoid the line of fire.

A few guards shot back, unable to see through the smoke. A green mist started billowing out from the atrium. The explosion had ruptured the gas grenades, which was now billowing into both the hallway and lab.

"Hit 'em with more," Barton said. "We'll choke 'em out."

Guards tossed more grenades into the lab, landing them near the blockade of tables that the infiltrators had set up. Good against bullets, useless against fumes.

Barton smiled. It was just a matter of time before they would have no choice but to come out through the only entrance.

****

Elise fired a few rounds through the greenish cloud then withdrew to the back of the room. She was already coughing. "We're in trouble."

"Thanks for pointing out the obvious," Luke said. He fired another round through the doorway. He ducked behind a table and loaded a fresh magazine. The lack of return gunfire indicated that the enemy was playing the waiting game. Unfortunately, it was a tactic that would prove successful. The ventilators were off. There was no other exit. The only way out was through those doors…right into the line of fire.

They were in the very scenario they were trying to avoid in Sublevel Four.

"I don't suppose you have any bright ideas?" Elise said.

"Working on it," Luke said.

Elise watched the cloud gradually fill the room. "Any ideas *now*?!"

"You *just* asked."

"Yeah—kind of a lot's happened since then…"

Luke sucked in a breath before the cloud embraced them. "Got no choice. Gotta make a go for it. That, or we blow the charges right here with us inside."

Elise almost said yes to that. "Wait… I have an idea." She opened one of the containers, pulled out a few vials of the virus, then lined herself up with the door.

"The hell are you doing?"

"Something to make them fan out," Elise said, rearing her arm back. Luke realized she had a point. It was worth a shot. If they got exposed in their escape, they'd have time to grab the vaccine and inoculate themselves.

"Hold up just another sec..." Luke pulled out the detonator marked for the explosives downstairs. *Something else to throw them off.* He pressed the button and felt the facility shake beneath his feet.

Even from this distance, the blast was deafening. Ceiling panels fell, lights flickered, and any staff member not already awake was now rushing out of their quarters.

"Do it now," Luke said.

****

Barton hurried to the juncture and peered into the connecting corridor. Smoke was spewing near the end of the hall. He could see structural damage. Parts of the corridor had caved in. There was the echo of collapsing debris.

The bastard had set up explosives downstairs and killed the specimens.

"Alpha Two! What the hell's going on?!"

"Standby, One."

"No, I want an answer right now, goddamnit! What was that blast?"
"Sublevel Four. He sabotaged our explosives and detonated a charge downstairs."

"And the specimens?"

"They—" Barton looked up at the ceiling, dreading the response. "There's no way they could've survived that blast."

There was a short pause.

"Capture them alive."

You've GOT to be kidding me! "Sir, they're not gonna allow us to take 'em..."

"I want them ALIVE! Do as I say. Or would you rather I gave your coordinates to the Turkish government? I'm sure they'd be pleased to meet you again after your little visit to their embassy in Libya."

The man was serious. He didn't make blatant threats often, but when he did, they were not simply for show. He was furious about the deaths of his pets, which had cost over a billion to produce and grow, let along create the product from their blood.

Barton singled out two of his men. "Prep tasers and masks. We're gonna go in and..." He heard the smashing of glass along the floor. Looking down, he saw the shards spreading out over a huge pool of red liquid. Another vial came out, smashing on the floor. A third struck one of the guards in the face, splattering its contents into his mouth and eyes.

"Contamination!" one of them shouted. The men fanned out.

"Hold position," Barton ordered. His next command was muffled by repeated gunfire as the two intruders stormed the hallway.

****

Their aim was fast and accurate.

Luke took the left while Elise took the right. They popped off rounds into the confused group of enemy soldiers, dropping one after another.

Elise reloaded, dropped to one knee, and placed two bullets into a guard. As he fell, she turned her aim to the next one, hitting him once in the vest. It wasn't enough to kill him, but foiled his attempt to shoot her, thus allowing that much-needed second shot which landed in his temple.

By now, killing had become second-nature. The training she had gone through in the past had finally come to use. With a swing of the pistol, she floored the guard who had been struck in the face by the glass vial, then pointed her muzzle at another who fired at her from the hall. His shot missed. Hers didn't.

She saw the one named Barton kneeling up ahead to her left. Knowing she had one chance, she pivoted and took aim.

In the blink of an eye, she felt two pricks, immediately followed by the tightening of every muscle in her body. She fell to the floor, convulsing from the electric current that surged through her body.

Double tap! Double tap! One to the body, one to the head. The two guards collapsed simultaneously, their weapons slipping from their dead fingers.

No sooner were they lying flat on the tile did Luke notice another duo advancing from down the hall. Both had rifles shouldered and pointed at him. With the slide of his pistol locked, he made the instant choice between reloading or diving for one of the dead guards' weapons. He chose the latter.

Luke hit the floor. Bullets whizzed overhead—bullets that would've struck him in the chest a millisecond earlier. He scooped up one of the M4s, pointed it down the hall, and unleashed a spray of bullets. Both combatants danced in place then collapsed to the floor.

The former detective rose to his knee and turned around. Elise was on the floor, shaking. Two wires stretched from her midsection, linking to a taser in Barton's grip.

The mercenary turned his gaze to the detective, dropped the taser, and turned to face him. Luke squeezed the trigger, only to hear that dreaded *click* of an empty weapon. Wasting no time, he threw the weapon like a tomahawk. Barton threw his hands over his face, deflecting the projectile.

Luke sprang into action. Barton, disregarding his instructions from Starch, went for his sidearm. It was kicked from his grasp before he could use it. Luke went on the assault, striking Barton in the face with a one-two punch combo, before landing a third strike to his center.

The merc absorbed the blows, returning with a swing of his own, which Luke successfully parried before throwing a kick to the ribs. The air blew from Barton's lungs, the impact knocking him back several steps. He recovered quick enough to anticipate Luke's next strike.

Luke threw another punch to the head, only for his arm to be caught and twisted. Next came the sensation of being lifted off of his feet before being flung over Barton's shoulder. He hit the floor, then grunted as the mercenary stomped down on his ribs.

He rolled to avoid the next blow then sprang to his feet.

Both men collided, each grabbing ahold of the other, simultaneously exchanging blows with clenched fists and elbows. A knee to the groin doubled Luke over. Barton seized him in a headlock, closing his airway while proceeding to knee him in the stomach.

Luke could feel the clouds roll over his consciousness. With moments remaining to break the hold, he went for his knife. Barton, seeing the weapon unsheathing, released his hold. Luke's grip on the knife barely lasted a moment, as the mercenary grabbed his wrist and twisted it. Barton kicked the weapon across the floor, then struck Luke in the face with an elbow.

Two more blows to the chin drew blood. Weakened, Luke was unable to stop Barton from pinning him against the wall. For the second time, he felt his airway close off as Barton rammed his forearm under his chin.

The merc stared him in the eye as he choked him out. "What a shame, Detective. There was a part of me that liked you."

Luke gritted his teeth, trying to grasp for breath, but received nothing. Not ready to quit, he tried to kick Barton's knee, only to feel the merc's weight atop his foot. He was pinned.

He couldn't outmuscle him at this point, leaving him with one final option. He reached for his vest. Barton went for Luke's wrist, pinning it against his abdomen.

"What do ya think you're doing? Got no more guns and knives…"

Luke grunted. Barton had pinned his wrist, but not before he grabbed what he needed. "Just—a party spoiler."

He watched Barton's expression turn to one of alarm when he realized it was not another knife, but a detonator in Luke's hand. He pressed the button, triggering a blast that shook the floor. The ceiling collapsed, the walls blowing outward. The interior of the lab caved in, sealing Starch's evil work inside.

Out in the hallway, debris rained down on both men. Simultaneously, they fell to the floor unconscious, surrounded by rubble, dust, and smoke.

CHAPTER 72

Lucid images of a burning vehicle haunted his mind. He was standing there, his face scorched, his skin red, his left eye white. It was nothing compared to the smoldering remains of his lifelong friend, who lay on the pavement in front of him. Pain and failure became one that night, their scars everlasting.

The fire was as hot as it ever felt. If Hell was on Earth, it started with those Molotov cocktails. In the dream, Luke simply watched as the flames transformed the body of his friend, erasing his identity, the cause of the closed casket, a reminder of the hate he earned from friends and family.

And himself.

No skin graft or eyepatch could hide the scars of failure. Nothing could wipe it from memory. There was nothing to do except live with it.

Like ripples in a pond, the images of his burning friend faded. Luke was surrounded by a vast blue world. In front of him was the humpback Melody. She and her young approached, flippers stretched out to the side, their song echoing far into the sea.

Forgiveness. Trust. Compassion.

Three words often thrown around as catchphrases. Yet, the whale expressed all three traits better than any human could dream of. It was riddled with scars, brought to the brink of death by humans, yet it didn't hold a grudge. It was a damaged soul and embraced the human stranger as though it could sense similar pain and despair. The creature offered forgiveness, trust, and compassion without a moment's thought. If only humans were so humane.

In the dream, Luke understood the fourth virtue the whale provided. Hope. There were brighter days ahead. Good would triumph over evil, no matter how impossible the road seemed. Those wounds should've been fatal, yet Melody survived. She beat those 'impossible' odds, spawned a child, mastered the ocean, and didn't hold a grudge.

The song reverberated in his mind, quelling the pain.

Beyond that song came a loud booming sound, like a hammer slamming against metal in the distance. Then came a feeling of mist against his face. The peace came to an abrupt end as something smacked against his shoulder…

****

"Wake up!"

Luke was on his knees, his vision gradually coming back to him. His head throbbed from where a piece of rock had hit him. He registered the smell of rusted steel, then took in the sight of the concrete walls lined with piping. Directly ahead was a huge pool of water.

He was in the submarine pen—the creature's holding facility.

The dorsal fin cut along the surface. The beast was swimming in circles, slightly faster than the pace of a normal shark. It was agitated. Luke knew this, not just by its movements, but the nervous expressions of the animal handlers at the desk. It would've been easy to assume they were uneasy due to the numerous explosions within the facility had their attention not been entirely on the shark itself. They hardly seemed to take notice of the two prisoners, armed guards, or even the furious Gary Starch as he stepped in front of Luke Jansen.

The doctor's hands were behind his back. His balding head was covered in dust. Either he was part of the rescue crew that dug him out from the aftermath of the lab explosion, or he had rushed to Sublevel Four to inspect his babies. Or, it could've been both, since the precious virus had been blown to kingdom come.

He looked over to Luke's left. "I suppose I misjudged you. I thought at worst, you'd simply refuse and attempt to escape. Not resort to terrorist tactics and destroy my work."

"Only someone as out of touch as *you*—someone who plans to murder millions—would consider what *we* did as terrorism."

Luke looked to the left. Elise was kneeled over at his blindside, hands cuffed behind her back, just as his were. She had a couple of cuts and bruises but looked okay otherwise.

He looked down at himself. The weapons and detonators had been removed. No surprise. They had patted him down pretty well. All they missed, or probably neglected, was the cigar tube in his flashlight pocket. Whoever checked him probably saw what it was and didn't give a sh:t as long as it wasn't a weapon.

Luke cracked a smile. *Priorities. Cuffed, on my knees, got over a half-dozen armed men in the pen with me...and I'm worried about letting this expensive cigar go to waste.* Maybe it was the lesson of the dream. Give yourself something to look forward to.

The crack of a small metal rod against his right shoulder ended his amusement.

"Get that smile off your face, mate."

He looked over his shoulder at Barton. The mercenary's face was bruised and cut. He was slightly lackluster. He probably regained consciousness only fifteen minutes ago or so. He held an expandable baton in his hand.

Luke shrugged. "Sorry. Just thought of something funny."

"I'm glad you're getting a last laugh, Detective Jansen. And I emphasize the word 'last'." Gary Starch paused only to look past his captive at the medical doctor stepping into the pen.

"Excuse me for interrupting. Just administering injections for anyone exposed in tunnel B."

Starch pointed at Barton. "Roll up your sleeve."

Barton did so. The doctor approached and opened the briefcase, revealing several vials of vaccine. He pulled out an injection gun, installed one of the vials, and raised it to Barton's arm. The merc showed no indication of pain as the needle entered him.

"All done. Anyone else?"

"The guards over there." Barton pointed to two men on the right of the pen.

"Don't forget the band-aids and lollypops," Luke said.

Barton struck him in the face. He then removed his knife and knelt down, nearing the tip to his eye. "Maybe you'd like to have it carved out."

"No, don't do it," Starch said. Barton hesitated, then stepped away. Starch leaned on the guardrail and looked at the Helicoprion. "I want him to *see* its jaw before it cleaves him in half."

"Oh, is that why we're here? Reduced to fish food?" Luke said.

"Absolutely. I figured you helping to sustain my creation will be at least one positive contribution to my plan."

"Yeah? What's the matter? Have a few setbacks today?" Elise said.

Gary Starch failed to hide his anger. He smacked the marine biologist across the face then struck Luke for good measure.

All it did was cause Luke to laugh. "I think we pissed him off."

Elise chuckled too. Might as well. She had no desire to spend her last moments crying and pleading for mercy. "Aw. Dr. Starch lost his virus. He's sad." She perked up. "Hey, you've still got the vaccine! You might still make a buck, even if the value has dropped significantly."

"The joke's on you, Dr. Sheldon. I still have my shark. The *purest* of my specimens. Thanks to my operations in the Antarctic, I found her DNA ancestor preserved in ice. Thus, its tissue was intact, allowing me to bypass the sequence gaps and develop a nearly pure genetic clone. With her physiology nearly identical to her ancestors, she carried the same diseases. I didn't have to dig her up from Jurassic limestone. She was ready and waiting to come back to life."

His self-indulgent monologue was interrupted as the shark slammed into the metal exterior door.

Luke felt the floor shake under his knees. The shark raised its head as it turned, slapping the door with its tail. The handlers rushed to the guardrails, armed with fifteen-foot poles with electric rods at the end. They touched the rods to the shark as it passed, shocking it. The beast jolted, swimming to the other end of the pen.

He looked over at Elise, who looked over at him. No wonder the thing was so violent. It was probably treated like this its entire life in captivity. Hence, everything it saw, it believed to be a threat.

Elise looked down and closed her eyes. She thought about her anger for the shark. Yes, it had killed Chad, and that was something she couldn't simply let go of. But now, it all came together. The shark wasn't acting as God made it—it was acting as *Man* made it. They had built this fantastic creature and turned it into a hyperviolent killing machine that was twenty-times more dangerous than anything that swam three-hundred-million years ago.

One of the handlers ran to the corner of the pool. "Dr. Starch, we need to get maintenance crews over here. It's gonna bust through this door as well."

Starch glared at him. "What are you talking to me for? Get on the radio."

Barton snapped his fingers at a couple of the other guards. "Get sedatives ready."

"Not yet," Starch said. "I'm about to calm it down. Bring in the other two."

Barton turned around, snapping his fingers at someone standing near the entrance.

Luke heard two men babbling as they were goaded toward the pen. Reggie Smith and Leo Parsons. They were still stripped down to their underwear, limping on their injured legs with their hands cuffed behind their backs.

Smith grew more frantic as he neared the pool. The shark continued moving in circles, its razor jaw coming in view as it made a turn along the corner. He stopped and looked at Barton.

"I didn't betray you."

"I sure as hell didn't," Leo said.

Barton walked up to the two men. "There's only *one* way this guy could learn the layout of this place so quick. He knew where to find the explosives and our dispatch center. One of you squawked, and as a result, you've hindered this operation."

"No!" Smith looked to the Doctor in hopes of finding some degree of compassion. His hopes were visibly crushed as Starch shook his head.

Even Barton was somewhat surprised. The doctor didn't like up-front murder, despite how that attitude contradicted his overall plans. But here he was directly ordering an execution, not only of the two saboteurs, but of two guards that failed to stop them.

"I'd like Mr. Jansen and Ms. Sheldon to see their fates play out before it's their turn," he said.

"Yeah?" Luke said. "Why not just feed them to whatever you're storing in the other pen?"

"You've already seen that specimen. Such a sad waste, that miraculous great white."

"Big ass great white," Elise said. "What was it supposed to be? Megalodon?"

"No, just a test subject for our accelerated growth technology. Worked wonders, both in setting the stage for us to grow the Helicoprion, but to misdirect public knowledge away from its existence. Except for the two of you." Starch forced a smile. "Now you'll wish you left well-enough alone." He looked at Barton and nodded.

First, the merc had one of his men stick an electric rod into the water. Mild electrical charges drew the creature's attention. As it closed in, Barton placed a hand on Smith's shoulder.

"No!"

"Relax. It'll be over quick." He pushed the man in.

Smith splashed, blood seeping from the leg wound. The Helicoprion fluttered its tail, jetting itself for the struggling prey. The spiral jaw found its target, cutting Smith in half in a single slice.

The water turned red as it proceeded to ravage the remains.

Parsons tried to resist, only to be doubled over by a gut-punch from Barton before being pushed in after his friend. And like his friend, he thrashed in a panic. The shark doubled back, spotted its prey, and closed in.

It grabbed him by the legs, raised him over the surface as though showing off for its creator, then bit down. The legs snapped from the body like toothpicks. Parsons' scream was drowned out by the water as the fish took him under. More body parts bobbed along the surface for a moment before sinking.

Gary winced at the grotesque sight, not at the suffering, but simply the gore.

"You alright?" Barton said.

"Never was the best around blood," Starch said.

Barton rolled his eyes then grabbed Luke under the shoulder. "You're next."

Luke was lifted to his feet and forced toward the edge of the pool. "Ah, eliminating loose ends. Just like with the shark. Just like with Vick. Was that *you* who killed him in the hospital, by the way?"

"Shut up." Barton shoved him forward.

"Oh, come on! You gotta tell the detective how you beat him. I gotta know before I die."

Barton knew Luke was bullshitting him, but went with it anyway. "Private contractor. You can thank your pal Norton for arranging that little job."

"Oh. I figured it'd be you, since cleaning up seems to be your job." He stumbled a few steps closer to the pool. "Kind of like, ah shit. What's the name of that town? No…*village*. Marikana! That was it." Barton stopped. Luke turned to look him in the eye. "Yeah. I saw the photo of you and your buddy Dixon standing there. Mass grave and all!"

Barton stood quietly for a moment. "You don't know shit."

"Maybe not. But it's interesting a high-value mercenary like yourself was seen at a site where a supposed outbreak occurred. What was the matter? Infect a few people, conduct a vaccine test, didn't work, so here comes Mr. Barton to eliminate loose ends? Am I close?"

"You gonna put him in the water or not?" Starch said.

Luke nodded at the doc, who was getting increasingly impatient—and *not* because he was eager to see his prisoners torn to shreds. "Kinda odd that photo got leaked. Almost as though someone wanted leverage over you in case you became more trouble than you were worth. Or if he needed a fall guy in the event somebody started asking questions about what happened over there. Considering first world governments see you as a terrorist, well…"

Barton turned his gaze toward the doctor.

Starch pointed at the water. "What the hell are you doing? Put him in the water."

"You motherfucker…"

"You're letting him get in your head. Aren't you trained to withstand this kind of shit?"

"Only if it's bullshit. When it's the truth, however… you look pretty damn nervous, Doc. Your hands are jittery."

Starch took a step back. He raised his hands, while glancing at the guards near Elise. He attempted to subtly wave to the guards for help, a gesture that didn't go unnoticed by Barton.

The two guards stepped forward, unsure who they had more allegiance to. Starch was the one with the money, yet Barton held grudges. And he was a faster draw than they were.

Elise watched the two nervous guards. One was directly in front of her, the other a couple of yards to her right. She took a moment to look back. There were no guards behind her. There were two on the right of the pen, standing beside a nervous medical doctor with the vaccine briefcase.

After taking a deep breath, she crouched as low as she could, being slow and quiet. Barton's attention was mainly on Starch, while monitoring the two guards in his peripheral. She pressed her legs together, and slid the handcuff link under them until her hands were in front of her.

She stretched her fingers and rolled her shoulders, testing her range of motion. There was about three inches of chain-link between her wrists. She questioned the absurdness of what she was about to attempt, only for common sense to bite back. *You're gonna die in the next two minutes anyway...*

Still crouched, she balanced her weight on the balls of her feet. Like a lion watching a zebra from the tall grass, she eyed the position of the guard's rifle. It was held at port arms, shaking ever-so-slightly in the hands of a nervous handler.

Elise leapt. She came down on his shoulder and grabbed the rifle grip. Hooking her legs around the guard's midsection, she spun him to the right with her bodyweight, forcing her finger into the trigger guard. The other guard quickly turned. By the time he saw what was happening, it was too late.

A spray of bullets tore into his chest, killing him instantly. Elise forced the weapon toward the other two guards, who quickly dove behind a couple of crates.

"The fuck?"

Barton ducked down at the sound of gunfire, turned around, and saw the guard fall backward on top of Elise. She stopped fighting for control of the weapon and was now focused on choking the guard out by pulling the cufflinks against his throat.

He went for his side arm, noticing a pivot in the other prisoner's stance. A hard kick landed square in his chest. It was like getting rammed by a bull. Barton hit the guardrail and teetered backward, gravity and momentum threatening to flip him head-over-heels into the water. He regained his balance, fixed his posture, only for the effort to go wasted in the next moment.

Luke closed the distance and thrust a second kick into Barton's chest. This time, the merc flipped backwards into the water.

Barton surfaced and immediately looked around to gauge the shark's location. It was at the other end of the pool. The dorsal fin angled toward him.

"Get it back! Use the rods! Get it back!"

The handlers rushed toward the far end with the rods in hand. Immediately, they stuck the poles into the water. The shark slowed, swimming in a tight circle, attracted by both the mild electrical surge and vibration of struggling prey.

The tug-of-war on its senses drove the creature into another frenzy. It lunged at the nearest target—the electrical charges. On many occasions, it had seen the silver objects extend into the water. They weren't edible, but the humans using them were.

The thrash of its tail shot the fish across the short distance at a speed even the handlers weren't expecting. The beast launched out of the water, its underside crushing the guardrail. One of the handlers squealed as the circular jaw closed over him. It cut halfway into his midsection, allowing the shark to lift him off the floor.

His partner attempted to run, only to be struck by the shark's enormous snout. The impact threw him face-first into the pavement, where his forehead caved-in like an eggshell.

The fish yanked its body to the right, taking its prize into the water. Using its inner mouth muscles, it retracted its jaw, sawing the human until the legs and groin separated from the rest of him.

With his hands still cuffed behind his back, Luke dashed for the handler desk on the left side of the pool. He leapt over the console right as the two guards on the opposite side emerged from behind cover and opened fire.

He sat upright, slid his arms so they were in front of his body, then peeked around the righthand corner. A few more bullets whizzed past him before the gunfire stopped. The men raced around the back of the compartment toward Elise. The guard she was choking kicked once more then went limp.

There was no time to rest. She saw the two men approaching, moments from aiming their rifles at her. She drew the unconscious guard's Beretta and fired, striking the nearest in the abdomen, then the chest. He stopped, looked at his bleeding torso, then fell to his knees.

The other was quicker on his feet. He dove behind a crate on the other side of the tunnel entrance, avoiding her shots.

Elise had no shot. The guy was behind cover and she was out in the open.

"Hey!"

She looked over at Luke, who waved with his cuffed hands from behind the console…which was at a better angle to pick off the guard. The gun scraped against the concrete floor as she slid it across the several yards of distance.

Luke snatched the pistol, took aim, and emptied the magazine into the rifleman.

Starch's voice echoed through the station. "I need armed response in pen station two! Immediately!"

"Team Three on approach."

"Team Four on the way."

Elise and Luke shared a glance. They would have dozens of men flooding the room in a minute or two. Even if they ran out into the tunnels, there was no avoiding the small army whose sole purpose was to kill them.

Luke winked at her. She knew that look. He had something crazy in mind. Crazy and unorthodox.

She watched him go for the console. He ran his hands over the controls, then found a lever on the left-hand side. The mechanical hum of the door made it clear what his plan was. *Oh, Luke, this is insane.*

"No! Don't!" Starch yelled.

Luke smiled at him, then cranked the lever the rest of the way. "Whoops!"

The door opened.

The Helicoprion turned, no longer interested in the other human in the pool, but now drawn to the sight of sunlight and the many smells that drifted in from the open ocean. Freedom. The drive to kill the other human vanished in favor of escape.

Starch ran to the guardrail and yelled out, as though hoping the shark would respond to his call. The dorsal and tailfin vanished under the surface. His only source of creating his pandemic was now out in the open sea.

He lifted his radio. "All teams, the asset is loose! I need all available hands to report to Dock A and commence pursuit."

With his eyes locked on the open doorway, Starch didn't notice Luke charging toward him until he was struck in the jaw.

Luke kicked the doctor in the stomach for good measure, then looked straight ahead. The medical doctor was frozen in fear, briefcase still in hand. Luke approached him. The man looked at the entrance, considered running, but realized he wouldn't outrun the one-eyed intruder.

He set the case down and raised his fists.

Luke perked up, then smirked. "You really wanna go down that road, Doc?" The doctor slowly lowered his hands. Cuffed or not, he knew this man would break every bone in his body. "Good choice. Why don't you leave that here?"

"It's all yours!" The doctor backed away then ran for the exit. Luke briefly checked the contents, confirmed there were eleven vials of vaccine inside, closed it up and met Elise by the entrance.

Using a key lifted from the guards, she uncuffed herself and then him. They stole the ammo from two of the guards, then ran out into the corridor.

Barton reached high. The damn ledge was three feet above the surface, forcing him to claw against the concrete in order to reach high enough to get his fingers over the corner. He hauled himself up, and saw Starch on his hands and knees, bleeding from the mouth.

"I oughta kill you right now."

"Shut up, you grunt. I paid you a small fortune."

"Means nothing," Barton said.

Starch stood up. "Guess what?! You ultimately won. See this?!" He waved his hand around at the dead bodies. "We're short on manpower. We've suffered tons of damage. We're going to have to hire whole new crews. I can't *afford* to screw you over."

"So that *was* the plan, huh?"

"No. It's called 'leverage'. You're a military man, don't pretend you don't understand."

"I understand my pay rate is gonna go up."

"If you catch the shark again and get that vaccine back, I'll make that happen."

Barton winced. "They have the vaccine?"

"Yes!"

"So what? You have more?"

"The lab was damaged in the explosion. The only reliable supply was what we kept in the infirmary!"

"Fabulous. And you diverted all our response teams to the shark."

"They're still on this island. The shark *isn't.* If we lose the specimen, then we're gonna have to start completely from scratch. I'll double your salary."

"Triple."

Starch pressed his hands to his temples. This ridiculous negotiation, at *this* time of all times, on top of the stress was fueling a razor-sharp headache. "Fine! Just do it!"

Barton wasted no more time with words. He grabbed a rifle and raced for the tunnel.

"And kill those pricks!" Starch called after him.

Barton pretended not to hear him. *Of course I'm gonna kill 'em. That cop is still gonna pay for what he did to Dixon.*

CHAPTER 73

The duo ran down the tunnel, stopping at each juncture to make sure nobody was there to greet them.

"Looks like your plan worked," Elise said. "They're going after the shark."

"Good. Let it take care of 'em."

"That creates a whole new set of problems, Luke. The Helicoprion is out there now. That means it could start a whole other outbreak."

"Not if we kill it first," Luke said.

Elise nodded. He was right. This was the only chance. Had the guards swarmed the pen, she and Luke would've been killed, and Starch allowed to continue with his sinister plan. They were the only two people on the planet with any chance of halting the oncoming threat.

They continued down the tunnel, coming to a wall of rubble that was once the lab. Much of the ceiling came down, blocking much of the pathway. The bodies of the dead personnel had been removed, leaving only their equipment.

Elise hopped over several pieces of rubble to get to the other side, only to realize Luke wasn't with her. She looked back and saw him digging through some ceiling tiles.

"Looking for souvenirs?"

He pulled out a vest, the one he took off Reggie Smith. "Not exactly." He strapped it on. "Might have a use for some of the material in it."

Elise shrugged. *Could've picked any other vest, but okay.*

They continued down the hall and made their way up a stairwell. They arrived at Sublevel-One, where several non-security crew members were racing about. Some were simply evacuating the facility, others were reporting for duty. Starch's call had been relayed to all channels, putting the entire island on high alert.

A utility worker stopped as he saw them approach. He pointed a finger. "Hey! It's *them*!"

A haymaker to the jaw silenced him. Two other workers approached, ready to take on the infidels themselves. The sight of the Beretta being drawn and pointed at them made them reconsider. Those fists opened into gestures of surrender before the two men spun on their heels and evacuated.

Luke and Elise continued down the corridor until they found a stairwell which went up to the surface structure. After ten feet of stairs, they were above ground again. The nearest exit took them back to the helipads. There was some residual smoke outside from the garage explosion.

One vehicle remained: the maintenance truck which had been parked over at the loading bay. It stopped to allow three security men armed with tranquilizer guns to climb into the bed for quick passage to the docks.

Luke sprinted for the vehicle, grabbing the third man before he could board. He pulled him back and knocked him to the ground with an elbow to the nose.

He hopped aboard the bed, where he engaged with the other two. One threw a swing at him, which Luke deflected before breaking his kneecap, dropping him.

The other hopped over his fallen friend to get to the enemy. He drew his pistol and pointed it at Luke's chest. His effort resulted in his wrist being twisted, his weapon lost from his grip, his arm over-extended, then snapped backward at the elbow. Both men were thrown off the bed of the truck like bags of grain. They landed atop their companion, flooring him a second time after he was halfway to his feet.

Luke leaned over the side to jump down and engage the driver, only to see Elise had already taken care of it. She struck him across the face with the pistol and pulled him out of the truck. A kick to the midsection put him on the ground.

With the engine still running, all she had to do was get inside.

"I'll drive," Luke said.

"I'm already in the seat," Elise said.

"Yeah, but you don't know the way to—" He ducked as he saw Barton, armed with an M4 Carbine, emerge from the building. Elise floored the accelerator, zipping out of the line of fire. A few rounds followed as they cut into the woods. One struck the tailgate, the others missed entirely.

Luke rocked back and forth, bouncing every time Elise hit a bump—which was practically every other meter. He rolled to his knees and leaned over the driver's side to yell through the open window. "Hey! He's not behind us anymore. You can ease up—WHOA!" He ducked back and avoided being slashed by a branch.

"What's that?" Elise called back.

"I said you can slow down!"

They emerged in a clearing that was one of the pathways. "Whoa!" Elise hit the brakes to keep from speeding past the trail.

Momentum sent Luke into the rear windshield. "Fuuuck!"

"You alright?"

"I'm starting to think I should've hijacked a boat and left your sorry ass here."

"You said slow down."

"Not come to a dead stop—oh forget it. Turn right."

"Boats are on the west side," Elise said.

"They'll be gone by the time we get there. I know of a better one."

Elise cut the wheel to the right and sped up the pathway.

****

Barton marched to the group of security officers. "Get aboard the choppers. We're going after them."

The one on the ground glared at him. His knee was bent to the side, his teeth clenched. "S—sir…I can't even stand."

The other one held his broken arm. "What am I supposed to do—"

Barton saw red. His temper snapped, ridding himself of any self-control. He pointed the Carbine and shot the guard with the broken arm in the chest. The other with the broken leg raised his hand to plead, only to take a round in the face. Barton turned toward the third guard.

"I'm ready whenever you are..." he said.

"Good," Barton said. He spoke into his radio. "I need flight crews here on the double."

****

They had arrived right on time.

The *Namesake* had already begun pursuit. Had they arrived thirty-seconds later, the tugboat would be right behind it. There were a dozen crew prepping it for the mission, with some on the pier handing supplies up to those on deck. The sound of a roaring engine drew their attention to the trail. They jumped out of the way as Elise raced onto the pier. Pallets and crates exploded into splinters as she smashed into them. Only when she neared the edge did she slam on the brakes.

Luke fired his rifle to the ground, avoiding killing anyone unnecessarily while hammering in the point that he *would* if they got in the way of them catching the shark. To his relief, the ground crew took the hint and fled.

The pair climbed up to the main deck. One tenacious maintenance man drew a Swiss army knife from his pocket and pointed it, only to see the muzzle of a rifle pointed back at him. He literally brought a knife to a gunfight. A small knife at that. With a nervous smile, he dropped the knife and went for the fastest exit possible, which was over the side into the water.

The rest of the crew quickly followed. After five consecutive splashes, Luke and Elise had the tugboat all to themselves.

"How nice of them to prep it for us," he said. He climbed to the flybridge and backed the boat out of the cove. On the console was a twelve-by-twelve computer monitor displaying a map of the waters surrounding the island. To the northwest was a red blip. As he predicted, the shark still had its tracking monitor installed. It was just a matter of catching up to it and putting it down.

He looked at his Carbine and final thirty-round magazine. Hopefully that would do the trick. He looked down at the main deck to view the other supplies. A flare gun, chainsaw—the very one the maintenance foreman was complaining about—tools, electrical rods, and an inflatable motorized raft.

The sound of numerous boat motors drew his attention to the west. All five security interceptors along with the *Namesake* and one of the maintenance vessels were speeding after the shark.

"I don't think these guys realize that Helicoprion is *not* going to take kindly to being forced back into its pen," Elise said.

"No. No it won't. But, if they can keep it in the vicinity, they'll at least accomplish something."

CHAPTER 74

Gary Starch arrived at the surface floor then sprinted for the east side of the building. A few crew members were loading supplies onto ATV trailers. There were three vehicles. One driver failed to hear his call as he sped for the loading dock, delivering gear to the tugboat crew.

"Damn it!" Starch turned to another driver standing next to the four-wheeler. "Hey! Are there any boats left?"

"One. M-Two. We're about to launch it. The others are already out after the fish."

"Good. I'll ride in the back. Let's go." He boarded the trailer and held tight. The crewman looked at him like he was insane, only to realize he *was*. Worse, the billionaire had acquired a pistol on his way to the surface.

"Hold on."

When they arrived at the main dock, M-Two's engine was running. The other vessels were hundreds of yards in the distance. Starch could see they were spreading out to take formation.

He boarded the vessel and snapped his fingers at the helmsman. "Alright. Let's go."

"Sir, it's dangerous out there. Perhaps it's best if you remain on shore."

"I need to make sure you guys don't screw this up. If that specimen gets killed, then this whole operation goes to shit." The gun twitched in his grasp. "Get moving."

The helmsman steered the vessel away from the dock, pointed the bow toward the objective, then pushed the engine to its max.

As they approached, the other crews communicated through the radio.

"Wolf Leader to Pack, continue fanning out. Boogie slowing down. Looks like it's responding to our electrical discharge. Wolf One and Two, hold position on our three o'clock, seventy-meters. It might not close in if we're all bunched together."

"Wolf Two holding position."

"Wolf One copies. Holding position."

"This is M-One. We and Namesake will hold back at your six."

"Ten-four. Standby with those winches. Have divers ready, because once it's drugged, it's gonna sink. If it drowns, the boss won't be happy."

"Goddamn right about that," Starch muttered. He climbed to the flybridge. M-One and the *Namesake* were about seven-hundred feet away now. Wolf Four and Five were two hundred feet to the left, Two and Three standing by on the right. After another few moments traveling at top speed, M-Two was less than a hundred feet behind M-One and the *Namesake.*

Wolf Leader was at the center of the group. A security crewman was sticking an electric rod into the water. Another stood on deck with a harpoon gun loaded with a cannister of sedative.

Starch looked at the monitor. The reader on the top right corner showed the creature at three-meters of depth.

The creature doubled its speed. That red blip was closing in rapidly. It wasn't curiously examining a mild electrical pulse—it *knew* that signal indicated human prey.

Starch grabbed for the radio. "Wait! It's—" He dropped the mic as the echo of an explosive impact filled the air.

The Helicoprion emerged from under Wolf Leader, launching the stern section ninety-degrees into the air. The two guards on deck were catapulted into the water, the helmsman clinging on for dear life as the boat appeared to 'teeter' on the bow before smashing back down.

The shark struck again, this time ramming Wolf Leader's starboard side. The boat capsized, its helmsman disappearing into the water. A moment later, he reemerged—in the shark's jaws. He threw his arms up at the sky, as though hoping God Himself would pull him free from the jaws of hell. The man received no such grace. Only pain. The Helicoprion coiled its lower jaw then whipped its head to the left. The torso detached from the rest of the body and flew across the ocean like a softball, splattering against the bow of the *Namesake*. Crewmembers turned to heave as the red glob dripped from the hull, clouding the water below.

All boats broke formation. Wolf Four and Five sped toward the struggling guards.

The Helicoprion darted to intercept. It dove several meters, only to angle back up and propel itself to the surface. It came up clear out of the water and smashed down on the deck of Wolf Four. Debris exploded from the boat like shrapnel as it cracked in half.

The fish fell in-between the two halves of the boat and shot straight for Wolf Five. The helmsman saw the dorsal fin rapidly approaching. No longer interested in saving the security man in the water, he gunned the engine. The guard waved and shouted, pushed away by the laps generated by the boat's hull. Those shouts turned into bloodcurdling screams as the shark's snout emerged.

He backstroked, kicking his legs at the angular face, only for his feet to skid off its sandpaper-like skin. There he was, spreadeagle on the ocean surface, with the shark's razor jaw closing in.

There was agonizing pain of his groin getting sliced, then his abdomen, stomach, lungs, and his head. Like two halves of a board sawed down the middle, the guard separated in two, each half drifting along the length of the shark's body.

The helmsman of Wolf Five looked back just in time to see the man get cleaved down the middle. Suddenly, there was a scream in front of him. It ceased abruptly with the arrival of a simultaneous thud and splattering sound. Glancing down at the starboard side, he saw blood and body parts in the water. He had just run over one of Wolf Four's crewmen.

"Look out!" one of the men on deck shouted.

The helmsman looked forward, and realized he was about to hit another guard. A sharp turn to starboard avoided splattering his brains over the hull…and instead put him right in the path of the *Namesake.*

"Oh—"

The impact sent shockwaves across the vicinity. Both fuel tanks ruptured at once, resulting in an enormous fireball from which razor-sharp pieces of debris were spat.

The mission was in chaos. Not a single crewman had survived the impact. The only bodies above water were on fire, held up only by floating debris. The air was permeated with the smell of burning fuel and flesh. Then came the sound of screams. The sight of the fireball was so horrific, yet oddly mesmerizing, that all other boat crews momentarily forgot about the shark.

It was the screams from the helpless crewmen in the water that snapped everyone back to reality. Those screams intensified as the triangular dorsal fin pierced the air. Twenty-feet behind it, the sickle-shaped caudal fin emerged, lapping water with each thrust.

There were three survivors still in the water. That number was reduced to two after a single bite decapitated the nearest swimmer. His headless corpse flopped along the surface before sinking. The shark closed in on the next. The man drew his pistol and fired several rounds point blank into its snout before the jaw closed over his arm. There was a brief *crack.* The water around him quickly turned red. The guard gazed in awe at the creature swimming past him, then at the bloody stump where his arm had been. As his brain registered what had just happened, the caudal fin smacked into him with enough force to drive his ribs out through his back. The impact launched him several feet through the air, right into the burning debris field.

The shark closed in on the third man. It opened its jaws to bite, only to jerk to the left after something stung its back.

Wolf Two sped near the creature, the guard on the forward deck firing a rifle into its back.

Starch was yelling through the radio. *"Cease fire, you idiot! I want it alive!"* His commands went unanswered. The fish had done too much damage. These men were only willing to risk their lives so much before reverting to fight-or-flight. For the crew of Wolf Two, it was fight.

The fish whipped to the right to engage the threat. As it did, its jaw slashed across the swimmer's face, opening his skull like an egg, emptying its contents into the Pacific.

More bullets stung its flesh, agitating it further. The Helicoprion charged the boat head-on. The helmsman kept the bow facing the shark in hopes that a direct collision would kill the beast on contact. Thirty meters, twenty, ten. He clenched his teeth, bracing for the tremor of impact.

That tremor was delayed by a mere second. The fish had banked to his portside, evading the head-on collision, and instead putting itself in position to smack the hull with its caudal fin. The curved tail hit the boat with enough force to fold a car in half. The hull caved-in several feet, splintering the deck. The boat rolled to starboard, nearly capsizing.

The men on board held on for dear life as the gunwale nearly touched the water. It rolled back to port and began to settle. The sense of relief on deck merely lasted a moment. Terror seized the crew as a mountain of water swept the boat. The shark struck the portside directly. This time, the boat capsized.

One after another, the three men on board were torn to pieces. Some were swallowed, others simply sank to the seafloor where they would be gradually picked at by the bottom dwellers.

"Disengage! It's gone nuts. We can't contain it."

Gary Starch watched as M-One and Wolf Three turned around and made a run for the island.

"No, no, NO!" He snatched the radio from his helmsman. "Do your jobs and catch that fish!" As he spoke, the helmsman started to follow. Starch's fiery gaze met his eyes. "What are you doing?"

"We—we can't catch it, sir!"

"The hell we can't. I'll do it *myself*." Starch climbed down to the main deck and grabbed a harpoon gun. He loaded a harpoon with a full cannister of sedative then climbed up to the crow's nest. "Get us close to it."

"I can't…"

"The hell you mean *you can't*?" The helmsman pointed. Starch looked ahead, then understood what he meant. When he said 'I can't' he meant it, as the specimen was pursuing the other boats.

It was not drawn by electrical discharges or blood in the water. There were no struggling swimmers generating vibration. It was going after the boats by *choice*. The beast was driven by vengeance, a need to rid the ocean of those who had kept it captive in a dark chamber for years.

M-One, being slower than the Interceptor model, had no chance of outrunning it. The crewman on the deck took aim with a harpoon. He waited for the shark to raise its head from the water to fire.

Even from this distance, Starch could see the look of amazement on the man's face as the harpoon bounced off its spiral jaw. The Helicoprion made its leap. For a brief moment, it appeared like a bird in flight. An expressionless bird with no colorful beauty, no graceful movement in its wings, or sense of soul. It was simply a killing machine bound by a need to kill.

And gravity, which brought it crashing down on the vessel. Its hefty mass flattened the transom and the guard simultaneously, pancaking him to the deck. The boat reared up. The helmsman on M-One's flybridge reeled backwards, plummeted to the main deck, then rolled head-over-heels like a tire wheel right into the shark's jaws. His squeal was as brief as his cleaving.

The shark fed on the parts as the boat submerged under its weight. After a few short moments, it was surrounded by water again. It wiggled its body off the boat and started chasing after the last, ignoring the vibrations of the crewman who had hidden down below, and was now trapped after the deck had caved in.

"Keep going," Starch said.

M-Three's helmsman reluctantly pursued. He didn't want to chase the shark, but unfortunately, he had the misfortune of having Starch on board. Then again, if he managed to help in successfully capturing the thing, that would certainly result in a pay increase, special privileges, and a promotion. It wasn't too farfetched, considering he had already moved up the seniority ladder by attrition.

They followed the shark, watching its dorsal fin chase the last remaining interceptor. Wolf Three angled to port and shot off to the north. The shark began to follow, only to divert its attention to a larger boat moving in from the cove.

"Finally!" one of the crewmen on deck said. "I was wondering when they were gonna back us up."

Starch raised a pair of binoculars and focused on the flybridge. He shook his head. "They're not here to assist. Helmsman, switch to the security channel. Get ahold of Barton."

****

"Looks like they've brought it straight to us," Luke said.

"I'm not sure that's a good thing anymore," Elise said. She was looking at the smoking wreckage in the distance. The fish had completely decimated the response teams. Only one interceptor and maintenance boat remained, the latter because it kept a distance from the action.

She moved to the side-deck and watched the fish. With her rifle in hand, she was eager to unleash it on the beast. The lever was switched to full-auto. She just needed it to get close. A spray of bullets straight into its head would do the trick.

The fish was taking its time circling them. It kept a distance of forty meters. Off and on, it would submerge. The unpredictable nature of its movements prevented Luke or Elise from pulling off a shot. Ammo was sparse and they couldn't afford to waste it on mere flesh wounds.

"Come on, you bastard. What are you so afraid of?"

"Bigger boat," Elise said. "It's like attacking a larger organism. It's proceeding with caution."

"Yes, I figured," Luke said.

"Then why'd you ask?!"

"I was trash-talking the bastard. Get with the program!"

Elise shrugged. "Oh."

The fish circled around the stern then slowly moved forward along the starboard side, still maintaining over a hundred feet of distance. Luke was about to take a chance with a shot when the thing dove. It reemerged a moment later where it made a turn ahead of the bow.

"Alright, I'm not doing this all day." He gunned the engine and closed the distance. The Helicoprion, determining this motion as an act of aggression, turned toward the boat. Two titans, one engineered of flesh, the other from steel, charged each other.

Luke braced for a collision that never came. He looked down in time to see the caudal fin disappear. The fish had dived underneath the boat. Probably behind them by now. Luke cursed and spun the wheel to port.

Elise went to the transom with her weapon in hand. The shark was nowhere to be seen.

"Where the hell did it go?" Luke looked at the monitor. The blip was right in the middle of the screen. Right on top of them. Or more specifically, *below* them.

The shark struck the keel. There was a crunch of hull. The tugboat lurched then rocked to the side. Luke clung to the helm, keeping himself from falling over. It was a luxury Elise didn't have. She fell on her stomach, then slid down the deck as a second impact rocked the boat to starboard.

Still gripping the helm, Luke swayed with the motion. He pushed the throttle to get the boat out of the way. No response. The engine had stalled. He tried restarting it but got no response.

"Not fair…" he muttered.

The spraying of water redirected his attention to starboard. The Helicoprion lifted its pointed snout up out of the ocean and smashed its neck on the gunwale, crushing it down to the deck. Elise scampered backward, narrowly avoiding being smashed by its chin. It snapped its jaws like a bird, its lower jaw moving in a bizarre whirling motion.

The tugboat teetered drastically to starboard. Seawater crept over the breach. The fish remained on deck, its fin lodged by the broken ledge of the wall.

Elise could feel herself starting to slide. She reached over for her dropped rifle, which slid millimeters from her fingertips. It slid toward under those jaws and through the breach, disappearing into the water. Inch by inch, she slid closer to those jaws. She clenched her teeth and watched that buzzsaw-like set of teeth come within inches of her legs.

Luke shouldered his Carbine and squeezed the trigger. A line of bullet holes popped along the shark's gill-slits and the side of its face. Blood splattered, the flesh shredding as though an invisible power tool was being run over it.

Sensitive nerves flared, igniting increased strength and desire to survive. The Helicoprion whipped its head to the left, tearing off another section of the gunwale as it escaped. A few more bullets chased it, nicking its caudal fin. The leveling of the boat forced Luke to abandon the attack. He grasped the rail to keep from falling, then looked down at his partner.

"You alright?"

Elise rose to her feet, then replied with a thumbs up.

The shark struck again from underneath, nearly flooring both of them again. Before the boat settled, it struck again. Then again.

It was operating like a battering ram, using gravity to wind back, then shooting forward for another strike All while out of range from those strange black stingers and their invisible projectiles.

Luke turned to the console. He twisted the key again. The engine turned over but stalled again. The fish struck again. Luke leaned on the console, frantically turning the key. The engine teased him by turning over but refused to spark.

Hearing the scream of bending metal below, Elise dove into the hatch. Water splashed under her feet. The thing had breached the hull.

"Shit." She climbed back up. "Luke, we're in trouble."

"Oh really?! Did it take a doctorate program to figure that one out?" He tried the key again, only to obtain the same result. He had to think fast, as the fish was not hesitating to turn the boat's entire underside into a crater.

Luke aimed his rifle over the side. Only able to catch glimpses of the shark down below, precise aim was impossible. He took his chances and emptied his magazine into the water. ONE lucky shot. ONE bullet needed to land in the right place. Between the eyes, into the brain. Just ONE.

The magazine ran dry, reducing the rifle to an expensive club. All they had left were their nine-millimeters.

Elise drew hers and fired it into the water. She leaned out as far as she could to get the best possible aim. Every so often, it would appear as it would prep for another strike.

The murky image jolted to the side as one of her bullets zipped down toward it.

There was no collision. The water began to settle.

Silence.

Elise looked up at Luke. *Did I hit it?* The widening of his eyes and pointing of his finger provided an answer. She looked down, saw the fish rising up, its teeth looking like an electric saw ready to cleave her in half. The Helicoprion broke the surface, shuddering the vessel. Elise fell back for a second time. And also for a second time, she lost her weapon, which spun in midair before plopping into the water.

The fish vanished again, pursued by a half-dozen rounds launched from Luke's Beretta. It shook the vessel with another impact.

"Damn it." Luke glared at his sidearm. It was useless at this point. The fish wouldn't emerge again until they were in the water. It didn't have long to wait—two or three more hits and they'd be in the water.

He looked at the computer monitor. It worked on a battery like a laptop. An idea came to mind. *A laptop that runs on electricity and a shark that's drawn to electrical currents...* Luke grabbed the monitor and tried pulling it away, but the screws connecting it to the console refused to let it free. He turned toward Elise.

"Where's that Swiss army knife that guy dropped?"

Elise checked the deck. Luckily, its red color made it easy to spot. She tossed it up to Luke who unfolded the screwdriver. The shark struck again as he unworked the screws. The first three came out quickly, the fourth offered resistance.

"Oh for CHRISAKE!"

Fed up, Luke grabbed the monitor and yanked it with all his might, busting the last screw. He heaved the monitor into the water. The light flickered as the water made contact with the electrical circuits, frying it.

The creature's silhouette moved over it like a massive cloud, studying the small disturbance.

Luke tucked the knife into his pocket and tried starting the engine again. "Come on, come on!"

After a few cranks, the engine finally came to life. Smoke spewed from the exhaust. Parts clattered from inside the boat, but Luke didn't care. He just needed to put distance between them and the fish.

He studied his potential escape routes. The last maintenance boat was up ahead on the left, and over to the right, the other interceptor was circling back. The helmsman had either regained his bravery, or realized there'd be no chance of escaping both the Helicoprion AND Starch's fury. A man of vast resources, Starch would undoubtedly have any traitors hunted down. The boat kept its distance, angling to port. There were two men on deck, one with a harpoon gun, the other holding a rifle.

Luke suspected the rifle was intended for him and Elise, yet, the group appeared deliberate in their attempt to maintain their distance. The droning sound from up above made it clear why.

"Hey, Luke? We're *really* in trouble," Elise said.

Luke looked back toward the island. Like two dragonflies, the chopper units were buzzing toward them. There was no doubt Barton knew they were on the tugboat. Either the dock crew reported it or Starch himself. It didn't matter.

"Seems I'm making a habit of being attacked by attack helicopters," Luke muttered.

Elise leaned against the cabin, defeated. They had endured all of this struggle only to encounter those choppers again. They had nothing to defend themselves with except Luke's pistol, and considering the altitude the choppers were keeping, it'd be impossible to do any serious damage. To add insult to injury, the damaged engines would quit on them at any moment, so escaping was out of the question.

One of the choppers angled to port, allowing the gunner to get a look at them. Elise held up a middle finger at Barton. What else could she do at this point?

=***

"Ha!"

Barton chomped on his favorite brand of cigar while watching the damaged tugboat below. He couldn't think of a better occasion to light one up. For years, he and Dixon smoked them together. Now that he was finally engaging his vengeance, that draw of the tobacco felt better than ever.

The shark had almost completed his work for him. He was glad it didn't, as that would rob him the pleasure of killing Luke Jansen himself.

In his hand was the same grenade launcher he used to sink the *Barracuda*. This time, with him standing right there in plain sight, Luke would not be able to pull off a miraculous escape. Barton would see to it that his grenades would land right at his feet. He envisioned the former detective's body parts flying in all different directions. The thought alone was satisfying. Now, he would experience the real thing.

The console appeared undamaged.

"Razor One, ascending ten meters. Waiting on your command, Alpha Two."

"Standby." Barton looked at the flybridge through a pair of binoculars. The console appeared undamaged, the radio functional. He changed the radio channel to maintenance. "Hi there, Jansen. I have to say, you have a lot of nerve showing your *face* around here!" He made sure his soon-to-be victim could hear his laughter as he took aim. He saw Luke pick up the console mic. To Barton's surprise, he was laughing back.

"Look who's talking."

Barton squinted. The guy wasn't just talking tough—he *meant* something by that.

****

Elise groaned. Seriously? Now of all times he decided to have a sense of humor?

"You had all that C4, you blew up half the island, yet, you didn't think to rig charges on those choppers…"

Luke chuckled. "What makes you think I didn't?" Elise looked up at the flybridge and saw him pull two objects from his vest. He extended an antenna. Detonators! She thought of when he'd sought out that particular vest when escaping through the rubble from the lab. That's why he wanted that vest!

"You son of a gun!"

"Just a matter of timing," he said. He held the device up, showing it off to Barton, before moving his thumb to the trigger.

****

The mercenary recognized the device. "Shit!"

Razor Two exploded above them from a charge taped to its underside. The fuel tanks ignited, the fuselage turning into a massive fireball. Debris rained down into the Pacific.

Razor One was next.

Barton unstrapped himself, abandoned the launcher, and dove into the fiery ocean below. He only descended ten feet before Luke detonated the charge on Razor One. The chopper exploded right above him, the force of the blast shooting him toward the ocean even faster.

He splashed down. Burning fragments immediately followed like a meteor shower. Shockwaves pushed him side to side for several seconds on end before all portions had completed their descent. He broke the surface and looked at the debris field around him. Some were still burning, the rest smoking. The only thing to serve as a life-preserver was a piece of hull that was previously the starboard side of Razor one. He swam to it and hauled himself aboard.

There was no sign of the fish. The tugboat was continuing west. Starch's vessel was moving toward him, but still had a few hundred feet to go. Wolf Three was closer.

He stood on the floating debris and fired a few shots in the air to get their attention. It worked. A crewman pointed toward him and the helmsman redirected the boat.

"Hurry up."

They closed within fifty feet then slowed to weave around a few pieces of debris.

Then the ocean exploded from underneath them. The boat was flung upward, its bow pointed directly at the sky. Following it into the air was the Helicoprion, which intercepted the ship like an astro-propelled rocket. The interceptor flipped end-over-end then landed upside down atop a piece of chopper debris.

One man somehow managed to remain on the boat the entire time, which resulted in him being crushed between the deck and hull.

The other two were flung. One landed on a jagged piece of rotor which punched through his torso like a gladius. The third managed to avoid the debris and struck the water. He emerged and started swimming toward his commander. Barton got on his knees and reached out, only to immediately retract his hand. The guard gave him a look of betrayal, then noticed the way he was taking a firing stance. He looked behind him and saw the dorsal fin. "Fuuuck…"

The Helicoprion seized the human, shook him side to side until he was thoroughly disemboweled, then continued toward the next one.

Barton officially held no regard for the mission, the pay, or the repercussions. He was simply a man fighting to survive

Bullets sprayed from the muzzle of his weapon, piercing the shark's snout and back. Blood spurted from its many wounds as it turned and dove. He continued firing at its shape in hopes of landing a lucky kill shot.

****

"No, NO! Goddamnit, Barton! I want it alive!" Starch yelled from the crow's nest. The mercenary either couldn't hear him or was simply ignoring him. Regardless, he was actively injuring his creation. His last remaining hope for his master plan to succeed. Or else, he would suffer years of setback on top of what the saboteurs had already caused.

Barton climbed down to the bridge and yelled at his crew. "Shoot him!" All three of them gazed uneasily at him. "You heard me! Shoot him before he kills the specimen."

The one on deck positioned his rifle. He placed Barton in his crosshairs and tried to steady the weapon. If only his nerves hadn't made him so shaky…

He fired a shot. He missed.

The mercenary standing atop the floating debris turned toward him. He slammed a fresh magazine into his own rifle and returned fire. He didn't miss. A half-dozen rounds shredded the deckhand's torso.

Barton continued returning fire. The two crewmen shot back. Starch ducked for cover as the helmsman absorbed a round in the chest. Knocked backward by the force of the bullet, the guard flipped over the guardrail and disappeared into the water.

Starch peeked in time to see the third crewman slump over the gunwale after taking a round to the head. Realizing he was next, Starch redirected the boat to the west and gunned the engine.

It was all a failure now. All there was left for Starch to do was take revenge on the bastards that ruined his plans. Judging by the thick black smoke coming out of their exhaust, they had moments left before their engine would fail.

He'd never killed anyone directly before. *That's gonna change today.*

****

"That's right. Run, motherfucker!"

Barton redirected his eyes to the water. The ocean started to calm. Too calm. Either the shark had moved on or was dead. He preferred the latter, just because of how pissed off it would make Starch.

A third possibility occurred to him.

Was it gone, dead, or *waiting*?

The ocean erupted behind him. He felt its snout ram between his shoulder blades, flinging him into the water. The weapon fell from his grasp and sank beyond his reach. Backstroking away from the fish, he drew his sidearm and took aim.

The shark had a piece of metal in its mouth, which it threw to the side, clearing the path toward him.

Barton fired. The fish took no notice of the bullets puncturing its snout.

"Get away from me, you FUCK!"

He screamed as the jaws sliced through his left knee. The severed limb flopped along the surface as the shark turned its head to bite the other. With ease, it removed Barton's other leg.

Unable to kick and weighed down by his equipment, the mercenary sank. Through the sting of saltwater and the veil of his own blood, he watched the shark circle around him. It was as though it was savoring the kill against the man who ruined its previous chance of freedom.

A flick of its tail tripled its speed. The fish launched its final attack on its enemy and ripped him apart within a few seconds. His ravaged body parts settled on the ocean floor, scattering along with his radio, helmet, and a pack of cigars.

****

Clank! Clunk! Sputter!

The engine died. Luke turned the ignition but received nothing. The boat was nothing more than an expensive floating device at this point.

"What's the plan now?" Elise said.

"I'm figuring that out," Luke said.

"Could we use the radio and call the Coast Guard?"

"Can't. Radios around here can't access that frequency. My feeling is Starch won't allow it in case somebody betrays him."

Water was starting to spill onto the main deck. They were sinking. All other options had been spent. They had to use the motorized inflatable and take their chances.

Luke climbed down and assisted Elise with getting it ready. Both jumped as a bullet smacked against the gunwale. Another whizzed by Elise's head. Luke saw the maintenance boat rapidly approaching from the east. At the controls was Gary Starch, now a one-man mission. One hand was on the throttle, the other aiming a pistol at them.

Luke pushed Elise to the deck then drew his sidearm. A bullet slashed his tricep, jolting his arm and shaking the gun from his grip. It splashed into the water.

Unarmed, he knelt behind cover. A few more shots hit the vessel before silence took over again. Luke recognized the thud of an empty magazine hitting the deck. Starch was reloading, providing a moment of opportunity for response. Luke had nothing to shoot back with. No guns. Not even a speargun. Just wits.

He seized the container of vaccine, stood up, and held it over the water. Starch reloaded his pistol, aimed to fire, but stopped himself as he saw the silver case.

Luke waved the precious case back and forth. "That's right. Go ahead. Shoot me! Hope you know how to dive, because if you kill me, I drop this, and there goes your precious vaccine."

Starch bared his teeth. More than ever, he wanted to squeeze the trigger. But more than that, he wanted to preserve his product. It was the purpose of the entire operation. That vaccine could be duplicated. It would take time, but less than creating it from scratch.

"Ten million!" he said.

Luke raised an eyebrow. "Say again?"

"Ten million dollars for the vaccine, plus your very own inoculation for any exposure you might've had. Then you get out of my sight! You can live in luxury. An early retirement, better than most people. For a man in your position, I say that's a generous offer."

Elise stood up. "A generous offer? From *you*?! You expect us to sit by and let you infect the entire planet?"

"The medical field is a business just like any other, Dr. Sheldon. Look at the world around you. Technology for example. It's not meant to benefit you. It's meant to *control* you. Feed you the propaganda the government wants. Social media, for example! It doesn't bring people together, it separates them. Reduces a human to a mere image and a few lines of text on screen. Makes it easier to unperson, thus tribalize groups. A divided people is more easily conquered. You think every product is designed to improve your life? No, it's just control. It's just a matter of who is holding the reins."

"Right. And an outbreak of this scale would elevate you to the top of the medical industry on a global scale," Luke said.

"Can you blame me?" Starch said.

"Yes," Elise replied.

Luke lowered his arm abruptly, threatening to drop the case. Starch jolted, his face wrinkling as he was ready to scream 'No!'.

"Oops. Did I scare ya?" Luke said.

"Give me the goddamn case!" Starch said. "Fifteen million. For each of you!"

Luke glanced at Elise then back at him. "Sorry. I would, but then I'd have to listen to her lecture me all the way back. She's a bit more moralistic than I am."

Starch rested against the guardrail. "Think about the position you're in. You're not getting out of here alive. You have no weapons. Your boat is sinking. You're probably up to your ankles in water by now. You've got nothing but that case!"

"I have *this*." Luke drew the taser from his vest and pointed it at Starch.

The doctor hollered. "Oh dear! Mr. Jansen, I might not be the most well-versed in firearms, but even *I* know you can't hit me with that. Those prongs would come close, but I'm sorry, I'm out of range!"

"I'd say you're close enough." Luke fired the prongs. Starch flinched, only to laugh again. As he predicted, the prongs couldn't reach him. They struck the water near the bow of his vessel. The weapon clicked as it emitted the charge.

Then it dawned on Starch what he was doing.

He looked to his right and saw the dorsal fin rapidly closing in. The snout lifted, those black eyes peering up at him. The shark struck the boat like a torpedo. The hull cracked like an egg, the boat rolling to port.

Starch fell into the water. He kicked and paddled, struggling to stay afloat. Never in his life was he a good swimmer. The boat settled on its portside, half-submerged, the underside split wide open, spitting gasoline into the ocean.

All of a sudden, he felt himself starting to rise. Then he was airborne, lifted by the shark's snout as it came up from under him.

Creator and creation were midair, the latter seizing the former in its jaws. The circular set of teeth came down parallel to Starch's spinal column and sliced through him effortlessly. Legs and arms expanded their reach as the two halves of his body folded outward, held together only by Starch's neck and shock-ridden face. The V-shaped doctor fell from the creature's jaws and splashed into the water. The Helicoprion splashed down, devoured its creator, then circled back. There was one last boat standing in its way before it was truly free.

"I always say overly ambitious people need to *cut* back a bit," Luke muttered.

They unfolded the inflatable and located the ripcord. Elise grabbed the handle and leaned down to give it a yank. As she did, she caught sight of the rapidly approaching dorsal fin through the breach in the gunwale.

The Helicoprion reared its head up and punched another hole, widening the breach and sending fragments shooting across the deck. Elise reeled backward as the boat rolled to port. She flipped over the side and splashed into the water.

Luke reached out to grab her but missed. He turned his attention to the snapping jaws in front of him. The shark threw its head back and forth, wiggling its way aboard the vessel, inching closer to him.

If only he had his pistol. A dart gun. ANYTHING! All he needed was something to fight with, rather than just wait and be shredded by the saw-blade-looking jaw.

A saw...

He looked to his left and saw the chainsaw under some debris. He lunged for it, lifted it from the water that had pooled in that corner of the deck, then yanked on the ripcord. The chainsaw started up on the second try.

Like an ancient knight fighting a dragon, he engaged the fish. He leaned back as it lashed its head at him. The shark understood the capabilities of its jaw. It wasn't just a tool for eating. It could slash enemies like a hatcher. All it needed to do was angle itself and swing its head.

After evading a series of slashes, Luke closed in.

"Taste *this*." He rammed the blade into the shark's mouth. Metal teeth clashed against bone teeth. Fragments sprinkled from the jawline and blood spilled from lacerations in the gums. The shark lurched again, its snout hitting Luke square in the chest.

He fell backward, immediately raising the chainsaw high to keep from slicing himself. The fish inched closer, shaking the boat with each wiggle. Its mouth closed in, ready to slice him in the same manner as it did Starch.

Luke rose to his feet, brought the tool over his shoulder like a baseball bat, then swung it across the shark's nose. A thick red line formed across its face. Luke attacked again. The saw came down on the shark like a fire axe. The right eye popped as the blade rolled over it, turning it into a squishy glob of loose flesh and blood.

The shark lurched, caught off guard by the sudden loss of one of its senses.

Luke stood, chainsaw at chest level, the blade dripping blood. "What's the matter? Have a problem seeing? Too hard having one eye?"

The fish jerked to the left and threw itself back into the water. It orbited the bow, moving in the direction of easier prey.

The waves that carried Elise were almost as strong as the shark that knocked her overboard. She drifted several meters from the tugboat. With Starch's maintenance boat being the closer vessel, she went for that instead of back to Luke. Years of swimming were put to the test here. She felt the sting in her leg, a reminder of the events that started this strenuous journey.

She kicked as hard as she could and grabbed the guardrail. Like climbing a rope, she scaled the bow deck of the maintenance boat.

"Look out!" Luke yelled.

The shark was directly underneath her. The bloodied jaw rose high, ready to snatch her off the ship like a grape from a vine. Gasping, she swung herself to the right. The one-eyed shark struck the vessel and fell back into the waves, then proceeded to circle back.

Elise climbed to the starboard side of the vessel, which now served as the deck. The smell of gasoline filled her nostrils. She sprinted toward the breach and looked down. Gas was drifting out into the water. The fuel tank had been ruptured during the impact.

She looked to Luke. "Is there a spare tub of gas over there?"

Luke looked around. "No. Why?"

"I know how to kill it!"

Luke could smell the fuel. Realizing what she was indicating, he looked around again. He held up the chainsaw. "This'll have to do. Unscrew the black cap and empty it over the deck." He propped himself on the gunwale and waited, rocking the chainsaw in his arms. The tugboat was slowly drifting in Elise's direction, pushed by the momentum from the shark's recent attack.

The boats closed within fifteen feet. He threw the tool with all his might.

Elise lunged for it as it skidded along the hull. She picked it up then ran for the breach, then started to unscrew the cap.

All they needed was enough gas spilled over the hull to create a steady fire that would ignite the leaking fuel, and explode the fuel tank.

The Helicoprion struck from behind.

Elise fell to her knees as the boat spun like a top. The chainsaw slipped from her grasp and skidded along the hull toward the water. "NO!" She lunged, hooking the tips of her fingers around the handle. The slightest slipup would make her loose her grip. Slowly, she worked it back, then secured a solid grip.

A dorsal fin emerged around the stern of the boat as she dumped the contents over the breach. The hull was now soaked with gasoline, untampered by seawater.

Now, all she needed to do was draw the shark in.

"Get ready!" she said.

"Hang on!" Luke was looking for something to use as a flame. As luck would have it, this stupid boat didn't have a flare gun. "Why am I surprised at this point? Not like anything else has gone according to plan since we've been here." He dug out his cigar lighter. "This'll have to do."

The shark lined up with its target. Raising its head over the water, it saw the human standing aboard the sinking vessel. She was close to the edge, well within reach of its jaws.

A thrust of its tail pushed it toward its goal. It would kill these people, then finally enjoy freedom in the open sea, where it would hunt and feed at its leisure. Any of these humans that crossed it would instantly meet the same fate as those who tried to stop it today.

Elise knelt near the slope of the hull, ready to spring out of the way.

"Move!" Luke shouted.

Elise waited. She couldn't flee too quickly, or else the shark would change course.

"Come on!"

It closed within thirty feet.

"MOVE!"

Elise waited. The shark closed the distance and raised its head. Only when the jaws slid up over the hull did she jump out of reach. Scampering on her hands and knees, she put distance between herself and the shark.

"Luke, now!"

Luke sparked a flame then reared his arm back Immediately, the flame vanished.

"Damn it!"

He tried again, only for the flame to die out after brushing against the air. *I should've figured. Not like how it works in the movies.*

"Luke! What are you waiting for?" Elise shouted.

The fish was resting right along the breach. Right on top of the gas puddle.

Luke tapped his vest and pockets for anything that could burn, ultimately feeling the rounded object in his left leg. He pulled the cigar tube out and freed the stogie.

He glanced at it, then at the shark, then lit it up. He bit the end off, took a long draw to get the burning end red hot. He clicked his tongue, registering the flavor, then glared at the shark.

"What a waste."

He tossed the cigar. It bounced once along the hull, skidded into the spilled gas, which ignited upon contact with the burning end. Flames danced around the fish. The trail of gas traveled into the interior of the vessel right into the fuel tank.

Elise sprinted to the stern and made a bounding leap into the ocean.

The boat exploded. The Helicoprion slumped to its side, its jaw slung, its body stiff. There, it rested on the floating hull of the boat, a charred husk of its former self.

The maintenance boat was split wide open, its fuel casting an orange curtain over the beast. The fire consumed its body, eating at the flesh and the virus it contained. The air bubbles holding them up ruptured, and the dead animal disappeared under the burning waves.

Luke took a deep breath, then slumped against the gunwale. He looked for Elise but saw no sign of her. He thought of the intensity of the explosion and the shockwave that must've hit her. Was she unconscious? If so, she was well on her way to drowning.

He put a foot on the gunwale, yanked his vest off, then leaned forward to dive.

"Giving me another striptease?" That voice came from his blindside. He turned to his left and saw Elise paddling near the transom. She was smiling. "I gotta say, I don't need a reminder of our first meeting."

Luke grinned, then helped her aboard. "You only say that because you like what you saw." To his surprise, she didn't offer a rebuttal.

The water was over their knees now.

They inflated the raft, got it into the water, then set course southeast.

CHAPTER 75

They made it nearly two hours before the engine sputtered. Luke yanked repeatedly on the ripcord. That couldn't have been all the fuel. The dying of the motor indicated otherwise.

He looked around and saw nothing but infinite blue around them.

"Damn it. I was hoping we'd see at least one boat by now."

Elise leaned against the hull. She could see the look of failure on his face. He was looking at the silver case. The vaccine vials were secure and undamaged, but it brought little consolation. There was no way they'd get back in time to get the vaccine to Brianna Raye.

"Listen, Luke. You stopped a terrible event from happening. You survived that damn helicopter attack, swam all the way to the island, and managed to *Rambo* your way through it. The Helicoprion's dead. The lab is destroyed. There won't be any worldwide chemical attack."

Luke nodded. He watched the ocean again. "Doesn't change the fact we're alone all the way out here. God knows where the current's gonna take us. No food. Worse, no water. We're in quite the pickle...*again.* Might be the title of my autobiography if we get out of this."

"We will. I know we will," Elise said.

They gazed in each other's eyes as they drifted. Both thought of the crazy events of the last several days and how it crossed their paths. Despite the doubt from their peers and the overwhelming odds of their enemies, they pulled through. Together.

Luke was the one to break eye-contact. He looked past her inquisitively. "You hear something?"

She turned around. She didn't see anything, but he was right: there were faint vibrations in the water. Hums. A song!

Several minutes later, the humpback breached in the distance.

"Looks like we'll have company," Luke said.

Elise watched the whale wave its fluke in the air. Another fluke rose beside it—a much smaller one. Its young.

She propped herself up on her knees. Her heart raced. Was it who she thought it was?

The whales moved in closer.

"Melody!" She laughed. "I guess you've made an impression on them with your dancing, Luke. Looks like they followed us northwest."

"How nice of them," Luke said. "Too bad they don't have a radio to call the Coast Guard."

A chill crept up Elise's back. "Hang on, I'll be right back."

Luke leaned forward as she slid into the water. "What are you doing?"

Elise swam toward the whales. Melody watched her approach, taking no mind as the human glided along her back. Elise found the tracker. She placed her feet against the whale and lifted it as hard as she could. The suction gave way and the tracking device detached from the whale's back.

She took a moment to swim alongside Melody and her young, thanking them for their help before returning to the raft.

"Alright, what are you up to?" Luke said.

Elise looked over the device. "You have a screwdriver?"

"Oh, sure. I'm a regular *Home Depot.*"

"Will you shut up and help me?"

"Sorry, I don't have—" He tapped his pocket, remembering the Swiss army knife dropped by the maintenance guy. "Would this work?"

She took it from him and found the flathead. "Perfect."

"Mind telling me the plan?"

"If I can mess with the sensor inside this thing, I can trick the reader into believing the whale's stressed out. With a little luck, maybe the Institute will get in touch with the Coast Guard and ask them to send a chopper out this way."

Luke perked up. "If this works, I might owe that whale another dance."

Two hours later, rescue choppers appeared over the horizon.

Elise glanced at Luke. "I'm gonna hold you to that."

Melody waved her flipper, continuing to show off for the humans.

Luke smiled. "I can live with that."

CHAPTER 76

It had been a long, but fairly low-key day at the office. Mostly just paperwork. Detective Norton liked these days. While most detectives despised paperwork, he didn't mind it as much. He would claim he hated it, but the truth was different. It was easy. Routine. He was a fairly creative person, so writing wasn't a difficult task. Plus it kept him in the office, away from the hysteria that had been taking over Amadea in the last couple of days.

Only when he arrived home and found a series of State Trooper vehicles parked in his driveway did the routine nature of his day come to an end. In the middle of the group was Chief Pino. By the way he was watching the driveway, he was specifically waiting for Norton to show.

Nervously, the Detective stepped out of his vehicle. "Hey, Chief? What's going on? Something happen?"

"Oh, something happened alright. Had a little call from the Coast Guard. They had to respond to a little incident roughly a hundred-twenty-miles northwest of here."

"Coast Guard? Northwest? A hundred-twenty—that's all the way out into the ocean. What does that have to do with my house? Why are the State Troopers going through it?"

"Well yes, it's in the ocean. An island, specifically. *Gary Starch's* island. You see, they uncovered some lab material over there that was…suspicious, to say the least. Especially considering everything that's been going down around here recently. So, they went through Mr. Starch's computer files and found some pretty damning stuff. The people he did business with. The people he hired, and the people *they* hired." He turned to one of the Troopers. "Mind if I have your phone…this is the right one, right?"

"Yep." The Trooper handed it over, then waited anxiously as Pino showed it to Norton. It was a video and audio feed, displaying a submarine pen, Gary Starch, the mercenary Barton, and Luke Jansen.

"Ah, eliminating loose ends. Just like with the shark. Just like with Vick. Was that you who killed him in the hospital, by the way?"

"Shut up." Barton shoved him forward.

"Oh, come on! You gotta tell the detective how you beat him. I gotta know before I die."

Barton knew Luke was bullshitting him, but went with it anyway. "Private contractor. You can thank your pal Norton for arranging that little job."

Norton stepped back, only to be stopped by two troopers who forced his hands behind his back and cuffed him. They removed his sidearm, read him his Miranda rights, then shoved him into the back of a police vehicle.

"Don't worry," someone else said, "once you tell us who that 'contractor' was, you might get a *slightly* reduced sentence."

Norton sneered as Luke Jansen stepped out of the house. "You cocksucking bastard! I'll kill you!"

"Yeah, yeah. Go ahead with the typical threats and insults. Though, get used to that particular one you used, you'll become quite experienced when you get to prison." The troopers went to close the door. Luke raised his hand, asking them to wait. "One other thing. Your wife's pissed at you too. I guess someone told her about all the fast food you've been sneaking in while you were at work. Probably should've used a public trash can…at least for the cigar wrapper." He slammed the door shut then walked away.

Norton shouted incomprehensibly, angry not only at them, but for himself for such a simple mistake.

Luke stood next to the Chief and watched the Troopers back out of the driveway.

"Nice work, Detective," Pino said.

"'Nice work'? No, 'sorry I misjudged you, Jansen. You rock. I suck. You deserve a ten-thousand dollar raise.' None of that?"

Pino smirked. "Maybe if you come to me first instead of losing your shit in front of the press—" He chuckled. "I'm sorry I misjudged you, Detective."

"Thanks." They watched the Trooper squad car disappear into the distance. "What about the rest?"

"Don't push it, Jansen."

Luke smiled then went for his vehicle. "See ya Monday, Chief."

CHAPTER 77

"The bombshell continues as Coast Guard Cutters surround the private island of Gary Starch. Formerly used as a Naval Research base, the island has reportedly been utilized as the housing facility for an extraordinary conspiracy that has led to the deaths of numerous Amadea citizens as well as the hospitalizations of hundreds of others."

Anthony Zach looked over his notes, then watched the camera, keeping an eye on the monitor behind the cameraman which displayed his news broadcast.

"Our report tells us that thanks to the Coast Guard, and the heroic work of Amadea Detective Luke Jansen and marine biologist Elise Sheldon, the criminal conspiracy was uncovered, as well as a working vaccine for the deadly outbreak in California. Mass production of this vaccine is already in the works, with medical professionals working tirelessly to recreate the formula and get it to everyone in need as soon as possible. With many patients in critical condition, and after accounting for the survivability rate as well as time it takes for testing, the CDC has given a green light for local hospitals to administer the drug. Early reports are stating that it is being met with great success."

Next page of script.

"We had the pleasure of speaking with Detective Jansen earlier today. Here is that footage."

He watched the monitor behind the cameraman as it switched from the live-feed to the recorded interview.

"The whales on the bus go 'round the town! 'Round the town! 'Round the town. The whales on the bus go 'round the town! All day long!"

"Crap! Crap! Crap!" someone shouted.

The feed returned to Anthony, who stared in stunned silence after seeing the B-roll footage taken from the docks.

He cleared his throat. "Um, sorry about that. Obviously, that wasn't the right footage. Bear with us a sec, and we'll show you the interview." He smirked. "I wonder how that happened..."

****

Brianna Raye woke up. She saw white directly above her. Heaven? No, it wasn't light. It was material. Tile. *Ceiling.*

A doctor rushed to her side. "There she is!" She checked her vitals. "Looking much better."

Brianna never knew she had lapsed into a coma. The pillows propped her up in her bed. "Mrs. Raye? Can you hear me?"

"Yes."

"How you feeling?"

"I—" She was surprised to realize she felt much better. Physically, at least. "What day is it?"

"Thursday. You've been out for a couple of days. Virus really took its toll on you."

"Wait… I'm getting better?"

"Yes, ma'am. You've missed a lot of news since Tuesday."

Brianna looked at the door. "What about my son? Glenn?"

"Hold on." The doctor and nurse continued taking her blood pressure and recording her heart rate. "Fever's gone. That's good."

"I need to know about Glenn. Please, tell me what's happened. Is he…?" She couldn't dare to even mention the possibility. If she had lapsed into a coma and nearly died, then he certainly was further along. "No…"

There was a knock on the door. One of the nurses opened it.

The doctor smiled. "Go ahead and bring them in. She'll be okay. The restrictions have been lifted."

Kirk and Glenn Raye stepped into the room, the latter still in his hospital gown. They ran to Brianna and embraced her with suffocating hugs.

"Alright, go easy," the doctor said.

Glenn, however, refused to let go. "Mom, I thought maybe you'd—"

"I'm fine. I'm just glad *you're* fine!" Brianna hugged her family once more then kissed her husband. "What happened? Sorry, I'm a little wonky at the moment. It's *Thursday*? There's a cure? What the hell's going on?"

"That guy you work with," Kirk said.

"The one with the eyepatch," Glenn said.

"Jansen?"

"You rang?"

They looked to the door. There he was, in his usual jeans and leather jacket, leaning against the door frame.

Brianna held back her tears. She didn't even need to know the specifics at this point. He was the detective she always knew from Los Angeles, the man who would move mountains to solve his case and keep his promises.

"Hey!" Glenn said. He pointed at the sandwich in Luke's hand. "That's *mine*!"

Luke took a bite. "Talk to your mom, kid. You have a lot to learn." He held the sandwich up, then smirked. "When you save someone's life, they owe you forever."

Glenn smiled, then hugged his mom again. She kissed his cheek then looked at Luke once more.

He backed out into the hall. "I'll visit you later."

"Stay out of trouble, *Luke*."

"How long you known me?!"

She laughed and continued hugging her family tight.

CHAPTER 78

Dr. Elise Sheldon gazed at her new research vessel. Per her request, Dr. Aaron Kent had the boat officially renamed the *Chad Samson.* She stood on the pier, mesmerized at the vessel and the spiritual harmony it gave her.

Chad was a posthumous hero. Though his death was tragic, it led to her meeting Luke Jansen, and eventually to the events that brought Gary Starch and his creation down. Thousands, maybe millions of lives had been saved thanks to her love for her nephew.

The Coast Guard reported recovering the body of the Helicoprion during the sweep of the island, and successfully recovered the charred remains of the other experiments. The computer files were intact, allowing them to figure out what Starch had been up to, and how he managed to do it. It was an investigation that would go down in history as one of the largest criminal conspiracies to ever take place.

It was noon now. The sun was high in the sky with hardly a single cloud to obscure its rays. The ocean was as blue as it had ever been, the horizon vast and peaceful. As the vaccine irradicated the virus, it felt that the ocean cleansed her soul. It was a true Heaven on Earth.

"I'll miss you, Chad." Genuine words, but not said out of grief, as she knew they would eventually be reunited. Until then, he would watch over her, along with his mom and dad.

"See an alien ship out there or something?"

Elise turned around. She had been so taken by the ocean that she didn't hear Luke pull into her driveway.

"Hi!"

He stepped onto the dock and looked at her new vessel. "Looks like you're not hesitating to get back to work."

"There's a lot of projects going on right now. Water treatment, recovering bodies of infected lifeforms. I convinced the Schmidt Institute to lead the charge. It'll be a lot of work, but we'll get the area cleaned of any infected organisms."

"Congratulations. You sure you're up to it?"

"I am! I really am. I've been sleeping well these last few days. I figured it's time to focus on a project." She walked up to him. "What about you? I figured you'd be up to your neck in paperwork."

"It's my day off."

"Yeah? How you spending it? Want me to buy you a drink?"

Luke shook his head. "Not craving one."

She looked at his scar. "No pain?"

"No." There was a glow in his good eye, something she hadn't seen before. She reckoned it was the first time it had shined in a long while. "I'm feeling…good."

"Excellent." She walked to the lot and picked up a couple of scuba tanks. "That means you're free. I need someone to head out with me to collect samples."

"Samples! Doc, it seems you always have some task for me to accomplish."

Elise smiled as she boarded the *Chad Sampson*. She faced the dock, crossed her arms over the guardrail, and gazed down at him. "I made a point to order scuba suits for a male partner, six foot, roughly a hundred-eighty pounds."

Luke returned the smile. "Well, if you insist..." He climbed aboard. "Where are we off to, Captain?"

She squeezed his hand then nodded to the horizon. "That way."

They both looked.

It was barely visible, but it was there. A whale breach far off in the distance. A humpback. Where there was one, there were often others.

Angels of the sea.

CHECK OUT OTHER GREAT DEEP SEA THRILLERS

LAMPREYS
by Alan Spencer

A secret government tactical team is sent to perform a clean sweep of a private research installation. Horrible atrocities lurk within the abandoned corridors. Mutated sea creatures with insane killing abilities are waiting to suck the blood and meat from their prey.
Unemployed college professor Conrad Garfield is forced to assist and is soon separated from the team. Alone and afraid, Conrad must use his wits to battle mutated lampreys, infected scientists and go head-to-head with the biggest monstrosity of all.
Can Conrad survive or will the deadly monsters suck the very life from his body?

DEEP DEVOTION
by M.C. Norris

Rising from the depths, a mind-bending monster unleashes a wave of terror across the American heartland. Kate Browning, a Kansas City EMT confronts her paralyzing fear of water when she traces the source of a deadly parasitic affliction to the Gulf of Mexico. Cooperating with a marine biologist, she travels to Florida in an effort to save the life of one very special patient, but the source of the epidemic happens to be the nest of a terrifying monster, one that last rose from the depths to annihilate the lost continent of Atlantis.

Leviathan, destroyer, devoted lifemate and parent, the abomination is not going to take the extermination of its brood well.

CHECK OUT OTHER GREAT DEEP SEA THRILLERS

PREDATOR X
by C.J Waller

When deep level oil fracking uncovers a vast subterranean sea, a crack team of cavers and scientists are sent down to investigate. Upon their arrival, they disappear without a trace. A second team, including sedimentologist Dr Megan Stoker, are ordered to seek out Alpha Team and report back their findings. But Alpha team are nowhere to be found – instead, they are faced with something unexpected in the depths. Something ancient. Something huge. Something dangerous. Predator X

DEAD BAIT
by Tim Curran

A husband hell-bent on revenge hunts a Wereshark...A Russian mail order bride with a fishy secret...Crabs with a collective consciousness...A vampire who transforms into a Candiru...Zombie piranha...Bait that will have you crawling out of your skin and more. Drawing on horror, humor with a helping of dark fantasy and a touch of deviance, these 19 contemporary stories pay homage to the monsters that lurk in the murky waters of our imaginations. If you thought it was safe to go back in the water...Think Again!

Printed in Great Britain
by Amazon

79040082R00193